DYING DAY

Robert Ryan

headline
review

First published in 2007 by HEADLINE REVIEW
An imprint of HEADLINE PUBLISHING GROUP

First published in paperback in 2007 by HEADLINE REVIEW
An imprint of HEADLINE PUBLISHING GROUP

5

Cataloguing in Publication Data is available from the British Library

ISBN 978 0 7553 2923 6

Typeset in Janson by Palimpsest Book Production Limited,
Grangemouth, Stirlingshire

Printed and bound in Great Britain by
Clays Ltd, St Ives plc

Headline's policy is to use papers that are natural, renewable and recyclable
products and made from wood grown in sustainable forests. The logging and
manufacturing processes are expected to conform to the environmental regulations
of the country of origin.

HEADLINE PUBLISHING GROUP
A division of Hachette Livre UK Ltd
338 Euston Road
London NW1 3BH

www.reviewbooks.co.uk
www.hodderheadline.com

For John and Gilly
and the men and women of The
British Berlin Airlift Association

Ihr Völker der Welt . . . schaut auf diese Stadt!'

(Peoples of the world . . . look at this city!)

– Ernst Reuter, Governing Mayor,
during the Berlin blockade, 1948–9

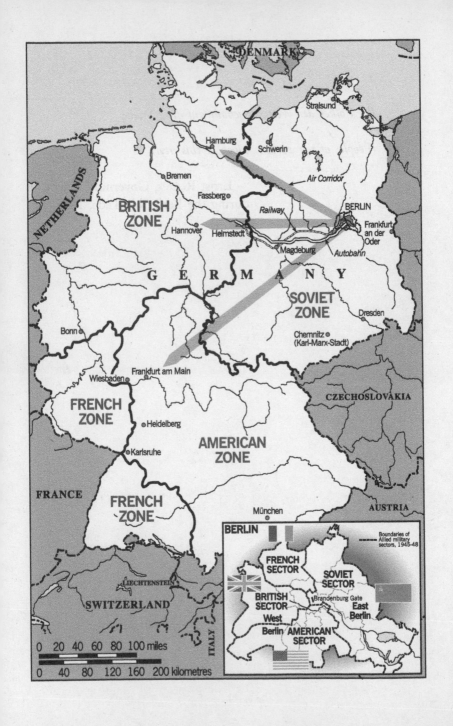

Prologue

Germany 1945

The once half-timbered city of Halberstadt was still burning when the small convoy passed through its outskirts. The USAAF Flying Fortresses hadn't left much of it standing, just enough to suggest it had once been a beautiful medieval city. As the Jeep bounced and bucked over debris, Alan Towers balanced the tatty copy of the pre-war *Baedeker* on his lap and turned the pages with numb fingers. He found the relevant passage, which identified Halberstadt as one of the oldest cities in Eastern Germany, founded by Charlemagne in the ninth century. 'And pounded to dust by the Americans in the twentieth,' he added.

It was a pity the picturesque houses were now smouldering shells, but Towers had seen enough destruction to be past caring about the loss of yet another *Altstadt* or a thirteenth-century cathedral, no matter what the quality of the woodcarvings. He was more worried about any snipers that might be lurking in the smoking ruins. He had lost a gunner to one three days before, and could still see in his mind the impossibly neat hole that had been drilled into the man's forehead, and the jagged, fist-sized wound that had been left when the bullet emerged out the other side.

'Stay sharp!' he shouted above the engine noise.

They were deep behind enemy lines now, even though there weren't many enemies to be seen, at least not in uniform. Just old men, women and children, all stamped with the same beaten, bewildered expression: *How did it come to this?* Well, you started it, Towers always thought.

It was doubtful that many of the civilians even realised it was a British convoy racing by them. The raiding-party consisted of two Jeeps, with Towers in the lead vehicle, followed by a pair of trucks containing their support troops and technical staff, with a third lorry empty, ready for loading with any booty they should find. It also contained shackles for restraining any reluctant prisoners.

The vehicles were all unmarked, apart from Union Jacks on the canvas roofs of the lorries. The biggest danger to them was from marauding Allied planes, not the Wehrmacht or the SS or the armed Hitler Youth they sometimes came across. It was fervently hoped that one of the tank-busting Typhoons or Mustangs that patrolled the area above might notice the markings *before* blowing them to kingdom come.

Leaving the town behind, the road began to climb into the foothills of the Harz Mountains, through trees still dusted white from the last of the season's snowfalls. The temperature dropped noticeably and Towers pulled his greatcoat around himself. If it got much chillier, they'd have to zip up the canvas door covers, even if it meant risking a slower response time to any attack.

The convoy was an offshoot of No. 2 T-Force (for 'Target'), a clandestine unit whose objective was to locate German scientists and their inventions and capture them before the Americans or Russians got to them. Towers was both the senior officer and the linguist of the group, with decent German and Russian, hence his position in the lead Jeep. They were also carrying an armed TAT, Technical Assessment Team, and a photographer, as well as the regular troops. Advanced German rockets, jets, chemical weapons, munitions, engines, submarines – anything of technological importance was within their remit. But the prize they were hoping for had proved the most elusive: the Foo-Fighters.

During raids over Germany, aircrew – mostly American but some RAF – had described strange lights in the sky, burning spheres or cigar shapes that would hover beside them and then dart away at incredible speeds. Initially dismissed as hallucinations caused by oxygen deprivation, identical incidents continued to be logged by returning pilots and gunners. And not all the oxygen supplies in the 8th Air Force could be faulty. Towers had recently discovered that the Americans had named the bizarre apparitions after the cartoon strip called *Smokey Stover*, in which the main character called himself a 'foo' instead of a 'fire'-fighter.

Clues to the location of the factories that might have created such 'weapons' had come from the Combined Detailed Interrogation Service, which had debriefed freed slave labourers. Some of those at the Volkswagen plant claimed to have once worked in the Harz Mountains on top-secret projects involving balls of fire – the so-called *Kugelblitz*. These installations, dug into the side of the hills to protect them from Allied bombs, were known as *G-Werke* or 'shade factories'. Of course the half-starved workers weren't the most reliable of sources. It might be nothing. But if they were right, the mountains might just turn out to be home to the Foo-Fighters – hence this dash behind the lines.

Corporal Dobson, his driver, dropped down a gear as the incline steepened and the haze from the scorched city thinned. The trees closed in, hugging the roadside; the thick columns of pines, and their proximity to each other, created patches of blackness that the grey daylight failed to penetrate. Behind him, Towers heard Cook, his replacement gunner, swivel his pair of ring-mounted Vickers K machine guns, covering one side of the woods; the gunner in the following Jeep would be pointing his weapons at the opposite side. Anything blinked in there, it would be torn to shreds.

Above the fumes of the engine, Towers caught the occasional

rich scent of damp humus from the forest undergrowth. He looked up at the watery sun, not quite high enough to clear the apex of the tallest trees. It was just gone noon, and soon it would begin its downward arc. It was important to reach the location while there was still light.

'How much more, sir?' asked Dobson, in his thick Scouse accent, clearly thinking the same thing. All the troops were drawn from a Liverpudlian regiment and they had been fighting together since D-Day. Even if Towers sometimes had trouble understanding them – and their sense of humour – he was pleased to have such a battle-tested bunch of men watching his back.

Towers checked the map, tracing the road from Halberstadt south towards Thuringia, and said: 'A couple of hours at most, if there are no problems.'

As the last word left his mouth, he saw the truck ahead. It was skewed to one side of the road, its rear flap furled up, and uniformed soldiers were moving around it.

'Kinnell,' said Dobson, in one of his trademark concertina-ing of words.

Towers reached into the greatcoat for his Browning pistol, and heard a loud click from the Vickers behind his head, but Dobson squinted through the windscreen and announced: 'Yanks, sir.'

'Buggeration.' In some ways Germans would have been preferable. At least they could have just shot them up and moved on.

'What'll I do?'

Judging from the way their vehicle had veered into the trees, the Americans had suffered an accident; this didn't look like a break for coffee or a piss. Some of the Yanks, on hearing the T-Force engines, took two steps into their path, weapons at the ready. Towers knew there was a clear code of the road here: the British should stop and help an ally in any way they could. But first, he had to make sure the Yanks didn't shoot them up, thinking they were Nazis.

'Can you play anything American?' asked Towers.

'Y'what, sir?'

'On the horn. I don't know – "Star Spangled Banner"? "Yankee Doodle Dandy"? Let them know we are friendly.'

'Sorry, sir.' The tone suggested that naked tap-dancing on the bonnet might have been just as appropriate. 'Er, there's a flag under your seat.'

'A what?'

'Union Jack.'

Towers scrabbled beneath the seat and found the bundle of cloth. He stood up, losing the shelter of the windscreen, and felt the sting of the icy slipstream on his cheeks. Stretching out his arms, he let the flag unfurl and began to shout: 'We're British! British!' The Union Jack snapped in the wind and folded in on itself, but it did its job: M-1s and carbines were cautiously lowered. From the corner of his mouth he said to Dobson, 'Slow up, but keep going.'

The convoy's speed dropped as it approached the rear of the six-wheel truck, and an American Lieutenant appeared from around the front of the 'Eager Beaver', as the workhorse was known, scratching his forehead. Towers indicated to slow even further. He dumped the flag in the footwell and gripped the top of the windshield to balance himself.

'You all right?' Towers yelled.

'Broken axle,' said the American.

'Bad luck.'

'Any chance of a ride?' the Lieutenant asked, eyeing up the rest of the British convoy.

They were level with him now. He appeared to be even younger than Towers, not yet in his twenties. 'Where are you headed?'

The American hesitated. 'Gernrode, more or less. There's a POW camp there needs liberating.'

Of course there is, Towers thought cynically – I don't think! These Americans would hitch a lift and then try to usurp his mission, perhaps by stealing the spare truck. 'Sorry,' he said, the lie slipping easily off his lips. 'I have an order to proceed to Ascherleben.' Then, with some truth he added: 'There's a sweeper unit some way behind with engineers on board. They'll sort you out.'

When the Yank realised the British had no intention of stopping, a crackle of rage came off him as he yelled: 'Yeah – but hey, you guys,' he began to jog alongside them, 'what the fuck do—'

Towers gave the signal to speed up and slumped back down in the seat. As the Jeep accelerated, so did the rest of his convoy. He was sure they heard far more of the ripe language from the Americans than he did. Nevertheless, that was a good result. He'd heard rumours that a US Operation Paperclip raiding-party – their equivalent of T-Force – was ahead of them. Now it wasn't. So, unless the Russians had advanced further than Intelligence suggested, his group would have the road to the *G-Werke* all to themselves. He just hoped the boffins in the lorry behind him knew what they were looking for, when they found the secret installation. Because the first T-Force to crack the secret of the Foo-Fighters would be the one that history remembered.

Part One: 1948

Cold Light

One

Laura McGill had never kidnapped anyone before. She wasn't even convinced of the best approach to the crime. She was too slight to use physical force, not without an accomplice, and she wasn't entirely sure how you recruited one of those. 'Fancy a bit of abduction, Thursday?' was not the kind of topic you raised over the bacon counter at Lipton's.

Still, she needed help of some description. Even though her target was in his fifties, he was still a man, and might be considerably stronger than her. It would be just her luck to choose an ex-Commando who could snap a neck with a flick of the wrist. Which meant she had to have an advantage. Such as a gun.

Which was how a pretty blonde in her mid-twenties came to be loitering on the south side of Piccadilly one spring evening with a Colt .32 in her handbag, pacing a few yards of pavement opposite Albany, the building where the target, a man called Rufus Napier, had his flat, or 'set', as she had heard them called. Napier controlled access to the files of the Special Operations Executive, or SOE, and seemed determined to keep them to himself. Laura intended to wrest from him the details of her sister's last mission.

The aim was to intercept him before he made it to the main gate of his apartment block, which was protected by a couple of burly ex-Guardsmen. She had already followed him on several occasions, and knew his routine. Napier invariably left the Home Office in Whitehall at 5.30 p.m. on the dot and always walked home, along Pall Mall and Lower Regent Street, no matter what the weather. Picking him up in Whitehall was a possibility, but there always seemed to be policemen stationed outside the government buildings, and several roving foot patrols. Plus parking inconspicuously was difficult anywhere near Number Ten and the Houses of Parliament. It was better to catch him at Piccadilly where she could park for up to one hour, right outside the Royal Academy, and intercept him just when he was slowing his brisk pace, in sight of Albany, and home.

Part of her accepted that what she was about to do was very wrong, but they had left her no choice. She had little experience of violence, not since her days in the Service at least, but sometimes it was the only option. Laura had spent the last few months dashing herself against the most implacable, uncaring bureaucracy in the world, feeling the frustration build in her until, almost inevitably, she had snapped. She was about to abduct the man who had blocked her every request to discover what had become of Diana. And part of her was looking forward to it.

The weapon in her bag had been given to her in Calcutta by Force 136, the local name for the Special Operations Executive, for 'personal protection' during the food riots there, and she had neglected to turn it in at the end of hostilities. She had even ignored the 1946 War Trophy gun amnesty. Laura never knew why she had hung onto it: perhaps this was the reason.

She jumped as the *London Evening News* vendor behind her yelled something incomprehensible about the forthcoming Olympics. Ahead of schedule? Behind? He shouted a second mangled phrase, an elongated moan she deciphered as 'West End Final'. Laura moved out of earshot, past the Simpson department store, towards the newly re-erected statue of Eros.

Of course, she told herself, it wasn't really kidnapping. It was more an enforced meeting with an unwilling participant. And she wouldn't even produce the gun unless she had to. There would be no ransom demands, no furtive phone calls or notes to Scotland Yard. All she wanted was fifteen minutes of the man's time, face to face, and then she would let him go. After that, he could call the police if he wished. But then he'd have to admit that a mere slip of a woman had bested him in broad daylight. He'd also have to admit why, and he wouldn't like that.

Even through the crowds, she spotted the tall, bowler-hatted figure of Rufus Napier as he turned the corner right on schedule, swinging his brolly so the ferrule made a bright ringing sound on the pavement. He approached on her side of the street, as he had the other nights, aiming to cross at the zebra just before Albany. She waited until he was level before she fell in alongside him.

'Mr Napier?'

His eyes blinked rapidly, as if the sound of his own name had startled him. He took in a woman with a long but attractive face, a little thin perhaps, and with two dark crescents under her eyes, but quite striking nonetheless. 'Yes?'

He carried on, not breaking stride, forcing her to almost run alongside him as they passed St James's Church. 'Could I have a word?'

He stared down at her for a good few seconds, as if trying to place the face. 'I'm sorry – you are?'

They were on the crossing now and she had to be quick. 'Laura McGill.'

'Ah.' She could see him wracking his brains, as the metal ferrule alternately tapped on the black and white stripes. 'The name is familiar.'

'I've written to you several times. I need to talk to you about my sister. Diana McGill.'

They reached the north side of Piccadilly and he stopped suddenly, causing people still on the crossing to spill around them as they stepped onto the kerb. A bus honked its horn impatiently as the zebra took its time to clear. 'I'm sorry, Miss McGill. I can't respond to enquiries outside of office hours. You need to make an appointment.'

'I've tried,' she hissed.

'Well, if you'll just ring my secretary . . .'

Now she felt her anger rise. She'd spoken to that damn woman a dozen times, had come to loathe her haughty, why-are-you-bothering-me tone. Before she knew it, the little automatic was in her hand, barely visible in the voluminous sleeve of her coat. She stepped in closer to obscure it further from public view. It was doubtful Napier had a good look at it, but when it hit the bottom of his ribs, he knew exactly what it was. She was so near now she could smell his peppermint-scented breath.

'Listen carefully to me,' she said. 'I'm pretty much at the end of my tether here.' She pressed the barrel harder into his chest and he moved away. 'Do you understand?'

When he didn't reply, Laura inclined her head in the direction of the Royal Academy. 'There is an Austin Ascot just along the street. See it? That black car.'

The Civil Servant nodded.

'We are going to get in it. You first, then me. Without any fuss or bother.'

Napier felt a burst of fear in his stomach. He had been the kind of spy who never moved beyond the shabby corridors and meeting rooms of St. James's, who had fought his war by sending coded messages and deciphering others' field reports, wielding nothing more deadly than green ink and mimeographs. Now that he'd been put out to grass at the Home Office, physical threats were the last thing he had anticipated. 'Are you insane?' he spluttered.

When she replied, her voice was small, but icy cold. 'Yes. You know, I rather think I am.'

Napier looked into her eyes for a second and, not liking what he saw in there one bit, moved obediently towards the waiting car.

TWO

Berlin

James Hadley Webb had chosen the Goethe, a shabby café in the middle of Hahnestrasse, as the rendezvous point with his Objective. It was a desolate road of mostly ruined houses close to the imaginary line that marked the transition to the Russian zone. The southern end of the street was blocked by the rubble left from the demolition of a *Flakturm*, a massive anti-aircraft tower, once bristling with long-range 128mm guns, but blasted level by the Red Army in 1945. Gossip had it that hundreds of bodies were still entombed in the air-raid shelter below. This explained why it had always been low on the priorities of the *Trümmerfrauen*, the women who cleared Berlin's streets and bombsites. The neglected pyramids of brick, steel and concrete meant there was no through traffic on Hahnestrasse. A man could escape on foot over the dereliction, if he knew how. Jimmy Webb knew how.

He also knew that the café had a rear exit that led into the 1920s' tenements which had been hastily converted back into habitable units with tarpaulin and plywood. Again, prior knowledge was needed to navigate the stinking maze of alleys and ruined courtyards. Webb had practised the route twice, earlier in the day.

Almost satisfied with his preparations, Webb gripped Alan

Towers's arm just as they were about to enter Café Goethe and pulled him back onto the street. The lad's eyes widened in an unspoken question and he pushed back a lock of his dark hair from his forehead. Webb sometimes thought Towers was just too handsome to be a spy. Whereas he himself was blessed with a perfectly acceptable but nondescript face, Towers in certain lights looked like an actor from the Rank stable of charming would-be leading men, with a hint of something dark and brooding, but in a non-threatening way. There was Spanish blood on the mother's side, so he'd heard.

'I think one of us should stay outside,' Webb said. 'No good both of us being in there.'

Towers wrinkled his nose, twisting those matinée looks. That was more like it, thought Webb. 'What, one of us should sit in the warmth, with *Kaffee und Kuchen*?'

'Yup. And it's my turn inside,' said Webb with a wink.

'When isn't it your turn inside?' Alan Towers shot back.

'When you get my job.'

'I was forgetting,' said Towers, the condensation of his breath streaming into the icy air. 'But I thought you skiers were used to the cold.'

Webb gave a peevish grunt. The very mention of skiing made him tetchy. At thirty-five, he was too old for the actual team, but a man of his experience should have been among the coaches for the British at the recent Olympics in St Moritz; however, he had been refused leave by London. It wasn't in the interests of national security to go gallivanting off, he was told. Well, what about national pride? The bloody French and Americans had taken most of the honours.

'Keep an eye out,' he said tersely now. 'Let me know when the Objective is in sight. Watch for a signal from the Sweepers, OK?'

'Righty-o,' Towers said, as jauntily as he could manage. He'd suspected this would happen; that was why he was wearing his thick Pesco thermal underwear.

Webb peered down the street and picked out the silhouette of one of Ernst Henkell's men. There was a team in place to act as 'Sweepers', designed to neutralise any tags that Otto, the Objective, might have acquired along the way. Otto was good, but it was worth double-checking that he was clean and unencumbered when he came across. The Sweepers were off-duty policemen, moon-lighting for dollars, who could intercept any suspicious characters by flashing their papers and detaining them for an hour or two on some dubious pretext.

Satisfied the safety net was in place, Webb entered, nodded to the café owner and took his place in the corner, near the window, just where it met the smoke-stained wall, with its tatty cinema posters for American movies. *Casablanca*, *Key Largo*, *Duel in the Sun*. Webb hadn't seen any of them. He wracked his brains for the last time he had sat in the cinema. Two years ago, he decided. He'd gone with Olivia to see *It's A Wonderful Life*. It had been her idea to go and they had argued, of course. He could recall the details of the row – hardly surprising, since they were always the same – but not the film.

The Englishman ordered a coffee and took out his hip–flask, ready to perk up the beverage when it arrived. There were no other customers, probably due to the fact that the Goethe was like an outpost of the Arctic. The iron potbelly stove was cold to the touch and in all likelihood hadn't been lit for days.

The mug was thumped down on the table and Webb rubbed his hands together and asked the scarecrow of an owner if there was any heat to be had. The man shook his head sadly. 'It was last warm in here in April 1942. A Monday, I think.'

Webb laughed politely at the man's deadpanning and made a mental note to send one of his lads round with the offer of some NAAFI coal at a reasonable price. It was always worth cultivating a new rendezvous or potential dead-letter drop. The promise of warmth bought you a lot in this bone-chilled town. Once he had gone, Webb tipped the whisky into his drink and sipped.

Through the grimy window he could just about spot the darker outline of Towers in the shadows, hidden away from the yellow cone of feeble light emanating from the nearby streetlamp. At the request of the lad's father, an old friend who had coached the British bobsleigh team back in 1936, Webb had rescued Towers from a dreary existence listening in on Russian Air Traffic Control. Poor old Towers had joined SIS after the war thinking he was going to be a spy and then he'd been shunted to the new Electronic Intelligence section. Eavesdropping on aircraft movements wasn't espionage as far as Webb was concerned. *This* was proper spying – out at the sharp end. Even if the pleasure was a little blunted when your Objective was tardy.

Webb checked his watch. He could afford to give Otto some leeway. It was a long, perilous trip from Saxony and the Czech border back to Berlin. What were a couple of hours either way? He thought of the desolate, dangerous places Otto would have passed through: Aue, also known as the Gate of Tears, Schneeburg, Oberschlema, with its radium baths, and Johanngeorgenstadt. His cover as a Socialist Unity Party labour organiser, responsible for meeting the ever-growing quotas for mineworkers, was as good as it could be. That is, barely adequate if you met the wrong kind of Ivan. And there weren't many of the right kind.

'You want something to eat?' asked the owner.

'Not yet, thank you. Perhaps in a while.'

'There's not much anyway,' came the glum reply.

'Not much' would be sausage, or at least a tube of sawdust impersonating a sausage, perhaps some bread, and a soup of some description. Add homemade cakes if there was a Frau Café Owner which, looking around the cobwebbed corners of the ceiling, he doubted. Still, he shouldn't have anything to eat no matter what they could rustle up. Webb had managed to put a few pounds on these last few months thanks to a combination of stodgy canteen food and the inclement weather, which had disrupted his usual exercise routine. It wasn't much of a gain, but he sometimes imagined he could feel the extra ridge of fat on his midriff slowing him down. That wouldn't do at all.

The rap on the window made Webb start. A second rap followed. It meant: subject approaching, all clear. Webb took a larger gulp of the coffee and unbuttoned his coat. It would be no fast draw, but a Browning automatic was weighing down the inside pocket of his suit jacket, just in case.

The doorbell clacked as Otto entered, followed by a swirl of the dusty wind, which he quickly shut out. Webb rose to his feet to greet the German. His first impression was how much more lined the face was, how sallow the cheeks. But the eyes still burned bright. Otto had been in the U-Boat Command, trained to use miniature submarines in what amounted to suicide missions. He had survived only because the war ended before he could be sent to attack Allied shipping. Now, virulently anti-Communist, he was Webb's best source on what was happening in the mines. Otto was one of a group of agents – the other major asset being a stay-behind network known as Librarian – that kept his creaking Special Operations Branch organisation a player in the Berlin game.

Webb pumped the German's hand. 'Otto! Am I pleased to see you here.'

'I am pleased to see me here, too. My God, Jimmy, I can't do that again. I think I have aged twenty years.'

'Nonsense. You look hail and hearty,' he lied. Otto smiled at the platitude. 'Coffee? And a schnapps?'

'Yes.'

Webb caught the familiar sour tang coming off the Objective. Otto was afraid. The smell of fear and agitation filled the room, as tangible as cigarette smoke. Well, it was to be expected. Webb's job was to reassure him, now he was home free.

Webb sat and swivelled in his chair towards the counter. The owner was nowhere to be seen. 'Hello! Service!'

'I went down a mine, Jimmy. My God. They are working people to death down there. Black marketeers, prostitutes, and intellectuals.

17

That is their punishment. Three years in the Gate of Tears. Better they should shoot them.' The voice was full of horrors remembered, and for a moment Webb could see the dark, dank tunnels, taste air that was gritty with lethal particles of radioactive rock. 'I heard something, Jimmy. Something scary.'

It was always like this. The rush to get it off their chest, to tell everything in the first ten minutes, was almost irresistible. Jimmy Webb knew he had to slow things down. Otherwise he would be swamped by a disjointed torrent of Intel, much of it rubbish, but embedded within the sludge might be sparkling little gems that were easy to overlook. It was like panning for gold in a riverbed of rumour, innuendo and conjecture, and it was best done at leisure, when the Objective had relaxed, and the stink of the job was no longer on him.

'Service!' Webb repeated.

His voice sounded hollow as it echoed around the deserted café. Webb felt as if icy fingers were playing down his spine. Something was wrong.

The fracture line exploded along the window with the sound of a gunshot. Webb whipped around just in time to see Towers bounce off the glass, arms flailing like a puppet whose strings had been severed. Otto was already out of the chair, and Webb slid his hand into his coat, his fingers closing on the Browning, but he was too slow. The two men who had burst in from the rear were already brandishing their Markhov pistols.

'Do not move! Keep your hands on the table.' The English was crude, the words slurred into one multi-syllabled bark, but the threat behind them was clear and authoritative.

Webb managed to ease the Browning a half-inch from the pocket before the first shot cracked out. Plaster fluttered down from the ceiling. 'Stop now!'

Webb did as he was told.

The third man, who came in through the front door, was a big specimen, well over six feet and broad with it. He was dressed in a heavy black overcoat, with a dark Homburg pulled down over his eyes. The shadow cast by the brim wasn't deep enough to hide the bulbous, pockmarked nose that disfigured the face. His leather gloves shone like liquorice. One of them was wrapped around a Walther P38.

'What is the meaning of this?' demanded Webb, turning on the full-bore bluster of an outraged Englishman whose home had been invaded. 'Who the hell are you?'

The man ignored him; instead he turned to look at Otto. The German's eyes were moist with tears and wide with fear. There was confusion in there, too. He was in the West, under the protection of the British Military Government. How could this happen?

'*Smyert Shpionam,*' the big man said softly, before the room filled with the boom of the Walther's discharge. Webb's body jerked with shock and he pushed back in his chair. Otto's head seemed to stretch out on one side before it exploded like a boil, flinging a grey-flecked wash of red up the wall.

The pistol turned on Webb, and, as he looked down the black hole of the barrel, he heard the expression repeated once more. Webb knew what it meant. *Smyert Shpionam*. Death to spies.

Three

As the Austin pulled away from the kerb, Napier turned to Laura and asked: 'What's to stop me jumping out and hailing the nearest policeman?'

She ground the gears as it jolted into second. It was her mother's old car and she was unfamiliar with the clutch, which had to be depressed right to the floor before the cogs would engage. It probably needed looking at. 'There's nothing to stop you jumping out.' She turned and flashed him a dazzling smile. 'Except I'm a very good shot indeed. Your lot trained me well.'

'My lot?' That could mean any one of a half-dozen clandestine departments he had served in.

'EW of SOE.' She had only been a glorified courier in the Economic Warfare section of Special Operations Executive, but even humble message carriers underwent weapons training.

'I see.' He had never actually been a member himself, but he was now the SOE Adviser to the Home Office, so he knew all about the courses devised by the likes of Dan Fairbairn and Bill Sykes, hard ex-Shanghai policemen. Courses that made you unafraid to kill or maim. He removed his bowler hat, ran a hand across hair oiled with Trumper's finest and muttered: 'This is very irregular.'

Laura didn't drive them far, just to Charlotte Street and

Schmidt's. She chose it because the waiters, the rudest in London, would ignore them, and, because of its Germanic origins, the place was still being boycotted by many clients, despite Schmidt himself having served in the British Army. You were always sure of a quiet table at Schmidt's.

'I'm going to buy you dinner, Mr Napier. It's the least I can do.'

Recovering some of his composure, Napier said: 'Do you realise the penalty for kidnapping a serving member of His Majesty's Government?'

The pomposity of the delivery almost made her laugh. 'I'll ask the judge for the dinner to be taken into consideration as a mitigating circumstance. Now get out, please.'

As she predicted, the restaurant was less than half-full. However, the head waiter had herded all the customers together in the same corner of the room, corralled like docile sheep. Laura insisted on a window seat, behind one of the restaurant's large square pillars, where even the waiters would have trouble spotting them. Not that they'd try very hard after she'd stamped her foot and made a little scene.

Laura refused all efforts to take her coat and they sat. Menus were placed before them, napkins snapped onto their laps and they were left in peace for what would probably be a good half-hour.

'Do you know much about guns, Mr Napier?'

'A little.' It was almost thirty years since he had handled one, in fact.

'Can you tell when an automatic is loaded?' She flashed the pistol at him, showing the hole in the bottom of the grip where the magazine should have been. 'I was never going to shoot you.'

He bristled a little, braver once he knew it had all been bluff. 'I never for a moment imagined you would. But why should I stay here now?'

Underneath the table, Laura slid the magazine she had removed only moments before back into place and pocketed the Colt.

Now she shrugged her topcoat off. 'Because I will scream and accuse you of acts so vile, the mere thought of them will make you blush.'

His mind flashed up various images unbidden and, sure enough, he began to colour. 'You really are quite a determined young woman, aren't you?'

'You have no idea, Mr Napier. You have no idea.' She made a show of studying the menu. 'The schnitzels are very good. The best in London, I'm told.'

'I've eaten here before, Miss McGill.' The old condescending tone was returning. 'I think we should have a bottle of hock and perhaps we can make some progress. Clear up any problems you might have. Then perhaps I can have my evening back.'

He arched back in his chair to afford himself a clear view of the room and snapped his fingers. Two waiters – surly, etiolated specimens in long white aprons – studiously ignored him for a few moments before they exchanged glances, then one of them sighed deeply and ambled over, walking as if the carpet was coated in Grip-Fix. Napier ordered the wine and, while he was at it, a brace of schnitzels. When the waiter had departed, he leaned back across the table.

'Now look here, miss, if you think for one moment—'

She, too, leaned in. 'I'll slap your face if you take that tone with me, Mr Napier. And I'll slap it hard. Then I'll scream the bloody roof down. Now we talk this over like two reasonable people, out for dinner. Agreed?'

His lips pursed together. Then: 'Agreed.'

'As I said before, this is about my sister, Diana McGill.'

'First of all, you do realise that the Special Operations Executive no longer exists?'

She rolled her eyes in frustration. 'Yes, of course I do.'

'It was disbanded with frightful haste at the end of the war. Its files were already in terrible disarray, with documents destroyed for no apparent reason, and then last year, there was a fire.'

The information took her aback, forcing an admission from her. 'I didn't know that.'

He nodded vigorously. 'Oh yes, at Baker Street. I was brought in to sort out the mess. It's sheer chaos, I can tell you. PFs – Personal Files – all mixed up with operational ones. There are gaps, terrible gaps. You are not the only relative concerned with the fate of their loved one.'

'Perhaps not. But as a former member of the organisation—'

He interrupted her, the implacable rubber-stamping bureaucrat once more. 'There is no special treatment for anyone, Miss McGill, not even former agents. No matter what their gripes.'

'If you had read my letters you would know all about my gripe.'

Napier let a flash of irritation cross his face and he jumped in once more. 'Of course I've read your letters. We have to file all new correspondence, so how could I *not* notice enough missives and telephone logs to fill up another cabinet. I now know the case like the back of my hand. Really. It doesn't help, you know.'

She suppressed the urge to apologise. 'You might have replied.'

'We did.'

'"Missing Presumed Dead. Investigations pending." What does that mean?'

'It means exactly what it says. Your sister was posted missing in April or May, 1944, if I recall correctly.'

'April.'

His eyebrows twitched upwards. 'Four years ago. What have you been doing, Miss McGill?'

'Apart from writing to half the departments in Whitehall? Watching my mother die, Mr Napier.' The Civil Servant blinked rapidly a few times, but said nothing. 'Cancer. It's rather time-consuming. But before she passed away, she asked me to discover what happened to Diana. I promised to do so. That's why I'm here.'

Napier picked up a fork, examined the tines and, apparently

satisfied with their cleanliness, put it back down. He took a deep breath and Laura knew a decision had been made. She never enjoyed playing the Final Wish of a Dying Mother card, but it was not only effective, it had the advantage of being true.

'So it's for your mother you are running around London threatening people with a gun?'

'Partly.' She considered telling him about the crushing feeling that she was responsible for Diana's fate. Her sister had recruited her to the Economic Warfare side of SOE, with a view to Diana running the China end of things, while Laura stayed in London and made sure the smuggling lines functioned. But Laura had bullied and sulked her way into a reversal of roles, so that Diana was the one who stayed in London.

And also the one who went across to France and disappeared. Laura said quietly: 'It's for my sake, as well. Mother is past caring now.'

Napier nodded. 'You signed the Act, I assume?'

'Official Secrets? Yes. And I know I am still bound by it.'

There was a lengthy pause while Napier harvested invisible specks of fluff from the starched tablecloth. 'What "investigations pending" means in this case, Miss McGill, is that your sister's file has a Blue on it.'

'A Blue,' she repeated. 'What's that?'

'In simple terms it means embargoed. It is highly classified and sensitive information, not to be released or discussed without clearance at the highest level. Which you won't get, of course.'

'Embargoed till when?'

'Twenty fifteen.'

'Twenty fifteen? My God, we'll all be dead by then.'

Napier smirked. 'I think that's the general idea, Miss McGill.'

'Laura,' she corrected absently. That didn't make sense. Diana had been sent to France by the Economic Warfare branch to discover why the supply lines of valuable goods smuggled from Switzerland across France had been severed. She was arrested and disappeared into what the Germans called *Nacht und Nebel* – Night and Fog, the shadowy world of prisons and concentration camps, where executions were arbitrary and any record-keeping of the shootings, hangings and gassings was frowned upon. There was nothing very contentious about that; it happened to dozens of agents. So why classify the file? 'What on earth for?' she asked.

'I would not be at liberty to divulge the reason. Even if I knew – which I don't.' He lowered his voice. 'More than my job's worth, as they say.'

I bet they do where you come from, she thought, but simply asked: 'Who put the Blue on the file? SOE or another outfit?' She meant MI5 or MI6.

He shrugged. 'No way of knowing. It was before my time. But it's still active.'

Laura felt the lick of hot anger again. 'Oh, why doesn't that surprise me?'

The embargo explained why she had been thwarted at every turn so far, why initially friendly contacts became cagey, distant and distracted. 'Look, Mr Napier, I wasn't lying when I said I had made a promise, but it wasn't only to my mother; it was to myself. Now, unless I pursue this, every day of my life will be a failure, proof that I can't even trust myself.' She felt her eyes sting. It was her turn to blink rapidly. 'Is there anything I can do? Anything at all to move forward?'

Napier shifted uncomfortably in his seat. Her tone suggested she might cry and he wasn't entirely sure he could cope with that. Being threatened with a pistol was one thing, coping with a bawling woman in public quite another. 'You've spoken to Vera Atkins, I assume? About your sister?'

Squadron Leader Atkins, the Intelligence Officer for SOE's French Section, had spent the last few years establishing the ultimate fate of SOE agents captured by the Germans, especially the women. 'I have written to Miss Atkins. At least she had the decency to reply to me. Strictly speaking, Diana wasn't one of her girls, but she'd kept an eye out for any sign of her and found nothing. No trace.'

'Which probably means one thing.' He tightened his lips and the blood drained from them. 'I'm sorry. Your sister was murdered and cremated.'

She shook her head furiously. 'You can't be certain of that. I'm not.'

'Perhaps you should be. Four years . . . I can't recall another agent who has turned up after so lengthy an absence.'

'I want to know exactly what happened to her, Mr Napier. Not conjecture.'

The wine arrived, dumped down without ceremony and already opened. Revenge for choosing their own table and clicking at the waiters, she assumed. They hadn't even been offered any bread as yet. Napier poured them each a glass and took a very generous swig. Well, he reasoned, it wasn't every night you were taken to dinner at gunpoint by an attractive woman. And one who was paying, at that. 'I can't tell you what is in Diana's file, Miss McGill, but there is nothing to stop you putting it together from scratch. What about speaking to Rose Miller?'

The name rang a bell. 'Remind me who she is, please?'

He hesitated. 'Diana's despatching officer. Lives on the Kent coast now, I believe. A word of warning, though – don't try pulling guns on her. It simply won't wash. Then there's—'

Two delicate, wafer-thin schnitzels appeared on vast white platters, along with a bowl of potatoes, sauerkraut and salad. Napier, suddenly hungry, began to attack his veal. Laura waited until they were alone once more before pressing him further.

'You were saying?'

'Yes.' He took some more wine. 'But I probably shouldn't.'

Laura winked at him. 'No, you probably shouldn't.'

Napier finally smiled. Part of him was beginning to have a sneaking admiration for the girl who refused to take no for an answer. Heaven forbid that every enquiry took this form, but it certainly made a change from dull Home Office routine. Still, he had to be careful. He hadn't crossed the line yet, but he was certainly picking up chalk dust on his turn-ups. 'Two other names. Neither in London, I am afraid. A boy called Raymond Bec in Paris has been recommended for the Croix de Guerre. Seems he had some contact with your sister – she is mentioned in the citation, as I recall. Then there is a chap in Berlin who put the whole shebang together. Must have known your sister. He'll be worth looking up.'

'What's his name?'

'James Hadley Webb.'

Four

Berlin

The moment the sound of the gunshot reached his good ear, James Hadley Webb kicked off, powering out of the depressions he had scooped into the cinders to act as starting blocks. He had already drained everything from his mind, suppressed the murmur of expectation from the crowd, the noise from the other track events and the breathing of his fellow athletes. He knew the secret to a good start from his competitive skiing days: to explode out of the blocks, to mimic the cartridge in the starter's pistol, to release all the energy packed into the muscles in one violent burst, not to worry about breathing or heart-rate or any other metabolic consideration. Oxygen was not a factor – the fibres would have to scavenge their energy without relying on fresh deliveries. It would all be over by the time the fully loaded red blood cells arrived at the muscle, anyway. This was short, sharp and brutal.

In the fraction of a second that his toes pushed down to lift him away from the start, he knew he hadn't given enough. It wasn't the instant detonation he was hoping for; there was more to be had. Somehow, he had failed to tap into that potential. He opened his eyes and willed his legs to pump, then pump harder, flinging his elbows back, feeling his limbs protest as the oxygen was sucked from the tissue and toxins dumped into his blood.

There was the tape, pulled taut across the track in front of him. He was closing on it, but not fast enough. *Don't think that,* his brain admonished him. *Don't lose the race in your mind – you can do this.*

As he chested through the piece of brown twine stretched between two wooden poles, standing in for the actual finishing line, Webb slowed and sucked in the cold morning air. He gripped his knees and put his head down, waiting for his heart to stop hammering on his ribcage, as if it wanted to leave his tortured body, like the first rat off a sinking ship. Sharp pains shot up the front of his legs – shin splints. The old curse of his skiing days, something no warm-ups or exercises had ever been able to cure him of. He shook each one in turn to keep the circulation going.

Webb looked at the shades of his fellow competitors, the ghosts of athletes long since run to fat, then up at the raked rows of empty stands, his imaginary audience of 110,000 gone, and over to the Führer-box, where Hitler would have sat, his gimlet eyes devouring proceedings, alternately thrilled and dismayed with his country's performance. Sometimes he felt as if the Führer was still there, looking down on his pathetic efforts.

He pulled off his singlet top as the ache in his chest began to subside, enjoying the feel of the cool air on his glowing skin. He looked across to Sergeant Withers, who had set up the tape for him, and was examining his stopwatch.

'Well, Withers?'

The physical fitness instructor scratched his head. 'Eleven and a half seconds, sir.'

'Damn. That's almost a second slower.'

The Sergeant nodded. 'You missed a few training sessions, sir. Can't expect the body to stay at race ready.'

'It's more than a few, Withers, and you know it. But thanks for letting me down easy.' Webb's aim was to get below ten seconds for the 100-yard dash. He was on the very track where Jesse Owens had embarrassed the Führer by winning with a time of 9.40. He'd heard that these days, Owens was reduced to running against horses and motor cars in fairgrounds, having lost all his money. It was a shame.

The Sergeant tossed Webb a towel and he wiped his brow, then his upper body. 'Thank you, Withers. I'll take a shower.' He nodded towards the tunnel that led to the changing rooms. 'Is the water on?'

'Sir. Tepid, rather than hot. Don't mind me saying, sir, it'd help if you had some competition. Real competition.' He pointed at his temple. 'Not just up here. I could arrange a few races, if you like. A couple of the lads are quite handy over shorter distances.'

Webb hesitated. These days he preferred solitary sports, racing against imaginary foes. But it made sense. You sometimes had to test yourself against others to bring out the peak performance. 'Possibly, Sergeant, possibly. I'll be in touch.'

'Right. Oh, and there's a message from Major Tyler. He'd like to see you in his office as soon as you are finished up.'

Shit and damn, thought Webb. That could only be bad news.

'The jig's up, James,' said Ralph Tyler, pointing the stem of his unlit pipe at Webb. 'Time to call it a day.'

'Pardon?' asked Webb, cocking his head to one side. 'Didn't quite catch that.'

'For God's sake, James, you had no trouble hearing me when I offered you a drink.'

Webb swirled the whisky in his glass and indicated the left side of his head. 'That's because I used my drinking ear. That one's fine. It's the other one giving me gyp.'

Through the grimy iron-framed office window behind Tyler, Webb could see the Osttor, the twin limestone towers guarding the entrance of the Olympic stadium complex, where he had just tried to imitate Owen. It was now the main base for the British MilGov, with hastily constructed barracks thrown up around the imposing structure to house soldiers, Military Police, engineers, clerks. And spies.

SIS had the better of it, of course, Tyler's office was in this former ticketing hall; Webb's domain, Special Operations Branch, was buried in the bowels of the stadium, not far from the laundry and kitchens. It reflected the comparative status of the two services.

Tyler shook his head, irritated by Webb's flippancy. The man spent far too much time talking to Americans, in his view. He began to scrape out the bowl of his pipe. 'The time for independent satellites has passed. We are bringing you into the main body of the Firm, James.'

Tyler, Deputy Head of Station for Berlin, was a grey man in his mid-forties, who seemed infinitely older. The tweedy three-piece suits, the pipe and the wispy combed-over hair all gave him the air of some distracted don. He had been, in his time, a formidable operator. Webb doubted he was still at the top of his game, but he still needed to be treated with respect.

Tyler spoke calmly and evenly now, as if the change he was proposing was a mere formality, a favour bestowed, even. His eyes, however, were hard as masonry nails, ready for the fight. 'I was saying,' he went on, 'that it is time to shut down your little outfit. Time for some consolidation. We're moving you to the main SIS staff.'

'Are you, indeed?' replied Webb, his own voice devoid of emotion. As far as he knew, only the JIC, the Joint Intelligence Committee, in London could dictate such a reorganisation. Of course, if he simply went along with the offer, threw his hat into the SIS/MI6 ring and handed over his networks, there was little the JIC could do about it. But he wasn't going to do that. He might have been damaged at the café, but he wasn't deranged.

'After that fiasco at the Goethe, you are clearly too exposed.'

From his tobacco pouch, Tyler fetched strands of Old Keg Empire and began priming the bowl of his pipe.

Fiasco was about right. The Military Police had arrived at the scene within ten minutes, summoned by Towers, who got off with a cracked cheekbone and sore head. At least he had a head to be sore: Otto was lacking most of his. Webb had been knocked unconscious but on awakening discovered that, thanks to a Walther being discharged close to his ear, a brass band had taken up residence in his cranium. Exercise might alleviate the worst of the ringing, the MO had said. Hence his return to the sprinting track.

'You're fine otherwise? Apart from the ear?'

Webb nodded. He had some fading marks on his neck and chest, but very little else. 'Badly bruised pride. Take a while for that swelling to go down.'

'Quite. And Towers?'

'Oh, he's claiming he'd like a transfer to the SIS catering division as soon as a vacancy comes up. Do you have one?'

Tyler's expression didn't change. 'Towers. Seems like a decent lad, keen to get on. Wasted in the Special Operations Bureau. We could do with a few more Russian linguists, rather than the rubbish they send us from the Joint Services School. You knew his father, I hear?'

Webb shrugged, wondering where this was leading. 'We met in Austria when I was a boy.' Charles Towers, another keen skier, had lost both legs in a V2 attack, which was ironic given his son's later career, trying to track that very technology across war-battered Germany. Although Charles still insisted on an annual bout of gentle bobsleighing, his Cresta Run days were over. Why bring up the father? Was SIS really interested in swiping his protégé? 'And I was joking. You can't have Towers.'

'Sweepers?' Tyler asked, veering off the subject. He knew that Webb would have put a catch team in place to see if the Objective had been tagged.

Webb paused before he answered. The old goat had probably

been doing his own digging into the event, so it was no use lying. Strictly speaking, such an incursion across the zones by the Russians was very much Tyler's concern. 'Outclassed, I think.'

'So your man Otto was tagged before he crossed?'

'It looks that way.'

Tyler took his time lighting the pipe, huffing clouds of smoke into the air for a few minutes. 'Look, you can see London's point when it says you Special Operations Bureau people are an anachronism we can't afford, James. When you start to lose men on our side of the curtain, it's time to centralise things.'

Webb was not going to fall for the old trick of attributing something to 'London', a vague catch-all that could mean anything from the Prime Minister down. 'This is all from Philby, isn't it?'

Tyler ignored the mention of Kim Philby, who had done a fine job of cornering the market in Soviet Intelligence by crushing any rivals within SIS. Instead, Tyler tried a conciliatory approach. 'You've always known you are operating on borrowed time. They want anything to do with SOE buried. And we'd be more than happy to have you and Towers. He's a good lad.'

Webb took a swig of his whisky. This was nothing new. SIS was always bullying the independents. SOB was a rump of Special Operations Executive that still had its own operating budget and London office. It was simple jealousy – the senior spying service hated any form of competition for resources. Or, indeed, glory. And he was fairly certain that, despite his apparent concern, Tyler would be quietly pleased by the killing of Otto at Café Goethe. It made Webb vulnerable.

'It was just a pick-up that went sour. It's hardly the first.' Webb had a long list in his head of SIS disasters he could wheel out if need be. 'It's no reason for me to roll over.'

'Not the first, but it has some worrying aspects.' The older man looked down at the notes on his desk. 'This phrase, *Smyert Shpionam*. Death to spies? Rather a dated little aphorism, even over there.'

The term had been contracted to the name SMERSH, one of the many rival military Intelligence organisations in the East. Its most recent role, immediately post-war, had been to hunt down hidden Nazis. As far as they knew, it was now disbanded and disgraced, absorbed into MGB, the Russian Ministry of State Security. Or perhaps not. It was difficult for even the spies to keep up with the power struggles over in the East.

Tyler examined his pipe, sucked a few times, tasting nothing but air, and relit it. 'You still have assets over there, don't you? Librarian people?'

Webb didn't reply. It was a rhetorical question. They both knew he had good agents giving him decent material. 'Librarian' was the code-tag for both the agents and the Intel that came across.

'Well, at some point we will have to arrange a debrief, so we can establish new control protocols.'

Webb felt a pinging in his brain, as if something had finally snapped. It was his patience. 'Over my dead body, Ralph.'

'It very nearly was, James.'

Webb stood up and drained the whisky from the glass. 'Thanks for the drink.'

'I'll expect full details of Librarian on my desk by next week.'

'Go to hell, Ralph. And leave me alone.'

'And what do you imagine you are going to do now?' asked Tyler smugly.

'I'm going to make some bastard pay for Otto.'

Tyler watched Webb as he picked up the bag containing his running gear and left without another word. He shook his head in dismay at Webb's crude outburst. Just as he'd thought. Too much time with Americans.

The day the American pilot Lee Crane arrived in Athens, a bomb had detonated in the Plaka, killing four people. The government had finally outlawed the KKE, the Communist Party, not unreasonably because the Reds were waging a civil war against it from plush offices in the centre of town. But KKE had retaliated for having its HQ closed by bringing its terror tactics to the heart of the capital.

As Crane raised the tower and asked for clearance and weather, even the guy on the radio sounded tetchy and scared. Welcome to yet another civil war, Crane thought. He'd just come from China, where the Communists and the Nationalists were killing each other by the thousand. He'd hoped Europe would be different. Apparently not.

It was a diamond-bright morning at 10,000 feet, but a finger of murky haze was still stretched across the sea in front of Elliniko Airport. As Tony Fitzsimmons, who was in the pilot's seat, banked for the approach, he said: 'Don't worry, Athens is a piece of cake.' Ex-RAF, Fitz had flown for Desert Air Force in Libya, Egypt and Tunisia and lived to tell the tale, so Crane guessed he knew what he was doing.

Anyway, it wasn't the pilot Crane was worried about. It was his plane. Fitz's crate was a converted Mitchell bomber, with more patches on it than Lil' Orphan Annie and a magneto on the port engine that liked to drop two hundred revs every so often just for laughs. Crane had picked up the co-pilot job from an agency in Cairo, who told him that there was a guy in Athens called Mikklos who might be able to help him get his own wings. He only hoped it wasn't the same guy who had sold Tony Fitz his plane.

They slid into the mist and Crane watched it streak past the side windows, like dirty strands of cotton wool. Then the Mitchell was clear, with the sea churning below its belly, and Fitz made the final turn to line up for the runway.

'Bit of an updraught as we come in off the water,' he warned. Sure enough, there was a lurch that flipped Crane's stomach just before the B-26's wheels banged onto the runway. Fitz taxied over onto the apron in front of the ground agent's hangar and went in search of a Customs officer. They were carrying coffee and cotton yarn. And that was all. Crane knew plenty of Cairo flights came with

35

added Lee Enfields and Vickers machine guns for one side or the other, so he'd checked over the B-25 personally to be sure it wasn't carrying that kind of sucker punch. He didn't want a detour into jail, especially not a Greek jail while there was a vicious war on.

As the props appeared out of the blur and wound to a halt, Crane began the post-flight check and filled in the logs, trying to ignore the cold beer that kept swimming into his vision and performing a little dance. He was drifting west, more or less, heading towards Berlin. There was plenty of work for flyers there, so he'd been told, and great broads. Although he wasn't looking for great broads, just one called Lorna McGill, and he'd heard from her old boss that she, too, was heading for the city carved up by the Allies like a pizza pie.

He finished the write-up and pulled out the piece of paper that told him the name of the bar on Syntagma Square where this Mikklos did business. He needn't have bothered.

'Captain Crane? Captain Lee Crane?'

The speaker bustled forward, wearing a white suit that had no place in a converted bomber on its last legs. Already he had streaked it with dirt and oil. Crane hoped he had a spare. And knew a good laundry. The Greek held out his hand. He was younger than Crane had expected, perhaps thirty, with a handsome face he chose to hide behind a moustache you could practise topiary on. 'Mikklos Christopoulos. I had a cable from Rani.' The broker in Cairo. 'He said you wanted to buy a plane.'

'Yeah,' Crane said. 'A C-47 or DC-3. One that still has a spring in her step and a modicum of self-respect. Not one with too many bad husbands and lousy lays on her books.' He used to have one just like that. Now she was scrap in a Calcutta yard, slowly being turned into cooking utensils. It was a crying shame.

'I know exactly what you mean. I have heard of several suitable aircraft.'

Crane felt a trickle of moisture down his neck and checked the cockpit thermometer. 'Shall we do this outside?'

'Sure, sure.'

They retreated to the apron, where Mikklos's driver fetched them lemonade from the trunk of a canary-yellow Dodge. It was warm and over-sweet but it would do until Crane came within hailing distance of a decent barkeep.

Now Mikklos took a good look at his potential customer, noting the scruffy forage cap on his head, the faded khakis and the battered leather jacket with the insignia that showed Crane had once flown transports in India and China. Crane knew what he was thinking.

The Greek wiped the pop bubbles off the shrub growing under his nose and said, 'Captain Crane, I am sorry to be so blunt. Assuming we find an aircraft to your liking, how will you finance this purchase? Will it be lease? A loan? Or will you pay cash?'

There was no doubting which he would prefer. Crane waited until the man had taken another gulp of his lemonade before he said softly: 'Gold.' The broker struggled not to choke or spray his new favourite client with saliva and soda. 'If that is OK.'

'Oh, that's very OK, Captain Crane,' he gasped. 'Very OK indeed.'

The pilot saw the little flash of greed in Mikklos's eyes and knew they were in business. Lee Crane was on his way to Berlin.

After he had picked up his signal traffic from the communications office at the Olympic stadium, Webb dismissed his driver and walked from the stadium to the S-Bahn, along the same wide avenue where the Nazis had paraded their Supermen prior to the games. He needed time to think. He'd never lost a man before, at least not like Otto, killed in front of him. Sometimes the lines went quiet, no further messages were received and you knew either the Objective had abandoned the job or been caught. But that was anonymous, distant and an inevitable fallout from the business. Nobody had warned him about the horrors of losing a man who trusted you, right before your eyes.

Webb had been a spy for a dozen years, ever since a man called

Claude Dansey had asked him to 'keep his eyes open' during the 1936 Winter Olympics at Garmisch-Partenkirchen and report back. He'd kept them open all right. Whereas the whole world had scrutinised the Berlin events, when the Nazis were on their best behaviour, the Winter Olympiad, deep in Bavaria, showed them at their most rabid. He still recalled the baying welcome Hitler had received, and the terrifying legions of Hitler Youth and Labour Battalions who had emerged from the blizzard that was blowing on the opening day. It was as if hell itself had opened its doors.

After that, he'd volunteered to help Dansey further, and the old man had arranged for him to spend a few months with Frank Foley in Berlin. Foley was ostensibly Passport Control Officer in Berlin – for which read MI6 Head of Station – and had caused a furore by issuing visas to Jews. Tens of thousands of them, it seemed, but nobody could ever be sure. There were certainly many, many families who owed their survival to Foley. Between them, Dansey and Foley had forged Webb's view of the espionage business.

Foley had burned with a Christian righteousness that Webb couldn't share, but he admired the man's trenchant bloody-mindedness in standing up to the Nazis. Nobody walked over Frank Foley. Dansey was less idealistic. To him espionage was a job – diplomacy by other, scurrilous means.

But both mentors encouraged him to follow his instincts, to trust the hairs on the back of his neck, the little nagging voice in the forgotten corner of the mind that was far too easy to gag. And what did his instincts tell Webb?

In the cold light of a Berlin day, it seemed to him that Otto's death was no mere bungle. That somebody was out to get him and SOB. He felt hunted, as if someone, somewhere had unleashed a pack of hounds that even now were sniffing the city's air, trying to locate him and bring him down. Losing Otto was designed to humiliate Webb, to make him vulnerable, more likely to stumble when the dogs fell upon him.

But who would benefit from his embarrassment? Major Tyler was too old a hand to give much away, but the attempt to absorb Webb, and Librarian, into SIS was a little too hasty for comfort. But even SIS wouldn't stoop so low as to murder Otto, just to create leverage. Part of him knew Tyler was right – SOB did have a limited time left as an independent organisation, but he still felt Librarian had important Intel to offer. After failing Otto, he had to make sure it was protected. No more bodies, that was his aim; no more sad, wasted deaths down to him.

There was a streak of anger now, burning fiercely, that insisted he avenge the dead German. His pride demanded it, even though he knew this was a dangerous consideration for a spy. But already the whispers within the over-garrulous Intelligence community would be saying that Webb was finished, ready for the scrapheap or a Whitehall desk job. Which amounted to the same thing. It was important he show them they had it all wrong. That Webb still had a bite or two left in him.

As he skirted a roped-off area of the car park – the blue and yellow tape was the kind favoured by the UXB chaps, so he gave it a very wide berth, – unexploded bombs being a daily fact of Berlin life – Webb examined the two signals he had brought with him. It was a nuisance having to use SIS communication channels, but cost cutting in London had meant the closure of their own secure link. Of course, he made sure his messages were double encrypted, so no casual operator could decipher them, but he suspected Tyler saw copies anyway and the code wasn't good enough to withstand a half-decent cryptologist.

The first message told him there was a woman causing a bit of trouble in London, it seemed, bandying his name about to all and sundry. The second was a signal from an old colleague, Rose Miller, saying the same woman, Laura McGill, had been in touch. Should she speak to her? He pocketed the sheets for later consideration. McGill? The name made him shiver with discomfort. That was just what he needed right now. Another bloody McGill.

By the time he had reached the S-Bahn station that would take him back to the centre, Webb had decided on a strategy and, furthermore, he had a half-decent plan for the evening: a drink, followed by a visit to a whore.

Five

Laura McGill travelled south from London to see Rose Miller with nothing more lethal about her person than a bottle of Very Choice Highland Mortlach. The Colt was left at home. She caught the train to Broadstairs from Charing Cross, a slow stopper that would call at all the stations along the North Kent coast. Still, it gave her time to prepare herself for the meeting.

She had with her two glossy red Silverine exercise books in which she had written all that she knew about Diana's mission to France, and the progress she had made. In fact, one of the pair was pretty empty, apart from a few doodles. In the other was a series of asteriks and arrows. *Go back to basics*, Napier had said.

Pleased to have a compartment to herself, she waited until her ticket had been punched by the guard and then spread out the books and her pens on the seat next to her. Many of the pages told a tale of dead ends, stony silences, blank stares, evasive answers. The SOE, SOB, MI5, SIS, CSDIS and GCCS – the Government Code and Cipher School – had all drilled their men and women well. Old slogans such as *Walls Have Ears* and *Careless Talk Costs Lives* were backed up by the full weight of the Official Secrets Act.

Even people she had considered friends had shaken their heads and regretted they couldn't help her, while at the same time wishing her luck. She knew what they were thinking: that this was the wildest of goose chases, that a woman lost in France and Germany for four years could only be dead. Their unspoken advice was to let her sister rest in peace. But Laura couldn't allow Diana to be dismissed so easily.

There had been other, more oblique ways to approach this puzzle. Diana was sent into France to investigate why a supply line vital to the war effort in China had been disrupted. Most agents were parachuted in, which meant a course at Ringwood, near Manchester. Those records were freely available. However, no Diana McGill appeared on the books, nor any female for the period during which she would have trained, March-April 1944.

Which meant she was probably flown in by Lysander. Again, that narrowed down the possibilities. Most of these single-engined planes hopped over the Channel from Manston in Kent or Tangmere in Hampshire. By the time Diana was mission-ready, Manston had been turned over to the USAAF and the black Lysanders were no longer based there. So all flights were leaving from Tangmere. There was an association of ex-flyers for 161 Squadron, the 'special duties' outfit that infiltrated and exfiltrated agents and who felt its role in the clandestine war was under-valued. This meant they were more open to persuasion when it came to discussing their missions. They didn't mind talking at all, in fact.

So through them she had managed to find a young pilot, Horrocks, who remembered a flight with a blonde woman around the right time. He mentioned a Frenchman named 'Raymond', another called 'Georges' and a British agent known as 'Astor'.

From the Friends of Maurice Buckmaster, an Anglo-French organisation which celebrated SOE's F (for French) Section, she confirmed that 'Raymond' was Raymond Bec, a young Resistant who had been recommended for the Croix de Guerre for his work in Paris Le Man and Taxi. The smuggling link had been broken somewhere between the latter two cities.

It wasn't much, as yet, but somehow she could feel herself getting closer to Diana; the ethereal figure that her sister had become was solidifying, and soon Laura might be able to reach out and touch her.

The dreary suburbs of South London slid by, an endless procession of washing lines sagging under the weight of clothes, and tiny backyards, each one with an outside privy and a concrete bunker for coal. These grimy terraces gradually gave way to more affluent semi-detached houses, with well-tended lawns, greenhouses and children's swings.

As the train sank into a cutting, robbing her of even that view, Laura reflected on the lengths the authorities had driven her to. She could scarcely credit her kidnap of Rufus Napier. But dealing with these people generated the kind of frustration you normally felt when trying to obtain a telephone line from the Post Office, reporting a leak to the Gas Board or applying for a bank loan – only multiplied a thousand times.

Her own intransigence was fuelled partly by guilt, she knew, because she was responsible for coercing Diana into taking the London job while she herself went out to China. As she had almost explained to Napier, it could have been *her* lost in France, but for the toss of a coin and a petulant sulk. But there was more to it than just remorse.

She also wanted Diana to know about the four long years she had spent nursing their mother, to hear her say, 'Well done,' to appreciate her sacrifice. Over and above that was a third thing. Diana was her sister and, even if she was sometimes infuriating and haughtily superior, not knowing what had happened to her was like having a missing limb, one of those phantom appendages that injured servicemen claimed they felt the need to scratch. She couldn't go through life explaining to strangers that, no, she wasn't an only child, but that she never did discover what had happened to Diana.

She was still pondering this when she fell into a fitful sleep. She dreamed of days before the war, with her sister and mother, summers in Dorset, Christmas at her aunt's house in Gloucestershire, of the sudden chasm between her and Diana as the latter developed breasts, curves and admirers. Little sisters were suddenly surplus to requirements. The dream darkened, into arguments and bitchy recriminations about hurtful gossip and borrowed clothes. Then she thought of their last real summer together, when Diana had a boyfriend called Hugh, the one with the Alvis, and how they would sometimes take Laura with them on their little 'tours', allowing her to sip cider in a pub garden and join in with their risqué jokes. Even in her half-slumber, she knew that was the Diana she wanted to find.

England gave way to China in a seamless transition. She could feel the heat of Kunming on her skin, and the acid burning in her throat, a memory of those vomit-flecked flights over the Himalayas – The Hump, as they called it. She also dreamed about Lee Crane, the American pilot who had betrayed, or at least, deceived her. This was a man she hoped never to see again, even in her slumbers.

Laura awoke thirsty and disoriented, forgetting for a moment where she was, shooing away imaginary mosquitoes. The train had stopped. and curlicues of steam pirouetted up past the window. They were in a station. She became aware of another person in the carriage, a middle-aged woman with an elaborate hat held in place with a silver pin. She was eyeing Laura with some disapproval, and the girl wondered if she had been snoring. Gathering up her exercise books, she replaced them in her bag and looked out through the sooty window at the new-style British Rail sign as it slid out of view. *Whitstable*. Not long now.

The station at Broadstairs was at the top of the town, away from the seafront and sands that drew the thousands of summer visitors who came for the perfect sweep of Viking Bay, the Punch and Judy shows, fish and chips and the celebrations of Charles Dickens. Today, though, a thin drizzle was falling and Laura was one of only a handful of people who alighted from the train. As instructed, once she had handed in her ticket, she used the public telephone in the ticket hall to call for a taxi to take her to the address Rose Miller had supplied.

The Ford Pilot appeared within five minutes; Laura identified herself by name and passed the slip of paper with the address on it to the driver as she stepped in. He was querying the name of the road when she became aware of somebody sliding in beside her.

'I'm sorry, this is my taxi—' she began. Her last impression as the gauze pad was forced over her nose and face and she was pushed down into the rear well, was of a conical hat held in place with a fancy silver pin.

Six

Webb walked into Johnny K's latest nightclub and took a deep breath, inhaling its atmosphere of Sobrainie smoke, Chanel Number 5, intrigue and lust. He loved this place; it reminded him of those months in Berlin in 1936, when he would hang out at Sabine's Cabaret, the Kit-Kat or the Red Fox. It was almost the same smell, although even by the time he left the city in early 1937, it was being replaced by the stench of fear, as the Nazis cracked down on such disruptive hangouts. But here, alive and high-kicking, was their progeny. Outside, Berlin might be in ruins, but in one of Johnny K's clubs, the spirits of 1936 still hung around the bar, talking about old times.

Johnny K had made his first stash of post-war money running SWING!, a club named in honour of the *Swing Jugend*, the German kids who had risked Nazi wrath with their love of 'degenerate' American jazz music. SWING! had been housed in the basement of a ruin on the Ku'damm; it catered for GIs who had drunk too much and clear-headed Fräuleins with an eye on the main chance. The house band had been a mix of displaced persons and a couple of Waffen-SS veterans who claimed the closest they had come to combat was providing the thumping soundtrack to various victory parades.

Those who remembered SWING! spoke fondly of the long

nights segueing into hungover dawns, the endless booze, the free sex (well, if not quite free, it was certainly dirt cheap), the transvestite cabaret that, shockingly, turned out to consist of genuine females, and the frequent raids by MPs. Late 1945 until early 1946 was a golden age for the Berlin underground club scene; like all such golden ages its lustre grew with each year. Webb, however, recalled SWING! as a sweaty dive where you felt you might catch VD from the furniture.

These days, Johnny K ran somewhere that epitomised the second wave of post-war clubs. The Blaues Zimmer was at the junction of the East/West border and the British and American Sectors – the latter had effectively been fused together for administrative purposes – maximising the catchment area for clientèle. Johnny K was what was known as a *Grenzhändler* – a border trader. He still operated in a basement, but this one had something other than damp brick walls growing mushrooms. The walls here were covered in a silky brown material and dotted with low-wattage lamps. The house band were pros, the bar well-stocked, the only accepted currency – unless you knew Johnny himself – foreign. Your Reichsmarks were no good here. At the rear was a 'cabaret' room, with a fluid divide between antics on the stage and at the tables. A flame-haired woman called Tante Greta, who wore dresses cut far too low for her age, controlled a door that led to stairs that enabled clients and girls to access the by-the-hour rooms on the ground floor.

When Jimmy Webb strolled in that evening, the place was already packed. He did a sweep of the room, clocking the usual mix of informers, pimps, journalists and spies that Johnny cultivated, and crossed to the bar. Ernst Henkell, of the Kripo, the slang for the Criminal Detective Division of the Police, was already there, perched on a stool. This particular *Detektiv* supplemented his income – which wouldn't normally stretch to Blue Room cocktails – by keeping Webb abreast of the political upheavals that shook the police service every two months, and by providing

Sweepers, although this particular sideline was in abeyance following the Otto fiasco.

Webb's deputy, Alan Towers, the bruise on his face almost healed, was whispering in the ear of one of the waitresses, who had a puzzled expression on her face. Webb could only guess what Pretty Boy was suggesting to her. Also at the bar was Bob Dolan, the man who had a job–title so long, it would be hard to fit it on a desk plaque. He was Assistant to the Director of the Something Something Something. It didn't matter what it said on his door: everyone knew Bob Dolan was former OSS, still very CIA, and Head of Staff D, the Communications Division.

'Jimmy,' the American yelled over the babble.

'Bob.' Ralph Tyler and his SIS cronies abhorred any kind of fraternisation with the Americans at 'desk level'. It was considered dangerous; liaison usually took place in the formal setting of the offices of SIS and the CIA in Frankfurt. Webb thought this restriction nonsense; he liked Americans and he enjoyed the way they spent their money. They weren't afraid to have a good time, something some of Webb's British colleagues seemed to have forgotten.

'Drink?' asked Dolan, right on cue. Towers, realising his boss was now in play, shooed the waitress away and gave his best sheepish grin.

'Whisky,' said Webb.

'Magda!' Dolan indicated the statuesque barmaid, whose cleavage was designed to take your mind off the price of booze. 'How's the ear, Jimmy?'

Webb shot a pantomime glance at Towers, who shrugged his innocence of talking out of turn. Berlin was a small village, as gossipy as any British market town.

'Oh, Alan here didn't tell me nuthin'.' Dolan sometimes played up his Texan accent, as if that would convince people he was just some dumb cowboy. It belied the fact that, although he could have been a pro baseball player, the lean, rangy American was a sharp-minded lawyer. 'Everyone here knows what happened. They were selling the whole story at the Prague the next day.' The Café Prague was where the bottom-feeders of the Intelligence community – the freelance tittle-tattlers – plied their wares. Most of the so-called 'Intel' was pure conjecture or out-of-date rubbish, but none of the agencies felt they could ignore the place completely.

'It's not worth five dollars,' said Towers dismissively. 'Although I heard CIA paid fifty.'

Dolan smirked. 'And worth every cent. We always like the lowdown on our friends' misfortunes.'

'These Americans have no concept of inflation,' said Towers to Webb, ruefully. 'Next thing we know they'll be paying good money to discover what type of dye Uncle Joe uses on his moustache.'

'Zubrovna brand,' Dolan whipped back with a victorious grin. 'Twenty-five roubles a tin. The best that funny money can buy.'

'Take no notice,' warned Webb. 'He'll be telling us the Russians have the bomb next.'

Dolan's face looked pained. 'Don't even joke about that, Jimmy.'

'Jimmy's had a nasty blow to the head,' said Towers, by way of explanation. The Russians' race to get a working atomic bomb was one topic always treated seriously.

'Yeah, so how is it, Jim?'

'It's not too bad, thanks, Bob. A bit of buzzing now and then. I'm going to have it checked out when I am in London.'

'You're off to London?' he asked as casually as he could.

'Relax. It's nothing. I'm not being promoted, demoted, briefed, debriefed or bollocked.'

There was a burst of applause from next door. 'New dancers,' said Bob. 'Fresh blood. These ones look like they've had a good meal in the past week rather than those dancing skeletons Johnny usually gets. Wanna look?' he asked. 'Before your chum Alan gets first pick?'

'Oh, really,' protested Towers with a self-deprecating smile that caused his cheeks to dimple. 'I have enough trouble with the waitresses here.'

'Only the ones you bang up.' Towers's jaw dropped and Dolan said: 'Only kiddin', Alan. Only kiddin'.'

Dolan had a reputation for two things: being able to down three martinis at lunch and still keep a clear head, and finding a new girl every week to amuse himself with. Webb suspected this was all a cultivated distraction from his less obvious talents. Still, Webb sometimes played games with the perceived notions of stiff Englishness, too.

'Alan here has been telling me about his days in T-Force,' said Dolan.

'The Phooey Fighters?' Webb smirked. His drink arrived and he swirled the liquid in the bottom of the glass and sniffed appreciatively. Dolan always got the good stuff out of Magda.

Towers winced at Webb's joke. His failure to find the legendary Foo-Fighters was a source of merriment to Webb and others. Those bright lights that streaked by bewildered bomber crews were rumoured to be the ultimate secret weapon, which was why T-Force had gone racing behind lines into the Harz Mountains. Sure, they'd located underground factories and advanced technology, but not the mythical Nazi 'Black Science' that was decades ahead of the Allies. That did turn out to be pure phooey.

'Just explaining the ribtickling lighter moments with the Reds,' said Towers sardonically. On his scientific fishing trips, Towers had seen enough of how the Russians behaved towards the Germans to dispel any romantic notions he might have held about their old Ally. The only ribtickling had been at the end of a rifle butt. 'Gentlemen, I was thinking of moving on.'

'Where to?' asked Dolan.

Towers moved his expert eye onto the pert backside of one of the patrolling waitresses. 'The Krypt – interested?' He made some stiff movements with his arms and mimicked Johnny K's accent. 'A little dancing, perhaps, make GI very happy.'

Webb had to laugh. 'No. I'll stick around. Did you bring the . . . ?' He let it tail off.

'Oh, right.' Alan took an envelope from his inside pocket and handed it over. 'All there.' He turned to Dolan. 'Sure you won't come to the Krypt? There's one girl there with an amazing act . . .'

Dolan shook his head. 'One bar is much like another to me. I'll prop up this one and proposition Magda.' The barmaid flashed him an in-your-dreams smile.

'Okey-dokey. Night, all.'

When Towers had left, Dolan ordered more drinks. 'How's Olivia?'

He had met the subject of Webb's on-off relationship when she had come over to visit him in 1947. The American and the Englishwoman had got on famously, although she had hated both Berlin and spying.

'I don't know,' Jimmy replied. 'She's one of the reasons to go back to London.'

'And a mighty fine one. Marry her, Jimmy. Before I do.' Bob Dolan suddenly lowered his voice. The Texan accent was almost completely absent now. 'We had someone snatched last week. Went into a camera store not far from here and they bundled him out the back. One of our G-2s.'

'Good grief.' A G-2 was an army intelligence officer; quite a catch.

'Not senior, but we've heard nothing more of him. I just want to say, you were lucky they only dealt with your man – Otto, was it?' Webb nodded. 'That they didn't take you.' There was real concern in his voice. 'Be careful, Jimmy. Berlin is a boil they want to burst. They might be starting to squeeze the pus out.'

Webb tried not to flinch at the rather queasy metaphor. 'I will, thanks.'

'What did Otto have?'

51

'Didn't have time to tell me. He'd been at the uranium mines. From the way he was speaking, I would guess they've upped production. You fart in public in the East these days, you get six months down the mines. Which is a life sentence, of course.'

'Shit.' They both knew that the uranium dug from the shafts on the Czech border was a vital part of the Russians' efforts to produce that A-Bomb.

Webb swirled the last of his whisky in the glass. 'I've got to go. Thanks for the drinks.'

'Any time. Anything I can do . . .'

Webb hesitated. 'I might take you up on that.'

'Meaning?' asked Dolan warily.

'I might need a Pavlovsky.'

'You're shittin' me.'

'I would not,' Webb said softly, enunciating carefully, 'shit you.'

'They're expensive.' Dolan wasn't talking cash. Intelligence was just as hard a currency as the Yankee Dollar.

'I'll find a way to pay.' Webb finished his drink, a large mouthful that made him shudder with painful pleasure. 'It's not certain yet. I might be barking up the wrong tree. I'll keep you posted.'

'Yeah. Remember – take care.'

'I will.'

As he left the club and climbed into the chill air of twilight, Webb heard an urgent voice behind him.

'Herr Webb – Jimmy. Can I talk with you?'

He spun to see Henkell, the Kripo man, bounding up the steps behind him.

After a moment's hesitation, Webb said: 'I'm after a cab. Walk with me to the corner?'

'Of course.'

Ernst Henkell had been a cop in Berlin before the war, based at the Alex, the Police Praesidium building to the south of Alexanderplatz. He had been thrown off the Force in 1936 because of his half-Jewish wife and had made a living as a security consultant.

He'd had a rough war, although not as rough as his wife, who didn't survive. When, in 1947, the German Police Force in the West was purged of former Nazis, Webb had been happy to sponsor him back to his old job. Henkell owed his *Fragebogen* – the much sought-after deNazification certificate – to Webb.

Webb leaned in close as the man spoke, so he could hear his words clearly. 'I just thought you should know about the Ami,' Henkell murmured.

'What American?'

'The one Dolan was talking about. Henderson. The G-2 who went shopping and got snatched.' Unlike Johnny K, there was no mistaking that this man was a native Berliner; the 'g' sounds were soft and sibilant.

'What about him?'

The *Detektiv* waited as a woman, carrying two heavy suitcases, struggled by. Her face was gaunt and the eyes had the look common to many Berliners, the dullness of long-term shock, that life should be reduced to this.

'He's dead,' Henkell said.

'What?'

'Oh, an accident, I think. A car taking him to Potsdam overturned. Some say the driver was drunk, others that a burst tyre was the cause. It was all over the Alex when I was there the other day.'

That put the Reds in a quandary. If they said he died in a road smash, then they had to admit to having him in the first place. Plus when it came to trading, as a rule of thumb, a warm body was better than a corpse. 'Why didn't you tell Dolan?'

Henkell touched his arm. 'Because I have nothing I need from Bob Dolan or the Amis. But you might.'

Webb nodded. It had become ingrained in them all, the little barter, the favour stored up for future use; everything had its value. Of course, this also racked up a credit for the Kripo man, should he need it. Webb reached for his wallet.

'Herr Webb, please.' He sounded offended. But then, everyone always did.

'Just a little Bowle,' suggested Webb. The name of the drink – a wine and fruit punch – was also slang for a sweetener or bribe.

'It's a favour.' The hurt seemed genuine. 'Remember those? They come free of charge. Besides, I owe you one.' Here was the real reason, thought Webb. An attempt to balance the books after Otto.

'No, you don't. But thanks, Ernst.'

'Welcome.'

They reached the intersection, the smashed buildings on all sides fading into a darkness that hid the worst of the scars, giving the random zigzag outlines a blue-tinged beauty. Across the road had been a C&A store and next to that, Schnabel's Pharmacy which, as well as medicines, had a section which carried British goods for the ex-pat community. This collection of stumps was where, in 1936 at least, the homesick Embassy staff went for their Marmite, Fowler's Golden Syrup or Brown's Blend Orange Crush.

A clanking Mercedes diesel taxi pulled up when Webb raised his arm. 'I'll see you when I get back from London.'

Then, once more, the friendly concern: 'You take care, Jimmy.'

James Hadley Webb did take care. He took care to make sure he was being followed. Whoever it was on his tail, as the Yanks said, wasn't bad, because whenever he stopped and made a show of consulting a map or asking a passer-by the time, there was no sign of him. But he was sure he was there. After twenty minutes, he spotted him, a shadow hanging far enough back that Webb couldn't make out much more than a silhouette. That was enough. He just wanted to be sure his instincts were correct. It was time to dump the tag.

In rapid succession he jumped two taxis, a U-Bahn, an S-Bahn and then walked the final two kilometres in a large loop that doubled back on itself.

At one point he thought that a black Volkswagen, that funny little jelly-mould of a car saved from extinction by the British Army, of all people, had made him when it came by twice. He noted the number as it clattered by, but it never reappeared. Just someone else lost in streets that no longer had landmarks.

Only when his feet were getting numb with cold did he finally decide he was no longer being followed and turned into the road that had been his destination all along. Americans called them 'cold-water walk-ups', grim tenements with four or six floors, no lifts, no communal heating system, one lavatory per floor and a warren of damp, depressing rooms. This street was unusual because one whole side had survived more or less intact, apart from blast marks and the usual smallpox of bullet holes.

He slipped through the door of number 30, past the ill-fed youths hanging around the stairwell and, no doubt like every other one of Karin's clients, pulled his hat down. Visiting a prostitute, a 'snapper', was not exactly uncommon in Berlin, but it still demanded discretion.

'She's busy!' one of the *Trümmerkinder* – the children of the rubble – yelled.

'You'll have to wait your turn.'

'Yeah, after us.' They collapsed in a fit of giggles.

Despite a strong desire to bang their lice-ridden heads together, Webb ignored the kids and carried on climbing, the slow plod of his steps on the bare treads echoing around the central shaft of the building. Karin's apartment was on the top floor. A painfully thin Frau sat outside, knitting, her faded, baggy overall suggesting a bulkier previous life. When she looked up at him, her face was like a skull with a taut, fleshy membrane stretched across it. She examined him, moving her head up and down, then nodded towards a glass door at the far end of the landing and said: 'Wait in there, please.'

This had never happened before. He checked his watch. He was exactly on time. Still, there was little to be done. He touched the brim of his hat and went to the waiting room. The door screeched as it opened. The frame was twisted, settled out of true, probably thanks to the bomb damage in the area.

The space beyond was little more than a cupboard, furnished with a rickety card-table and a shabby cane chair. The only internal light source was a bulb screwed into a wall socket. From a shelf, he took a dusty copy of *Stars and Stripes* and flicked through it, wondering why he found not one of the many cartoons remotely funny.

He heard someone clump along the landing, but could only make out a vague shape through the frosted glass. Had there been another client before him? Webb insisted she kept thirty minutes free before his slot. Bumping into a familiar face in Karin's doorway would be a tremendous embarrassment, after all.

Karin was in her mid-twenties, a woman who in normal times might have had a decent job in government, teaching or in the health services. But with inflation making wages worthless within a week and a two-year-old boy with suspiciously Slav-like features to look after, she had taken the same route as many of her fellow Berliners: servicing the basic needs of the Occupiers. He wasn't sure who the old woman was – he never asked and she never told him – but he suspected it was her mother. There would be no judgements of her choice, except by snot-nosed street kids like those below; it was simply accepted as necessary.

Sometimes, it was hard to recall how much he had despised the Germans just three years ago, when he felt they had brought all this on themselves. These days, he found himself wondering more and more if people like Karin, Magda at the Blaues Zimmer, Ernst Henkell, and the woman knitting on the landing truly deserved this scrap of a life. Were the deprivations they suffered justified? There was no doubting the enormity of the Nazi crimes, but as his admiration for the phlegmatic Berliners had grown, Webb's initial certainties about retribution and recompense had wavered.

He opened the envelope that Towers had given him. Inside

were a dozen signed chits enabling Karin to draw clothes, light-bulbs, candles, food and fuel from the NAAFI. Another commodity that was better than cash. A sharp rap on the glass told him his number was up. He stood, adjusted his coat and went to see his favourite prostitute.

Seven

As soon as Laura opened her eyes she felt her world lurch. Something bitter rose up from her stomach and she gagged, spitting onto the floor and wiping the stringy dribble from her mouth with the back of her hand. She closed her eyes again and moved up onto all fours, aware of a floor that scratched at her skin. It was rough and gritty and cold. Concrete, she guessed.

She knelt there for what seemed like five minutes before lifting her lids again. Yes, concrete. Ridged and coarse, stained from splatters far older than the dark circle she had hawked up. She risked raising her thumping head to examine the room. It was painted in a dark green gloss, although it was covered with a scarring of chips and scratches, some of which were an attempt to form words. Three pipes ran down the wall in front of her, fat as sewage conduits. A faint gurgle of liquid came from them. She could smell something putrid in the air. Were they leaking?

In one corner of the room was a cream iron-framed bed, of the kind used in hospitals, and on it a mattress any self-respecting medical establishment would burn. The same went for the greasy pillow. Two striped blankets were folded on the bed. Apart from that uninviting cot, the only other furniture was a steel bucket which, although empty, was obviously the source of the faecal smell. It hadn't been disinfected, probably in an age.

There was a door, metal by the look of it, the skin wrinkled like an orange, a patina from a thousand futile blows and kicks. In the middle, at head height, was a round disc. A peephole, no doubt.

A bare bulb on a fitting attached directly to the centre of the ceiling, with no cord, gave the only light. There were two slits high on one wall, which might once have contained glass, but they were painted over with the same lurid green paint as the rest of the cell. The covering was intact because they were too high to reach to scratch away and see if daylight was behind them.

Laura shuffled backwards and propped herself against the bed, pulling her hair away from the mattress. She had on a blue shift dress of thick cotton, with a tie at the waist. The scratchy, over-boiled knickers weren't hers either, nor the vest that was the only other piece of underwear. She concentrated on breathing deeply, trying to purge her body of whatever chemical it was the woman with the hatpin had used to knock her out. Had she been Rose Miller? Something told her no. That woman had been in her late forties; Rose Miller was ten years younger at least. Still, she'd been fearsomely strong and professional. Someone had trained her well. And that someone must be the Government.

Laura fought off a sudden wave of panic that caused her to shudder. *Keep calm*, she told herself. *Take it one step at a time.*

Talking of which, what time was it? The train had pulled into Broadstairs just after eleven. The cab had arrived at around twenty past. How long had she been unconscious? She didn't feel too groggy, so she suspected they hadn't used a vast amount of the knockout drops. Let's say it is one o'clock, and take it from there, she thought. She would try and keep some kind of mental time, even if it was off by a few hours.

So, next question. Where am I? A prison of some sort, that much was clear. But whose? And for what? Kidnapping? Possession of a firearm? But shouldn't she have been arrested for those crimes, taken to a police station and charged? And given access to a solicitor? Not drugged and abducted.

Which meant this wasn't a police matter. That she was here because of the Blue. This was the old catch-all, DOR, Defence of the Realm. Now she really did start shivering, as the panic bubbled up inside. She'd trodden on toes by going after a Blue file. And those toes were no doubt encased inside the highly polished Oxfords of MI5 or someone similar.

'Shit!' she shouted out loud. Her voice seemed to die as it hit the green walls, as if even an echo wasn't allowed. 'Shit,' she repeated, softly this time.

OK, check the internal clock. About one-fifteen. Lunchtime. She was probably hungry, although it was difficult to decide whether the abdominal pangs were hunger or fear. She was also thirsty, her throat still tainted by the residuals of chemicals they had used on her. But there was no sink and no jug or glass of water.

She stood and paced, counting to estimate how long a minute was, and then sat again. She was in that position, head on her knees, when she heard the rattle of keys and the clicking of the levers in the lock. She leaped to her feet, the words and questions log-jamming in her throat. Before her stood two women in quasi-military uniforms, all epaulettes and buttoned pockets. They made a regular Laurel and Hardy team. 'Stan' had hair pulled back so tightly into a bun it appeared to have stretched her face smooth, giving her the look of a burns victim. Behind her, Hardy filled the doorway, mostly with a bosom that might be called matronly on another woman. On this scowling bitch, it looked like a lethal weapon. Laurel was gripping a metal tray with food in her right hand, but Olly held a pole, like a sawn-off broom-handle.

'Where the hell am I? What right—?' Laura began heatedly.

The pair said nothing, just withdrew, taking the tray and its food with them. The lock was thrown again, and she could hear the sound of retreating steps.

She began to count, and estimated that fifteen minutes had passed before they returned, the same unreadable expressions on their faces. This time Laura stood and tried to be less aggressive, more conciliatory. 'I'm sorry I shouted. I just need—'

The door slammed shut once more.

By now, her mouth was as dry as those Broadstairs sands she had been heading for. She smacked her lips and roiled her tongue, but seemed unable to generate any saliva.

When they returned for the third time, she stayed on the floor, not looking up. She heard the ringing of metal on concrete as the tray was lowered, followed by the slamming of the door.

Desperate as she was for a drink, and something to eat, Laura stayed where she was for a few more minutes, trying to contain her anger at herself. Eventually, she helped herself to the water, bread and soup. Whoever they were, they had already won the first round.

Eight

Alan Towers looked up from his desk as Webb tapped on the door. 'Sir?' He always addressed his boss formally within the confines of their office, but outside, Jimmy didn't mind Christian names. However, he knew that such familiarity would threaten to bring the MilGov roof down if overheard during working hours. Webb was clearly on his way out. He had on his overcoat and the dark chocolate 'Attaboy' Trilby he favoured. There was a brown-paper parcel under his arm, secured with twine.

'I'm off,' Webb announced.

'Anywhere nice?' asked Towers.

'The Opera.'

This could only mean the Staats Opera, over in the East. 'Really? What is it?'

'Glinka – *Russlan and Ludmilla*.'

Towers shrugged. 'Never heard of it.'

Webb smiled. 'Put it this way. I'm glad only one ear's working properly.'

'Watch your back over there,' said Towers. 'And front and sides. By the way, the hat-check girl at the Opera—'

'Please, Alan. We can't all have your stamina.' Or looks, he thought. It was always going to be easy for Towers in Berlin. If bulldogs like Dolan had no trouble finding girls, how much

62

easier for someone who looked like he could understudy Laurence Olivier. Still, at least he didn't flaunt it under Webb's nose too much.

Webb took a car-pool Mercedes and driver and cruised around town for an hour until they were both sure there was no tail. He had the Corporal drop him near Tiergarten. As he walked briskly through the still, chill air, he thought about Karin, the prostitute, and wondered if he could do more for her. He had known her brother, before the war, when the lad had been a part-time musician in the Ku'damm clubs. He had been killed in the Battle of Britain, a gunner in a Heinkel, downed by a Hurricane. When Webb had realised what his sister was doing for money, he offered her a decent sum to act as a cut-out, someone who receives and moves on messages without actually knowing what they are. Not enough cash or NAAFI chits for her to give up prostitution altogether perhaps, but enough that she could be choosy, and stay off the dangerous streets.

So they always spent his allotted half-hour drinking coffee and playing chess. He could give her more, but surely that would just make her a kept woman and the situation might become even trickier. He imagined it would be best if she climbed out of the trap herself. Perhaps he would give her a little more of a shove, though.

She had made it clear that he could also avail himself of her services as part of the deal, but Webb had refused. She was attractive, and he was no prude, but he was a professional. He knew only too well the dark places where the mix of business and sex led.

As he approached the crossing point he carefully removed his wristwatch, a Jaeger, and placed it in his inside pocket. He also had on his second-best topcoat and a rather scruffy pair of brogues. Hardly the dress for Covent Garden, but if you were crossing into the East, even if it was for opera, it was better to look dowdy. He threaded his way between fragments of fallen Doric columns, the remains of some once-grand building, pummelled into dust and a flotsam of architectural motifs.

Before he reached the blackened, skeletal hulk of the Reichstag, Webb turned right through the darkened arches of the Brandenburg Gate, still standing, but hardly intact, towards the Opera House. The three Russian soldiers on duty eyed him warily, wondering if he was worth a shakedown. Before they could move he tossed them a pack of cigarettes and said: '*Padarok.*' Present. Sometimes, it backfired, and they all wanted a present; this time he got a sardonic salute from the biggest of the group, a grubby-looking Tartar.

Ahead, flanked by a pair of hammers and sickles on plinths, was the vast illuminated poster of Uncle Joe in beaming, benevolent mode, with his creepy suffer-little-children smile plastered over his face, welcoming you to the Promised Land of the East. The effect was undermined completely by those black, shark-dead eyes of his, which told you things the false smile never could.

The streets here were empty compared to the West. 'Dead trousers', as the locals said. The Opera House, though, still thrived, the one bright spot along the darkened street. A crowd of mostly uniformed men and smartly dressed women milled around the double steps leading up to the terrace, smoking and laughing. The gaiety seemed inappropriate, given the surroundings. Webb went through the main door and found the cloakroom in the basement. The girl wasn't very busy, she explained, because the theatre was so cold that most people liked to keep their coats on. Even the performers sometimes, she said. He took her advice and gave her just the parcel, accepting a small red ticket in return and leaving a generous tip. He couldn't help but wonder if this was the very girl that Towers had mentioned, but he doubted it. She was too plain for Alan's discerning eye.

Inside the auditorium, wind whistled through gaps in a tarpaulin that had been stretched over part of the roof. As it snapped in the breeze, it dislodged pieces of gilt and plaster that rained down like tiny snowflakes onto the front two rows of the stalls. Webb's seat was at the end of the very back row and he took his place, wondering why Max wasn't there already. Still, getting across from Karlhorst took time.

As the audience filtered in, the air grew fouler. There was little hot water and no soap or toothpaste in the East. By the time the auditorium was full, the stench of unwashed human was ripe enough to make him retch. He tried hard to breathe through his mouth.

As surreptitiously as possible he turned and surveyed the entrance. No sign of his man Max yet. He was sure that Karin would have got the message across, and the Opera was the next due meeting-place, one of a dozen that they rotated, for fear of slipping into careless habit.

Fifteen minutes later, the overture to *Russlan and Ludmilla* began. Despite his misgivings Webb rather liked it, stuffed as it was with Russian themes and folk songs, and the crowd applauded at regular intervals as they recognised some patriotic ditty. He had a restricted view of the action on the stage, though, as many of the Soviet officers in the audience had not removed their enormously high-peaked caps. Nobody seemed to object; or, more likely, they were too scared to.

The overture finished and there was a flurry of activity as late-comers were admitted. Webb had to stand to let a flustered woman, her face red from exertion, past, but the seat next to him remained empty. *Come on, Max.* On stage, a lone female had burst into song. Ludmilla, Webb supposed. Max wasn't coming. Either he'd never got the message, or he'd been blown or he'd deemed it too dangerous. Whatever the reason, it wasn't a good sign. Webb hardly listened to the rest of the first act, waiting impatiently for the interval. It wouldn't do to just walk out mid-aria; that would only get him noticed.

After what seemed a Wagnerian age, there was a break and

Webb strolled out with the crowd, slipping away downstairs to the cloakroom. The parcel was too valuable to abandon.

Mistake. The girl had gone. His package was on the counter, opened, the precious blocks of Lifebuoy soap neatly stacked, apart from one. That tablet was being sniffed with exaggerated appreciation by a man dressed with the full broad-shouldered ostentation of a Russian Colonel.

The C-47 that Mikklos Christopoulos was offering was not in Athens but in Thessaloniki. They took the train there, a cramped six-hour journey, during which Mikklos alternated between paperwork, telling Crane what a fine aircraft he was about to buy with his gold, and lamenting the state of Greece. He was disappointed when Crane had to tell him he didn't physically have the gold. Oh, it existed all right: it was part of booty he had helped extract out of China.

'But you don't have it on you?' Mikklos asked, exasperated.

Crane laughed. 'If I had it on me, I couldn't get out of the seat. Or walk. You know how much that stuff weighs?'

Mikklos waved a hand. 'You know I didn't mean literally. I mean, did you bring it with you?'

Crane lit a cigarette, his third of the journey. 'Mikklos, I may be a dumb Americano, but even I know that the way to a long and healthy life does not involve flying around the world with a suitcase full of ingots. Sooner or later someone is going to want to carry it for you. With or without your permission.'

'I suppose you are right.'

'It's in a reputable bank in Calcutta and they will wire you the equivalent sum in any currency you wish. I don't take delivery until the transaction is complete – OK?'

'OK.' The train began to squeal as it hit a gradient. They were chugging up the side of a mountain, leaving the plains below. 'Where did you learn to fly?'

'Back home. Air Force. Before the war.'

66

'You saw action?'

Crane almost smiled. He'd been with the Flying Tigers fighting the Japanese, then flying cargo over The Hump, between Calcutta and Kunming, fighting off Zeros and the most capricious weather in the world. But he just nodded and said: 'I saw action,' in a tone that shut the topic down. He'd fill him in later if need be. Mikklos went back to his books, and Crane pulled down his forage cap and dozed. He'd seen scenery before.

Thessaloniki looked like an interesting town, with the kind of busy waterfront that always threw up rowdy bars and fascinating characters, but it was four in the afternoon when they arrived and Crane was keen to see the plane, so they took a cab straight to the airport. He could sightsee later.

The airstrip was south of town but on the coast, with the sea lapping at the side of one of the crumbling runways. The buildings looked ramshackle and neglected, and Crane hoped this wasn't a portent of things to come.

It wasn't. The C-47 was parked in the open, and had a few weeks' worth of salt-spray on her that should have been removed daily, but apart from that he liked the look of her. Crane soon discovered exactly when this C-47 had rolled off the Douglas production line, even without consulting the log. It was 8 June 1944, just after D-Day. He knew this because three of the riveters had scratched their names and the date on the fuselage, right next to the large red lever that was the emergency cargo-door release – something fitted to a few of the later DC-3s.

Three women – Mary-Lou, Susie D and Martha P – had used a fine power tool to etch their signatures on the panel. Underneath the names they had urged: *Go Get 'Em, Boys*. There were hearts and kisses. He wondered what became of the trio. Back to their pre-ordained lives as suburban housewives, he reckoned. *Thanks, girls, here's the kitchen sink.*

Whatever the three riveters were doing, after an hour going over the plane he raised an imaginary glass to them, because they, and their fellow workers, had bolted their plane together real well. She was no virgin, but she wasn't any kind of raddled whore either.

Unusually, there was no name on the nose, no hint that she had been christened, no flamboyant sketch of a scantily clad woman. It was bad luck to change the name of a plane, but he guessed that didn't apply when you could find no sign of a moniker in the first place.

After the long visual, looking for defects that might enable him to drive a harder bargain, and finding none, Crane sat in the pilot's seat. Every plane has an individual aroma and all control surfaces a unique pattern of wear. He checked for signs of abuse, of worn metal and broken Bakelite, sniffed for the ghostly scent of old electrical fires or short circuits. Nothing. Just a healthy mix of leather and ozone and oil and grease.

Through the windshield he could see Mikklos sitting in the shade of the hangar, drinking a beer. He gave a thumbs-up, but Crane ignored it. He began the pre-start check, but even before he fired her up, Crane knew he would take her. He also knew what he'd call her: *Three of a Kind*, after the trio of riveters who had left their names for him to find. He allowed himself a shiver of giddy pleasure. It was good to be in love again.

Webb made to turn to leave the cloakroom, but there were two soldiers blocking his way, both armed with stubby submachine guns. 'Sorry, just looking for the Gents,' he said to them, then repeated loudly: '*The Gents*. Lavatory. Toilet. Er, *Tyaner*.'

'Mr Webb.' The Russian cut through his bluster with a surprisingly high-pitched voice, considering his large jowlish face and barrel-chested bulk. 'Please.'

Webb let out a breath and stepped back to the counter, where the Colonel was stacking and restacking the soaps, as if they were a child's building blocks, and with just as much glee as a three year old.

'Soap,' he said.

'Yes,' replied Webb.

'Very valuable over here. For this much, I could buy . . .' His eyes rolled heavenward. 'You can imagine.'

'Yes. It was for my auntie. Not my real auntie – Tante Leni we called her—'

He tutted at this fabrication. 'Max isn't coming, Mr Webb.'

Webb furrowed his brow theatrically. 'I don't actually know anyone called Max.'

'Max Borchart. He has been detained.'

Webb knew he didn't merely mean 'late'. Poor Max.

There was a metallic buzz from above, just audible. The bell for the next act. Webb shifted uneasily. Now he really did need the Gents.

'You like the Glinka?' the Colonel enquired.

'Very nice.'

'I prefer his other opera – *A Life for the Tsar*. But it is not played so much now.'

'I suppose the title is a little out of touch with today's reality,' offered Webb.

The Russian laughed and held out his hand. 'Colonel Nikolai Zakharovich Grusenko.'

The Colonel had a fine white scar across his forehead and a prominent mole below his nose that Webb had to force himself not to stare at. He was a bit of a pug, but he gave him back his fingers without crushing them. 'James Hadley Webb.'

'But Jimmy to your friends.'

'I don't think we are quite yet that, Colonel.'

There was another burst of laughter that caused a shaking of the jowls. 'No. But acquaintances – work colleagues, perhaps.'

'Except we work on different sides.'

'Sometimes, perhaps, sometimes. Ah, listen.'

The opera had restarted and, by some quirk of the acoustics, the orchestra was perfectly audible in the cloakroom. The Colonel began to hum tunelessly. Clearly, he was not a member of the Red Army Choir.

'What do we do now, Colonel?'

The Russian frowned as he looked down at the green tower before him. 'I cannot take this soap.'

It was Webb's turn to laugh. A Russian Colonel in the East with two armed guards could do pretty much as he liked. 'Please, be my guest.'

'No. It would be stealing. I must give you something in return.' Colonel Grusenko scratched his head in an exaggerated fashion, before he clicked his fingers. 'I have it.'

From beneath the counter he retrieved his own parcel, about the size of a misshapen shoebox, more crudely wrapped than the Lifebuoy had been, but also done up with string. Webb hesitated.

'Don't worry, it doesn't explode.' The Russian held it up to his ear. 'See? No ticking. For you.' He held it out and, cautiously, Webb took it with both hands. 'There. We are even. Goodnight, Mr Webb. My men will escort you back to the border, just in case any of these German rogues cause you trouble.' He gave a wink. They both knew it wasn't the Germans that late-night strollers had to fear.

They didn't exactly frogmarch him to the Brandenburg Gate, but the two soldiers set up a brisk enough pace that Webb almost broke into a jog. Luckily, his recent sprinting meant he wasn't too puffed by the time he bade them goodnight. The pair made no reply, just watched in silence as he crossed over into the West, as if they were seeing a drunk off the premises.

Webb caught a cab to his flat, where he lit the fire laid by his housekeeper. A perk of his cover at the Board of Trade Office of Requirements was a decent supply of coal. He knew the Frau helped herself to a few lumps each time she prepared the grate, but he couldn't begrudge her that little hidden tax. While he waited for the place to warm up, he poured himself a small scotch.

First Otto and now Max. The cold, calculating part of him knew

Max was no great loss tactically. His primary role was to brief Webb on the developments in the structure of Soviet Intelligence. Webb had wanted to see him to discover the identity of the SMERSH people who had killed Otto. Was the organisation really back in business, or was that just a red herring? Max knew nothing about Librarian or his other circuits in the East. And there were too many cut-outs between Max and Karin for them to trace the message back to her. No, in the grander scheme of things, Max was an acceptable casualty.

So why did he feel so wretched? Because he could imagine the kinds of procedures being performed on him to make the man talk. The fact that he had nothing to give the Russians that they didn't already know wouldn't help. They would assume he was lying or stalling.

'Bastards,' he said out loud. All of them, fucking bastards. Especially that grinning gargoyle Grusenko. What was he playing at? It was time to see what he had given Webb in exchange for his Lifebuoy.

The parcel from the Colonel was wrapped in reused corrugated cardboard and held together with very coarse brown twine that was unravelling. Webb gave the package a preliminary squeeze but could find no hard edges to offer him a clue as to what was within. Using a pair of nail scissors, he snipped at the twine until he could unfold the outer wrapping.

Within it was a pass-the-parcel-style confection consisting of layer after layer of brown paper and newspaper. He cautiously unwrapped each one, until he came to the final sheet of thin onion tissue. Now he took off his overcoat and moved towards the fire. The thin sheets yielded to his fingers and he found himself holding a glove. A man's glove. A glove that shone like liquorice in the hearth's spluttering flames.

Webb turned it over in his hands, and became aware that there was something inside. He prised apart the wrist opening and tipped it up, giving the glove a little shake. He recoiled as something

ROBERT RYAN

clammy dropped into his palm. He examined it for a few seconds before he realised that it wasn't a pickled walnut or an exotic fungus. The lump of gristle had a covering of skin over part of the surface. It was a nose. A pockmarked nose he had last seen poking out from under the rim of a Homburg at Café Goethe.

Nine

Laura's mental clock told her it must be well into night-time, but the hideously bright bulb showed no sign of being extinguished. When she was convinced it was at least ten o'clock, she pulled the frame of the bed across the floor, as quietly as she could, so that the head of it was directly under the ceiling rose. Then she climbed gingerly onto the mattress and stepped with one foot onto the metal crosspiece. At first she lacked the nerve to balance fully, and although she could touch the light if she jumped up and down, it was not enough for her to be able to unscrew the bulb.

After a deep breath, she propelled herself upwards, placing both feet on the metal strip, her arms windmilling for balance. She stood there, swaying for a few moments until she was certain she wouldn't topple. Then, gingerly, she stretched above her head, holding her knickers in her hand to protect her from the fierce heat of the bulb.

She'd just got hold of the Osram and was twisting it when the door flew open and the outraged yells from the two warders made her slip backwards. She fell clumsily onto the edge of the bed and from there, straight onto the floor, feeling her ankle bend under her as she landed. Pain flashed up her calf, and she cried out, but was ignored. Laurel and Hardy simply threw the mattress off the bed, turned the frame on its side and marched off with it, slamming the door behind them.

The urge to cry again overwhelmed Laura, but she managed to hold back the tears; instead, she found herself lying bare-bottomed, on the floor, a blanket thrown across her, laughing at the ridiculousness of her situation, until she fell into an uneasy, pain-wracked sleep, her dreams invaded by the creaking of contracting pipes and the tap-tap of tiny, brittle legs on concrete.

'I ought to knock your blasted block off.' Robin 'Tin-Eye' Stephens was panting, his breath coming in clouds as he snarled at Webb. The latter had barely managed to get out of his car before Stephens had sprinted across the cobbled square, his eyes blazing with fury, the ever-present monocle flapping around his neck. 'Come to gloat, have you?'

The night after receiving his puzzling gift, Webb had flown in an RAF Dakota to Hanover, from where he intended to catch the evening BEA flight to London. Before that, however, he had borrowed a car from the SIS HQ and driven out to Bad Nenndorf, a once-pretty village eighteen kilometres out of town.

The town consisted of tiny black-and-white cottages interspersed with a few swanky merchant houses, many of them surprisingly intact, but the cobbled central square, which held the Town Hall, the bank and the magistrates' courts, was in total disarray. Abandoned filing cabinets and broken furniture littered the cobbles; three large Bedford trucks were being loaded with desks, chairs, lamps and more filing cabinets. There was the smell of burning in the air, and smouldering heaps of charred paper marked the spots where documents had been torched. The British Army was abandoning Bad Nenndorf.

'I'm not here to gloat, Robin. I'm not the gloating kind. Is there somewhere I can get a cup of tea?'

Webb waited while Stephens calmed down. He might be a xenophobic thug, but he was a well-mannered xenophobic thug. He wasn't going to refuse a chap a cup of tea.

'You've got a nerve.' Tin-Eye shook his head and grimaced as he refitted his monocle. 'C'mon.'

He led Webb across the square to the Town Hall and up a flight of cracked marble steps to the first floor. The place was empty and echoing, the wooden panelling and plaster of the walls disfigured where posters and maps had been carelessly torn down. The last time Webb had been here, the cluster of administrative buildings around the main square had been a hive of activity, especially in the cellars, where torture the Gestapo would have approved of was regularly used.

Stephens found them an office that still had a desk and two chairs, and rang down for a pot of tea.

'Where are the prisoners?' asked Webb.

'Some are in Hanover, others in Hamburg. Some they've set free.' The latter was said with a sneer.

Stephens had been a brilliant interrogator during the war, regularly breaking German spies who had had the misfortune to be landed in Britain. He ran Camp 020 – Latchmere House in Ham, where those suspected of working for the Abwehr were incarcerated and 'turned' by Stephens and his team. At Bad Nenndorf, also known as No 74 Combined Services Detailed Interrogation Centre, he had overstepped the mark. His rampant mistrust of foreigners had finally got the better of him, and he was convinced that most Germans were not only still closet Nazis but were also personally responsible for Dachau, Auschwitz and Belsen. Apart from those who were Communist spies.

His over-brutal methods of flushing out the latter had drawn complaints even from his own men, and Webb had been part of the inspection team sent in to check the veracity of rumours that Stephens was using starvation, sleep deprivation, humiliation, thumb- and shin-screws. The rumours turned out to have understated the degree of physical intimidation deployed at No 74 CSDIC. So much so, Stephens was now facing a court-martial.

'I'm sorry about the tribunal,' Webb said truthfully, if only because he already knew its outcome. Stephens would be acquitted; the Allied forces couldn't admit to torture, not so soon after Nuremburg. It would be a sham.

Stephens nodded. 'Damned nuisance, that's all. We were doing good work – who else is going to find all the agents the Reds have dumped on us? SIS? I don't think so. Your lot?' He gave a mirthless laugh. 'You have trouble keeping your own people alive, so I hear.' Did he mean Max or Otto? It must have been Otto. The jungle drums in Germany were fast, but not swift enough to have delivered the news about Max. 'No, you were far too hasty in closing us down.'

A batman arrived with two mugs of tea and some Marie biscuits. The betrayal gave Webb time to consider his reply. Stephens was a bully, an intimidating physical presence with a legendary temper, but Webb knew it was always best not to pander to him or his fits of stage-managed apoplexy.

'It had gone too far, Robin. The men would say anything just to get some sleep or some food. You'd crossed the threshold. Robust treatment became cruel intent. Some of your men were little better than gangsters.'

He watched the tight-lipped mouth quiver for a second, and then Stephens relaxed. 'I can't agree with you, Webb. Loss of nerve, if you ask me.'

'They will ask you, Robin, they will.' He sipped his tea.

'If you're not here to gloat, to what do I owe this pleasure?'

'I want to see your debriefing files from 1945.'

'They are not here.'

'I should imagine not. Are they still in Germany?'

'As far as I know, they are in the London Cage.' This was a large house in Kensington Gardens that was still used to hold high-ranking prisoners, for interrogations and for court-martials.

'Are they catalogued?'

'Of course they're bloody catalogued! Who do you think we are – SOE?'

'*Touché*. Robin, I'd like your permission to spend a day sorting through them.' There were other ways to open the CSDIC files, but Stephens was the surest route to free access.

'What are you looking for?' He held a hand up, freezing the reply. 'Actually, don't tell me. It wouldn't be the truth anyway, would it?'

Webb grinned as he reached for his mug of tea. 'Probably not. But if I give you some idea of the area involved, perhaps you can point me in the right direction?'

'Of course. And I'll type you up an access chit before you leave.' Bully he might be, but Stephens would never obstruct an investigation by a friendly agency. 'Is that it?'

'No, not quite.'

'It never is with you chaps, is it? What else can I do for you?'

'I would like to find me a tame traitor.'

Stephens furrowed his brow, his curiosity piqued. 'Really?'

'Yes. The truth this time.' Webb put down his tea, anticipating the reaction his reply would generate. 'I need someone killed.'

Laura estimated it was the second day. Her ankle felt better and she had managed to sleep, having selected the side of the mattress with the fewest stains, using one blanket to cover her head and the other to keep warm. At one point she awoke, shivering, and she reckoned that must have been three in the morning, the lowest ebb in the body's cycle. She was pleased when breakfast was delivered at what she reckoned to be approximately 7 a.m. It was reconstituted egg, a piece of cold toast and lukewarm sweet tea, but she ate and drank it all.

Shortly after that, she became aware of the itching on her scalp. It ran along her hairline, with other hotspots behind her ears. Scratching didn't appear to do much good. She must have picked up something from the bedding. The moment she thought that, her armpits and her crotch began to itch as well, but she reckoned that could just be a sympathetic response. The thought of body lice and nits was disgusting, but, again, she forced herself not to cry, and not to fantasize too much about a long, hot bath. Sooner or later, she knew, they would tell her why she was here. She just had to hold out until then.

In the meantime, she still had to tackle the problem of the bucket and the lack of toilet paper. At least she was no longer noticing the stench from the metal container; in fact, Laura suspected she didn't smell all that sweet herself by now. But there was no point in making it worse by neglecting basic hygiene. It took her the best part of what must have been an hour to rip the cover off the pillow and to tear it into small squares. Not ideal, but it would do. She bundled the wiry stuffing into the corner behind the door, and hid the fragments of material under the mattress. She didn't want Laurel and Hardy marching in and removing her lavatory paper, the way they had the bedframe.

The pipes gurgled and rumbled once more. She was about to use the bucket, when a thought occurred to her. She took the pail over to the pipes and, using the handle, tapped on one of them. It made a dull sound. It was asbestos or concrete. The middle conduit, though, rang lovely and hollow. Using the handle of the bucket, she tapped out a message in Morse. Even after four years, it was still there, and she was surprisingly fast. *Where am I? SOS*, she banged out three times.

She had given up hoping for a reply and was steeling herself to squat over the bucket, when she heard the rat-a-tat of a reply. She rushed over and listened intently, mouthing the letters to herself. B. E. Q. U. Then a pause. Bequ? Bequest? Be quick? Yes, be quick.

The next letters rang out. Laura's heart sank. BE QUIET. She listened to the rest with growing anger. THERE IS NOBODY HERE TO HEAR YOU. She turned and kicked the bucket as hard as she could, bending back her big toe, causing her to cry out. But it made her feel better, all the same.

Ten

Henley, England

Maudsley Court, where Webb stayed when he needed to be near London, was one of the more modest Special Training Schools used by the SOE. Some of the houses the outfit requisitioned were so grand that insiders joked that SOE stood for Stately 'Omes of England. Maudsley, however, was a rather undistinguished early-Edwardian house in several acres of ground, surrounded by high walls on three sides and the river on the fourth.

James Hadley Webb walked down the sloping grass towards where the dirty Thames lapped at the remnants of a wooden jetty. The sun was hot on his face. He removed the V-neck cricket jumper he had slipped on over his shirt and threw it across one of the garden benches as he passed.

At the water's edge he broke up some of the crust of bread he had saved from breakfast and threw it out onto the river. Two flotillas of ducks turned and steamed eagerly towards him.

Maudsley had once been a prison, of sorts. It had housed those SOE operatives who had failed their training. In the final stages of their courses, often after many months of intense and lonely tutoring in arms, explosives and subterfuge, the potential agents were put in an off-guard situation in a bar or restaurant, where a

charming, attractive WAAF or friendly fellow officer asked, casually, about what they had been up to. A surprising number admitted
something close to the truth, thereby disbarring themselves from
any secret mission.

Those who had proven too loose-tongued were sent to Maudsley,
where they were incarcerated until any sensitive knowledge they
might have acquired was no longer relevant. That was often only a
matter of weeks, but longer-term detainees were despatched to
Inverlair Lodge, in Inverness-shire, where the Cameron Highlanders
made sure they remained quarantined. Both SOE and SIS had used
Maudsley and Inverlair – known collectively as the Velvet Prison –
on many occasions.

Webb shredded the final pieces of crust and tossed them to the
scrabbling ducks. The act of pulling apart the bread made him think
of the way his organisation was disintegrating. He had more than
a hunch about why he was under attack now. He had spent the
previous day at the London Cage, digesting dozens of interviews
conducted at the end of the war, looking for the person behind this
campaign to discredit him. He thought he might have him, but
this was a time for softly-softly. He couldn't use Tin-Eye's
methods. This was going to be more like riding to hounds – he
needed to flush the quarry out into the open. And for that,
he needed Dolan, the American, and his deep pockets.

'Sir.' It was Becker, the elderly butler-cum-batman who had run
the house during the war and was acting caretaker until the owners
reclaimed it. He had joked that he was one of the few butlers in
the world authorised to carry a revolver and use it on the guests
if he thought it appropriate. He probably would have, too.

Becker came further down the slope, making sure he spoke loud
enough for Webb to hear. 'Sir, you have a visitor.'

'I do?' Who on earth knew he was here? 'Does he have a name?'
'It's a young lady, sir. She said to tell you Olivia is here.'
'Is she indeed?' He was half-excited by the prospect and half-
dismayed at having been tracked down so easily. 'Where is she?'

'Right here, Jimmy.' She was dressed in a full blue skirt, matching blouse with white hat and gloves. She stood on the stone terrace, bracketed by two enormous urns that sprouted ferns which looked to Webb like a series of giant green tongues. 'Mr Becker says you are having trouble hearing.'

'That's rich,' Webb said to the old man, who smiled.

Webb began the climb back up the sloping lawn towards where she stood. She was speaking at an exaggerated volume. 'Mr Becker has kindly offered us tea. Shall we take it out here?'

He pounded up the steps to the terrace, pleased to note that his heartrate hardly rose from the exertion. All that sprinting was doing him good. Perhaps he'd put in a spot of rowing on the river, something he hadn't tried since Cambridge.

Olivia was already fussing over the furniture, wiping down the chipped white metal chairs and dusting the leaves off the table. 'There,' she announced, sitting down and removing her hat. 'Come and sit down. I SAID COME—'

'Olivia, I can hear you,' he said. 'I'm not Harpo Marx.'

Her brow furrowed. 'Isn't he dumb? I don't think there is a deaf one.' She pointed to the faded remainder of a bruise on his neck. His hand went to it instinctively. It was one of the blows from a Russian gun barrel. 'Been in the wars, Jimmy?'

'Something like that. Accident.'

She raised an eyebrow, a silent quizzical interrogation that also managed to be alarmingly cute. He kept mum.

'I worry about you, Jimmy, I really do.'

'I'd rather you didn't.'

'I'm going to have a cigarette. Do you mind?'

'Not at all.'

'Do you want one?'

'I'm trying to cut down. I'll watch.' It was never onerous to observe her, a Vivien Leigh-ish dark beauty who might be past the mid-point of thirty, but who could still pass for a girlish twenty-five when she wanted to. Olivia's father had made his money in paper. She had been part of what was considered to be a 'fast set' before the war, with parties on the Riviera, in Biarritz and at Burgh Island in Devon. She still displayed the same slim figure from back then, and a pair of lips that . . .

. . . *that got you into trouble last time. That cost a man his life.*

'How did you know I was here, Olivia?'

'Oh, I used to be a spy, you know.' She winked at him. She had undertaken some low-level work at the outbreak of the war, reporting on the reaction of the appeasers at Cliveden to hostilities against Hitler. 'And I was married to a journalist. There are ways.' She lit the cigarette. 'I thought you might be pleased.'

'I am, but you should have given me some warning.'

'Why – so that you could have made an excuse?' She sounded hurt.

Olivia was talking about his last visit, when he had flown in and out of London without calling on her. 'That was unforgivable. But I was working then, Olivia, and I'm working now. Just for a day or two, then I was going to get in touch.'

She flicked ash off her cigarette. 'I know you are good at your job, Jimmy. I just wish you were a little less focused sometimes. Or at least, more focused on us.'

The tea arrived and she blazed a grin at Becker, who as a result made a hash of pouring the first cup. He scuttled off and Webb said: 'You've got him all flustered.'

'It's nice to know I can still get someone flustered, even if it is only octogenarians.' She hesitated before asking the next question, unsure of how to approach him. It was often like this for the first hour or two. Webb's absences from anything like normal life were just long enough to make readjusting to each other an awkward prospect. 'Can we do something today? Or will you be working?'

He shook his head glumly. 'I'm going to Kent.'

'Why's that?'

'I've had a woman detained under the 1930 Mental Deficiency Act.'

Olivia laughed but stifled it when she realised he was serious. 'Can you do that?'

'Oh, yes. You get a tame MO to sign the committal certificate – and bang! You're locked up until someone says you are not mad any more. Which might be never.'

She looked shocked. 'How frightening.' She dropped her voice. 'Remind me never to cross you, Jimmy. I wouldn't like to end up in the loony bin.'

'I'd never commit you.'

She sucked on the cigarette. 'Or to me.'

Webb found himself chortling and Olivia joined in, blowing smoke from the corner of her mouth in an insouciant manner she could only have picked up from American movies.

'Want to tell me? About the woman? I'm still bound by the Official Secrets Act, Jimmy.'

To his surprise he did, going right back to Otto, talking freely about Karin, the opera, and the strange gift of a nose.

'How grisly,' she interrupted. 'Why?'

'We have a file on Grusenko, of course. He is in charge of cross-border security for the central section of Berlin. My guess – and it's only a guess – is he didn't want a tit-for-tat developing. If hit teams start crossing the divide willy-nilly, bumping off agents – well, it'll be chaos. Retaliation will follow retaliation and before you know it . . .' He paused and let her fill in the gap. 'What SMERSH did was against the accepted rules. So Grusenko got the retaliation in first.'

'And the girl in Kent? What does she have to do with it?'

'Nothing yet. And I want to keep it that way. She was poking around in my business, making waves, and this isn't a good time for distractions. I had to head her off.'

'Well, if you don't mind me saying so, it was rather an extreme way of heading her off.' He didn't disagree. It had simply been the most effective method available to him. 'Will you let her go?'

'More tea, sir?' Becker had appeared at a discreet distance, pointing at the cups that now contained nothing more than a slick of the tiniest leaves in the bottom.

'Yes, please,' said Olivia. 'But fresh cups. I'd like to read these first.'

There was just a hint of a raised eyebrow from the butler. 'Certainly, madam.'

She reached over, took Webb's cup and stared into the debris at the bottom.

'Tea leaves? You can't really do that, can you?'

'Yes, it's easy. The trick is to predict something you know will come true.'

'Such as?'

'Such as a drive in the country. A pub meal, perhaps. See what develops.'

'And back here for a nightcap?'

'A nightcap?' She adopted a horrified expression. 'What on earth would Becker say?'

'Becker is the soul of discretion.' He cleared his throat. 'I've missed you, Olivia.'

He leaned over and she allowed herself to be kissed. It felt like bare electrical wires on his tongue, a flash of pain and pleasure. His hand went to her leg, and he could feel the tops of her stockings and the tantalizing button of her suspender. He risked prolonging the kiss, but she twisted away. She ground out the cigarette.

'Are you all right, Olivia? You seem a little tense.'

She slumped back in the chair, letting out her breath in a long stream. 'Jimmy, I look forward to seeing you so much – but then I never know what to do for the best. We're like a couple of hedgehogs, aren't we? Skirting around each other. Can I stay? Please?'

'I have to see this girl—'

She placed the back of her hand on her forehead in mock histrionics. 'You would desert me for a mental deficient?' Then, seriously: 'Can't you delegate, Jimmy? It's important.'

He should say no. It would be unprofessional not to be there personally for the debrief, but then again, it might be better to run this one at some remove.

Eventually, he nodded his assent. 'I'll make a call.'

'Good.'

After all, he rationalised, who knew what demons seeing another McGill might release at this moment? Guilt about what became of Diana McGill? That would not be advantageous; guilt and spies made for unhappy bedfellows.

Webb allowed himself a rueful smile. That wasn't always true. He might be responsible for the death of her husband, and feel terrible about it, but that rarely stopped him bedding Olivia.

The scarred metal door swung open and, for once, there was someone in the frame who wasn't Laurel or Hardy. Laura looked the newcomer up and down. Late thirties, almost six foot in height, slim, with a good figure hidden beneath a calf-length tartan skirt and a pleated blouse, hair pulled back and held in place by a large tortoiseshell clip. Under her arm was a buff folder. This was no Neanderthal warder.

Laura repressed the urge to speak. Her experiences so far suggested she should wait until the woman made the first move. She struggled to her feet and stood facing the door, aware of the frightful mess she presented. She smoothed down her skirt as best she could.

'Miss McGill?'

'Yes.' Her voice sounded croaky and rough. She cleared her throat and repeated, 'Yes.'

'I am here to apologise.'

It could be a trick, she thought. Don't rise to it. Start with something safe. 'Where am I?'

'The Danescliff Secure Institute, Kent. Not far from Dover.'

What? A mental hospital? But she wasn't mad. Not in that sense anyway. But she only said: 'Why?'

'You were detained under the Mental Deficiency Act. It was that or criminal charges. Threatening behaviour. Possession of a weapon. Abduction. It's better this way.'

For whom, she wondered. 'I see. Am I free to go?'

'Not entirely. Not yet. We still have some questions.'

'About what?' It came out far louder than she intended. She cursed the tiny note of hysteria that was there, too. The woman didn't bat an eyelid.

'Let's get you cleaned up and then we can begin.'

'Where is my apology?' she demanded.

'I beg your pardon?'

'You said you were here to apologise.'

'Oh, that. Yes, James Hadley Webb sends his apologies that he can't be here in person, but he is unavoidably detained. He's asked me to conduct this session on his behalf. I'm Major Rose Miller.'

Major of what, she wondered. But before she could ask the question, the unmistakable silhouettes of Stan and Olly appeared behind her.

'If you'll just follow these two ladies, they'll make you somewhat more presentable.' She wrinkled her nose. 'I will see you then.'

She turned and Laura heard the clack of her retreating heels. The impassive Laurel and Hardy entered the cell, and now she could see that both of them were wielding sawn-off broom handles. She blinked back tears of frustration. So it wasn't over yet.

Webb woke up alone. Tea had given way to claret and the claret led to the bedroom. There had been sex, more hurried than he would have liked, and they had lain in bed, watching the sun fall behind the trees that lined the opposite bank of the river.

'Why do you stay over there?' she had asked as she lit up her second cigarette of the day.

Webb thought for a moment. 'Because if there is another war, that's where it will start. Berlin is the powder keg.'

She touched the bruise on his chest, another souvenir from the Goethe, and he winced. The ribs underneath were still tender. 'Is there going to be another war?'

'Not while the Russians don't have the bomb. That's our big stick.'

'And when they do?' She sat up, the sheet falling down to expose her breasts and he felt himself stir once more.

'If. Not when,' he grunted.

'Don't be naïve, Jimmy. You know they will. It's inevitable.'

He couldn't argue with that. 'Then I suppose our job is to make sure we delay that day by as much as possible.'

'You know, I think you'd like another war. Not a nuclear one. But you spies, you hate the peace, don't you? All this grey uncertainty and fudged morality. Give me a good Fascist to fight, you think. Your kind thrive on war and on subterfuge. That's why you are in Berlin. Because it's as close to a war as you can find.'

He was taken aback by her combativeness. 'That's nonsense.'

'Is it?'

'Mostly nonsense.'

Her voice had lost the sharp edge. 'What would it take for you to move back here, darling? To London.'

He had taken the cigarette from her and helped himself to a lungful of smoke, biding his time. 'I'm not sure what I'd do.' Broadway Buildings is a nest of vipers, so I'd like to avoid that. Broadway Buildings was the SIS Headquarters in St James's. 'What do you see me as doing back here?'

'I think you could do anything you set your mind to. In a way, you would be facing the same dilemma most men faced in 1945 and 1946. What to do for the peace? You've just delayed the decision by a few years.'

'Part of me thinks I'm only really qualified for what I am doing.'

'For the rest of your life? Is that it, slowly accumulating a tally of dead men – Otto, Max . . .'

The missing name had hovered between them, unspoken, but no less powerful for that.

'Come home, Jimmy.'

'I can't. Not yet. You could come to Berlin. I'd like that.' *But would he? Could he balance having business and pleasure in the same space, or had he grown too used to this compartmentalisation?*

Webb had watched the mesmerising ripple of her breasts as she shook her head vigorously. 'I hate the place. It's so grim. So venal. No. Ask for a transfer.'

'I can't. One day, I promise. Soon.'

'Soon.' She had made the word sound empty and treacherous.

He had leaned over and kissed her and they made love again, slower and gentler this time and afterwards he had fallen asleep, content. Now he faced an empty bed. And it was too early in the evening to stay put. He threw back the covers and got dressed.

He found a note in an envelope from her on the dresser downstairs and pocketed it, unread, not wanting to spoil the glow that had settled around him after their lovemaking. He could guess the contents. It would be a continuation of their pillow talk, urging him to give it all up, to grow up and get a real life. She had a point. He certainly didn't want to end his days like the wraiths who haunted the corridors of SIS, shadowy figures who once 'did something in the Great War', now long forgotten. But for the moment, he was still active, he had Librarian, and he had to protect that source. And the thought of giving it up to become a bank manager or some other pillar of a parochial community frightened him more than anything Colonel Grusenko and Co could do to him.

He dined alone on Becker's rather glutinous steak-and-kidney pie and finished off the claret. The rest of the evening was unremarkable save for one phone call, from Rose Miller. She was about to interview the girl. How much should she tell her? Everything, he said. Everything? Well, up to a point, he had replied.

Only now did he feel a pang of guilt at his dereliction of duty in not debriefing the McGill girl himself. Unable to find sleep, Webb padded down polished stairs glistening in the light of a new moon, crossed the hall and fumbled for the light switch in the kitchen.

There was a scrabble as a field mouse made itself scarce. Webb opened the larder and checked that the pest hadn't managed to penetrate its defences. Then he carved a slice of bread and spread it with honey, while the vast black iron kettle, a remnant of the days when Maudsley catered for twenty or thirty, huffed its way to boiling on the hob. Once it had managed a head of steam, he sat down at the kitchen table with a mug of Ovaltine and made some notes, listing possibilities and options. Suddenly, he was impatient to be back in Berlin.

It was only when he had finished and read over them that he noticed what he had scribbled in the margin, twice: *Olivia*. As he burned the pieces of paper, he held the blackening sheets in one corner, at just such an angle that her name was the last thing to be consumed by the flames.

Eleven

Lee Crane didn't recognise the kid who walked out from around the front of the plane and hailed him in broken English. Crane was standing back admiring the illustration of three Queens – hearts, diamonds and spades – he had commissioned as nose art. Fifty bucks it had cost him, but the guy had done a good job. 'I make breasts too big?' the artist had asked when he had finished.

Crane had started to answer when he realised the kid was ribbing him. He'd used photographs of starlets in *Life* magazine to capture not only the cinched-waist shape but also the careless come-hither grins of American women. 'No, the breasts are just fine,' he'd answered with a wink. 'They almost make me homesick. Or lovesick, I'm not sure which.'

Now it was coming up to ten in the morning, a beautiful day with the sun sparking off the sea, but he was keen to be gone, to take the plane down to Athens to pick up a cargo for Crete, the first of his hops en route to Berlin. He'd been in town for almost a week, waiting for the money transfer and the sale documents to be approved by Mikklos's lawyers.

He'd spent the time in a room at the misnamed Macedonia Ritzy, hanging out in the port bars, listening to theories about who murdered George Polk, the CBS correspondent found floating face down in Salonica Bay, and gruesome tales about the civil war.

The conflict seemed to boil down to right-wing gangs with one set of initials burning down the villages of left-wing gangs with a different set of initials, then vice versa.

Mikklos had tracked down a co-pilot for him, a German who was keen to get home to Hamburg and only too happy to take a paying job. He'd flown Junkers, the triple-engined transports that had carried paratroopers to Crete, but had also done some time on Boeings and he'd seemed like a fast learner. He was also keen to leave the country: the Germans were still spat upon and even attacked in certain quarters of Greece. Mind you, it was no picnic being an American, either.

For his part, Gunther had few questions, apart from: Where? When? How much? And why Berlin?

A woman, Crane had answered. A German woman? *No, English.* They left it at that. Crane didn't mention that when he saw Laura McGill, he would make sure he stood well back. They had history.

Whoever this Greek with a mop of curly hair and ingratiating smile was, though, he certainly wasn't the Gunther Barkhorn he was expecting.

'Captain Crane,' the kid repeated, his hand outstretched. 'Sorry I am late.'

Crane took the hand out of politeness and said: 'You are?'

'Your new co-pilot, Andreas Xidopoulos. At your service.' He gave a mocking salute and stretched his smile even wider.

Crane frowned. 'I don't think so.'

'Yes, yes. Mikklos sent me.'

Crane walked under the C-47's wing and made a display of checking one of the tyres, his back to the newcomer. He picked gravel out of the rubber for a few seconds. 'What happened to Gunther?'

'He got into a fight in a bar with some American sailors.'

'American sailors?' Crane straightened up and emerged from under the wing into the sunlight. 'Idiot.'

'Yes. He is in hospital. Broken bones. So Mikklos called me.'

Did he now? Crane thought. Without calling me first? These Greeks had a funny way of doing business. 'You got a flight log I can see? Papers of any kind?'

Andreas shrugged, spreading his hands wide. 'Everything is in Athens. Mikklos will vouch for me.'

'But you have flown?'

'Of course.'

'C-47s?'

A pause. 'No. But twins. Fiat. Marchetti.'

'Italian planes?'

'Yes, why not?'

Crane just said: 'Where the hell is Mikklos?'

'He has gone back to Athens. To get your cargo ready.'

Crane thought for a moment. It looked like he was over a barrel. He pointed to *Three of a Kind*'s open door. 'OK, I need to give you a shakedown.' The guy went to protest but Crane held up his hand. 'You really want to fly with a pilot who'd let any stranger take the controls just on his say-so? I don't think so. You want to show me what you can do?'

Andreas considered. It certainly wasn't an unreasonable request. 'Of course, Captain.'

The young Greek bounded towards the door and Crane was behind him in three quick steps. He used the butt of his .45 on the neck, smacking down twice, hard, and jabbing him in the kidneys with a fist for good measure as he went down.

The air exploded from Andreas's lungs as he hit the apron, banging his head with a sharp crack. Crane heard a cry from behind, an alarmed mechanic, no doubt, but ignored it. He kicked Andreas in the stomach and felt the boot go deep. The Greek whimpered and curled up in a ball, knees to his chest. Crane knelt beside him. Only now did he flick the safety off the Colt and he held it opposite the Greek's right eye, so he could see right down the barrel. 'Just stay real still, Andreas.'

'What are you doing?' he gasped. 'Captain . . .'

'Shut up.'

Crane frisked him and found a snub-nosed revolver under his shirt, which he slid over the apron, out of reach. 'What was that for?'

'These are dang—' He closed his eyes as a spasm of pain shot across his abdomen. 'Dangerous times. We carry protection. I think you ruptured something.'

'Let's hope so.' Crane stood. 'You know, I was in the Sani Bar last night. All the girls were complaining that they hadn't seen a Yankee ship for weeks. Just diplomats, journos and cops who wanted to talk about the death of George Polk. They were so desperate they started hitting on me. There are no American sailors in town. And I know that the Commie air force, such as it is, consists of Italian planes left over from the war. Is that what you learned to fly? What was the deal here?'

'I don't know what—'

'You want me to kick you again?' Crane pulled his foot back.

'No, no. It was just a few extra boxes for the flight. That's all.'

'Weapons?'

He nodded.

'For Crete?' But that didn't make sense. The Reds weren't fighting in Crete. 'Or somewhere else?'

Andreas's eyes flicked away. 'I think I've cracked my skull.'

'Excellent. Was it the mountains?' The ELAS – Communist – strongholds were in the mountainous north of the country, on the Bulgarian, Yugoslav and Albanian borders. 'That's it, isn't it? You were going to take us to the mountains.'

'Mikklos was saying how this American who bought his plane had flown in the Himalayas.' Crane cursed. He'd opened his big trap about The Hump to the agent one night in some seedy dive after too many beers. Where was the harm, he'd thought at the time. 'We have units in the mountains who need resupplying, and no pilots who are good enough to get in there. The strips are very poor and very high.'

That sounded horribly familiar. Crane had hoped never to have to face strips that were very poor and very high after he'd left China. 'How were you going to persuade me?' He jerked a thumb in the direction of the revolver. 'With that?'

'I was to offer you money first. If not . . .'

'Jesus fuckin' Christ.' Just then, the worried Greek mechanic appeared at the edge of his vision and Crane turned and hissed, 'Go away! Private argument. He screwed my wife.'

The mechanic opened his mouth, but seeing the gun, thought better of it and made himself scarce. He was probably secretly pleased that a handsome countryman had been cuckolding a Yankee pilot.

Crane turned back to the prostrate Communist. 'And once I had delivered the goods?'

'The Royal Hellenic Air Force have converted this kind of plane to bombers. We thought we might do the same.'

'With or without my permission, right?' Andreas didn't reply. Crane tried to sound reasonable. 'Look, kid, I don't understand your war. I don't want any part of it. Not for money, gold or glory. Understand? And I don't fly with a gun to my head. Ever. Now get up.'

'What are you going to do?'

Crane kicked him again, but it wasn't much more than a nudge. 'I ought to fly you over the Aegean and do an Icarus on your ass. But I'm not. Take me to Gunther.'

'He is in the hospital. Really.'

Damn. If the German really had been worked over, that was going to delay him. Berlin suddenly seemed a long way away once more. 'How bad is he?'

Andreas rose to his feet, still doubled over. Crane took a step back, in case he was braver than he looked at that moment. 'Not too bad. Not much worse than me, Captain.' He touched his head and winced then examined his fingers for blood. There wasn't any. Just an egg-sized lump, Crane reckoned.

'Ok, let's go and take him a get-well card and some grapes. You came by car?'

'Yes.'

'You drive. And I know the way to the hospital. If you do anything stupid, I'll blow your nuts off. Understand?'

The Greek, his face a picture of contrition, nodded. 'Yes, Captain.'

Twelve

Laura McGill felt wonderful. Like a long drink after days in the desert, the hot shower and clean clothes reinvigorated her. And shampoo. She doubted it would shift the lice, but at least now she felt as if she had clean hair with nits, rather than a nest of filthy straw housing them. She was under the water so long, she heard Laurel bang on the shower-room door with her stick. 'C'mon, missie, the local reservoirs are nearly empty. There's a towel and hairbrush on the shelf.' It was said in a soft, educated Scottish accent. That was a surprise.

She didn't even mind that the towels were thin and scratchy or that the fresh clothes were no more attractive – or less coarse – than the discarded ones, or that the hairbrush was full of some other inmate's blonde strands which she picked out before using it. She felt human again. All she needed was a toothbrush, and she'd be ready to face the world. And some talcum powder.

She was led along corridors painted an alarming shade of pea-soup green to an interview room. It had little furniture, other than a desk with a bentwood chair on either side, but it did have a window, albeit a barred one. And it was dark outside. By her reckoning, it was still afternoon. She'd been hours off in her estimates of time passing. But was she slow or fast? Was it last night, tonight, or tomorrow night? She gave up trying to work it out.

'Wait here, please,' instructed Stan, who closed the door behind her.

Laura crossed to one of the chairs and sat, hands on her lap, fingers intertwined, as if she were waiting for an interview with the headmistress. She closed her eyes and revelled in the feeling of scrubbed skin and brushed hair.

'Right.' Rose Miller burst in with a no-nonsense bustle and put the file down on the table in front of her. 'Let's get started.'

'On whose authority—'

'Please don't speak. You can answer my questions, that is all.'

'No.' She tried hard to make it sound final.

'Miss McGill—'

'No. That's not any kind of deal. I want to know why I was brought here and treated so abominably. It was like, like . . .'

'Bedlam. I know.' But the woman didn't care overmuch about Laura's treatment, that much was obvious. 'Have you ever been in touch with either the French, German or Russian Embassies?'

'No.'

'You are certain?'

'I'd have noticed.'

Rose Miller didn't react to the sarcasm. 'What about approaches from affiliated bodies? Have you, for instance, been contacted by trade delegations from any of these countries? Friendship Leagues? Foreign-language courses? Political discussion groups?'

'No. No. Up until a few months ago I was nursing my mother.'

'You can recall no encounters with foreign nationals?'

She put as much emphasis on the negative this time as she could muster. 'No, I cannot.'

'So who put you up to this mischief?'

Laura rapped the desk in irritation. 'Mischief? I want to find my sister. How is that mischief?'

'You mean, you want to discover what happened to her. Her burial place.' The woman's words were designed to shock Laura with the reality. *She's dead, you know*, she was saying.

'I want to find my sister,' Laura repeated stubbornly.

'By fair means or foul, it seems. You have to understand that if a member of the public starts to investigate restricted material, especially if they use pistols to kidnap Civil Servants, it triggers all sorts of safeguards.'

'Like this place?'

Rose nodded. 'Yes. We had to be sure you weren't being duped. Used by others.'

'And are you sure now?'

'We could find no evidence of you being a tool of foreign powers, willing or otherwise.'

Laura allowed herself a sigh. 'Good. So can I ask you a question without you thinking I'm Uncle Joe in disguise?'

Rose considered this request for a moment. 'You can try.'

'Why is the bloody file restricted in the first place?'

Rose gave a soft laugh, and spoke as if she were addressing a child. 'I can't tell you that. If I did, it wouldn't be restricted any longer, would it?'

Laura felt the old familiar frustration of dealing with these people, whose neural pathways were designed by Escher. 'I suppose not.'

Rose pushed the thin folder in front of her across the table. 'Here.'

'What's this?'

'Your sister's PF. Personal File.'

'The one with a Blue on it?'

The corner of Rose's mouth turned up into the shadow of a smile. 'Not that one. This one has been filleted.'

'When Laura reached across, she saw that her fingers were shaking like fish bait. She pulled the file closer and flipped it open. It contained six typed sheets. She flicked through them. The document detailed Diana's recruitment, her training, posting to China, return, and the subsequent mission to France to reconnect the broken smuggling line. There was also a *Combat Casualty*

Notification stating that Diana had been posted missing, along with the date. A later addition was stamped with the all-too-familiar initials MPD. *Missing Presumed Dead.*

All the way through, however, pertinent names and places had been blacked out with thick ink, making them unreadable. The whole thing was like a half-completed crossword puzzle. Even so, to see her sister described by her trainers as 'tough, resourceful, mildly flirtatious, resilient' – brought tears. She tried to stop herself, but she couldn't stem the flow. Her nose began to run and Rose passed over a handkerchief. Laura allowed herself a good blow. More resilient than her, that was for sure.

'Sorry.'

'No need to apologise.'

'It doesn't tell me much,' she sniffed.

Rose waved a dismissive hand. 'No. They usually don't.'

'Do you know what happened to her?'

'We know what happened to her dance partner.'

'Her what?'

'Her dance partner – slang for conducting officer. He was a chap called Philip Maxwell. Very dashing, very Clark Gable. He was there because Diana hadn't undergone the full training for operating in France. She needed an old hand to help. But he'd hurt his ankle on his last jump, which—'

'Is why they went across by Lysander.'

Rose Miller raised her eyebrows in something that could have been surprise. 'Quite.'

'What happened to Philip?'

'Jimmy Webb, the man who put the mission together, was a friend of Philip's. At the end of the war, Philip was MPD, too. Jimmy followed a trail from the cells of Avenue Foch in Paris to Karlsruhe gaol. And then . . . have you heard of Flossenburg?'

'Wasn't it a concentration camp?'

'Yes, but primarily a labour camp, next to a quarry where the Germans worked the prisoners to death. It's also where they executed Admiral Canaris, the Head of the Abwehr, for his part in the plot against Hitler. It used to house fifteen to twenty thousand. By the time the Americans liberated it, there were only two thousand living. Philip had been hanged two days before they arrived.'

Oh God, Laura said to herself. Here it comes. Her throat was desperately tight as she asked: 'And Diana?'

'Would you like some tea?'

Taken aback by the sudden change of tack, Laura could only nod her head. After she had asked at the door for Laurel to fetch a pot, Rose Miller sat down again. 'Jimmy Webb should be telling you this.' Was that a note of disapproval that he wasn't? 'He interviewed all those who met Philip and Diana during their last days. It's not in the PF – the nitty-gritty never is. I won't apologise for what we have done to you, Laura; it was necessary. But I can offer some recompense for a few days' discomfort.' Rose reached over and took the file back. 'Do you want to hear the real story of Diana's mission?'

A shiver of fear went through Laura as she said very quietly: 'Yes, please.'

Part Two: 1944

City of Blood

Thirteen

Tangmere, 1944

The cottage reeked of stale bodies and unwashed feet. Even downstairs, away from the narrow, thin-mattressed beds crammed into the small bedrooms on the first floor, Diana McGill could smell the suffocating scent of scores of men and women, many like her, no doubt, excited and terrified, their brains numb from playing their cover stories over and over again. *My name is . . . I work at . . . I am in town to visit . . . I have permission to travel from . . . no, my mother was from . . .*

It was, she supposed, fear that she could smell most strongly. Three years' worth, soaking into the fabric of this nondescript building opposite the entrance to Tangmere Airfield.

She was sitting in the corner of what would have been the cottage's living room. Now it was Ops, mostly occupied by a table covered in maps, with pride of place given to a green scrambler telephone. In the dining room across the hall, she could hear the chink of cutlery. A meal was being laid out by the FANYs, the nursing corps who did little if any nursing, as far as she could see. Diana wouldn't be able to eat. She kept thinking of condemned men and last suppers.

A hand touched her knee and she jumped. 'You all right?'

Philip Maxwell was standing over her, his face jaundiced and angular in the weak bulb. The matinée-idol looks had become shadowed and sinister, like something from *Nosferatu*. The carefully trimmed moustache had gone too, replaced by two-day stubble.

'I hope so. Is it always like this?'

'The waiting? Well, we've been unlucky with the weather.' It was a full-moon period, but they had already missed one chance to cross to France because of fierce storms ripping down the Channel. They'd progressed so far as to be shown the clumsy-looking Lysander that would carry them across, before the operation was called off. Then they'd been driven back to Mrs Bertram's house, where Diana had spent a fitful night. After dark, they'd been brought to the cottage again, slipping in the back way once more, like thieves in the night.

'Cigarette?' he asked.

'Yes, please.'

'It'll be your last decent one. Nothing but phony Gauloises from now on.' He passed her a Craven A, lit it, and then put the rest of the packet to one side. He was dressed in work clothes, washed and boiled to a thin, scratchy grey. She had on a skilfully patched floral dress, which spoke of years of make-do-and-mend. Her underwear, the contents of her small pressed-fibre suitcase and the products in her washbag, including pre-war sanitary products scavenged from goodness knew where, were all equally authentic, suggesting four years of increasing deprivation. Even her nails had been shaped by a Parisian manicurist borrowed from the Ladies Department of Truefitt & Hill in Old Bond Street, who also advised on appropriate hairstyles.

Her French wasn't perfect – she would have to pretend to be from Alsace if questioned closely – but it would pass muster for most casual encounters. Philip's, though, was flawless. His father had worked as a salesman for ICI across much of the South of France until Philip was fourteen. Even his shrugs were perfectly Gallic.

Diana sucked in the cigarette smoke and held it for two seconds before releasing a thin stream. She thought about Laura, out in Calcutta at the Saturday Club or dancing with the Flying Tigers in Kunming and felt a pang of envy, which she quickly dismissed. It had been her idea to go over and find out what had happened to break the supply line between Tours and Le Mans. Nobody had made her. She was pleased that Philip was along, though, a safe pair of hands, an old pro who had already bested the Germans.

There was a cooing from the corner of the room and a rustle of wings. She had two pigeons to take with her. The mission wasn't important enough to warrant an SOE radio operator, who were in woefully short supply, so she had two winged chances to get a message back home, relying on the birds supplied by a young lad in Ramsgate.

'You want to run through the cover stories again?' he asked. 'Stop the mind working overtime?'

On the aerodrome, an engine coughed and caught, the racket terrifyingly loud and throaty, the vibrations thrumming through the cottage, even at that distance.

Maxwell copped an ear. 'Not a Spit – a Typhoon,' he said. 'I think. Our Lysander doesn't sound quite that powerful, I am afraid. So, how about that run-through?'

'I'll be all right,' she said with a smile. 'I'm sure I recount Suzanne's story in my sleep.' Suzanne Galliard was the name on her identity card; 'Celeste', her codename.

'As long as you recite it in French,' Philip warned.

The door to the cottage snapped open, causing her to start, and Rose Miller ducked inside, the leather of her new flying jacket squeaking. 'We've got the go-ahead. All set, weather fine the other end. So if you are going to eat, best do it now. Here . . .' From her pocket she produced two ticket stubs and gave them to Diana. 'A concert in Tours last week. Put them in your bag. And this.' She passed over a make-up compact.

105

'It's gold – just in case you need extra funds. Philip, you still have . . .'

'The cufflinks? Yes.'

Diana opened the compact and weighed it in her hand. It was tremendously heavy. 'Thank you.'

Rose sniffed the air. 'You've none of those cigarettes about you?' she asked sternly.

Both shook their heads with conviction. Maxwell pointed to the discarded packet.

'Good. No more British cigarettes, chocolate or toothpaste. Right – let me look at you.'

Diana stood up and Rose did a thorough job of frisking her, checking labels and pockets and her teeth, for anything that looked at all suspicious. It was the second time this had happened: she had been undressed and scrutinised by a FANY officer, and Maxwell by a grizzled Scotland Yard detective earlier in the evening. When Rose was satisfied that even Diana's fillings were suitably continental, she turned to Maxwell. 'Look after her.'

'I will,' he replied. 'Don't worry. We'll be sending Percy Pigeon back calling for a lift in a week.'

Rose nodded, hoping it was true, but said nothing.

Diana picked up her case and the blue pigeon box and they stepped outside into the chill air, thick with fumes from the still-revving Typhoon, the slipstream from the prop buffeting them through the wire perimeter fence. A cloud of grit swirled through the air as the pilot released the brakes and it taxied forward. As the bulky shape moved out of the way, beyond it, just visible in the deliberately feeble hangar lighting, was the spindly and fragile outline of the black, high-winged Lysander that would carry them to France. The pilot was walking around it with a diffused torch, carrying out a pre-flight visual.

Diana felt her feet grow heavy as she plodded towards the staff car that would carry them through the main gate and across to the plane, her limbs signalling that this was a very, very poor idea.

As if he could read her mind, Philip laid a hand on her shoulder. 'Don't worry. It's always the worst part, just before take-off. Once you are underway, with no turning back, it's better. Trust me. And anyway, I'll be there to watch your back.'

Yes, she thought, thank you. But who watches yours?

Fourteen

Soucelles Landing Field, Occupied France

The old Resistance hands claimed it was harder to spot someone in the light of a full moon than on a moonless night. Raymond Bec, crouched against a tree, wasn't convinced. However, he certainly had trouble picking out the others folded into the dark corners of the field where the plane from England would touch down.

There were four of them out there: himself; Georges Court, the *chef du terrain*, in charge of the landing sites; Captain 'Carson', as his codename had it, an organiser for the British and adviser to Georges's MAGICIAN circuit; and the man known as Major T, General de Gaulle's emissary, who had been over on a fact-finding mission and would return on the plane. No matter how hard Raymond Bec stared, he could not detect their hiding-places. Maybe those old bastards were right about the full moon and its deep shadows.

He shifted position. It wasn't a cold night, but the ground was damp and he could feel his muscles stiffening. He had to be up at dawn to begin work on the Germans' lorries, many of which were out of action due to sabotage. Raymond had avoided service in Germany under the STO, the compulsory labour scheme, by making himself an irreplaceable asset to the motorised infantry unit at the Le Mans garrison. The Wehrmacht mechanics were often baffled by the idiosyncratic design of the French lorries and cars they had requisitioned, whereas Raymond had been working on them since he was nine. It was quite a lucrative business. One night, he helped the Resistance slash tyres and put carbonundrum in the oil tanks. The next day, he was paid handsomely, albeit in the despised *Reichskreditkassenschein*, Occupation credits, to help sort out the damage.

An owl hooted somewhere across the fields. Ahead of him, he saw a rabbit freeze, then dart for cover. Raymond massaged his calf, which was exploding with pins and needles. All the time, he listened for the plane. There had been a false alarm an hour previously, but even he had recognised it as a twin-engined aircraft. They were expecting a Lysander. Georges had not even flashed the signal. It could have been an Allied aircraft, a Hudson, even, sometimes used for Resistance infiltrations, but just as likely a Junkers or Messerschmitt nightfighter. It hadn't circled, so Georges had wisely assumed it wasn't looking for them.

Now, even before he heard the Lysander's engine, he saw the Morse signal flash from Georges's torch. He stamped his foot to put some life back into his leg and pushed himself off the tree. On the ground ahead was the fire he would light on Georges's signal. As he broke cover he saw the others emerging into the silvery moonlight. The drone was louder, and there was a winking light from above as the plane came over their heads, the motor straining as it banked.

Like the others, he listened to the little aircraft make its turn, ready for the approach. The field would already have been photographed and shown to the pilot, who would know where every tree and shrub was.

The beam of Georges's torch flicked around the site, alerting them to ignite the beacons that would create an L-shape pattern. Raymond ran forward and struck a match, which fizzled out. He tried a second and a third. The quality was appalling. Finally one caught and stayed lit and he touched it to the kindling. There was a whoosh as the precious gasoline caught. He backed away as the wood began to crackle and spit.

Raymond could hear the plane clearly now, the engine note lower and rougher as the power was cut. Any minute, the landing light would snap on, briefly bathing the undulating surface of the field, and the Lysander would bump down and taxi to a halt.

Any minute now, he repeated to himself.

The nine-cylinder radial was so noisy, he could no longer hear the popping of the firewood. He could, though, see the black, high-winged shape streaking through the moonlight towards him, like that owl descending on the jittery rabbit.

Any minute now.

As it dropped to the ground, and Raymond Bec realised the landing light wasn't going to come on, the engine seemed to scream at him and he sprinted to the left as the noise and the wind swept over him. He threw himself horizontal, and there came the sound of metal shredding through branches and leaves and the deep thud of an aeroplane smacking into a tree. Wood, steel and glass splintered in a building cacophony until the terrible sound stopped dead, replaced by the soft creak of the fuselage as it slowly settled into its new, twisted position.

'Mother of God!' Raymond yelled. He pulled himself up and ran towards the plane, its distorted form all too clear in the dying flames of the beacon. The others were there already, scrabbling at the doors, trying to yank them open. Raymond could smell petrol, and his eyes were stinging. There were fitful sparks coming from the engine.

The door on his side opened with a screech and flapped back. Inside the crushed space of the cabin was a tangle of arms and legs. He could make out a woman's face, with a dark line running down it. Blood. He took out his clasp-knife and began hacking at straps.

110

It took some minutes for the two passengers and the pilot to be dragged clear of the plane. All the time, they were making a noise far beyond what was prudent for any reception committee. The two men and the woman from the Lysander sat down on the grass, stunned. Raymond dabbed at the blood on the woman's face, but she pushed him away. Georges and the Englishman who wasn't the pilot shook hands with a curt nod each. 'Welcome back,' said Georges to Philip Maxwell. 'I wish it had been a happier landing.'

'*You* wish? What the bloody hell was that?' snarled the pilot.

'Sshh!' said Raymond.

'Sshh my arse. Verity is going to kill me when he finds out I've lost a plane. Who laid out that flare-path? It was too bloody close to the tree.' He glared at Raymond.

'Please be quiet!' snapped Georges. 'We can argue about this later.'

'Why didn't you put your landing light on?' retorted Raymond.

'Because it could be seen from miles around.'

'So can the beacons,' insisted Georges. 'The landing light makes no difference. Now be quiet.'

'I agree. I fear this is not the place for such concerns.' It was Major T, the man who should have been exfiltrated on the now-ruined plane. 'Someone, somewhere will have raised an alarm.'

Georges stroked his stubble. 'We cannot go to the cottage nearby; it's too dangerous. We must put some distance between us and this wreck.'

'No,' said the pilot with vehemence.

'We have to leave,' Raymond stated.

'And I have to burn the plane,' the young Englishman told him.

'That guarantees interest,' Georges objected. 'And pinpoints us.'

'I must burn the plane,' the pilot insisted once more, wagging his finger at Georges.

'We should get the detonators and charges out first,' said Captain Carson.

'And the suitcases,' chipped in Diana.

'What detonators?' asked the pilot.

'You were bringing detonators. And more plastique.'

The pilot shook his head. 'No. I brought two passengers and two . . . Christ.'

The flyer strode across the field to the plane, rummaged inside and produced the blue wooden box containing the pigeons. 'They're alive,' he announced. The pair began cooing.

'Bloody hell,' seethed Carson. 'Birds. What use are they?'

Georges stroked his chin again. 'Fear not. I do an excellent *Pigeon à la Rouennaise.*'

With only three bicycles between them, they trudged the four kilometres to the barn of a friendly farm before the crude timing device that Pilot Officer Horrocks had set up ignited the aircraft. Diana wheeled one of the bikes, while Raymond carried the battered brown suitcase for her. As they crested a low hill and saw their destination below them, there was a dull thump from behind, followed by the whoosh of exploding fuel. They could no longer see the landing field, but the horizon danced with an orange glow. The six forlorn figures slid into the farm building and, in the half-light from the moon, found themselves somewhere to slump down.

'What a fiasco,' said Horrocks. 'How do I get back now? You have a radio operator, I presume?'

Georges said: 'I suggest we get some sleep before we think about this.'

'Christ Almighty.' Horrocks folded his arms and began mumbling to himself.

Raymond scrabbled over to Diana. 'You are all right?' He pointed to the drying blood on her head.

'Yes, thank you. It's nothing. I am a little cold, though.'

There are some blankets here. Just try not to smell them. And you, are you all right?' he asked Philip Maxwell.

'Yes. I suppose every Jerry for miles around will be crawling over the area.'

'Not so,' put in Georges, who had been listening. 'There isn't the manpower. Perhaps some gendarmes will come out, but I doubt we will be uncovered. However, it will make travelling difficult – there will be more of a watch at the railways.'

Raymond undid the top of his hipflask and passed it to Diana, who took a sip. It was cognac and it tasted wonderful. She passed it to Maxwell, who took a longer slug.

'Thank you,' Philip said. 'Look, I know we've all had a bit of a shock, but in my experience . . . ' He hesitated, looking over at Carson, whose patch it was. The other Englishman was staring at his feet, deep in thought, so Maxwell continued, 'I think Georges is right. Let's get some sleep. Things will look better in the morning.'

'Celeste, these papers are not right.' Georges turned over her *carte d'identité*, in his hand, angling them so he could read by the rose-hued glow of the sunrise. The fresh country air was tainted by the stench of burned rubber and canvas, carried on the breeze. She had come outside to use the ancient water-pump so she could wash the blood from her forehead, and Georges had followed her out. He handed the pass back.

'The stamps are fine, but the texture is not. It is the wrong material, I think. Too thin, and too new-looking. We must tell London to be more careful,' he said with concern in his voice. 'I can get you a better one in Le Mans.'

'Thank you. But I thought I should start at Tours. Our business begins there.'

'Perhaps, but that pass won't fool many people. I think it is prudent to change it. Is Astor's from the same batch?' he asked, using Maxwell's codename.

'I think not. His is old and battered.'

'Good. Most people's are. You had best come with us to Le Mans and get a replacement. I assume the pilot has no papers?'

She shrugged. 'I can't imagine he expected to be staying.'

From his pocket, Georges extracted a bundle of ID cards held together with an elastic band. He flicked through them, before settling on one with a photograph that looked vaguely like the flyer. 'This will get him past a sleepy policeman. But he, too, must obtain decent documents as soon as possible. He won't survive a proper check.'

'What about these?' She showed him the ration book and the medical certificate that London had prepared, which would give her the excuse of being in any area to seek out a specialist.

'Not bad. But not that. It is also not in order.' He pointed at her hair.

She grabbed a few strands. 'What's wrong with it?'

'Very blonde. Good if you are to pass as a German, perhaps. Not so, French – not in this part of the country. You will stand out too much. I am sorry to say this, but you can be too pretty in this business. German soldiers have a habit of checking women's papers when all they want is a good look at them. They are men, after all. And the Schloks like their blondes.'

He took her arm and directed her away from the barn, towards a small stand of lime trees. They were shaded from the road by an unkempt yew hedge. He took out a pack of cigarettes. 'I think we can risk one.' He smiled as he handed the medical certificate back. 'Even in your condition. You must be hungry?'

She hadn't thought about it, but realised she was. 'I can manage.' She took a Gauloise and lit it from his.

'It's one of your Firm's fakes', he told her. 'Not quite as good as the real thing. Make sure you cup it – like this.'

'Your Captain Carson doesn't say much,' Diana remarked.

'No. He is disappointed. The last consignment of detonators and plastique parachuted straight into the arms of the Germans. This one doesn't arrive. The trains still run. He is angry.'

'He wants to blow up a train?' she queried.

'Yes. He is an impatient boy.'

Something in his voice betrayed his true feelings. 'You don't agree?'

'If the Germans drove the trains, I might agree, but they don't. Frenchmen do. If the Germans didn't undertake reprisals, then I might agree, but they do. Only last week there was an explosion at Ascq, near Lille. No Germans were actually killed, but a troop train was derailed. The SS nevertheless beat the local railway employees, and then descended on the village. They killed eighty-six men between fifteen and fifty before the German police stopped them. It was a massacre. And for what? The line was repaired in eight hours.'

She shook her head in dismay, unsure what to say.

'Plus your Firm, they want two things that are contradictory. Incompatible. You want sabotage. OK, we blow things up, make lots of noise, produce plenty of dead Germans. You also want us to lie low until the invasion and gather arms and men. Well, fine, but then we shouldn't draw attention to ourselves by destroying trains and factories. You see? Which is it to be?'

'I see. And you think it best to keep a low profile?'

He nodded. 'We should be *naphthalinés*,' Georges said. 'Mothballs, lying low until the time is right to strike. Two, three months, the British and Americans will be here. We will get the Action messages. The BBC will inform us: "the goat is anaemic"!' He winked to let her know this wasn't a genuine message. 'Then it will be full war, and we can blow up what we like.' A thought occurred to him. 'Are you here to blow things up, Celeste?'

'No, I'm—'

'Don't tell me, I don't want to know. I am not sure I wouldn't talk under friction. None of us can be. What you don't tell me, I won't blurt out when the Schloks give me the bath.'

Diana shuddered. The 'bath' was, she knew, a favoured Gestapo torture of holding agents underwater until they near-drowned, then reviving them. It was a terrible death once; to suffer it over and over again was probably unbearable. 'All I was going to say was, I am not in the sabotage business,' she told him.

'Good. You have your death-pill?'

She touched the seam of her dress. She could feel the two bumps of the L-pills, the cyanide tablets that would spare her too much of what Georges called 'friction'. Taking one, she thought, would require as much bravery as facing torture.

'What about the others?' She pointed at the barn. 'What are their stories?'

'In there? Astor, you know,' he said, using Philip's codename once more. 'I know him of old, too. He is a good man. He was here in 1943 during the collapse of Prosper. You know about that? Disaster. But he did everything right. I trust him. Major T? He's a politician.'

'How do you mean?'

Georges cupped his hand over the tip of the cigarette and inhaled deeply once more. He pointed up the hill, to a series of low buildings now visible against the lightening sky. 'We can perhaps go to the farm soon, get some cheese. The farmer is no fly.'

'Fly?'

'Friend of the Schloks. Collaborator. Major T is here to check out the nature of the Resistance hereabouts, whether they should continue to get precious weapons. If they recognise de Gaulle, fine. If they are Communist – well, the General will create trouble. I have been in England. I have seen the politics. They tell me as a Frenchman I should not work for this section or that. I tell them to go . . .' he cleared his throat '. . . take a running jump. You will find that when this is all over, the Communists will not have lifted a finger against the Germans. According to people like Major T, that is.'

'And is it true?'

He tensed as the thin-bladed knife swept from behind and under his chin, dropping the cigarette in panic. It tumbled into the grass, where it continued to glow.

'If I were a German, I could have killed you,' hissed Carson.

'If you were a German, you'd be dead.' Philip Maxwell stepped forward, the ungainly silenced Welrod pistol held at arm's length.

Georges staggered forward as Carson released him. He put a hand to his sparse beard and it came away with a drop of blood. 'Idiot.'

'Who is an idiot, smoking out in the open?' Carson stamped on the smouldering butt. 'Your voices carry for miles. So does the smoke.'

Diana stole a glance at Maxwell who nodded his agreement. 'I'm sorry, it was my fault,' she said. 'I came out here. Let's go back inside.'

Diana left, flanked by her guardians, leaving Georges cursing them. It was his country; he knew where the danger lay, and it wasn't with smoking. A sleepy Raymond Bec strolled out to find out what all the fuss was about, one hand down his trousers, scratching himself.

Georges shook his head and pointed to the trio who were stepping into the barn. 'Take a look. The English. It always comes down to this – one woman, two men. Every time. So the men start playing Tarzan to see who gets the mate.' He banged his chest with one fist. 'I have seen it again and again. No French organisation would ever make that mistake. You know what Vera Atkins said to me in London?' He grinned at Raymond. 'She said, "At least you French just copulate and have done with it".'

Raymond nodded sullenly. 'I will look forward to that part of my life, Georges. Meanwhile, the pilot, Horrocks, is complaining again. He still blames me for placing the flare too close to the tree. You want me to contact Peroux?'

Peroux was MAGICIAN's 'pianist' or radio operator – an incredibly vital resource, one Georges was loath to risk. He thought for a moment. 'We will use the birds the woman brought; send a message that Horrocks needs a pick-up. Same message on both birds, just in case. Tell them to confirm through Peroux that they understand.' Listening was a lot less dangerous than transmitting. 'We can hide Horrocks for a few weeks until arrangements are made.'

'I do not think he will be an easy house-guest.'

'No. But worse than that . . .'

'What?'

He linked his thumbs together and mimed the flapping of wings. 'There goes my pigeon pie.'

Fifteen

After a bad-tempered council of war, made worse by the fact that there was no sign of the farmer – and, therefore, breakfast – the group decided on their tactics. They would split into two parties. Georges, Maxwell and Diana would cycle to Ettriche Station, the others would walk to Tierce, which was nearer and an easier touch. Papers were rarely checked there, so the pilot had a good chance of getting through. All would board the same train, from Angers, which would take them to Le Mans.

A soft rain was falling as the cyclists set off, some twenty minutes after the walkers. The roads were mostly empty; they passed one *gazogène*, a charcoal-powered car, and a couple of pony and traps. As they cycled, Diana explained to Maxwell what Georges had said about their companions.

'Well, I can't blame Carson,' said Maxwell. 'It is a frustrating enough existence at the best of times. You need a little action to keep you going. Bad luck about your identity card, though.'

'Yes.'

'While Georges sorts you out, perhaps I should go down to Tours?'

'No. Let's stay together. We can always do it in reverse – find out why the package never arrived in Le Mans.'

'Righty-o.'

'FRENCH!'

Maxwell blushed, appalled that he had just uttered the expression in English. He also hadn't realised Georges was so close behind. 'Sorry.'

Georges tutted. 'It's about another three kilometres. Pay attention! Your documents will be checked when you go through the barrier. Go when I go, when there are maximum people. Just follow my lead, eh?'

They both nodded and cycled the rest of the way in silence.

There were two gendarmes at the station, but no sign of the Schloks. They were ten minutes early for the train. Georges bought his ticket separately from them; Maxwell purchased two to Le Mans in his confident French. Nobody gave them a second glance. The sleepy policeman on the barrier waved Diana through, and only gave Maxwell's card a cursory once-over.

The stationmaster made a crackly announcement that the train would be late because of 'terrorist' activity near Angers. A groan went through the people on the platform. Diana suppressed a smile when she heard Georges curse loudest of all.

There was no waiting room, only a kiosk selling acorn coffee and grey-ish pastries, for which, a handwritten sign announced, no coupons were needed. It neglected to mention that this was probably because the main ingredient was sawdust. Nevertheless, her stomach demanded that she have one. Diana had ordered and made to pay when she recalled that all she had with her was a 5,000-franc note. It was the smallest note London had issued her with. As soon as she hesitated, Maxwell smoothly stepped in and took care of it with coins. He gave her arm a little squeeze of reassurance.

Diana moved away to rest on the wooden counter that was screwed to the side of the station wall and tried to stop her hand from shaking as she raised the cup to her lips. She sipped and wished she'd asked for a rum, which could be had off-ration. Maxwell joined her and they made the kind of inconsequential small talk that would convince any eavesdropper that they were monumentally dull, full as it was of fictional friends and relatives and their tedious comings and goings.

Georges also bought coffee, and grumbled to the serving woman about who exactly the Resistance thought they were fighting – the Germans or honest working Frenchmen. He turned with his coffee and Diana saw terror flick cross his face, just for a second, and then it was gone. Then she became aware that someone was staring at her.

The man had pursed his lips, as if about to kiss a cheek, and was looking her up and down shamelessly. He was a repugnant specimen, close to six foot and either bald or with severely cropped hair beneath his Trilby. His face looked lopsided, like a modern painting – by Picasso, perhaps – with one eye lower than the other.

'Albert!' Georges exclaimed to him. 'How are you?'

The man turned, irritated at having his appraisal interrupted. Recognition dawned on his twisted face. 'Henri?' he asked of Georges.

'Yes,' Georges confirmed the alias. 'How are you? Can I buy you a coffee?'

Slowly but effectively, having broken his concentration, Georges – or Henri, as he clearly sometimes was – steered the deformed man to the service counter, where he bought him coffee and a rum.

The man stole one further glance at Diana as the train huffed around the corner and into view, wreathed in dirty smoke. She felt hot cinders catch her face as clouds of steam and muck rolled along the platform.

She and Maxwell took a carriage in the centre, while Georges and his newly reacquainted friend went towards the rear. 'Who do you think that was?' she asked Philip.

'I don't know. Milice? Georges seemed keen to get him away from you.'

Joseph Darnand's Milice assisted the Vichy government and the

Germans in anti-Resistance actions. There were thousands of them and the worst were said to be so enthusiastic in their pursuit and torture of their fellow-countrymen, they sometimes shocked even the Germans.

Diana and Philip had chosen an empty compartment and hoped they would have it to themselves. However, before long an old woman with a large suitcase joined them. Philip helped her heave it onto the luggage rack. The bulging tendons in his neck suggested it was weightier than he had expected. The woman smiled her thanks and gave him an apple in return for his hernia. Diana suspected the case would be full of farm produce to sell on the black market in Le Mans.

The train pulled away with a jerk and the woman produced an old, creased copy of *Je Suis Partout*, the collaborationist newspaper. It had been fingered so often the ink was worn away in places. While the old woman was apparently engrossed in it, Philip reached across and squeezed Diana's hand. She smiled and nodded, trying to convey that she was doing fine.

The train accelerated, stopped with a squeal, and then pulled away once more, gathering speed. Philip stared intently out of the window, examining the track and other rolling stock. After crawling along for a quarter of an hour, they were shunted into sidings while an empty troop train clattered by. This was followed by a series of tanker trucks, each one marked with a sequence of numbers and letters that Philip wrote onto a slip of paper. The training, she supposed, and the months of clandestine living in France the previous year, meant he took note of everything that might be of value to London.

As they moved off once more, she saw evidence of Allied bombing raids. Le Mans was an industrial city and a major rail centre. It had, she knew, been targeted relentlessly, both from the air and, thanks to the Resistance, the ground. Along one section, a locomotive lay at the side of the track, its boiler eviscerated by high explosives, several of the bogeys missing. There were carriages, too, including, sickeningly, one just like the model they were travelling in, equally devastated. She prayed it had been empty at the time of the bombing.

Twenty slow, jerky minutes later, they pulled into Tierce Station. In the line of waiting passengers, she spotted Major T, de Gaulle's spy, casually reading a cheap paperback. She turned her head away from the window as they drew level, anxious not to betray any sign of recognition. They heard doors slam, and new arrivals walked past the doors, sometimes staring in, but none entered. One of them was Raymond, but again, she paid him no attention.

The train sat hissing for a further ten minutes, eventually answering her silent prayers by creeping forward. There were, Georges had told her, four more stops. They would alight at the station before the main terminus, because there would be less attention there.

She felt eyes on her once more through the door, and fearing the ugly Milicien, turned, but it was Georges, a look of concern on his face. He was moving slowly as the carriage rocked, exaggerating the problem this caused. He mouthed two words to her: '*La Geste.*' The Gestapo. They had boarded the train.

It might not be the Gestapo, of course. The name was used to cover all kinds of organisations: it could be agents of the SD or the Abwehr or any one of their French imitators. It all boiled down to the same thing: someone checking papers with a suspicious, critical eye. They would be especially vigilant after the burned-out plane had been found and the 'terrorist' activity in the vicinity.

She prodded Philip and repeated what Georges had said. No emotion showed. He, in turn, tapped the woman next to him. 'Madame. The papers are being checked. Are you in order?' As he suspected, her eyes swivelled upwards to the case in an involuntary tic. Still, she nodded and said she was.

Diana heard a distant shout from down the train, but could not discern what it meant. A gendarme streaked past the window, heading towards the rear. Someone was in trouble. The pilot, perhaps? He had little French and a dead man's papers.

She excused herself and said she was going to visit the toilet. Philip began to say something, but closed his mouth. She knew what the warning would have been: *'Hiding in the lavatory will not save you.'*

She slid open the door and looked out. The paper-checkers had not reached their carriage yet. She moved along the corridor and found the cubicle, slipped in and snicked the catch across. She tried to close her nose to the ammoniac stench rising from the sodden floor. Frenchmen's aim, it seemed, was no better than the average Englishman's.

From her bag, she took the suspect *carte d'identité* and fingered it, cursing London's error. She folded it back and forth a few times to try and remove the newness, but only succeeded in putting very recent-looking creases in it. So, she thought, time for Plan B. She began to cough, softly at first, then increasingly loudly, until her throat began to ache.

As she hacked away, Diana scrabbled around in her handbag and found the hook-ended nail file (stamped *Hélène, Paris*) and looking into the mirror, pulled down her lower lip to reveal the glistening fleshy part. She closed her eyes and stabbed the end of the small file into it and began to draw it back and forth, grinding her molars as she did so. When she opened her eyes, she smiled grimly at the sight that greeted her, streaking her teeth with blood. She coughed once more.

The hammering on the door came two minutes later – a brusque demand for tickets and papers. She slipped the latch and opened it a crack and pushed her hand, clutching the papers, through the gap. The swarthy man on the other side leaned his weight against the door to get a better look at her. As he did so, Diana coughed into her handkerchief, splattering blood over it. The man recoiled and she waved her medical certificate at him. He took one look at the word *tuberculose* and thrust the identity card back at her. She grabbed it and, mumbling apologies, worked her way back to the compartment. The Germans, she had been told, had an irrational, almost pathological, fear of TB.

She sat down opposite Philip, who looked suitably alarmed and fussed over her. The old woman hid behind her newspaper. All their papers were given a cursory glance and the Gestapo moved on.

Having alighted a stop short of the city and switched to a bus and then foot, they did not reach the safe apartment until gone four o'clock in the afternoon. They had all made it except Horrocks, who had jumped from the train, hence the gendarmes' panic. If he was caught, she hoped he had the sense to claim to be anything other than the Lysander pilot. Still, at least he couldn't betray the safe house.

Diana's lips throbbed from the self-laceration, and the constant fear had made her bowels loose. She had survived a wave of stomach cramps on the bus, but only just. Still, after being shown to her room, she lay down on the quilted eiderdown and fell into a deep sleep.

When she awoke, her tongue was playing with the swellings on her inner lip. Georges had slipped into the room, with a blanket for her, and he froze as her eyes flickered open.

'Sorry,' he said.

The curtains were tightly drawn and the only illumination came from a low oil lamp. It gave everything a very gloomy air, thanks to the heavy furniture with its crude ornamentation, which looked like gargoyles in the soft light, and the dark, embossed wallpaper.

She rolled over, sat up and pulled a hand through her hair. 'What time is it?' She sounded as if she had just spent an hour in the dentist's chair.

'Almost ten. I was hoping you would sleep right through the night. How is the mouth?'

'Thaw,' she mumbled.

'Astor told me what you did. It was quite a stunt.'

'Yeth.' She made an effort to enunciate correctly. 'Yes. Lucky, too.'

He nodded gravely. 'It always helps.'

'Where are the others?'

'The pilot turned up. He, too, has luck on his side. Some friends found him before the Germans. He is safe. Raymond has gone home to his parents. They know nothing of what he does. The Major is in another safe house a short distance away. Your two Englishmen are locking horns a few floors below us.'

'About what?'

'Well, nominally about how best to sabotage a railroad. Astor keeps his eyes open, eh? He has pinpointed where we could destroy the heart of the points on several lines. Then, we watch which one the Germans repair first. It tells us their priority line. That way, we know which one to blow up come the invasion. I think he might even have persuaded Captain Carson.'

'He isn't here to help sabotage things.' There was a touch of irritation in her voice. Philip was meant to be looking after her, not Carson.

'No. You said.'

'How long to get me a new identity card?'

'Twenty-four to forty-eight hours. Perhaps more.'

She shook her head. She couldn't stay cooped up in a dingy room that reeked of camphor for two whole days.

'If I could perhaps help you ... ?'

'No.' She realised she had snapped at him. 'Sorry. As you said, the less you know the better.'

'That was then, when we were too close to a burning plane. But you are right. I only know where all the aircraft land, who comes from England, who goes, where the safe houses are ... but perhaps your mission is more important than that.'

She laughed at his mock humility. 'Well, perhaps not. And, I suppose as I said to Astor, there is no reason not to start at this end rather than Tours.'

'End of what?'

'The supply chain. Vital materials for the war effort. It doesn't matter what. It runs up through here to . . . well, I suppose that doesn't matter either. But it is broken. The message confirming the delivery to the two sisters in Le Mans never arrived. I could start with them.'

'You know where they are?'

'Yes. They aren't hard to find – they are identical twins.' The pair had escaped from France just before the Fall, but had volunteered to go back in early 1943, explaining their absence by claiming they had been staying with their aged parents in Cannes. Diana had helped the two middle-aged ladies work on their tans, using sunlamps to back up the deceit.

'Twins? Do you mean the Malbrecs?' he asked.

'Yes. You know them?'

'Of them.' He rubbed the stubble on his face. 'They were arrested over a week ago.'

Sixteen

'The Malbrec twins were kept for two days at the Hotel Marianne.' This was the SD Headquarters in Le Mans, and much like Avenue Foch in Paris, the once-innocent name had acquired a sinister ring. 'They have been shipped to Paris for further interrogation.' The Major shrugged. 'It is all my people could find out.'

Georges, Raymond, the Major, Philip Maxwell and Diana were sitting at the rear of a café on rue Reine-Bérengère in the old town, not far from the river. The private back room, separated from the main seating area by fancy Art Nouveau glass doors, was decorated with photographs from the famous Le Mans race. These mostly consisted of white-overalled men sitting nonchalantly on their Bugattis and Alfas, smoking and laughing in the face of highly flammable liquids. One of them showed Auto Union drivers giving the stiff-armed *Heil Hitler* salute; another, head-and-shoulder shot, more prominently displayed, was signed by its subject, the handsome and flamboyant Robert Benoist.

Carson was stationed outside the café at the pavement tables, keeping watch for any untoward activity. He would warn them if one of the periodic swoops by gendarmes, Gestapo or Milice looked imminent. The *salon privé* had a rear exit that could act as a bolt-hole. Only Horrocks, the frustrated Lysander pilot, was not present; his lack of French was a liability and he had been parked up until

Georges could produce some decent ID or London arranged to fetch him.

'Why were they arrested?' asked Diana. 'They are two nice old ladies.'

The women were actually only in their late forties, but in their matching black dresses, sensible shoes and headscarves, they had always seemed positively antique.

'They were harbouring partisans,' the Major explained. 'It was an FTP safe house.' This was the *Francs-Tireurs Partisans*, the Communist Resistance movement. 'Locals noticed all the comings and goings. They thought the women were black marketeers and denounced them. Apparently, the Germans couldn't believe their luck when they found armed men and a transmitter.'

Diana groaned. Every link in the supply route had been warned not to compromise it by branching out into other Resistance activity.

'Which prison are they in?' asked Georges. 'Fresnes?'

The Major ran a hand lightly over his oiled hair. He was dressed elegantly and expensively in a double-breasted pinstriped suit, which fitted perfectly with his cover as a black marketeer. 'Saint Denis.'

Raymond let out a little whoop, strangled when Georges shot him a warning glance. Outside in the main salon a few heads turned, but the curious soon went back to stirring their filthy coffee.

'My brother is in Saint Denis. The town, not the prison,' he added hastily. 'He is . . .' Raymond lowered his voice '. . . one of us.'

Le patron came through to the *salon privé*, cleared the dirty cups and they ordered another round of drinks. 'I will need this room for lunch,' he explained. 'I am expecting some VIPs.' The wink told them they were Germans. It was a warning to clear out soon.

'What can we do for them?' asked Diana when the owner had left, trying to keep desperation from her voice. The thought of the pleasure the SD might take in torturing identical twins filled her with horror.

'I hear the prison at Saint Denis is more porous than Fresnes,' said the Major.

'Meaning?' asked Philip.

'Open to bribery,' Georges told him. 'Yes, I have heard this, too.'

'My brother has another way.' Raymond murmured about a tunnel being excavated to the prison.

'How far is it from completion?' queried Diana.

'Only weeks,' insisted Raymond.

Philip snorted. 'We don't have weeks.'

'Maybe days,' the lad added, with what was clearly hopeless optimism.

'How big a bribe do we need?'

'To get someone released from under the noses of the Schloks?' Georges held his finger and thumb several inches apart. 'A million francs perhaps.'

Diana blew her cheeks out in frustration. She had only brought fifty thousand across. 'I don't know where to get that much money.'

There was a growing silence until Philip cleared his throat and said softly: 'I do.'

Paris and its suburbs smelled not of fresh bread and coffee, but horseshit and charcoal from the *gazogène* burners used to power cars and trucks. The fumes wafted over Diana, sticking to her skin. She had been on the street for thirty minutes, and already felt as if she needed a hot bath. She was sitting at a café table in Place du Marché in St Denis, nursing a coffee that tasted of nothing but chicory. Her stomach rumbled. Living, like the rest of the French, on just over a thousand calories a day was proving difficult. She touched her hair, shocked for the tenth time that hour that it was shorter, and darker, than when she had arrived.

At another table was Maxwell, scanning the lies in *Le Figaro*, a

Gladstone bag clamped between his feet. Across the square, beneath the plane trees, she could see Georges, talking to a *vélo-taxi* cyclist, involved in what appeared to be a good-natured argument. The *vélo-taxi* man was Raymond's brother, Jacques. Raymond himself was on the opposite side of the *place*, having picked up a few days' work at the local garage, performing the miracle of turning ordinary cars into *gazogènes*.

Seventy-two hours had passed since her discovery of the arrest of the Malbrec sisters. In that time, Philip had arranged to meet his 'banker', with whom he had deposited SOE cash during his last sojourn. Georges, true to his word, had provided a better identity card for Diana, as well as some hair dye and scissors, and Raymond had come ahead to arrange for this meeting. She, Philip and Georges had enjoyed an uneventful train ride to Gare du Montparnasse the previous day.

The prison where the sisters were being held was several streets to the west of them, surrounded by flaking, diseased walls which were high enough to prevent even a glimpse of the former convent within. They were topped with several coils of barbed wire and powerful lights. The gates were massive iron-and-wood double doors, with a smaller entrance cut into one of them. A brace of German soldiers was on permanent duty, with a patrol of gendarmes making circuits of the walls four times an hour. Diana had inspected the tunnel in the basilica and, although it was a brave effort by Jacques and others, progress was so slow she couldn't see it being finished until it was no longer needed – once the Allies had reached Paris. Which is why the group had resorted to the original plan to free the Malbrecs: bribery.

The man who walked briskly across the square and up to the café was in his fifties, with a bushy moustache that needed trimming, and stained, protruding teeth. He looked Diana up and down and dismissed her. She calmly moved her handbag so it was positioned close to her on the table and unclipped it. The knurled handle of a pistol was just visible.

The man approached Philip's table, made a comment, as arranged, about the headline, which claimed the Allies were being pushed back down Italy. Philip folded the newspaper. The man she assumed was a warder sat and ordered a Houblonnette, the pathetic excuse for a beer that had been adopted from Belgium when raw materials to make the genuine article became scarce.

Diana strained her ears, but could not hear what was being said between the two men. When his drink arrived, the warder downed it in three large gulps, reached under the table, took the Gladstone bag and walked briskly from the square. After a moment's hesitation, St Denis appeared to snap back into life. Philip returned to reading the newspaper. Diana clipped her handbag shut and drained her cup of chicory. Georges climbed into the *vélo-taxi* and was pedalled off at a brisk pace. A new brittle sound drifted over the *place*: Raymond, hammering at the rear of a small Peugeot, making space for a boiler.

They were on.

Two days later, the network was to be in position to receive the sisters. The man with the bad teeth had not been a warder or prison clerk but 'represented' someone who was. The message had come through that the Malbrecs would be substituted, in a contrived bureaucratic mix-up, for two prostitutes who were due for release. It was imperative to get them out of St Denis town before this bungle was discovered, so Raymond had borrowed a *gazogène* Renault van from the garage. His brother would pick up the liberated duo in his *vélo-taxi* and deliver them to a nearby rendezvous point, where Raymond would be waiting with the van. Diana would travel with them into Paris, where they could lie low while it was decided whether it would be safe to go back to Le Mans. She would also debrief them. Meanwhile, contact between them and other Resistants must be kept to a minimum. Anyone who was arrested by the Germans must be viewed as compromised, even the sisters.

Georges would not be in on the action. He had to return to

his base of operations to keep an eye on Carson and to make sure the pilot got back across the Channel, along with de Gaulle's Major T. Plus, he explained, there were arms drops to organise and a new landing field to find, the one with the wrecked Lysander now being off the list permanently.

In the meantime, Raymond had arranged for Diana and Philip to stay in a tiny *pension* that, in peacetime, had accommodated pilgrims to the Basilica. It was cramped and low on luxuries, but nevertheless they spent the day before the operation in Philip's room, smoking and sharing a chocolate bar that Georges had left them.

Diana sat in the window, legs tucked under her, watching the doorway of the church, fretting whenever German soldiers passed. Tunnelling was continuing at its agonisingly slow pace. Philip, convinced the scheme would never work, had suggested it might better be used as an arms dump, ready for the big push when the invasion came. Raymond and his brother said they would at least consider that option.

The sun had broken through the thin clouds of morning and the trees were in vibrant leaf, dappling the pavements with a mosaic of shadows and light. It was hard to imagine what those sisters were going through less than a mile away. Diana knew she should be furious at them for setting up as a safe house. Still, she couldn't really blame them; waiting for a parcel once every few weeks and making sure it reached Brest must have seemed like a minimal contribution to the war effort. Yet they had been told they were vital bombsights for the RAF. Wasn't that enough? In truth, the genuine contents were in many ways even more valuable than that.

'What did you do? Before the war?' Diana asked Philip.

'Journalist. *Daily Express*. One of Beaverbrook's Boys.'

'Was that fun?'

He smiled at the memory. 'Yes.'

'Are you married?' she asked.

A nod came in reply.

'Do you miss her?'

Philip shifted uncomfortably. 'It's best we don't—'

'I won't ask her name. Or what she looks like. Or what she does. Although I'm not sure what value it would be to the Germans if—' She stopped the sentence. She didn't want to think about where it was leading.

'Yes, I do miss her. I'd promised her I wouldn't come across again.'

'I'm sorry.'

'For what?'

'For being the one who made you break your promise.'

'Well, if I was going to do so for anyone, I'm glad it was you.' Diana noticed he had reddened slightly. He was, she thought, very handsome, even if he was doing his best to disguise the fact by not bothering to shave. She found herself in the usual quandary with married men. She had no wish to encourage them to be unfaithful; on the other hand, there was a wicked curiosity to discover if they did find her attractive. Even as she was doing it, she realised it was more than a touch adolescent.

'What about you?' he asked in his turn. 'Is there a sweetheart?'

She shook her head. 'No, not really. A few non-starters. The war . . . it rather gets in the way, doesn't it?'

'How's your lip?'

She wondered if he was changing the subject. Or was he thinking about her lips – and what he'd like to do with them? She reached up and unfurled the lower one, displaying the dark red weals.

He winced at the sight of them. 'Ouch.'

'Difficult to stop my tongue playing with them.'

'Must be.' Philip stood up, banging his head on a low beam. He rubbed his scalp furiously.

'Ouch back,' she laughed.

'Bloody hell, what a pair. I hope we'll still be in one piece tomorrow.'

The reminder of what was to come jolted her. She lit her fourth cigarette of the day. 'Will it work?'

'A million francs opens a lot of doors. Even prison ones.'

'What if our friend with the bad teeth doesn't deliver?'

'I promised him that I – or a friend of mine – would hunt him down and shoot him like a dog. And then his chum inside the prison.' The tone of his voice and the look in his eyes suggested he would do just that. 'When he left the café, Georges had the go-between followed. We know where he lives. Georges has let him know we know. I can't see there is much else we could do.'

'We should have cut the banknotes in two. Given him half now, half on delivery.'

'And you're telling me this now because . . . ?'

'Because I only just thought of it.'

He laughed. 'I think a million taped-together francs might raise some eyebrows at even the most dubious bank. And if they looked too closely . . .'

She let out a small shriek. 'They're duds?'

'Hand-printed by our man in the Holloway Road, apparently. Under the supervision of a French treasury official, so it's as good as the real thing. It might even *be* the real thing in one sense. Still, fake or not, it's a lot of spending power. Look, I am going to get some fresh air before I give myself concussion on this ceiling. Do you want to come?'

'A stroll in the park? Is it safe?'

'It's a beautiful spring day. We'll be just like sweethearts – if you know what I mean. Good cover story. Two is always safer than one.' He was blustering.

She swung her legs off the windowsill, fetched a precious stub of lipstick, applied it, then stood on tiptoe to kiss him. He turned his face away and her mouth hit his cheek, leaving a slash of scarlet. 'There you are. Now we look the part.'

She slept badly that night, afraid and alone, shivering even though the sun had warmed her room beneath the eaves for several hours and there was no need of extra blankets. What had she been playing at, teasing him like that? Philip had responded badly to the kiss and they had walked around not like sweethearts, but lovers who had just had a tiff. He thought she was being flippant, not taking the work seriously enough.

That wasn't true. It was just a momentary release of tension, idle thoughts while pretending they weren't agents of a foreign power in a hostile country. Diana *was* serious about the mission. She wanted to get back to London having succeeded in putting the Swiss Line back together and running like, well, clockwork. *And* having returned Philip to his wife in one piece.

Around two in the morning, the room was illuminated by vivid flashes. She could hear the rumble of rolling thunder. It took a while for her to realise these were bombs falling – on the marshalling yards, probably. They were the favoured target around Paris.

The bombing raid lasted for three hours. When Diana finally dozed off in the grey dawn light, she had made a determined decision to be a consummate professional from now on. Of course, she couldn't have known just how little time she had left to prove anything to Philip Maxwell.

Seventeen

As it had twice a week for the past four hundred years, the market had arrived in St Denis. Eight rows of brightly coloured awnings, faded and patched these days, marched across the sunlit *place*, shading the goods laid out carefully for inspection. Lazy dogs snoozed under the trees, swishing at the flies that circled them. A child on an ancient tricycle pedalled furiously up and down. There was even a game of *boules* on the dusty strip to the left of the square, with a group of onlookers carefully smoking their precious cigarettes.

To Diana's eyes, the almost timeless scene was spoiled by the preponderance of German uniforms and the haughty, well-dressed figures of the 'grey mice', the female volunteers from the Reich who did secretarial, clerical and telephonic work for the Occupation.

There was also a scarcity of food on the tables. The meagre piles of fresh fruit, vegetables and eggs had disappeared early in the day, before full light. After that went the other rare items: nearly-new toothbrushes, perfumed soap, razor blades, combs, lacy underwear, carpenter's nails, cigarette lighters, shoe polish and brushes, yarns of wool, lipstick and face powder. Everything that had once made life so easy, so bearable, so civilised.

What the Germans were poring over now were people's

heirlooms, their dowries and the detritus from attics and cellars. The pickings were slim, but every so often a family, at the end of its tether, would decide to sell some precious memento. The Occupiers had, over the past four years, grown adept at this; they knew that a few sausages, some bars of Wehrmacht Swiss chocolate, maybe even a purloined rabbit or chicken, bought them far more than mere money. This had led to Paris, effectively, eating its own heritage.

It was close to midday and the soldiers were leaving as the stalls were dismantled. Diana, unable to face any more coffee, which coated her mouth with a gritty residue, ordered one of the saccharine-heavy flavoured waters that passed for an apéritif and tried to stop biting her nails. She had got into the habit of clenching her fists, so as not to expose them too much. No self-respecting Frenchwoman, especially a Parisienne, would allow them to deteriorate so far. She made a note to book a manicure as soon as possible. Falsies might even be in order. The woman from Truefitt & Hill would be furious with her.

She watched Philip cross the road towards her, looking, to her, self-conscious in his unseasonable raincoat. But then, she might just be over-sensitive because she knew what he had hidden under it, slung by a strap from his shoulder, so its shape was lost in the garment's folds and flaps. Philip killed time buying cigarettes at the *tabac*, gossiping with the old war-veteran owner, who was so pleased of the company he sold him a rare pack of Boyard Caporal Ordinaire.

Raymond's brother Jacques cycled past at five to twelve, skilfully ignoring the man who tried to hail him, and disappeared in the direction of the jail. What was more natural than for two newly released prisoners to jump in a passing *vélo-taxi* and flee the place of their confinement as quickly as possible? Jacques would appear just as the little inner door opened, a heaven-sent messenger.

With a cough of smoke from its brazier at the rear, Raymond's van appeared right on cue and slid to a halt in front of the café where Diana sat. She shifted position. Under her jacket was a Welrod silenced pistol. It carried just a single shot, but its soft hiss would attract far less attention than the noisy revolver in her bag. Not that they wanted a gunfight. This whole affair would only be considered successful if they got away without attracting undue attention. Or shooting anyone.

The Cathedral's bell began to strike the hour and Diana stood. She had already paid the bill; she had been primed that it was customary in France now to settle up at once, in case of a raid, either by Allied planes or German thugs. She walked from the Café du Marché towards the street where the exchange would take place. Behind her, she heard the Renault van move for a final circuit of the square. Raymond was looking for suspicious characters, singly or in groups – anyone paying too much attention to their surroundings. At the periphery of her vision, she saw Philip fold up the newspaper and slip it under his arm, and fall in ten metres behind her.

The last stroke of twelve seemed to hang heavy in the air, the decaying chime reverberating around the buildings. It made her heart beat faster. Her feet hurt within a few paces. The crude wooden clogs she had bought to blend in with the locals had rubbed unsightly blisters into her flesh. To make matters worse, a band of pain had taken hold around her head, squeezing like a too-tight hat. She forced herself to breathe deeply, letting oxygen get to her blood, telling herself that Philip was covering her back, and not to draw attention to herself by walking too fast.

The shops in the designated rendezvous street were closing for lunch, the wooden shutters coming down one after another, each with a noise like a drum roll. Then she saw Jacques's *vélo-taxi* turn into the road, four hundred metres ahead. She shaded her eyes and could just make out the two shapes in the rear. The sisters.

The Renault van growled by, apparently on another test drive, the engine spitting and snarling in protest at the low-grade fuel it was forced to run on. Diana risked a look around, knowing it was unwise. People rarely glance over their shoulder if they have no care in the world, only those worried about followers. Philip had slowed, but was still there, his coat flapping open, so he could swing the Sten up if need be.

Apart from the odd storekeeper still shutting up shop, they had the road to themselves. As the van slowed and then jerked to a halt, she picked up the pace, ignoring the sharp pains from her feet. The *vélo-taxi* had drawn alongside the Renault. Raymond was already out, opening the rear doors, pushing a board in place to shield the women from the brazier assembly that powered the vehicle and occupied half the cargo space.

The sisters, dressed in identical black as always, emerged stiffly from the *vélo-taxi* and followed Raymond's directions to climb in. Jacques passed by without a glance at Diana, as if, having made a little cash, he was intent on getting to his lunch. Perhaps he was. She looked again at the women as they clambered inside.

And then she was into a headlong dash, as fast as she could manage, almost throwing a clog in her haste. Raymond looked at her in horror and swiftly darted to the driver's side and dived in. The engine was still running, the rear door open waiting for her to climb in and join the sisters. Philip had sprinted to her side.

'Diana?' he gasped. 'What's wrong?'

'Get them out, get them out,' she hissed through her teeth.

'What?'

'It's not them. It's not the sisters. We've been duped.'

As she reached the Renault, the two women had already thrown off their shawls, revealing their hard, chiselled faces and dead eyes. The telltale legs were curled up beneath them. They were sheathed in expensive seamed stockings – the real thing, not just beige paint – of the kind the sisters would never have worn, that ended in very unspinsterish high-heeled shoes. As soon as she had seen those legs, Diana had known that catastrophe was upon them. They had paid a million francs for a pair of whores.

Eighteen

Diana reached into the Renault and grabbed a handful of coarse dyed hair. 'Out! Get out!' The prostitute raked her wrist with her fingernails, drawing blood, but Diana held on, yanking harder. The first one stumbled out into the road, cursing and spitting. Philip extracted the second in a gentler manner.

'Where are they?' asked Diana, a tremor of anger and despair in her voice. 'Where are the sisters?'

'Who?'

'The sisters who should have been released.'

The second *fille de joie* shrugged. 'The old women? Pah. Gone.'

'Gone where?'

'We don't know. They were taken away at dawn. They are probably in Germany by now.'

Diana, unable to contain herself, slapped the woman as hard as she could. The prostitute staggered back and was about to spring forward, when Philip made sure she could see the Sten. 'Lose yourselves. Now.'

After a second's hesitation the pair tottered off.

Beyond them now, the group saw the low, sleek shape of a Citroën Traction Avant slide across the road, blocking it. Raymond yelled something. They turned to see a truck taking up a similar position at the other end of the thoroughfare. They were trapped.

'Get in!' Raymond instructed. 'Now!'

The pair launched themselves into the space vacated by the prostitutes and Philip slammed the door. Raymond pressed the accelerator immediately, while Philip struggled to release the strap of the Sten. He used language and expressions in both French and English Diana had never heard before.

'Hold on.'

The Renault lurched forward, then swerved into an internal courtyard and bounced over rough, ancient cobbles. Through the windscreen Diana could see there was an arch at the far end of the space, leading onto another street. It was an old drive-through coaching inn. The jolts threw her against the board that lay across the brazier, and she could feel the heat on her cheek. She was pushed back against Philip as Raymond spun the wheel to the right and emerged onto a clear street. He let out a little whoop. The coast was clear, for the moment at least.

'What now?' Diana asked.

'We head for a safe house. There is one not far from La Villette.'

'Jacques?' She didn't have to expand on her concerns for the brother.

'He will say he just picked up a fare as instructed. Do not worry. He might have an uncomfortable twenty-four hours, but he won't say anything, no matter what they do.'

That hadn't been what she meant, but she kept quiet. She was biting her lip again, nibbling at the place where she had made it bleed in the train. She tasted the first copper tang of blood.

Philip Maxwell was peering through the ventilation slats in the door. 'How long, Raymond? To the house?'

'I'm heading east. I will pick up the canal and follow it down. Twenty minutes.'

Philip checked the Sten once more, making sure it was on single shot before removing and replacing the magazine to guarantee a snug fit. Diana extracted the small revolver from her bag. If it came to it, this was going to be no time for one-shot silenced pistols like the Welrod.

'What went wrong?' she asked him. 'Who betrayed us?'

Philip shook his head. 'The jailers. It's more likely they couldn't pull the switch. They didn't want us asking for a refund, so they tipped off the Germans or the Milice.'

'But you told them you or Georges would kill them!'

'My guess is that they'd rather take their chances with us than the Gestapo.' Philip turned to look at her. He reached across and touched her wrist and showed her the end of his finger. It carried a fragile globule of blood. 'I'm sorry if I was, you know, off-ish the other—'

'Sshh.' Diana wiped the three parallel lines on her wrist with a handkerchief and pulled her sleeve down to hide the wound. 'There is nothing to be sorry about.'

He gave a wry smile that suggested there was always something to be sorry about.

'Canal. Hold on,' said Raymond. He made the right turn as smoothly as he could. Philip pointed his weapon away from them as they slid around. They didn't need an accidental shooting right at this moment.

Diana kept peering anxiously ahead. They all shared the same fear: roadblock. If the telephone lines were working – and they weren't always, thanks to Resistance sabotage – then the Germans would have called ahead and sealed off the routes into the city. They might not have expected them to come this far east, but then again, they just might have anticipated it.

'La Villette coming up.'

'And I think someone is behind us,' said Philip as calmly as he could.

'So do I,' Raymond confirmed. Diana looked through the door slats, and saw the familiar inverted Vs of a Traction Avant grille. 'We can't lead them to the safe house.'

'No.'

The van gave a shudder and a hiccup. 'Shit,' muttered Raymond.
'What?'
'Brazier's failing.'
'Can I stoke it?'
'Not on the move.'

The van lurched once more and kangarooed a few metres before settling down. But Diana could feel they were slowing.
'I'm losing power. This is flat out.'
There was the snick of the Sten's bolt being pulled back.
'No,' said Raymond. 'You'll lose in a head-to-head fight.'

An empty livestock truck came out from a side turning, muscling its wooden-slatted way into place behind them. They heard the Traction Avant's horn blare. Raymond made a fast left, over a canal bridge. Ahead was the Métro for La Villette and streams of people were emerging from it, colliding with an equally large group trying to descend the steps into the subway. The van stuttered once more and Raymond pulled over. There was no sign of the pursuing Citroën.

Now Raymond spoke so fast, Diana had trouble following him. 'Get out. Merge with the crowd. Take the Métro to rue Grenelle. Ask for Michel at the Bar Joséphine. Tell him Raymond has bought a cat. A Persian. He will help.'

'What about you?' she blurted.

Raymond swivelled and grinned. 'I have no gun. My papers are in order. There are thousands of vans like this. I am on a test drive for the garage. Please, it's best. I can manage – trust me.'

They were out in seconds. Philip quickly added charcoal to the brazier, burning his hand, and closed the doors. The van made a gurgling noise as Raymond pressed the pedal, so both of them pushed, Philip using just one hand, to try and shield the Sten from view. The engine slowly cranked itself up and fired. Raymond stuck a hand through the window in a farewell wave, then made his way through the sea of people flowing across the road and disappeared.

Diana and Philip turned towards the large, ornate M sign that marked the La Villette subway. That was when the rough hands grabbed each of them, pinning their arms to their sides, marching them away from the Métro and safety.

Nineteen

Diana McGill had always wondered how she would react at this moment – when, as they said at Beaulieu, the game was up. She had expected to go into a hotheaded funk, for terror to grip her insides. She anticipated screams and sobs and the white heat of pure terror. Instead, it was like a glass of iced water dashed in her face, clearing the mind, bringing a sudden, terrifying clarity to the situation.

There were three captors. Two were broad-shouldered hulks of men. The one clutching Philip had a bald head and one of those moustache-less beards she had only ever seen on fairy-tale giants. He was dressed in a blue smock of heavy cotton. She couldn't see the man gripping her that clearly, but she had an impression of a hard-muscled body and she could smell him, a musty feral odour tinged with garlic and aniseed. The third of the trio was directing them. He, too, was wearing a smock, but his was a cream colour, with a green armband. It was also spotless. He had a mop of reddish hair and freckles, and when he spoke he showed teeth that were far too regular to be genuine. So far he had uttered but a single word of contempt for them: 'Idiots.'

From over the heads of the crowd, she heard the mournful moan of a whistle. 'Shift B has finished,' said Ginger. 'Good.'

'Where are we going? What is the meaning of this?' demanded

Philip. The inflection sounded like the genuine outrage of an innocent man to her.

'What is the meaning of *this*?' returned Ginger, poking at the Sten gun which still hung under Philip's raincoat. He gave a toothy grin.

As they moved into the body of the crowd, Diana began to notice that most of the labourers wore smocks of some hue. Those heading directly towards the Métro, though, had one distinctive feature: they were all covered in blood, from shockingly fresh sprays of crimson, to old, crusted scabs like deposits from a claret bottle.

'Who are you?' asked Diana.

'People who know what a hidden Sten gun signifies.'

'She knows nothing,' said Philip, jerking his head at Diana. 'Let her go. She can't help you.'

Ginger cursed as oncoming workers buffeted him. He stopped and squinted at Philip. 'She can't help us? We are helping you, you fool. Not that you deserve it.'

As they continued, Diana asked softly: 'Resistance? Is that who you are?'

'FTP,' he snapped back proudly. Communists. 'The Métro is crawling with Milice and Gestapo. And look.'

She turned her head. With a grating of gears, a Wehrmacht Henschel truck nosed its way into the workers, parting them. In the rear of the lorry she could see the glint of sunlight on coal-scuttle helmets. Elsewhere, she could make out the *képis* of regular French cops, bobbing above the sea of heads as they emerged from a *panier à salade*, a salad basket, the French version of a Black Maria.

It all seemed a disproportionate response for a couple of Resistants on the run. This must, she decided, be one of the swamping operations, in which the various arms of the Occupier saturated an area in the hope of capturing deserters, black marketeers, subversives and those avoiding compulsory work in Germany.

They had just been unlucky to get enmeshed in it. She hoped that Raymond had not underestimated his abilities to talk his way out of a corner.

'It's a sweep,' Ginger confirmed. 'You will be run to ground in minutes.'

'Where are we going?' Philip repeated.

A second truck, a Hanomag, appeared. Chains rattled as its tail-gate dropped and the troops began to dismount. 'The only safe place around here,' he replied. Diana heard the yelp of dogs, the snap of leashes nearby. 'Hurry. If there has been sabotage, they might be taking *Sühnepersonen*'. Atoners, it meant: hostages by any other name.

A ripple of panic spread through the crowd and the workers began to jostle into a tighter pack, funnelled towards a gap in a tall, wire-topped brick wall. It looked like the outside of the St Denis prison, Diana thought glumly. There was another element making her uneasy, carried on the wind. A smell like the one from her captor, only far stronger. It was the stench of piss, shit and fear. Ginger saw a dawning in her eyes and nodded. 'Welcome to the City of Blood.'

As the mass of workers approached the gates of La Villette, Diana could see armed German guards patrolling. Above and behind them, standing on soapboxes, were French overseers, scanning the faces of the crowd. As each individual approached, he or she held up a blue canvas-backed card.

Diana felt her arms freed, and saw that Philip's captor had done the same. They both quickly worked some life back into their wrists. Ginger flashed his work pass at the nearest supervisor, and then passed the card to Diana who repeated the gesture. The over-seer glared at her, but Ginger emitted an odd three-note whistle. It was clearly a signal of some description, for the overseer lowered his eyes. He didn't even look their way when Philip and his thug repeated the charade. The nearest German guard was too busy making sure he wasn't jostled to notice any subterfuge.

Once inside the vast compound, which she judged to stretch across several acres, Diana could hear what had been masked by the chatter of humans. It was a mix of lowing, grunting, bleating and squealing. All around the complex were pens, each containing hundreds of animals. They represented more food than Paris had seen on its tables in four years.

'The meat is mostly for the Wehrmacht and SS units,' Ginger explained. Ahead of them was a squat building with a shallow sloping roof, supported at the overhang by ornate cast-iron pillars. Steel fences created corridors that led from this elaborate shed to the animal pens. It was an abattoir, an exceptionally pretty one from the outside, but still clearly a slaughterhouse.

'There's five of these buildings,' said Ginger. 'The Wehrmacht Supply Corps and the Office of German Procurement have taken one to four. Paris makes do with that little one over there. It's mostly for horses, a taste the Germans don't share. Except, I hear, on the Eastern Front.' He made an unpleasant sound that might have been laughter.

La Villette was, he told her, one of two slaughterhouses in Paris, the other being on the Left Bank. This was by far the larger. It was supplied by rail and canal; the animals were often moved in and their products shipped out, under cover of darkness. Some of the meat went to the city, some to the Atlantic Wall coastal defence units, a portion to the various German units elsewhere in the country. Other, choice consignments, packed in ice generated by the huge plant at the southern entrance of the City of Blood, headed east, by rail from Gare de l'Est, to Germany itself. Just like eighty to ninety per cent of everything else France produced.

'We are in slaughterhouse number four,' Ginger said. 'Everyone here is designated by the colour of their smocks, aprons or armbands. The most skilful butchers wear white or cream smocks and aprons. The slaughtermen wear dark red. Follow me.'

They stepped through hangar-style sliding doors into a living tableau from a Bosch or Brueghel painting. The vast hall was partitioned off into discrete areas by low whitewashed walls. Each individual section was crammed with scarred butcher's blocks and tables. Everywhere carcasses glistened red and bone-white. Flies patrolled in squadrons, their passage disrupted only by the fans rotating above each workstation. These had long strips of Fly-tox paper attached to each blade, creating a whirling chemical corona.

Above their heads, routed to avoid the fans, was a complex series of moving metal links, like enormous motorised bicycle chains. These carried rows of hooks of various sizes, most of which were already baited with flesh. The larger system was designed to move whole or half-carcasses from the slaughter area for initial butchering. The smaller models took this moveable feast, now reduced to various cuts, towards the packaging area at the far end – at least, Diana estimated, half a kilometre distant.

The metal links and the fans squeaked and rattled; butcher's knives flashed against sharpening steels; from the slaughtering section came the thud of captive bolts and the plaintive squeal of doomed animals. Steam hissed in the scalding rooms, where chickens were dipped ready for plucking and then hooked onto the overhead belts to be delivered to rows of women who sat at long benches, covered in feathers and guts, their blades and scissors snick-snacking in unison. Cleavers thunked through bone into wood; blood, destined for *boudin noir*, gurgled into steel channels and was collected in troughs.

Diana felt something bitter rise in her throat.

Ginger saw her expression. 'You see why the Germans rarely enter this place. Like most people, the first they want to know about where their food comes from is when a pork chop is plopped onto their plate. Come.'

He threaded between the blocks, exchanging ribald or sarcastic remarks with his fellow workers. Nobody gave Diana and Philip a second glance once he had thrown each of them a green smock and they had slipped them over their heads. Just a couple of fresh recruits, lambs to the slaughterhouse. 'I am guessing you aren't up to butchering a rack or a salmon cut yet. We'll start you on offal.'

'The lowest of the low?' asked Diana.

Ginger grinned. 'No, they are the ones who clean up after you. Just cut the fat off the kidneys, pull the membranes from the livers and slice into lobes, clean up the sweetbreads. Or at least, look as if you are. At the end of the shift, you can leave with us.' He indicated the streets outside. 'They should be clear by then; the sweeps only last a few hours.'

They moved to an area close to the killing rooms, where piles of still-warm innards steamed in large circular enamel trays. A group of women were sorting the piles, selecting stomachs and guts for sausage casings, slicing out organs and tossing them onto a second table, where workers quickly trimmed them up. Eventually, the various cuts of offal were piled into canvas sacks and placed on the hook system.

Diana and Philip slithered over a floor sticky with mucus and blood and Ginger found them a station at the offal-trimming table, in front of the shiny raw material of their new work. He fetched them a couple of wicked-looking knives, gave them an expert sharpen and told them to get on with it.

'I'll be over there, showing some finesse,' he smiled.

As he turned, Philip muttered: 'Thanks, er . . . Thank you.' He knew better than to ask the man his name.

Ginger shrugged and nodded towards a pyramid of digestive tracts. 'Thank me after ten hours of doing that.'

Diana wondered just how many thumbs she actually had. No matter, she'd managed to cut them all within thirty minutes. The other men and women eyed them suspiciously at first, but one rotund woman – being well-fed was probably a perk of this job – demonstrated how to hold the knife and slice through densely packed fat. As she parted the intestines and connective tissue, there was a sucking, glutinous sound that almost made Diana heave.

Eventually, though, Diana discovered that some of her thumbs really were fingers and the mountain of gore shrank to a small cairn. Having mastered one job, they were moved from extracting kidneys onto removing cheeks and tongues from an enormous bucket of cow heads, slowly accumulating a patina of animal parts, a blend of blood, fat and gobbets of flesh that she even managed to get into her hair.

Then, mercifully, there was a break, ten minutes in which many simply stepped away from their stations and lit up cigarettes. Diana staggered outside to gasp some fresh-ish air – even the odour of farm animals was preferable to the greasy atmosphere inside. At least here you were smelling the exteriors of the poor creatures.

'You OK?' asked Philip, handing her a cigarette.

She brushed a strand of stiff hair back in place. 'How do I look?'

He raised his eyebrows and lit her a Boyard.

'That bad?'

'You look fine.'

'Steady with the compliments, there, young man. You could turn a girl's head.' When she tried to actually rotate it, though, she realised her neck was stiff. She massaged it with her free hand, enjoying the deadening taste of the strong tobacco smoke in her mouth. 'When do you think we can leave?'

'We might as well stay until the end of the shift. As long as the Métro is cleared, our man is right – travelling en masse with this lot,' he jerked his thumb behind him, 'should be as safe as it gets. We should get to the bar and undercover well before curfew.'

She held up her palms and examined them, marvelling at the way the lines were now picked out by a reticulate of ingrained blood. 'As long as the place has running water, hot or cold, I don't care.'

Philip gave a grin, but it froze on his face and then melted away. She followed his gaze to where the compound's gates were being pulled back to admit a black Traction Avant and a compact Opel troop-carrier. The two fugitives hastened back inside, just as the signal sounded that break was over.

As she passed Ginger, Diana muttered: 'Schloks.'

He moved to follow her and came alongside, slipping his knife back into the leather belt of blades slung around his waist. 'Here? Inside the compound?'

She nodded. His sour expression told her this was not usual. 'Many?'

'Ten, twelve – and a couple of Gestapo, by the look of it.'

'They cannot check everyone. There are a thousand people working here. It would take them days. Just get on with your work.'

The next task was severing sweetbreads from a morass of fat, fibre and membrane. Once again Jacqueline, the corpulent woman, instructed them in the correct technique. Both of them kept their heads down, applying themselves to the job, not daring to look up. The hangar gates squeaked back at one point and they heard shouting in German, but nobody approached their section of the shed. 'Perhaps they are looking for someone else,' said Diana.

'Perhaps.' The terse reply suggested Philip thought not.

Then the doors slid almost closed once more and she let out the breath she had been holding for far too long. Her ears caught the sound of the Opel truck starting up. The Germans were leaving.

'Almost there,' said Philip. 'Four hours to go.'

'You know, I didn't even ask what the wages were like,' she replied.

He began to chuckle to himself, relief making him light-headed. 'I think I'll be eating a lot of cheese from now on.'

'I think I might insist on visiting a dairy farm first.'

'Yes.'

'Gaspard.'

Philip glanced at Diana, thinking it was she who had uttered the name.

'Gaspard.' It was Jacqueline. She was indicating with her knife a tall, dark-haired man moving between the stations. He had on a pristine white jacket, with some sort of crest on the breast pocket. His eyes were darting back and forth, examining faces, and now and then he would click his fingers. The subject of his attention then showed their La Villette work pass. 'Supervisor,' Jacqueline said, before spitting: 'Milice spy.' Part of the Vichy police force's work was suppressing the black market. La Villette was certain to be a prime source of illegal meat. Then she added: 'Pig.'

Gaspard the Milicien moved slowly but thoroughly through the main butchering area, making sure he didn't miss a single man or woman. Behind his back, Ginger gestured with his knife to Jacqueline.

'Of course.' She turned to them. 'The scalding rooms are finished for the day. When he isn't looking, slip in there. He will not notice. We can close the gap here.'

They waited until Gaspard picked on a young lad, questioning him closely, before they padded across to the enclosed scalding room and slipped through the ribbons of synthetic rubber that filled the doorway. Inside was hot and airless and as clammy as a Turkish bath. The cauldrons, although no longer heated by the gas-jets underneath, were still steaming. Rows of empty hooks swayed above them, marching off along the ceiling until they exited through an aperture and descended to the now-empty plucking area.

Philip looked around. There were few places to hide, except behind the cauldrons. To be found skulking down there was certainly an indication of guilt of some description. There was an exit to the outside, where the chickens that had gained a day's reprieve were kept, but the grilled door to that was held by a hefty padlock.

From beyond the walls came the three-note whistle Diana had heard Ginger emit at the gate when he cowed the overseer. It was clearly a warning from him.

'What shall we do?' she panicked.

'Come here. Please don't be offended.' Philip pushed her against the stained wall, loosened his belt and let his trousers drop to his ankles. 'Sorry.'

She smiled what she hoped was a reassuring smile and tugged at her skirt, pulling it up over her thighs, until Philip could press himself close enough to make the act look genuine. As she heard the rubber strips swish apart and then snap back, Diana pulled his head to hers and clamped their mouths together.

'You two!' yelled an exasperated Gaspard. 'For God's sake!'

Philip leaped away, looking shocked. He reached down for his trousers. 'Pardon me.'

'Pardon me?' The Milice man put his hands on his hips. The hope that he might be either indulgent enough to let them get on with it or too embarrassed to intervene looked forlorn indeed.

'Show me your papers. *Now.*'

Diana smoothed her skirt down and looked at the floor in a suitably contrite manner. Philip stepped forward towards Gaspard, who barked: 'Stay where you are.' It was too great a distance to sprint and Philip hesitated. The Sten was tucked under the table outside, hidden by offcuts. Her handbag and pistol were with it.

'Sir, please, forgive me. I . . . it was my fault. I have a wife –'

'Papers!'

'– and children.' Again he moved closer but Gaspard stepped back. From his jacket, the man took a long silver whistle and managed two blows on it, when there came a soft spitting sound, like a smoker clearing tobacco off his lip. The shot gouged through the side of Gaspard's neck and his hand flew up in shock. He tried to blow the whistle but no sound came from his mouth. Instead there was a hideous bubbling from beneath his fingers. When he released his hand, the arc of frothy blood splattered noisily up the wall, and then pulsed out across the floor. He was staggering already, as his life spurted away. With the single shot gone, Diana tossed the now-useless Welrod into the nearest cauldron.

'We must get our other guns.'

Philip remained frozen, unable to leave the man dying so noisily in front of him. Milicien or no, it was a horrible way to go.

'Oh, shit.' It was Ginger, looking horrified as Gaspard thrashed around in the pool of his own blood, smearing the concrete. 'Oh, shit.'

'Who was the whistle for?' asked Philip, kicking it away.

'Alarm. If they heard it, they'll call the troops back,' said Ginger. 'We don't have much time.'

Diana marched past him.

'Where are you going?' demanded Ginger.

'To get our weapons.' Now she had ditched the Welrod she was keen to fetch her revolver. 'Time for us to go.'

'Not quite.' He slid a ten-inch blade from his belt 'Bring a couple of cleavers.'

Diana was about to ask why, but then she looked down at Gaspard and realised what Ginger intended to do. She was about to move on from offal to butchery after all.

With the aid of the two burly companions who had helped them earlier, Ginger stripped Gaspard of his clothes while Jacqueline hosed down the floor and walls. The body was pale, but covered in a continuous growth of black hair, that thickened across the genitals and chest. A butcher's block was manhandled into the room, so the job in hand could be performed without too many prying eyes witnessing it.

'Help me get him up,' Ginger said to Philip, who bent down and gripped an ankle. Diana also grabbed a cooling limb, but found it simply rotated out of her grasp and she staggered back. The carcass was astonishingly heavy and awkward. 'OK. You,' Diana realised that Ginger was pointing at her, 'turn on the grinder. It is just outside, to your left. Green button.'

'You're going to mince him?' She tried to keep the horror from his voice.

'Not all of him. *Go.*' The lifeless form was slapped onto the table.

As she hurried out, Diana heard three swings of a cleaver, the squeak of steel on bone, and then a final blow that hit wood. There was a thud as something heavy fell to the floor. The head. They were going to mince the head.

The industrial grinder started with a roar, its internal blades hissing as they swished over each other. They produced chunks of flesh, which fell into a cavity where a mechanical ram moved the pieces to the fine mesh and squeezed them into the enamelled receptacle. She listened to the noise, as if mesmerised, but in reality preferring it to witnessing what was going on in the scalding rooms.

Eventually she had to go back inside, to face up to what she had done. As she entered the room she was forced to choke back bile. The three butchers were working at full tilt. Gaspard's viscera lay coiled on the floor, like some hideously bloated serpent. She could see organs, somehow more livid and raw than those of the cattle. And the smell . . .

Pull yourself together.

'Head, hands, feet, grinder,' instructed Ginger. Seeing her frozen to the spot, Philip scooped them up, his face set to impassive.

Just an animal, she thought, as his kidneys and liver were set aside. That's all we are: animals, an assembly of muscle, bone and organs, no different from the cows in the pens outside. Just a lot cleverer, that's all. And far, far more evil.

She took a breath, steeled herself and stepped forward, picking up a handful of sliced arm, cringing at the feel of still-warm meat.

'What are you doing?' Ginger asked.

'I'm taking it to the mincer.'

'Don't be ridiculous. Dealing with the head and extremities will blunt the blades. I'll have to change them. Anyway.' He held up a bloody rack of ribs with a grin. 'This lot are going to feed our friends in the Wehrmacht.'

Before the horror of what he was saying could sink in, an urgent voice hissed: 'Troops. Coming our way.' It was Philip, his raincoat, Sten and her bag bundled under his arms.

The smile vanished; Ginger went to the scalding room's exterior door, checked the padlock and reached up above the doorframe. He produced the key and undid the clasp. 'We'll finish off here. Good luck. Head to the canal and take the towpath. It will take you down to the Métro at Jaurès.'

'Will anyone miss him?' asked Diana, indicating the fragments of a man still remaining on the block.

'Gaspard? We'll make sure they don't. Move.'

Philip pulled on his coat and he shook sticky hands with each of the three before they dived out into the twilight. The animals in the pens were quiet now, just soft shufflings and snorting coming from them. Philip tugged at Diana and they began to walk quickly, heading for the next of the giant abattoirs. Each movement of her clothes released more odours, the stench of human blood, flesh and viscera rising from the folds of the smock. She scrabbled to pull it off and tossed it to one side with a shudder. Philip did the same.

They crossed the open space between the slaughterhouses without being spotted, and moved through thickening shadows. In the distance she could see the blue glow of Paris's paltry blackout streetlighting coming on. Inside the houses of death, lights had started to blaze, but shutters were being lowered to mask them.

'Come on.' They walked west, straight towards the canal. The moon had already risen; the sun was making its last effort to illuminate the sky. It would be dark soon.

'Halt! You two, stay where you are!'

The three soldiers were sprinting between the pillars to their right, weaving as they came, featureless wraiths in the gathering gloom. Philip swung up the Sten and fired, taking them by surprise. It barked four times, joined by her revolver on the final round. One soldier flung his arms up in the air and they heard a rifle clatter down. The others dived for cover. Philip and Diana were sprinting long before there was the sharp burp of returned fire from a machine pistol. Diana felt the air snap and pop around her. Philip risked a short burst on automatic to keep the Germans' heads down, the Sten's barrel spitting yellow and orange.

They reached a grass bank that sloped away from them at a steep angle. At the bottom lay the dark, limpid waters of the canal. They slid down onto the towpath, out of sight of their pursuers. To their left was a lock complex, to the right, a tunnel, its mouth a black hole. A trap waiting to be closed, thought Philip.

Diana tried to calm the noise in her head, a humming created from the rushing of blood and the explosions of discharged weapons. She looked at Philip, wanting to give, and get, some kind of reassurance, but he was too busy taking in their surroundings, looking for an advantage, an angle to play. Philip wasn't going to be taken cheaply. She had to make sure she played her part.

The lock gates were open, and the snout of a boat was edging through, its engine putt-putting it forward. Philip knew he had seconds to decide what to do. Those German soldiers would be moving forward, probing whatever he had to offer as defence. Not much, was the answer. And this boat was one with fuel, rather than being horse-drawn, which meant 'special consideration'. Which guaranteed the barge was on German warwork.

They were sandwiched.

'Wait here,' he said.

He scrambled up the bank. Sure enough he could see four, no, five, black shapes, crouched very low, but moving in their direction. He knew firing would give their position away, but he had no choice. Two small bursts in an arc and he slithered back to the accompaniment of the flat crack of Mauser rifles.

By now the boat was free of the lock and pulling level. 'Diana. We have to split up.'

'No.'

'Yes.'

She put a hand on his shoulder and he winced. 'You're hurt.'

'Yes.' It was no good lying. He was trying to keep a lid on the pain, but the left side of his body felt like it had been dipped in acid. Over her shoulder he could see the grizzled bargeman at the tiller, his eyes saucers as he watched the two fugitives. Philip moved Diana aside and stepped to the edge of the towpath.

'Let me look at the wound.'

He shrugged her away. 'Nothing to see.' Philip examined the man at the tiller. He would have to take a chance. He whistled to get the bargeman's full attention and gave the clenched-fist salute of French Communists. The man looked taken aback. Philip repeated it and, after a further hesitation, the bargee flashed the gesture back in reply. Philip felt a surge of relief.

'The woman only,' said Philip. 'Please.'

Diana began to wave her arms in protest, but he held her back. 'Please. For France.'

'English?' the man asked.

'English for France.'

'I have a son in the camps.' It was a cry of helplessness. There were still thousands of French POWs, working as forced labour in Germany. It was possible, with the right connections, to buy out a son or brother, but the fee was far beyond the means of a bargeman. In the meanwhile, the imprisoned relative was a permanent hostage, a powerful weapon of control for the German Occupiers. It could even make you toil for them, however reluctantly.

'We are working to free him. For France,' insisted Philip.

The boat travelled on towards the dark mouth of the tunnel. It had moved several metres before the man nodded. 'For France.'

The tiller was moved and the barge slid closer to the canal edge.

'Jump.'

'No.'

'Please.'

'I can't.'

Ignoring the burning pain in his shoulder, Philip tried his best to throw her across the narrowing divide. He only partially succeeded, and Diana was forced to leap or land in the water. She

160

hit the canvas cover over the deck heavily, driving the wind out of her body and sending up a ghostly cloud of dust, which hung in the moonlight.

'God bless you,' Philip said, to which the bargee shrugged. He didn't need any English God to bless him. *'Vive La France.'*

As the tunnel swallowed the front of the barge, Diana struggled to her feet. From her pocket she extracted the revolver and threw it to Philip, who fumbled it and let it drop on the path. Then she scampered towards the cabin at the rear. Just before the dark took her, she blew Philip one last kiss.

Now his shoulders slumped and he let the wave of suppressed agony wash over him, shuddering as it did so. He could feel blood running down his upper arm. His fingers told him a bullet had passed through his bicep. He needed a doctor. That made him a liability for Diana, for any Resistance group. It was best she went on alone, best he stayed here and did what he could. Philip bent and picked up the pistol. He moved towards the tunnel, his steps so heavy it felt as if he had lead shot in his soles.

As he reached the entrance he peered in. He could just make out a grey shape moving through the water inside the tunnel. Weak light was penetrating the airshafts that dotted the bore at intervals, picking out the silhouette of the barge. 'God speed, Suzanne or whatever your real name is,' he prayed. As he tucked himself into the wall, he thought about his wife, about how she would feel when she got the inevitable letter saying they had lost contact with him. If she would cry or, as he half-expected, refuse to believe it.

The first steel head appeared over the grassy slope, up to his left, the helmet catching the strengthening silver rays now beaming over Paris. He loosed off a revolver shot at it, aware he was unlikely to hit anything at that range.

He scrabbled deeper into the tunnel. How long before they thought of grenades? Or would they want to take him alive? He leaned against the tunnel's dank brickwork and the pain from his shoulder that flared across his chest was so intense it made him yelp. He slid down to the ground, ignoring the pools of water soaking his trousers. Sweat prickled on his forehead. He wasn't asking much of his body. All he had to do was hold them off for twenty minutes or so, to give Diana time to get really clear. He fired off a shot with the Sten, then the pistol once more. Let them think there were still two of them to take down.

A machine pistol chattered and bullets pinged through the tunnel and hissed into the water. A cloud of mortar drifted down over him. He blinked the dust from his eyes and returned fire, alternating his weapons, until the revolver clicked on empty. Now he could see muzzle flashes as the bullets zinged over and around him, forcing him into a huddle. The Germans were closing.

He just hoped his wife Olivia wouldn't take his death too hard.

Part Three: 1948

The Red Sector

Twenty

The story took them through two pots of tea and by the time Rose Miller had finished, Laura felt drained of all energy.

'Thank you,' she said. 'For telling me.'

'Your sister was a brave woman.'

Is, she almost corrected. Is a brave woman. 'What happened after the barge?'

'We don't know. Jimmy Webb tracked Philip to his final incarceration, but Diana? *Nacht und Nebel*. Night and fog. I'm sorry.'

That was the answer to everything, wasn't it? Night and Fog. Well, night was followed by day and fog always lifted eventually. 'So there was no trace at all?'

Rose Miller put her fingers together in a pyramid. 'Numbers eighty-two to eighty-six Avenue Foch were the buildings in Paris where most captured SOE agents were taken for interrogation. There were floors where some were kept *en secrèt*, that is, apart from other prisoners. In one of the logs, there is a set of initials noting a prisoner delivery. The initials are SG. Suzanne Galliard was your sister's alias.'

Laura swallowed hard. She had heard of terrible things happening at Avenue Foch. Rose Miller read her expression. 'It doesn't mean she was tortured. Not all of them were, by any means. But once they left there under a Night and Fog order, anything could happen.'

Laura closed her eyes and felt the room spin. She was exhausted. She needed to lie down and digest this.

'There is one slight hope of finding out the truth.'

Laura forced herself back to full alertness. 'How?'

'Jimmy Webb has discovered a guard who witnessed . . . well, a guard who might know what became of her. You'll have to judge for yourself.'

A guard? At Avenue Foch – or Flossenburg? 'Where is this guard? Can I see him?'

'I think you need to get some sleep first. I have selected a more comfortable cell for you.'

'Can I see him? Please?'

'If you feel strong enough.' Rose took a deep breath. 'It won't be easy, but yes, you can see him. I'll make the travel arrangements and give you a contact.'

'Travel arrangements? Where am I going? Berlin?'

'No, not Berlin. Paris, you lucky girl.'

James Hadley Webb waited until the lumbering Lancastrian was on its final approach to Gatow before he opened Olivia's letter. It might, he reasoned, take his mind off the buffeting as the converted bomber – much more suited to carrying high explosives than Civil Servants, in his opinion – dropped jerkily into the thin clouds. He was surprised to see through the tiny, scratched window that the countryside below was bathed in sunshine. Perhaps the back of that ghastly winter had finally been broken.

My Dear Jimmy, the letter began.

A familiar headache started around his temples. He folded the single piece of paper once more and slipped it into his jacket. It was no good, he thought, he still couldn't read it. He was flying back into the arena to do battle; he didn't need his resolve knocked back by specious but seductive arguments. Not when he could still smell and taste a lingering echo of the author. And not when she was so wrong.

He'd dwelled on her accusations and decided that, as far as he was concerned, he was fighting for the future, not rehashing the past nor craving the security of wartime. At least, he prayed that was the case. It was sometimes hard to tell. You couldn't be a spy and a human being, it seemed, except in rare cases. If you were to succeed in espionage, you had to put your humanity to one side. But did there come a point where you could no longer access it? He hoped he hadn't passed that point with Olivia.

A sharp pain in his jaw made him squeeze the arms of his seat. The Major next to him shot him a glance. 'Ear trouble,' Webb explained.

Out of the window he saw a glint of sun on metal, then it was gone. He was reminded of Towers's Foo-Fighters, the flaming apparitions that Allied bomber crews insisted they had seen over Germany. Moments later he glimpsed it once more, a now distinctive shape that made him groan. Not again.

'Ladies and gentlemen,' came the Captain over the intercom, his distorted voice barely audible above the roar of the four engines. 'We're almost at Gatow. Some of you may have seen one of our former Allies' aeroplanes off our port side. It may be back. They like to fly quite close. It's the Russians' idea of fun. Well,' he drawled, 'have you seen their women?'

There was a general guffawing from around the plane. Even the WAAF across the aisle managed a weak grin. It was bravado: everyone on board knew about the Viking incident.

The smile was wiped off her face as the Lancastrian shuddered and yawed. A booming filled the passenger area, and papers seemed to fly across the space of their own accord. Webb was lifted in his seat, his bottom hovering in the air, and he scrabbled for his restraining belt. He came down with a thump, but his stomach stayed where it was. He strapped himself in.

'Good God!' said the Major. 'Bloody Reds. It's a pity this thing doesn't still have its gun turrets. I'd like a pop at them.'

'Sorry about that,' said the pilot. The silver fighter, which bore no markings other than a red star on its fuselage, took up position off the port side of the Avro and waggled its wings mischievously. It was both handsome and sinister, with its functional swept-back wings and high tailplane.

Up until now, Webb had never seen any Russian jets, only Yak prop jobs, one of which had already collided with a BEA Vickers Viking, killing all on board, after it had buzzed the airliner. The Russians blamed the British pilot for turning into their plane, which they claimed was making its approach to Staaken, the nearby base in the Soviet zone. That might be so, but it ignored the fact that the disaster wouldn't have happened if the Yak hadn't started playing silly buggers.

This jet fighter certainly looked the part of the aggressor. Webb had no doubt the design was mostly copied from captured Nazi blueprints and produced by the German engineers the Russians had exported East. They had had Serov units combing the defeated country, their own equivalent of the scientific raiding parties of which Towers had been a part.

In an eyeblink the jet plane had gone, accelerating away in a blue streak of raw power. In its place was a Gloster Meteor, a British jet, sent up to guide the threatened sheep home. After the Viking incident, Gatow had considered giving every incoming plane a fighter escort; perhaps, thought Webb, it would be prudent to resurrect the practice. There was a scattering of applause at the sight of the friendly shape, and jittery, relieved conversation began between strangers.

As the Lancastrian rattled its way down the flight path, below them Webb could see the lakes gleaming in the sunshine and the green tops of the Grünewald Forest. Jutting out from the canopy was the flaming orange tower of the still-intact Kaiser-Wilhelm monument, then it was a quicksilver flash of the Havel and they were bouncing onto the ground at Gatow to more applause. The plane taxied onto the apron, bucking over its uneven brick surface, squeezing its way between Dakotas, Halifaxes and Skymasters.

'Welcome to Berlin,' said the pilot over the speaker as the engines whined down. Webb peered through his condensation-streaked window at the small crowd waiting for the passengers to disembark. To one side of them stood two RAF Military Policemen, flanking the diminutive figure of Ernst Henkell, the Kripo *Detektiv*, who was scanning the windows of the airliner, looking for a familiar face. Something told Jimmy Webb that this was no coincidence. They were waiting for him.

Twenty-one

Paris

Laura McGill felt dowdy and frumpy. Her clothes still had the severe, military-influenced cut of English fashion, if it could be called that. In the hour she had been in Paris, she had seen evidence of the New Look everywhere and not just around the expensive salons of Avenue Montaigne. Even when she had alighted at Gare du Nord in the gloomy 10th *arrondissement*, the clothes showed signs of Dior's daring influence – the shoulder padding, the complicated jackets, the softening of the edges into something more feminine. She had seen such clothes at society gatherings in London, of course, and in the pages of magazines, but here in Paris, it appeared to be universal.

Lucky old Paris, she thought, as she searched for the address given to her, albeit somewhat reluctantly, by Rufus Napier. Not in what the city had gone through, of course, but how it had come out of it. London and other capitals were still disfigured by bomb-sites, great gap-toothed holes in their skylines. The City of Light looked as elegant as ever. It had its scars, naturally, but they were buried deeper than London's.

And what, she thought, about her own scars from her experience of being detained as a 'mental deficient'? It was three days since she had been released, and the physical memory of her ill-treatment was fading fast, but not the feeling that she'd been taken to the edge of the precipice, eviscerated, then sewn back together. A few more days of such treatment and she might have broken totally. Would anybody ever write 'resilient' next to her name, as they had about Diana? She doubted it.

Never again would she make judgements about those who blurted out names and places while under genuine abuse.

After all, she'd hardly been tortured. They had simply started stripping away her dignity, layer by layer, trying to make her increasingly vulnerable. And all because she asked about the wrong file. What were they capable of doing when faced with something that involved a real threat to the realm?

Laura found the apartment block she was seeking on a shabby left Bank street populated mostly by butchers and hardware stores. A shrunken, black-clad concierge waved her through the door and she took a fragile birdcage lift to apartment fifteen. She could hear the wailing baby as she walked along the landing. The door was opened by an harassed-looking young woman with a sobbing child in her arms. Her dress was covered in dried milk and crumbs, and her eyes were red-rimmed from sleeplessness. The baby took a deep breath and emitted a lusty howl.

'Yes?' the mother demanded over the racket.

'Does . . .' Laura turned up her own volume. 'Does Raymond Bec live here?'

'Why?' the woman asked with an aggressiveness that took Laura aback. 'Why do you want him?' Exhausted, with an inconsolable baby, she was no doubt considering all sorts of unpalatable reasons why a young, fresh-faced single woman should turn up on her doorstep.

'It's about the war.'

She brightened slightly. 'His medal?'

The Friends of Maurice Buckmaster had put Raymond forward for a Croix de Guerre for his Resistance work in St Denis and

Paris. It was how Laura had tracked him down. 'No, sorry, I have no news on that. But Raymond – your husband,' it was a guess, but the woman didn't contradict Laura, 'knew my sister in the war. I won't need long with him.' That was true. She had an appointment with the French Secret Service at lunchtime. Laura adopted her best hangdog look. 'She's still missing, you see . . .'

The woman's features softened into something approaching sympathy. 'Of course. Forgive me. Come in. Raymond! We have a visitor.'

After an hour and a half – longer than she intended – with Raymond Bec, Laura took her leave and located a Renault cab, giving the driver the address of the Directorate de Surveillance Territoire, the DST, on a quiet side street near the Eiffel Tower.

The DST offices were discreet and smart, a world away from the cramped make-do-and-mend accommodations that SIS and MI5 had to tolerate. The grizzled old soldier on the desk said that Inspector Bevier was expecting her and she should go up to the third floor. He gave her a numbered cardboard tag on a piece of string, waited until she had placed it round her neck, then directed her to the lift.

The door to his office was open, and Jean-Marc Bevier was staring out of a picture window that seemed filled with M. Eiffel's giant Meccano kit. But his attention was held by something at street-level. He didn't turn when she tapped to get his attention. 'Enter.'

'Inspector Bevier?'

He turned around with exaggerated slowness, as if he wanted her to admire his profile framed in the light. He was youthful-looking, with a face that suggested he hadn't quite shed his puppy fat, topped with a thick mop of carefully coiffured dark hair. He wagged a finger at her and announced: 'Mam'selle. There is a crisis.'

'Crisis? What sort of crisis?'

He spoke as if barbarians were not only at the gates, but had made it as far as the elevators. 'Miss McGill, you are late. Nevertheless, if we go downstairs, now, we will catch lunch over the road in that brasserie. If we wait any longer – puff, gone. What do you say?'

She hadn't eaten much since the queasy overnight boat-train crossing, and breakfast had been a bowl of bitter coffee at Raymond Bec's apartment. The thought of a decent meal made her stomach gurgle. 'I suppose . . .'

'We can talk there. I can tell you about the piece of scum we have in custody, and you can tell me about your quest.'

'Quest?'

'For your sister's killers.'

'Killers?' What did he mean? 'I don't follow.'

He didn't reply, but swept a jacket from the back of his chair and had it on in one smooth movement. 'Come.'

There were oysters followed by a simple, but succulent beefsteak, and the place really did fill up to bursting point dead on one o'clock. Inspector Bevier was a good listener, with a subtle line in prompting. Laura found herself telling him about a distant war in China, a sister lost somewhere in Occupied France and the over-whelming urge to find her.

'And you?' she asked, when she had exhausted Diana's tale.

'Me?'

'The war? Were you here?'

'London. With de Gaulle. Liaison. Not as glamorous as your war.'

'Mine wasn't glamorous.'

Bevier laughed. 'It was from where I am sitting. China, the Flying Tigers, Calcutta – I think that's glamorous. Now, how about some dessert? I suggest Tarte Tatin.'

'Inspector, this is very nice, but I am keen to get on – to see this prisoner.'

'I know. So we eat our tarte and we go.'

He wasn't going to move until he had finished lunch, that much was obvious. The French, she thought, insisting on satisfying their stomachs above all else. 'Did you like London?'

'Did I like London?' he repeated with a smile on his face.

'Let me guess. You still crave steak-and-kidney pudding and Mackeson stout.'

'No. I craved steak-and-kidney pudding while I was there. Any real meat. Most of the time I got whale. And what's that pink stuff?'

'Blancmange?' she offered.

'Spam.' He shuddered.

'Do you think people dined on oysters and Tarte Tatin in Paris during the war?'

'Good point. I think many people here would have loved the opportunity to eat Spam and whale. But to answer your question, yes, I liked London. I enjoyed what it stood for, the people. Everything but the food. And South African sherry – is there a more disgusting drink in the world?'

'Wincarnis,' she said firmly.

Bevier nodded and smacked his lips, as if he could taste the medicinal tang of the fortified wine. 'Yes, you win again.'

The desserts arrived, no more than three or four mouthfuls each, but delicious.

'Tell me one thing,' he said. 'The supply line that was broken – what was it carrying?'

'You don't know?'

Bevier shook his head. 'I have no idea.'

Laura paused, as if she were divulging privileged information. But it was a long time ago and she hated the obsessive secrecy she had found in London. Where was the harm? 'Watches.'

'Watches? Wristwatches?'

'Diamond ones. Rolexes, mostly.'

'It was smuggling?' Bevier looked shocked. 'Your sister risked her life for money?'

174

Laura shook her head. 'The watches were meant for me, in Kunming, China. They were used to bribe the local warlords to carry on fighting the Japanese, rather than reaching a settlement with them.'

'Really?'

'Yes. Or sold for a fortune to get local currency at more than even the black-market rate. So, we assumed someone at Tours had opened one of the packets and discovered they weren't the bomb-sights we'd pretended, and absconded with them.'

The Inspector shook his head, amazed at the subterfuges of war. 'It had to be watches?'

'Not any old watches. It had to be Rolexes. Or South African diamonds. Those tribal warlords are more sophisticated than you might think.'

'Amazing.'

Coffee came strong and black and Laura gulped it back in one, keen to move on. 'Shall we go?'

He seemed to hesitate. 'Are you sure?'

Laura sighed. 'Please, Inspector, let's get this over with.'

Twenty-two

The Berlin city morgue was, officially, still housed at Entrance Two of the old 'Alex', the Police Headquarters on Dircksenstrasse off the Alexanderplatz. However, that was in the Russian zone and, as with most police matters, the Allies had set up their own independent system to run in parallel. The British mortuary was in the once-leafy streets of Charlottenburg, among the apartment blocks and mansions confiscated by the Army back in 1945.

This morgue was a conversion of an old garage. It had once been a rather grand affair, where affluent locals stored their Mercedes, Hanomags, Borgwards and Horches, and at one time boasted a bar and a gymnasium. Now, the latter was partitioned into administration offices and pathology labs. The main workshop housed the post-mortem rooms, all marble slabs and steel troughs; where once oil had been drained and radiator fluids changed, bodies were now sucked dry of blood and topped up with embalming fluid.

Henkell signed them in and led Webb down a corridor and a set of iron stairs into the blue-lit basement, where the racks of car spares had been replaced by wooden pallets holding covered cadavers. It was icily cold, and Webb felt his ears go numb. Two morgue attendants, both so thin they looked as if they might join their charges at any moment, shuffled around, their soiled gumboots squeaking on the floor. The air reeked of formaldehyde and carbolic disinfectant, and Webb took out a handkerchief to wipe his stinging eyes.

The *Detektiv* began to point at the shrouded forms. 'Raped to death. Drunken Americans, in all likelihood. Killed for some meat. Bar brawl. Starvation, starvation.' The *Detektiv* let his fingers touch one of the cloths, gently brushing the covered head. 'Raped. Fifteen years old.' He spat the words. There had been so many assaults on German women in the early years that US and British females had taken to wearing armbands to show they weren't *Fräuleins* available for a cigarette or there for the taking. 'This one, robbery. We think. That one, suicide.' He stopped and with a small flourish said: 'This one is yours.'

Webb tried to remain impassive as the policeman pulled back the sheet, but he felt himself start at the condition of the corpse. He had seen bodies before, was used to the waxy pallor that death lent, but this was something different.

Karin's skin was covered in marks the colour of blueberries. Elsewhere there were black and brown circles, and across her chest ran garish red lines, some opened at the edges, like macabre smiles. And her face . . .

His eyes instinctively flicked away.

'Dear God.'

Henkell sighed. 'Indeed.' He yanked the sheet back to cover the mangled face. 'She had been savagely tortured. Cigarette burns – the smaller marks you can see – under her arms, on her breasts and—'

'Please.' Webb held up his hand. 'I can imagine.'

'Can you? So, you admit to knowing her?'

'What on earth gives you that idea?' he spluttered.

'She was alive when they finished with her. Barely. She crawled out into the hallway, where her mother found her. She said just two words.'

Webb waited while the *Detektiv* played with the pause, hoping to build the tension. When he didn't rise to the bait, Henkell said: '*Tell Jimmy*. That's what she said: *Tell Jimmy*.'

He felt sick to his stomach, but managed to say: 'I'm hardly the only Jimmy in Berlin.'

'We interviewed the kids in the hall about her regulars. They talked about an Englishman – and we had a description.'

'Are you suggesting I had something to do with this?' Webb asked indignantly.

'Being in England at the time is a decent enough alibi. And even if you were a suspect . . .'

'Your hands would be tied. Prosecuting agents of the Crown is not a good career move.'

The *Detektiv* narrowed his eyes. 'You see how difficult my job is? Half the suspects will be above the law.'

'So you do have suspects?'

Henkell ignored the question. 'Is a statement from you out of the question?'

The very idea, Webb thought, not even bothering to answer.

'There is something else. A boy – he saw it all. He won't speak about it.'

'He's probably too young to say very much about anything. Which is what kept him alive, I suspect.'

Henkell pointed a finger, which Webb had the urge to break. 'You know his age, then?'

He shook his head. 'She is a young woman. He can't be that old.' Bloody policemen, he thought, all thinking they are Hercule Poirot.

'You are aware she was a prostitute?'

'That hardly makes her unique in Berlin, does it?' Webb wanted to flee from the place, to purge the smell from his nasal passages with something strong and aromatic. He thought of the Johnnie Walker he had brought back from London with him.

There was a hiss of a high-pressure hose as one of the attendants set about dousing a newly arrived body. Webb looked over as the man began to whistle a jaunty and anachronistic pre-war tune about strolling under Berlin's limes. The attendant felt the disapproving gaze and the melody died on his lips.

'You know, don't you?' said Henkell quietly. 'You know who did this.'

'No,' he said truthfully. 'No, I don't.'

'Don't feed me that cabbage, Jimmy. Do you know why she was tortured like this?'

Webb didn't answer. He didn't have to; the flinch told the *Detektiv* all he needed to know.

'Is this your fault, Jimmy?'

Otto. Max. Karin. Philip. Yes, it was his fault. The net was closing in on him and these murders were all his fault. Henkell was right to be suspicious and outraged, because somewhere along the line, his carelessness had killed Karin. He had thought she was ring-fenced, with nobody in SIS or SOB knowing of her existence. But somehow he had put her, in espionage parlance, into the Red Sector – the danger zone.

The Englishman turned on his heel, then halted. He half-spun, glaring at Henkell. 'You breathe a word to anyone, I'll have you in Spandau.' He put as much menace as he could muster into his voice. 'It's a client who got out of hand. Understood?'

'It is my job—'

'It's your job on the line, Henkell. As you said, she was a snapper. This was done by a pervert who paid her for something a little special and got carried away. Do the paperwork and bury the slut.'

He stopped once more. He knew that German citizens still tended to be interned in tarpaulins, coffins being expensive and almost impossible to come by. *You can't be a spy and a human being at the same time*, his conscience reminded him. *Well, perhaps sometimes you have to try.* 'I'll get a casket delivered from the Board of Trade.'

The *Detektiv* nodded, his face impassive, the Englishman's largesse confirming all he suspected. Karin had been one of Webb's agents and it had cost her her life in a most gruesome fashion. This city, he thought, devours its own. Who would be next?

Webb had to take a detour to get home. Red flags were flying, and he was told there was a UXO – unexploded ordnance. The bomb squads had cordoned off two blocks in Wilmersdorf. It happened almost every day – an old RAF or USAAF bomb, a Russian shell that had failed to detonate, an SS 'Werewolf' booby-trap; the city's rubble was still throwing up lethal puzzles for Royal Engineers to solve. Occasionally he heard the flat crump of one detonating, and prayed that it was a deliberate, controlled explosion, rather than a disposer who had severed the wrong wire or a kid who had got too curious about a piece of shiny metal on a bombsite.

Back in his apartment on Ludwigskirchestrasse, on a warm evening that hinted at a decent summer ahead, Webb threw back the windows, unscrewed the top of the Scotch and poured himself a generous measure. When he had chased some of the chill of the morgue from his body, he took his drink to the armchair in front of the table that supported his radio and gramophone.

Before he'd left for England, he had been listening to the West Berlin radio station, RIAS, and the American Forces Network, rather than the BFN, with its predictable mix of Robert Farnon, Spike Jones and Eric Coates. On the US airwaves, late at night when sleep wouldn't come, amongst the mix of propaganda and preaching, Webb heard music the likes of which he had never experienced before. Thumping 'coloured' blues from performers with strange names such as Son House, Howlin' Wolf and Blind Lemon Jefferson. And, slotted in between Tommy Dorsey or Benny Goodman, a new kind of jazz, which seemed to consist of rivers of notes tumbling over each other. Dizzy Gillespie, Charlie Parker, Fats Navarro, and Earl Hines were the names that stood out, but there were dozens of others. It was a whole new world to a man whose musical taste normally ran a tiny gamut from Bach to the Billy Cotton Band.

This was not a night for wild jazz, though. After waiting for the tubes of his black-market gramophone to warm up, Webb put on a recording of Beethoven's Third, one of the shellac discs in the six boxes which came as part of the package.

Settling down for the Funeral March, he let a wave of melancholia wash over him as he thought of Olivia and of Philip, her husband, and the terrible fate that befell him. And of poor, poor Karin. Webb raised a glass to her, a woman he had grown fond of these past months. A brave girl, doing what she could to survive and feed her family. All she had to do for him was to pass on messages to a fictitious aunt in Potsdam, messages that eventually ended up with Max Borchart. Another casualty.

Karin had trusted him, and he had let her down. But how? Had he not managed to lose the tag at their last meeting the previous week? Or had they traced her back from Max? Unlikely, since that was a tangled trail of cut-outs and dead-letter drops, but he couldn't discount it altogether.

'Tell Jimmy—'

Tell Jimmy what? The identity of her tormentors? That she had betrayed the source? Explained the code embedded in the messages to Max?

No. For one thing, she knew nothing about the code or Librarian. All she could give them was mundane details. And the brutal extent of her injuries suggested to him one thing, that the incomplete statement went like this: *'Tell Jimmy I didn't speak, didn't break. Tell Jimmy I didn't let him down.'* Yes, that was it; it had to be. She'd stayed true to the end, not even yielding the basics.

So it behove him to make sure her life – her fortitude – was not entirely wasted. The alcohol was swishing around his brain now, and he could feel a fug of gloom falling on him. More lies, subterfuge and perhaps even death would be necessary before long, he knew. The murders of Otto and Karin were direct attacks on SOB, a way of telling him they were on to him. Well, that might be so. But the game wasn't over yet, not by a long shot.

He finished his drink and went to bed on his foam-rubber-filled mattress. It was something he insisted on. When he had been searching for Philip Maxwell he had come across the mattress factory at Ravensbrück, where the hair of murdered women was used for stuffing. He had been fussy about what he slept on in Germany ever since. He fell asleep quickly, strangely confident that he would find a way to strike back at those who had killed his assets.

Twenty-three

Paris

Laura McGill opened the carton of cigarettes and offered the man across the metal desk from her a Capstan. He took it, and while she fiddled with the lighter she checked her heart-rate was steady rather than jittery, and as she reached across with the gold Dunhill Unique, she was pleased to note that her hand didn't shake. Apart from the tiniest desire to push the flame into one of the man's eyes, she was calm and in control.

They were sitting in the basement of the former SHAEF HQ on Boulevard Suchet, now used by DST as a detention centre. The walls were bare, the whitewash flaking and yellowed, the bulb unshaded, the air tinged with Dettol. In the corner was a sink and a draining board with chipped enamel mugs on it. It looked as much like an interrogation room as she could hope for.

'I would like to make it clear that I am speaking to you of my own free will,' Charbonneau said in lightly accented English. He had thinning brown hair, heavily oiled, and a rather sharp face etched with lines. He'd probably been good-looking once, but his skin was pallid and tired. He looked older than the birth-date on his file suggested.

Laura pointed to the door. 'It's not locked. The guard outside will escort you to your cell whenever you are ready.'

The Frenchman scanned the ceiling and tugged at one earlobe nervously. He was worried about microphones, she realised.

'We can change rooms, if you like. Your choice. Any one you nominate.'

'Perhaps they are all bugged,' he said with a shrug.

She smiled as if this were ridiculous. In fact, he was right, but she wasn't going to admit it. Laura wondered if his whole life was like this, suspicious and hunted. She hoped so. That was a reasonable enough punishment for a man like this. 'Then we can do this in a bar, across the street, with armed guards, and hope one of your old inmates doesn't come in and recognise you.'

He winced, then relaxed. He interweaved his fingers as if he were about to pray. 'Miss McGill, you have to understand, that once Alsace was annexed . . .'

She waved a hand to stop him. 'You were a German citizen, I know. You are not on trial here, Philippe.' The use of his Christian name almost snagged in her throat. 'All I want is information.'

'So I understand.'

'Good.' She had been thoroughly briefed on him by Bevier on the way over. Both his file and affadavits were on the desk in front of her.

'How can I help?' he asked solicitously, as if offering street directions to a stranger.

Laura opened the buff folder, reading so she didn't have to stare at his face while she spoke. She coughed once to ensure her voice would be flat and unwavering and began. 'You were a guard at the Lasshofer camp in Alsace, a subcamp of Natzweiler-Struthof, from early 1944 until October of that year.'

'That is correct. I must stress that my duties—'

She jumped in quickly. She didn't want to hear justifications or even remorse. Just the bare facts. 'As I said, I am not here to make accusations or review your conduct. I believe that has already been done.'

'Yes.'

'And you are awaiting the decision of the magistrate as to whether there is a case to answer.'

'That is correct. But I am confident—'

'I am solely interested in what happened the day and night of May the fifteenth, 1944. Do you recall where you were?'

'Of course. I was at my post in the camp.'

'And you remember the four women who were delivered there that day?'

Charbonneau suddenly chortled, as if this were somehow amusing. Laura took a deep breath, keeping her anger in check. She mustn't make him clam up, as the Americans put it so succinctly, by losing her temper now. 'It was memorable,' he explained hurriedly, seeing her expression, 'because it was a male camp. A work camp. Women were very unusual.'

'Do you recall any details?'

He took a drag on the cigarette. 'They arrived at about three or four in the afternoon, by car, with an escort of two plainclothes men – Gestapo, probably.'

'Germans, then?'

'I always assumed so. I never heard them speak.'

'Go on.' Her willpower broke and she lit her own cigarette, hoping the smoke would calm her and help mask her true feelings.

'They were taken to the processing hut, and they emerged a while later, still in their civilian clothes, but without their cases. I suppose there were no female uniforms for them. They were taken by one of the Sergeants down to an unused barracks. Away from the men.'

'Can you describe them?'

'They were all quite young, I would think. Thirty, at the most. Hard to tell – they all looked tired, and thin. There was a brunette, quite tall . . .'

She looked down at the folder. 'Sylvia Reeve.'

A shrug. 'If you say so. I don't know their names. Didn't ask. A shorter brunette with very cropped hair.'

Elaine Roscoff, the file claimed. Laura's throat was dry now.

Charbonneau had screwed his eyes up now, trying to picture the scene. 'The third was about five foot eight, fair, with green eyes – very striking green eyes.'

'Dorothy Carlisle.'

Another shrug. 'I don't recall much about the other, the fourth girl. A blonde. Yes, a blonde. She had hair down to here.' He marked a spot on his upper arm. 'But I didn't see her face very clearly.'

Someone, perhaps Bevier, had pencilled in: *Diana McGill* followed by a question mark.

As steadily as she could, Laura prompted: 'Go on.'

'OK.' He finished his cigarette by stubbing it out on the dimpled surface of the table. 'I thought nothing of it until that night. I mean, it was unusual for our camp to have women, but there were so many prisoners being moved after the Americans landed. There was so much panic, anything was possible.'

'But you did see them again? The women, I mean?'

For a second she thought he wasn't going to answer. His jaw clenched and his mouth became a slit, all colour drained from the lips. Then he let out his breath in a low sigh. 'Yes. There was a noise at about midnight. I had been reading. I didn't sleep much in those days. From my barracks hut I could see the main parade-ground and . . .'

'And what?'

'May I have another cigarette?'

She dealt him one and lit it for him again. This time there was a slight tremor to the flame, but she didn't think he noticed.

'And some water?'

Laura rose, selected the least chipped enamel mug and filled it from the butler sink in the corner. He took two sips before he answered. She wanted to dash the mug from his mouth. 'Ready?'

He nodded. 'At the edge of the parade-ground, where roll call took place, was a gallows and circle of chalk. It had been dug out, about four metres across, perhaps one metre deep.'

'The chalk being to soak up the blood.'

'Correct.'

'Of the executions.'

'Yes.' The voice was smaller now, ashamed, but hers had grown steelier.

'Go on.'

'I heard footsteps and what I thought was a cry. One of the dogs barked. I looked at my watch. It was just gone twelve. I stood on a chair, so I could see out of the window, and there were the four women, with some of the German guards and Wessler, the SS Lieutenant. And Severin, the camp doctor. You know what happened to them?'

It was Laura's turn to nod. Bevier had told her. 'Severin was tried and executed after the war. Wessler was shot by the Resistance, I believe.'

'Yes.'

'Tell me what happened.'

'I think you can guess . . .'

'Tell me what you saw.' She tried hard to keep her true feelings from her voice. 'Never get annoyed or indignant,' Vera Atkins of Special Operations Executive had told Laura when she tutored her in interrogation. 'They expect that,' she had said. 'They'll have heard it all before. Calm, dispassionate, that's what throws them.' Laura kept her breathing as deep and regular as possible as Charbonneau continued.

'The four of them were marched towards the circle. They were cold. They no longer had their coats, and they huddled together for warmth. They knew what the circle meant. Even in the camp lights at night, you could see the stains on the chalk . . .' He coughed and looked at his cigarette accusingly. 'I should give up. Wessler took one of the women, the short-haired one, and pushed her into the circle. He made her kneel down and took out his pistol . . .'

Suddenly, she wanted this over. 'And shot her in the back of the head.'

'No.'

'What do you mean?'

'One of the women, the one that was a blonde, she yelled at him. Wessler turned, listened to what she had to say, and agreed to whatever it was. I couldn't hear, but I can guess, because then all four of them knelt down in a ring, and the blonde organised them so they were holding hands, like children. And Wessler walked around and . . . as you say, he shot them, one at a time. He shot the blonde last. The doctor certified them dead and they were taken away by trustees, I assume to the bunker, where the furnace was.'

Laura quickly wiped away the moisture from her eyes. 'And that was the last you saw of them?'

'Yes.'

Laura closed the file as calmly as she could and stood up into the light.

'You understand I was just a camp guard,' the man blustered. 'I had been wounded in—'

'I know.' She kept it short and simple, trying to hide the quiver in her voice. 'Thank you. The guard will see you back to the holding cells.'

'Yes. Of course.' He didn't move, though, as she gathered up the papers, and he spoke very quietly. 'They are all dead now, the ones who did it. There is nobody left to blame.'

'That's not true,' Laura hissed, and saw surprise flicker in his eyes. She could only imagine what her face looked like at that moment. Not a pretty sight. 'That's not true at all. Somebody has to pay.'

She walked briskly from the room and nodded to the guard, indicating that he could enter and take Charbonneau away. Then she half-ran down the corridor and into the dismal lavatory, where she locked herself inside the white-tiled cubicle and allowed the tears to flow and the sobs to wrack her body.

Laura didn't speak until she had downed the second *marc*, feeling it sear her insides. Bevier nursed a beer, biding his time. They were in a large old-fashioned brasserie, a few streets away from the former SHAEF building.

'Thank you,' she said at last. 'For letting me see him.'

'I'm sorry. It must have been difficult.'

'Those poor girls.'

'Yes. I'm sorry about your sister – but it was quick, at least. It wasn't always so.'

'You were listening in, weren't you?'

He hid any grin with beer then wiped foam off his upper lip. 'Just to see if he added anything new in that situation.'

'Did he?'

'No. So what now? Back to England?'

'No, I think Berlin. To see this Jimmy Webb.'

He finished his drink and signalled the white-aproned waiter for two refills. 'I thought you might have had enough. You probably know everything by now. What is to be gained?'

'I still have to find my sister.'

His eyes widened a little in surprise. 'But she will have been cremated.'

'Maybe. But not in the manner I just heard. My mother used to tell me fairy tales, Inspector, I know them when I hear them.'

He looked offended. 'Fairy tales?'

'The brave women kneeling in a circle, holding hands, the quick death. The people who ran these camps were not in the business of letting people die with dignity. The exact opposite, as you well know.'

He took the fresh beer and played with the foam on top, idly creating a series of peaks with his index finger. 'You think Charbonneau made that up?'

'I think he sanitised it, made the deaths more palatable for me. Whether he did it of his own accord or under your tutoring, I am not sure, but I do think you listened, to ensure he stuck to the script.'

Bevier gave a shrug that managed to be both insolent and insulting. 'I think you are perhaps, what is the word, paranoid?'

'Suspicious, certainly. I am sure four female agents did suffer terribly and were executed. I am sure Charbonneau witnessed it. Whether from a distance as he claims is a moot point. But whoever they were, however they died, Diana was not among them.'

There was a distinct frostiness now as he spoke. 'And how can you be so sure?'

'I haven't been entirely straight with you, Inspector. You were not my first port of call in Paris. Before I came to see you, I went to see a brave young man called Raymond Bec. He confirmed the story told to me by Rose Miller. But he added a few very important details. Such as in April, my sister had cut and dyed her hair. By May, it would not be so long, and it would not be pure blonde.'

'Perhaps Charbonneau got that part wrong.'

'In which case, how can I believe everything else?'

'I think perhaps you are hiding the truth from yourself – refusing to accept that your beloved sister is dead.'

She stood. 'And I think my time in Paris is over, Inspector. Thanks for whatever help you gave me.'

Bevier watched her leave. He downed his beer and then took her *marc* as a chaser. At least some good had come of it. The damned woman was leaving Paris. This end of things could rest easy.

Twenty-four

Berlin

The bank that Ralph Tyler, the Deputy Head of Station, took Webb to was off the western arm of the Ku'damm, one of those colonnaded late-nineteenth-century buildings that exuded the arrogance of enormous wealth. The image of invulnerability had been rather dented of late: the blackened façade and the columns were pock-marked by bullet holes. One corner of the roof had been patched up with wood and tarpaulin, where a Howitzer shell had taken a bite out of it. The over-sized entrance to the bank – you could have driven a tram through it – was guarded by a pair of British soldiers, but once inside, these were replaced by Americans, trap-faced members of the National Guard.

'Why are we going?' he had asked Tyler on the drive over. The older man had puffed and steamed and sucked for a few moments until a cloud of pipesmoke billowed around the office. Webb didn't like this. It was far too convivial. Which suggested that SIS had somehow got one over on him. He could see it in Tyler's eyes.

'You spend a lot of time with your friend Dolan, don't you?' the Englishman asked.

'I see him from time to time, yes. Socially.'

'Then you know that quaint American expression: "the shit is about to hit the fan"?'

It sounded comical pronounced in Tyler's clipped Oxbridge accent, but Webb wasn't laughing. 'I've heard it.'

'Well, Jimmy,' Tyler had replied, 'it's a big fan this time. And an awful lot of shit.'

Once inside, the banking hall was as grim as the exterior. The serving counters were gone and the wood panels of the ceiling taken down for tinder, leaving a bare marble space that was echoey and dusty. This was no longer a temple to mammon, thought Webb, more like a mausoleum. Yet these Yanks were here to protect something.

Tyler showed his pass several times, and signed in at a desk manned by a formidable US Staff Sergeant before being allowed downstairs.

'As you can see, we have had to use storage facilities where we can find them. This place had a good, large vault, so the Cousins requested its use.'

There was a capacious lift, also operated by a guardsman. When it reached the basement, their credentials were checked once more.

A National Guard Captain saluted them and took them through two layers of freshly installed steel bars with much opening and re-locking of doors. Finally they were at the vault, guarded by a foot-thick door, bristling with bolts. Inside, laid out on shelving, were wooden crates. Each one was stamped with the words: *US Medical Corps: Penicillin* or *Sulfonamide*. Webb felt even more alarmed, but tried not to let it show.

'And I thought there was a shortage of drugs,' he said, puzzled by such hoarding.

'There is,' replied Tyler. 'Captain, I believe one of these is open.'

The American nodded and pulled the face from one of the cases. Within were three-inch-thick bricks wrapped in greaseproof paper. Tyler reached inside and took one, handing it to Webb. He unwrapped one corner, then looked at the rows of crates, furiously performing mental arithmetic.

'Over a million pounds here alone. More elsewhere.' Webb examined the stack of notes, weighing it in his hands. Now he knew why Tyler had called him in. It was to gloat. To show Webb that he was closer to the inner sanctum than Webb, despite his hobnobbing with Bob Dolan. It was important not to be rankled by such point scoring. 'What are they called?'

'Deutschmarks. They will replace the Reichsmark right across the free zone. It will kill the black market stone dead.'

'And the Russians?'

'Wanted no part of it, as usual. Currency reform was put before the Allied Control Council in January and Sokolovsky rejected it out of hand. They've buggered us about ever since.'

Marshal Vasily Danilovich Sokolovsky was chief of the Soviet military administration, and one of Stalin's 'Iron Guard'.

Now Webb knew what Tyler had meant about shit and fans. The Russians would see the new currency as a declaration of economic war. 'But we are going ahead anyway,' he mused. Tyler nodded. 'How will they react?'

'How do you think?'

'Like a bear with a sore head?' The Reds could teach the average four year old a thing or two about sulking.

'I think that is a fair assessment. May I?' Tyler took the money from Webb and allowed the Captain to put it back in place.

'How far will they go?'

Ralph Tyler shrugged, and what he said next made Webb shudder. 'Three days ago, B-29 bombers in the United States were put on standby for redeployment to bases in England. Read into that what you will.'

Another piece of inside information Webb had not been privy to. 'It feels a little like we've made our home in a bull's-eye, doesn't it?'

Ralph Tyler nodded his agreement. 'Perhaps.'

Webb grabbed Tyler's arm and pulled him out of the Captain's earshot, their feet ringing on the tiled floor. '*Es geht um die Wurst*,' he said in a low voice.

It was an old Berliner expression which translated as: *The sausage is at stake*. Or: *This is the Big One*. He'd called Berlin a powder keg. This stack of new money was about to light the fuse.

'Yes, I believe you are right. Whether we go to war or not will be decided over the next few months.'

Tyler hadn't brought him along just for the ride, Webb decided. He'd risked showing him all this for a reason. 'Ralph, you didn't bring me here just to show me the colour of your money, did you?'

'The colour of my money? Is that another Americanism?'

'It might be. Ralph—'

Tyler held up a hand. 'Of course I didn't. That Board of Trade cover you have is quite a handy device for scrounging this and that. To build up some supplies, just in case.'

Webb twigged immediately. 'You want to warehouse food?' 'Warehouse' was an accepted euphemism for using black-market and smuggling contacts.

'And medicines. Yes. Operation Counterpunch. The Americans are already ahead of us. But I hear good things about Towers and your lads. Contacts at the Krypt, the Blue Room, the Alex.'

Webb tried to read Tyler's face, to see if there was more, but the expression remained impassive. 'We'll do what we can.'

'Excellent.'

'On one condition,' Webb said.

The old dog was one jump ahead of him. 'A truce. I let you run with Librarian for a while longer? Because if there is a crisis, it will provide invaluable insight into how things are in the East. It will also give you the opportunity to discover who killed Otto. Is that what you had in mind?'

Webb laughed and, surprisingly, Tyler joined in. 'That'll do for now,' Webb said.

Twenty-five

Ernst Henkell's summons to Kripo HQ in the Eastern sector was a nuisance, but not entirely unexpected. The Chief of Berlin Police, Paul Markgraf, was determined to ensure that he was recognised as such, even though power had devolved to Assistant Commissioners in each of the Allied zones. Every Kripo man was called back periodically and harangued about where their loyalties should lie, and how they should not be corrupted by their temporary landlords. They were then given a small task to perform, usually innocuous, just to test their allegiance. Ernst always turned his over to the Office of Internal Affairs for guidance. He didn't want to be rounded up as a Soviet spy. This time, it was bound to be something about the new currency. The Russians were furious, had tried to block it as legal tender in West Berlin, but had been over-ruled by the Magistrat.

So Ernst Henkell ordered a car and driver from the pool and made sure he had a pack of cigarettes to slip the border guards, just in case, and signed off the paperwork on the dead prostitute while he waited.

There had been a funeral and Jimmy Webb had organised the coffin as promised. It was the gesture of a decent man. He liked Jimmy Webb – he couldn't imagine any of the hard-assed Americans or the callous SIS men giving an old Occupation Mark

195

for the life of Karin Thurgau – but his luck seemed to have changed lately. For the worst.

The phone rang and the desk told him a car was outside. Henkell made his way out of the police building, climbed into the Mercedes and settled down for the ride. The city was shrouded in grey half-light; the authorities were trying to conserve power, just in case the main supply from the East was switched off because of what the Russians called 'technical difficulties'.

Every so often the Reds liked to show whose sector it was by halting and checking vehicles. The driver told him there were such hold-ups near the Brandenburg Gate. With the *Detektiv's* permission, the driver headed south, into the American sector at Kreuzberg and then back north, taking them over the quieter crossing point at Friedrichstrasse, then north to join Unter den Linden.

The Alex, one of the few habitable buildings on the otherwise decimated Alexanderplatz, was ablaze with light. The reorganisation of the police force was going ahead day and night. The creation of a new secret police – the K-5, a Gestapo by any other name, Henkell thought – was a priority. Now he had heard there was to be a new unit, the Alert Police, a heavily armed militia housed in barracks, ready to crush any anti-social behaviour, such as a strike in the uranium mines or food riots on the streets.

The driver passed the time running through his repertoire of anti-Russian jokes, all of which Henkell had already heard. It was polite to laugh at the punchline, which inevitably illustrated another example of Ivan's ignorance or brutality. Still, he was glad when the car pulled into the courtyard at the side of the Alex's Entrance Four. Henkell climbed out, gave the driver a cigarette and asked him to wait.

The Sergeant on duty told him he was expected, up on the sixth, no less, at Assistant Commissioner Drager's office. Walking past interview and incident rooms reverberating with the clatter of heavy typewriters, Ernst took the stairs, breathing in the once-familiar odour of the building where he had toiled for three years back in the 1930s. It hadn't changed much. Perhaps it was a little scruffier and stuffier, with floors sub-divided into yet more cubby-holes. The sixth, though, had space, with just a dozen large offices, including Markgraf's.

The secretary's desk outside Drager's room was empty, so Henkell knocked on the door and was told to enter. The moment he stepped inside, he knew he was in trouble. There was no sign of Drager. Instead, three plainclothes Russians lounged around the desk. They had been playing cards, and a half-empty vodka bottle was in plain view. One of them stood, removed his cigarette and said: 'Ernst Henkell?'

'Yes.'

'We are from the MGB.' Henkell felt as if icicles had crystallised in his blood. This was the Ministry of State Security, the counter-Intelligence group that was growing rapidly at the expense of the older MVD, the Ministry of Internal Affairs. 'You are under arrest for continued Fascist activities contrary to the interests of the Socialist Unity Party of Germany. Close the door.'

Jimmy Webb's telephone rang at just gone midnight. He lay still for a second, hoping it would stop, but the tone seemed to grow more insistent. He slid out of bed, crossed into the hallway and unhooked the old-fashioned earpiece and candlestick. He pressed the perforated disc to his good ear and spoke into the flared end of the black rod in his right hand. 'Yes?'

It came out as a croak. Now he could taste the whisky and he remembered he'd finished off the bottle earlier in the evening.

'Yes?' he repeated.

'It's Alan.'

'Ah.' He expected Towers had found a coalmine under the old Reichstag or some such piece of luck. They had eight warehouses full of supplies now, much of it thanks to Towers and his little team. If the worst came to the worst, they could feed the British sector for all of a week. 'What is it?'

'I want to read you something.'

'Go ahead.'

'This came in by teleprinter to the news agencies.'

'Just read it,' Webb said irritably, the taste of stale alcohol unbearable. He was longing to brush his teeth.

'It reads: "The Transport Division of the Soviet Military Administration is compelled to halt all passenger and freight traffic to and from Berlin tomorrow—"'

'What?' Webb snapped. 'Read that again.' Towers did as he was told.

'"... From Berlin tomorrow at 0600 hours. Water traffic will also be suspended, coal shipments from the Soviet zone will also be halted and the electrical power supply from the Soviet zone to the Western sectors will be switched off".'

'Bloody hell.' It left Berlin totally isolated, every source of support blocked.

'Yes. Looks like this is it.'

'*Es geht um die Wurst.*' Webb agreed. The sausage was indeed at stake. The city was under siege.

Part Four: 1948

Shining Hour

Twenty-six

There was bad weather over most of Germany – heavy skies, rain squalls and shifting fronts. The C-47 he had christened *Three of a Kind* took it in her stride, thought Lee Crane, just like he'd been promised. Gunther, now completely recovered from a beating by the Greek Communists, had also delivered the goods. He was a solid, quiet presence in the right-hand seat. At Athens, they had established that Mikklos had nothing to do with the attempt to dupe him into taking Andreas, and the Crete cargo had paid them well, as had a second lift of foodstuffs from Rome to Munich. They were coming into Frankfurt empty, though; Munich had nothing left to export.

The rain had settled over Rhein-Main Airport and the C-47 danced a skittish two-step as she dropped through 6,000 feet at the outer marker. Crane identified himself as one of General Tunner's boys, an ex-Hump pilot who knew a bit about ferrying supplies into beleaguered areas. Tunner had been in charge of air operations from India to Kunming, where Crane had spent his two years trying not to fly into a Himalayan mountainside. Now, he explained, he'd come to volunteer his services, since his old pal the General was running the airlift.

'Then welcome, welcome, welcome,' said the controller sarcastically, after he'd acknowledged the call sign and position. 'The

201

Operation Vittles HQ is to the left of Hangar D. You are clear for final approach. Wind ten knots from the north-east. Visibility two miles but falling. It's wet down here. Over.'

As the tail wheel dropped onto the runway asphalt and they slowed, there was no 'follow me' welcoming jeep, just frantic indicating by ground crew for him to get off the runway and onto the stand, with vocal support from the ground controller in his ear. Crane did as he was told, put on the parking brake and let the engines run down. As he began the post-landing check, he said, 'Well done, Gunther. You sure you won't come all the way? Could sure use an extra pair of hands.'

The German shook his head. 'Berlin? Are you crazy? I'll hitch a ride back to Hamburg. See my mother.'

'Good luck.' Crane handed over the last of the German's wages, a wad of US dollars held with a rubber band. 'And thanks.'

Gunther took the cash. 'Thanks to *you*. It's been fun – mostly. And I got a new-shaped nose.'

It was true that the boys in Athens had remodelled it slightly. 'Suits you. Makes you look interesting,' Crane told him.

'We'll see what my mother says.' Gunther laughed. He unbuckled, shook Crane's hand, pulled his kitbag off the rack and left him to it. Crane's head was buzzing. He was tired after the best part of three days in the air, but he had a job to do, a bit of boring routine. But, as the saying went, look after your plane . . .

After he had finished the check, Crane walked down the fuselage and wrenched open the cargo door. He stepped out into the drizzle and watched a four-engined C-54 come down the flight path he had just followed; behind it, another set of lights wobbled through the clouds. They were certainly packing them in.

'You on turnaround?' an Infantry Corporal barked at him from within his slick oilskins. Crane tried to reply but another C-47 started up for a taxi, drowning out his words. A tractor towing a trailer of what looked like duffel bags crawled by, heading for another cargo plane, its door cranked open as far as it would go, waiting to swallow the load.

When the racket subsided, Crane spoke. 'I said I just got here.'

The Corporal pulled his hood back and looked him up and down, taking in the battered leather jacket and the oil-stained khaki pants. He nodded at the unfamiliar insignia on Crane's right arm. It was the Star of India and the sun of China, above a set of red-and-white stripes. The patch showed he had served in the China-Burma-India theatre, but the Corporal had no way of knowing that. 'You Air Force?'

'Not any more,' Crane replied.

'But you're a pilot?'

He jerked a thumb over his shoulder. 'Well, I flew this one in.'

The Corporal nodded. 'That'll do. You'll get a forty-five, we'll have you on your way.' He yelled something at a group of men in baggy coveralls. Crane didn't recognise the language. 'Lithuanian,' the GI explained. 'We got Lithuanians. They got Poles at Wiesbaden. Keeps the DPs working and fed, everybody's happy.' The millions of Displaced Persons made for a ready supply of manual labour all across Europe.

'What's a forty-five?' Not a Colt .45 he figured; and anyway, he already had one of those, under the left-hand seat.

'Forty-five-day commission. Get you in the Air Force real quick, get you flying Operation Vittles.'

The rain began to ease and Crane looked up at the bruised sky. Summer in Germany didn't seem quite as pleasant as summer in Athens. Still, he wasn't here for the weather.

The Transportation Corps HQ, the outfit which supervised Vittles – the plan to supply besieged Berlin by air – was indeed a converted trailer, hastily extended by the use of steel sheeting usually used to clad runways. Inside, in a haze of cigarette smoke, dozens of men were scribbling orders, pinning up requests, writing on charts and demanding action RIGHT NOW at the top of their voices.

'You!' An Air Force officer pointed at Crane. 'What plane? What group?'

'A C-47. I'm not with a group. I'm looking for Carl Robertson.'

'Major Robertson? He's at Tempelhof. Take a docket and get a cargo loaded.'

'Not so fast. I just got in. I ain't got a crew.'

'Crews we got, planes we ain't. Yours serviceable?'

'Yup, but—'

'You know Tempelhof?'

'No, but—'

'Reynolds!'

Reynolds, a clerk with a nervous twitch and eyes that needed a lot of sleep and soon, poked his head through the crowd. 'Get this man an experienced crew and a cargo. Coal or flour if you can.'

'Sir.'

The next thing he knew, Crane was outside, with a piece of paper stamped *Group B* in his hand and a refuelling ticket for up to 108 gallons. As Reynolds led him across to the aircrew quarters, Crane said: 'I'm not, technically, in the Air Force or Army Transport.'

Another aircraft started engines, a ragged looking C-47 that had seen many better days. Crane listened intently for a second, stripping the seemingly featureless cacophony down to its component parts, examining each brick in the wall of sound. He didn't like the whine coming from one of the Pratt & Whitneys. It sounded like a bearing.

'Well, technically, this is all insane,' said Reynolds. 'So don't worry.'

'How long has the blockade been on now?'

'Ten years. Oh, pardon me. Ten days.'

As they walked past the loading area there was a puff of what looked like smoke and then a white cloud rolled over the loaders. A flour sack had burst. There were curses and recriminations and then the Corporal restored order with a few choice phrases of what Crane supposed must be Lithuanian.

Reynolds said: 'Berlin has two and a half million people. It needs, get this, more than six hundred tons of wheat a day. One hundred and nine tons of meat and fish. About three thousand tons of oil and coal.' He pointed to the duffel bags being loaded into a C-54. 'Coal's what's in the bags. So, ideally, we gotta move four to five thousand tons a day in all. Us and the Brits, that is, because the damn French don't have any planes worth jack. Course, the Brits fly into Gatow.' His face soured. 'We got Tempelhof.'

'What's wrong with Tempelhof?'

Reynolds laughed bitterly. 'I'll let your co-pilot tell you what's wrong with Tempelhof.'

At the end of a frustrating day, James Hadley Webb decided to visit the Blaues Zimmer. It was strangely quiet. Each table was lit by a fat candle, but there were no customers to bathe in their glow. Paraffin heaters had been used to raise the temperature, but they had left an unpleasant chemical odour. Dean Martin singing 'Walkin' My Baby Back Home' echoed around the room, the crooner's voice lost and lonely. Two of the cabaret girls from next door sat at the bar, shawls wrapped around their shoulders, complaining to Johnny K about the lack of business. Six stools along was Towers, nursing a gin and tonic.

The owner, as immaculately turned out as always, raised a hand, pleased to see someone, anyone, enter his place.

'Johnny.' Webb knew he should despise the man as a fop and a parasite, but he couldn't. Better smooth, slippery Johnny than the hatchet-faced thugs who ran the Krypt.

'Jimmy.'

'Quiet tonight.'

The German made a face, and an attempt to lift the takings. 'Bottle of champagne?'

'Whisky and soda.' Webb heaved himself onto the bar stool

next to Towers. 'Is there anything more miserable than an empty nightclub?'

'How about a frightened city?' responded Towers. 'You heard the radio vans?'

Webb nodded. To counter a sudden outbreak of the jitters, loudspeakers had been mounted on trucks and driven around the Western sectors relaying the message that the Allies were going to stand up to the bullying of the Soviets. It helped that the news had reached them that the new Mark had already had a stabilising effect in the rest of Germany, with scarce goods such as stockings and toiletries, fresh fruit and vegetables, cigarettes and alcohol on open sale at relatively reasonable rates. The black market was in retreat. If Berlin was allowed the same chance, some kind of normality might be possible here, too.

'Any joy on Ernst?' asked Towers.

Webb took a hit of the whisky and let it warm his insides. 'I have spoken to the Assistant Police Commissioner, the Kommandatura, the Alex, the British-Soviet Liaison Officer, Tyler . . . nothing. They say they haven't got him. I have a driver who says he delivered him; the Alex say he is mistaken.'

'And you don't believe that?'

'They never owned up to having Henderson when he was kidnapped shopping for a camera on Unter den Linden. Or the Schneiders, taken at the pet shop on the border. They beat up a policeman yesterday in Wedding. Took him off to God knows where. Remember Tremper?' This was a seventeen-year-old reporter, ambitious and articulate, arrested by the Soviets when he published a piece about Police Chief Markgraf, hinting at a Nazi past. The boy was badly roughed up before the Russians finally admitted they had taken him and released him in Potsdamer Platz.

'Well, let's hope he doesn't catch a cold.' The Russians had a trick where they beat up prisoners, stripped them, and then showered them with freezing water from a hose. Then they could claim the victim died of 'pneumonia'.

'Quite,' Webb said absentmindedly. As he thought about the release of the young reporter, an idea began to form.

'Alan, I want you to be very careful. I mean that. Being close to me is a dangerous occupation at the moment. The roll call of the dead and missing is getting longer by the day. I don't want to wake up and find you're on it.'

'Gosh, me neither. And I am careful,' Towers insisted. 'But you reckon there's nothing we can do for poor Ernst, wherever he is?'

'Oh,' he replied with a sly grin. 'I wouldn't say that.' Webb drained his glass and signalled Johnny for a refill. The alcohol was, for once, lifting his mood. He'd been on the back foot far too long. He wasn't going to lose any more men or women. It was time to counter-attack.

Twenty-seven

Lee Crane found out what was wrong with the Tempelhof approach for himself. The airfield had been built in the middle of the city and so was now surrounded by the ruins of tower blocks. The first step was to take a bearing on the outlying Fulda Beacon. This went *dit, dit, dah* ad nauseum, a Morse cycle of Fs and Ds. Over the Beacon, you dropped through 5,000 feet, turning to 57 degrees magnetic and clearing Soviet territory. Then, you had to make another turn over the Wedding Beacon, lose another 500 feet in altitude, kill your airspeed, and make two more turns. The final approach came over the Neuköln cemetery, at a steep angle Crane really didn't like, with an oversized brewery chimney to avoid. Finally, you dropped in low over the barbed-wire fence and barely had time to register the gaggle of ill-fed, scruffy kids standing on the mounds of rubble to your left, frantically waving at each incoming aircraft.

Then, your plane slammed onto the runway, which was badly churned from a fully loaded transport landing every four minutes. You had to taxi as fast as you dared to the unloading area, where German ground-handlers poured into your aircraft and stripped it bare. The engines had barely stopped ticking before the Ops people then told you to get the hell out of there and go back for another load, pronto.

That was what was wrong with Tempelhof.

After he had parked up, John Harvey, his temporary co-pilot, congratulated him on the landing. 'Not bad for a Tempelhof rookie.'

Crane shrugged. He'd landed on strips in China that were worse.

Harvey said: 'Nice plane. Try and keep it that way.'

'What do you mean?'

'What Berlin needs more than anything is coal. Coal and flour. They pack the coal in duffel bags, but, shit, they leak all over the place. The dust settles on the screen, you try and wash it off, it scratches the glass. The scratches act as prisms which cause flares at night that blind you. The dust also gets into the control lines, the engines, everywhere, and if it rains, it turns into mud, then cement – so don't carry coal if you can help it. Flour isn't much better.'

In fact, this time they had got away with a cargo of pasta, sugar, graham crackers, Spam and red wine, the latter for the French who, Harvey said, didn't deserve such consideration. They claimed it was as essential to them as Coca-Cola to the Americans, but he didn't buy it.

'You think the Air Force will lease this plane off me?' asked Crane.

'I dunno. But I do know half the C-47s are laid up because of windshield or electrical problems. The rest have engines older than Methuselah. And spares are rarer than a woman without the clap – and that's damn rare. This is a nice crate. If they do take it on, make sure you get top dollar, because those guys are going to bat the shit out of it.' He yawned. 'I'm beat. Look, there's a hostel over the road from the terminal, I'm due eight hours' shut-eye. You gotta sort your status out, but you wanna fly with me again,' he held out his hand, 'I'll be there.'

Crane found Roberston in the Tempelhof Ops office, as besieged with people as the one at Rhein-Main. Robertson looked up from his desk, saw his old Flying Tiger Wingman, flashed a grin and said: 'Tell me you brought me a C-54.'

'Gooney Bird.'

209

'Shit. Three, three and a half tons, max. C-54 does ten.'

'The C-54 is not three times the plane.'

'You're biased. Coffee?'

Crane looked at the frenzied activity around him. 'You got time?'

'No, of course I ain't got time. Let's go.'

Robertson threw down a piece of paper and the two of them walked from the crowded office, across the apron and into the main terminal. The hall showed signs of bomb damage, but the grandeur of the place still impressed. It had all the hallmarks of Nazi architecture – the brutal, squared-off columns and the over-sized windows designed to make mere humans feel insignificant – but it was still handsome, in a slightly sinister way.

Robertson led him upstairs, to where a canteen looked out over the wings of the crescent-shaped building and the airfield. It was dark and inhospitable out there, but the planes didn't stop coming, screeching down in a spray of mud and dirt.

'See that?' said Robertson. 'The perforated steel plates that make up the surface have sunk under the impacts. Bang, bang, bang. Every time a plane comes in, the plates go into the rubble. This runway won't last two months, but we can't afford to close it until we have built two others to replace it.'

He fetched them both coffee and ushered Crane to a window seat, where he could keep an eye on proceedings. Robertson had been a Flying Tiger for Chennault, fighting the Japanese over China even before the US had entered the war; prior to that he had flown in Spain. He was hitting fifty, and usually looked younger, but right now, he seemed a decade older.

'Gooneys are no good, Lee, not in the long run. We need planes with a bigger capacity.'

Crane sipped at the coffee. It was surprisingly good. 'I like my C-47.'

'I ain't going to turn you away, Lee. Not at the moment. But we've been promised C-54s and C-74s soon. Our C-47s are falling apart on us. You could convert?'

'And give up the Gooney? I just bought her. She's solid.'

'Tunner wants the C-47s out of the picture. I'm sorry. He's trying to put some order into this chaos. He needs something with a bigger capacity.'

'Come soonest, you said,' Crane reminded him, with a hint of sullenness. 'Great broads, good money.'

'Yeah – well, that was before I knew what it was really going to be like. We are making this up as we go along, Lee.'

'I know. Will this work – the airlift? Transporting five thousand tons of material a day?'

'Tunner made it work on The Hump.' Robertson didn't need to add that they'd had thirteen bases in India and six in China back then. Or that they had a lot of sky to move around in, not three narrow air corridors where the Russians just might shoot you down if you strayed off-course. 'At least there are no Himalayas in the way.'

'You know, I'd rather the mountains than that brewery chimney. Can't you demolish it?'

'The owner says the beer is essential for morale. He could be right. But to answer your other question: will an airlift work? Well, if we let the Russians chase us out of Berlin, then they'll just keep pushing till they have moved us out of Germany altogether. They're bullies, Lee. This is our Munich. We gotta stand up to them. The airlift has to work.'

'How many planes you lost standing up to them so far?'

Robertson lowered his eyes. 'Some. There's not a lot of room for pilot error. And two or three missions a day is too many.' There had already been fully-laden aircraft that had ploughed into apartment blocks or crashed short of Berlin, crumpled into a field on the Soviet side. 'The Russians have just announced live firing manoeuvres by their new planes in the air corridors. Plus there's a fog problem. I don't know why, but it can be clear all over the city and a pea-souper at Tempelhof.'

It sounded bad, but no worse than The Hump, when giant

storms and Japanese Zeros came looking for the unwary. 'Well, I'm here now. I might as well get a forty-five and get on with it.'

'A forty-five? In which case you can't fly a civilian plane. You'd have to mothball your Gooney.'

Crane sighed. 'You know, I'd forgotten about the red tape.'

'There's more since your time.' Robertson thought for a moment, hesitated, and then spat it out anyway. 'Look, what about flying for the Brits? Operation Plainfare. They're using Dakotas. Trying to do a hundred and sixty flights a day, but failing miserably at the moment.'

Crane wrinkled his nose. He didn't have a very high opinion of the British.

'I know. But they aren't the assholes they were in Burma and China. They are contracting civilian flyers, so you won't have to take a forty-five. They pay better, too, for once. Uncle Sam slaps you in uniform and then screws your wages. They pay commercial rates for planes. Plus for our guys there is going to be no leaving your aircraft in Berlin from now on, order of General Tunner.'

'What does that mean?'

Outside, the rain began in earnest once more, whipping at the windows like buckshot. Slowly, the runway disappeared under spray. Robertson stood. They'd be stacking over Berlin soon. This was the kind of visibility in which accidents happened; there weren't yet enough high-intensity beacons to land safely on instruments alone.

'As of 08.00 tomorrow, you land here at Tempelhof, you unload, you get a clearance slip and a weather report, and you fly back. If you're lucky, a couple of cute Fräuleins will come out with hot-dogs before you leave. No sightseeing or fraternisation in the city at this end. You get a bed if you're too tired to go back, at one of those flop houses over there. I think we've got the bugs there on the run, just about. But seeing Berlin? Forgetaboutit.'

'Jesus.' Now Crane remembered why they called Bill Tunner 'Willy the Whip'.

'Yup. With the Brits you get to go into the city between tours if you wish, let off a bit of steam. And you fly into Gatow. No brewery chimney.'

It was the leave that clinched it. He needed that time in Berlin. Still, he said: 'I came all the way from Asia to fly with you, Carl.'

Robertson looked into his face and grinned. 'No, you didn't, you lying bastard. That's a crock if ever I heard one.'

Lee Crane laughed. No, he hadn't, he reminded himself. He'd come all the way from Asia to find a woman called Laura McGill.

Twenty-eight

Potsdamer Platz, once the social and cultural hub of Berlin, the site of the first traffic-lights in Europe, where cosmopolitan cafés, cabarets and cinemas entertained Berliners in the 1920s and 1930s, was a blasted plain. The tramlines had been relaid, but elsewhere the square's former landmarks, such as the ultra-modern Columbus Haus, lay in fragments, like a child's construction set that had been wantonly kicked to pieces.

The black market on Potsdamer Platz wasn't as large or comprehensive as the one in front of the Reichstag. There, you could buy anything from a forged ration card to a one-careful-owner condom. Here, the pickings were slimmer. The 'market' consisted of threadbare offcuts of carpets or tattered tarps spread out on the ground, with the usual depressing array of goods placed on top. You could snap up an Iron Cross (Second Class), a dented Leica, a wind-up Schuco car or an old Lüger pistol for next to nothing. It was the onion or carrot next to them that was going to clean you out.

Haggling over any food was fast, furious and occasionally violent. There were also the cigarettes – thin tubes with a few clumps of tobacco held together by the saliva of the Lord knows how many people: they were recycled from hundreds of discarded butts. But, thought Webb, if you needed a smoke that bad, you weren't going to be too concerned about its provenance.

Ralph Tyler and Jimmy Webb stood behind a makeshift barricade on the British side of the plaza, surrounded by a platoon of soldiers plucked from the 1st Battalion of the Sherwood Foresters, all of whom were carrying loaded Lee Enfields. Along another edge of the square were the Americans, a full battalion of MPs, each with either carbines or 'grease guns'.

The customers and vendors all looked nervously at the numbers of armed men, but the trade carried on anyway, driven by desperation on all sides.

'You think they'll try anything?' asked Webb.

'We'll see,' Tyler replied. 'But for God's sake, stay back. It's not a good idea to be too conspicuous.'

The previous day, Russian police had raided the square, arresting dozens of people and, when the crowd started hurling rocks, firing into it. Fifteen had been wounded, the dark varnish of their dried blood still visible on the cobblestones. It was a mark of the city's resilience that the market had returned the next day, as busy as ever.

'We had a couple of interesting walk-ins at Platanenallee yesterday,' said Tyler, as if making idle chitchat. He was talking about the MilGov Administration (Information) Centre near the Olympic Stadium. A 'walk-in' was usually a term for someone offering his or her services as a spy, but Webb guessed that wasn't what Tyler meant.

'Oh, yes?' A plane buzzed overhead, climbing quickly from Tempelhof now it had shed its load.

'Yes.' Mischief glinted in Tyler's eye. 'A young lady asking for you. Rather attractive, by all accounts.'

The McGill woman, Webb thought. She hadn't fallen for the story in Paris. He'd arranged with Tin-Eye Stephens and the DST to find a former concentration camp guard – which Charbonneau really had been – to feed her a story that would convince her that her sister was dead. It had been Diana McGill he had wanted 'killed', at least in Laura's mind, so, it had seemed the only way to shut her up for the time being. He gave a theatrical sigh. 'Another paternity claim, no doubt.'

Webb was pleased to see this wrong-footed Tyler for a second, until he realised it was a joke.

'The second walk-in?' he asked.

'An American pilot, looking for the same woman.' Tyler shrugged. 'Name of Lee Crane. You know him?'

Webb shook his head. 'No, don't think so. What did the desk tell them?'

Tyler laughed. 'You know the one thing the information desk is adept at, is *not* giving out any information. They said they would "see what they could do".'

An American pilot? Looking for Laura McGill? It might just be the change in his fortune he needed. Manna from heaven, so to speak.

'Thanks,' he said to Tyler. 'I'll get Towers onto it. You have an address for these people?'

'They signed in. Addresses should be there in the book—'

At that moment, his head whipped round, as did that of everybody across the square. Trades were halted in mid-haggle and even the dogs dropped their shoulders and ears in fear. There was the distinctive crunching of hobnails on cobbles, echoing over the ruined space. The Russians were coming.

Lee Crane had problems. Sitting in the aircrew rest area at Wunstorf – a collection of army-issue chairs and tables under a canvas awning – he watched the fiendish activity at the cargo stands as the German loaders formed human chains before each plane, carefully slotting boxes and crates in until the chief indicated the aircraft couldn't carry another peanut. Around him, tired pilots dozed in the chairs.

The weather had cleared and transports were taking off every six to eight minutes, bound for Gatow. Robertson had got him transferred to the British base, as promised. Of course, he'd forgotten to mention that the only chow was British rations. And then the British had really got to work on him.

'Trouble is, old chap,' the clipped voices played in his head, *'your radio doesn't work on RAF frequencies. Gatow is an RAF base, not civilian.'*

And then: *'Oh. I see you have a Greek airworthiness certificate. Well, you are approved for a lower load than the military Dakota, and all our material come pre-loaded on pallets at maximum carrying weight. We can't start adjusting and reweighing just for you.'*

And finally: *'We don't actually need any one-man bands.'*

He had hitched a ride on a jump seat into Berlin the previous day and met exactly the same attitude at the half-dozen offices he had visited, trying to track down Laura. *'Two and a half million people in this city. Needle in a haystack, old boy, unless she is working for MilGov. Is she working for MilGov?'*

'I have no idea.'

'Can't help you then. Try . . .' and they had named some other obscure government organisation with an office across town. He'd given up and got drunk on Mortimer beer in a smoke-filled *Eckneipe* near the Ku'damm.

A man in stained brown overalls, wiping his hands on a rag that had to be dirtier than his hands would ever be, ambled over. He bellowed at one of the snoozing pilots in an English accent: 'All right, Captain Thorpe, you are on fully loaded, fuelled and cleared for take-off in twenty minutes.' Crane suddenly paid attention. Ground crew wouldn't know an aircraft's status, and this guy didn't look like a dispatcher.

Thorpe snuffled awake. 'Right. OK. I'll just go and splash some water on my face.'

The pilot staggered off, still half-asleep, and the newcomer examined the other figures, in case any of them were on call. He stopped at Crane.

'This is my relaxation area. RAF crew over there.' He indicated a long, low wooden hut.

'Sorry. There was a free seat.'

'Oh,' he said, taken aback by the accent. 'American?'

'Yup.'

'Pilot?'

'When they let me.'

The tone changed when he saw the insignia on the shoulder. 'That's CBI, isn't it?' Crane nodded, impressed he should recognise it. 'Are you having problems?'

Crane explained why the RAF didn't like him, trying to stay as polite as humanly possible.

'You have an aircraft of some description?' the man asked.

Crane nodded towards his silver bullet gleaming in the sun. 'That C-47. Or Dakota, as you call it.'

'Is it for sale?' The Englishman might look like a grease-monkey, but he certainly didn't sound or act like one.

'No. But it's for lease.'

'Where have you flown?' he almost demanded.

'Here and there,' Crane began and then stopped himself. This was no time for false modesty. 'I was with the Flying Tigers. The real ones, before the USAAF stole the name.' He touched the patch on his jacket. 'Then The Hump, followed by supply missions for Merrill's Marauders. After the war, I mostly skydogged jungle strips in South-East Asia.'

The man grinned. 'So you can fly a little?'

Crane winced as an ungainly Avro-York came in heavy, burning rubber scars onto the runway. 'Better than that.'

The Englishman stroked his chin, leaving oily streaks. 'Radio's no problem. I can get you a set of crystals out of one of mine that's laid up for the time being. The certification is a piece of cake – two hours' clerical work. I've got a dozen Haltons, converted Halifax bombers, but we are low on spares. If you fancy doing a couple of runs over to England as well as Berlin . . .'

'They don't seem to like one-man bands around here.'

218

There came a dismissive wave of the rag. 'Oh, you don't know how to handle these bloody penpushers. I'll put you on my books.'

'I'll need some time off in Berlin. Personal reasons.'

Now he looked suspicious. 'How much time?'

'A few hours every couple of days.'

'OK. We'll see how it goes. I didn't catch your name.'

He stood and offered his hand. 'Lee Crane.'

'Nice to meet you. Freddie Laker.'

It was an armed group of the Alert Police that marched into Potsdamer Platz, snubby submachine guns or Mosin Nagant carbines at the ready. They were flanked by regular police units and, on the fringes, a number of plainclothes observers. The group funnelled into the square at double-time and fanned out. The black-market traders and their customers stood frozen, penned in on three sides by Russians, Americans and British. They all eyed the one escape route left to them.

An officer detached himself from the body of the Alert Police and strutted across to the Americans. His voice carried over the hushed plaza. It sounded like the clunk of machinery, hard and grating.

'Police Commissioner Markgraf requests your assistance in clearing this illegal gathering of economic criminals.'

The Americans' reply was lost, but from the twitch of the Russian's shoulders, as if he had been punched, they knew it was a 'no'.

Webb turned and caught the eye of the Captain of the Foresters. 'Ready?'

'Absolutely. On your signal?' He raised a small swagger stick. Behind him, three men appeared, dressed like the other soldiers in the uniform of the Sherwood Foresters, but somehow more poised than their fellow squaddies, moving quickly on the balls of their feet to the barrier. Rather than Lee Enfields, this group had a Sergeant with a Thomson submachine gun and the others were carrying pistols only. This trio came from The Special Air Service, the SAS, which had a unit based out at Spandau who were keen to do anything that helped keep the boredom at bay. Like giving the Russkies a good kicking.

Webb said to the Sergeant: 'You know what to do?'

Sergeant Gallagher had a fleshy face, with small eyes and a nose that was bent by regimental boxing matches. His chest looked as if a steel plate had been welded over it. Webb was glad he'd never had to face him in the ring. 'Sir! You'll be along later?'

'Of course. Good hunting,' replied Webb.

'Leave it to us.'

Things moved quickly after that. The Russians began to break up the market with kicks and clubs, and, once Webb had given the Captain the nod, the British threw down the barriers and streamed across to try and intercept them. The Americans did the same.

The scene became chaotic when a volley of rifle shots – later identified as British rather than Russian weapons – were fired over the heads of the crowd. There were squeals, high-pitched and terrified, from the women. A submachine gun – this one a Soviet SKS45 – was fired into a section of the mob, wounding two men and a woman. Grease guns blasted into the sky by way of reply, the long deafening burps causing more panic. Bodies, uniformed and civilian, swirled around Potsdamer Platz in a grotesque dance of terror, while orders were barked from all sides calling for calm.

Within five minutes, the black market had vanished, the traumatised Berliners scrabbling over rubble or through the Allied soldiers and police to escape, and the various military groups had returned to their respective lines. The air was thick with the smell of cordite. Slowly, the opposing groups backed off, leaving Potsdamer Platz empty and wind-sheared once more, the debris of the market tossed around like tumbleweed, the only sound the constant drone of aero engines above.

It took the Russians a good thirty minutes to discover they were a man down. Webb had gone on the offensive, thanks to the SAS. He had snatched himself a Russian. And now he had something to trade with.

Twenty-nine

The Hotel Charlot, over in Wedding, the former Communist stronghold of old Berlin, now part of the French sector, had not enjoyed a good war. Outside, the façade was criss-crossed by wavy lines of bullet holes that joined together to become jagged craters around each window and doorway, where the fire had been concentrated. Shrapnel had splintered the steps, and the Art Nouveau tiles inlaid into each tread were crazed and chipped. The foyer was covered with brown and yellow wallpaper, peeling in places to reveal black mould. In Laura's room, the bed sagged like a broke-back nag, its brass plating long since tarnished and flaked, the mattress a lawn of wiry horsehair poking through the ticking. The sheets were thin and rough, and still contained the fine traces of sand that was used at laundries in place of soap. The floor, which lacked a carpet, creaked and groaned with every movement.

An S-Bahn rattled nearby, filling the hotel with its clanking. She couldn't actually see it; instead she had a marvellous view of what seemed to be a precariously unsupported wall, its elaborate stone window frames empty, like a skull's eye-sockets, the rest of the building apparently vapourised around it.

As Laura McGill struggled to open the warped drawer of the bureau, she couldn't fight the feeling that she was wasting her

222

time coming to this sad shell of a city. Every name led to someone else. Rose Miller, Raymond Bec, Jean-Marc Bevier, Philippe Charbonneau and now Jimmy Webb. No doubt Webb would lead to another set of shadowy figures, with the promise of the truth about Diana always residing at the next set and the next and the next. It was like one of those slow-motion running dreams, except she was not trying to escape from a threat, but make headway towards her elusive sister.

She cursed herself for her lack of resolve, reminding herself what sort of life Diana must have had, the deprivations she must have suffered these past few years. It would make her own time in the mental hospital look like a picnic. And she was thinking of giving up because the chest-of-drawers was warped? *Do you think your sister ever gave up hope?*

I'm not my sister, she told herself.

You can say that again.

The drawer came free with a pained squeak, and she was pleased to see that at least the liner was relatively fresh. She unloaded her blouses, underwear and two precious pairs of unladdered stockings into it.

There was a tap at the door. 'Just a minute,' she shouted, and wiggled the drawer shut once more.

She opened the door to a young man in a smart grey suit. He smiled nervily.

'Miss McGill?'

'Yes.'

He pushed a strand of his fringe back into place. Here it stayed for almost a whole second. 'My name is Alan Towers. I'm with the Board of Trade.'

'Are you selling something?'

'Not really.' His eyes sparkled. 'Is there something you need?'

'Not really.'

He glanced left and right down the dingy corridor. 'I'm not a tinker, honest. Do you mind if I come in?'

She opened the door and stepped back and he shuffled inside. 'I can leave – it open?' he offered.

'No, close it,' she told him. 'Boiled cabbage was never my favourite aroma.'

'No. Quite.' He smiled again and she thought how young he looked, like a schoolboy. The lines around his mouth and the odd lump on his cheek suggested he was somewhat older than that, but she could imagine him as a young prefect, in blazer and flannels, calling for a fag or leading the First XI out onto the pitch. Not unattractive, she decided, surprised at herself for noticing.

'I'd offer you a seat, Mr Towers, but . . .'

'Alan, please.' He looked around the bare room. 'You don't get a lot of seats in Berlin. There's something of a shortage. We have to fly our own in. Most of the furniture in the hotel probably went for firewood at some point. You are lucky to have any at all.'

'What can I do for the Board of Trade?' She said it in a way that left no doubt as to what she thought of his cover story.

Towers hopped from foot to foot. 'Well, it's more what the Board of Trade can do for you. I believe you are seeking Mr James Hadley Webb?'

'Yes. You know him?'

'Well, he is my superior. The thing is, he's frightfully busy right now, as you can imagine,' he pointed up to the cracked ceiling, 'what with the airlift and such. So he wondered if you could tell me what it is about and, possibly, I might be able to help.'

Help how? Was this lad another diversionary tactic? Sent to make love to her and take her mind off her sister? 'I don't think so. And please don't treat me like that.'

'Like what?' He looked genuinely perplexed.

'As if you don't know who I am or why I am here.'

Towers smiled once more and this time it stayed on his face. He stopped the annoying English dithering act and straightened his tie. 'I'm sorry.' The voice was deeper, less eager-to-please. He looked at his watch. 'Well, I'd rather not stand here all day, to be frank.'

'We could talk in the lobby. There are seats there.'

'Ooooh, no. No talking in lobbies, not in Berlin. If walls have ears, lobbies have eyes.'

'You're rambling, Mr Towers.'

He laughed at this. 'Yes, I am rather. Shall I apologise again, or is that enough for one day?'

'I'd lay off it for the moment.'

'Good idea. Have you eaten?'

'No, not yet.' Why did people want to keep feeding her? The thought of food, though, made her hand go involuntarily to her stomach. 'I haven't had lunch.'

'Have you, in fact, eaten since you arrived in Berlin?'

She smiled. 'That's not as simple as it seems, is it? I've had black bread and black coffee.' She had found a Kneipe the night before and had almost been tempted inside by the smell of Bratwurst, but when the door swung open, she saw it was full of ruddy-faced men and cigar smoke and raucous, perhaps even lewd, laughter. Her nerve had failed her and she had fled.

Towers ran a hand through his hair. 'Thing is, you need to be attached to a mess. Every civilian working for the MilGov is assigned somewhere to dine, if that is the right term. It's airlift rations, I am afraid. Powdered egg and mashed potatoes. Corned beef. All the McConaughey you can eat.'

'Sounds fine to me. How do I get attached?'

'Well, that's not straightforward either; it can take days. And in your case . . . well, you aren't actually working for the MilGov, are you? If you are ever desperate there is the man who sells Frankfurters at the Gedächtniskiche. You have to be quick, as he sells out in a jiffy. He's a police informer as well, but that's by the by.' Towers made a pantomime sigh, as if he had just come to a monumental decision. 'We can go to my mess, if you wish. Then I'll get you assigned there. Shouldn't be too difficult.' For a pretty girl, he seemed to be saying.

'So, are you inviting me for McConaughey, whatever that is?'

'Meat and veg in a tin. If you fancy that.'

He winked, which was a surprisingly nice effect, she thought. If he had been sent as a would-be seducer, he wasn't a bad choice. Not that he had much of a chance, she reminded herself. But after three days in solitary and that charade in Paris, a little civilised company wouldn't go amiss.

'Or if you prefer, there's *Kasseler*,' he went on, 'which is smoked pork chop. Or liver and onions with apple, which is better than it sounds. Then there's *Wiener Schnitzel*—'

'Stop, stop. And where do you find all these delicacies?'

He spread his arms wide in a gesture of plenty. 'I have a car and driver downstairs. I shall show you, Miss McGill.'

Laura picked up the jacket she had slung across the bed and slipped it on.

'There's just one thing,' he warned her suddenly. 'If the head waiter calls me by some other name than Towers, don't let on.'

She had to laugh at that. 'Are you a spy, Mr Towers?'

Assuming a voice that, unknown to Laura, echoed Jimmy Webb's, Alan told her, 'My dear girl, anyone who is anyone in Berlin is a spy these days.'

The nest of basement rooms that formed part of the British holding cells was beneath the old Olympic swimming-pool complex. New lowered ceilings, with integral microphones, had been added, as had heavy, lockable steel doors to create the cells. There had been no repainting though, and the plaster walls still sported an inappropriate aquamarine blue. Here and there, they were stained a darker hue, with what could be splashes of blood.

Webb sat in the guardroom with Tyler, sipping weak coffee, waiting for the news of their abductee. The Special Air Service team had snatched him from the square and, under cover of the mêlée, bundled him into a Jeep and brought him here. They had turned him over to John Findlay, a Russian speaker who had been in the city since 1945. Findlay was one of SIS's finest interrogators; he'd trained under Tin-Eye Stephens during the war, although he'd never moved beyond 'robust' in his techniques.

'I'll send the SAS boys a crate of something,' said Webb.

Tyler nodded. 'You owe me for this too, you know.'

Webb grinned. 'I know. It had to be done. I need a bargaining chip.'

'It's dangerously sentimental of you, Jimmy. All for a Fritz copper as well.'

'Regular Shirley Temple, that's me.'

Findlay entered from the cell corridor, sweat on his brow, and an unlit cigarette in his mouth. He was barely five foot six, but stocky and well-muscled, and he looked as if he might burst out of his suit. There was a threatening virility about the man. The Scot picked up the box of Swan Vestas from the table and looked down at Webb.

'You're a bloody lucky man, sir, you know that?'

'How so?'

Findlay struck a match and lit his cigarette. 'His name is Vatnik. A Major. He's KI – a political co-ordinator. Straight out of Karlshorst.' This was the old hospital in East Berlin converted to an Intelligence HQ by the Russians. 'He was assigned to assess the effectiveness and loyalty of the Alert Police. Poor bastard.'

'So, they'll want him back?'

'Oh yes.' The interrogator nodded. 'And soon.'

'Can you get anything from him?' asked Webb. Findlay and Tyler knew what he meant: order of battle, troop deployment, long-term aims of the blockade. Even tiny fragments were all grist to the mill.

Findlay sucked on his cigarette. 'He's scared shitless. Once he's been over here, he's tainted. They won't trust him.'

'Can you get anything from him?' Webb repeated. What happened to the Major back in the East was no concern of his.

'Och-aye, in a couple of days.'

'You'll have twenty-four hours.' Webb fixed Tyler with a no-nonsense stare. 'And Ralph, I want you to share any Intel with Dolan.'

Tyler and Findlay exchanged glances. Dolan might be a senior figure in the CIA's Communications Division at Dahlem, but he was also a rival. 'Frankfurt won't be too thrilled. Why do you want to pass *him* anything?' asked Tyler.

Webb rolled his eyes in frustration. 'Because I want something back from Dolan, of course.'

'Are you going to tell me what?'

No, he thought, because only the Americans had the resources to do what he had in mind. With the Intelligence from the Major and the news Ernst had given him about the accidental death of Henderson, the kidnapped American, he had a couple of corkers to trade on. But all he said was: 'I want them to arrest an American citizen for me.'

'Who?'

'That pilot called Lee Crane.'

Thirty

Lunch was at a black-market restaurant on the western borders of Wilmersdorf. It was an anonymous residential house, larger than the norm, perhaps, but the only thing to really distinguish it from its neighbours was the sheer number of cars blocking the driveway and spilling into the street. There were three floors, a pianist, a head waiter who simply called Towers 'sir', steak and potatoes and a bottle of Hock. Conversation between them had been steady and pleasant. Laura went through the history of her sister and then talked about some of her own time in the Far East.

Things had only become strained when she pushed Towers on his wartime record and why he was in Berlin. He managed to deflect most of the questions. After lunch, back in the car, he instructed the Sergeant who was behind the wheel to take them further west, out almost past Gatow. They drove beyond the wrecked city to one of the parks that ringed Berlin. The driver parked up in a designated bay and Towers asked Laura to follow him, grabbing an old gas-mask case as he got out of the car. Curious, she followed him off the gravel and onto a track.

The path led them up a hill, through a copse of trees, which showed the livid scars of crude hacking at branches, for firewood. 'Had to put armed guards on the parks in the end,' explained Towers as they pushed on through the scrappy bushes. 'Otherwise there wouldn't be a tree left for miles around. You OK? Bit slippery here. Nearly there.' He paused to look up as an Avro Tudor came over them, inbound for Gatow. A Dakota was close on its tail.

Laura was enjoying the smell of the place, the sensation of lungfuls of air untainted by cement and brick particles and the undertow of decay. Everything in the centre, she realised, was contaminated by grit. Berlin was a city of dust.

They cleared the undergrowth and moved onto a low ridge, which gave them a vantage point over the countryside spread out before them. To their right was the sprawl of Gatow, the planes wobbling like toys on wires as they came in to land. To the left was the bomb-mauled town of Potsdam, and the estate that housed Sans Souci, Frederick the Great's palace, its dome just visible over the treetops. Ahead was a long stretch of potato and cabbage fields, which she could smell on the wind.

'See the wire fence?' Towers asked. 'That's the border. You are looking at the East. Here.' From the gas-mask bag, he took a pair of binoculars. 'Take a peek over there.'

She followed the line of his finger, pressed the field-glasses to her eyes and turned the knurled knob in the centre. A watchtower swam in and out of focus. She adjusted the screw and it sharpened. She swept away from the tower and along a line of wire-topped walls. 'The camp? Is it a camp?'

'It was one of the German command centres. The RAF bombed it pretty comprehensively. Now it's a barracks, housing the 112th Shock Battalion.'

'It looks like a prison.'

'It is. And every so often, they escape.'

She lowered the glasses, puzzled by the hardness of his tone. 'I don't quite follow, Alan.'

He clenched his jaw, and she watched the muscle twitch. 'I hope you'll forgive my crudeness, Laura, but every single man in that barracks is infected.'

'With what?' she asked, thinking he meant TB.

'Venereal disease.'

Laura willed herself not to blush.

'Sorry to be so blunt. You want to sit down?'

There was a wooden bench with a seating slat missing, so they perched on it. Laura could see a farmer with a horse heading from the fields. The afternoon sun was warm on her face, which was still flushed from the alcohol, and she took her jacket off.

Towers took his time retying his shoelaces while he spoke. 'The rape problem, immediately after the war, meant that there were so many cases of the disease, it was easier to group them all together. Over lunch, you asked me why I was still here in Germany.' He cleared his throat. 'At the end of the war, we were all racing to get whatever we could from the German factories. We knew the V-weapons were just the tip of the iceberg. All of us wanted whatever scientific secrets we could get hold of. The Americans had Operation Paperclip, ours was Operation Overcast. Have you heard of the Foo-Fighters?'

She shook her head, wondering where the diffident young man who had picked her up from the hotel had suddenly gone. There was flint in the voice, a desire to be heard and to make his point.

'When the Allies, specifically the Americans, were flying over Germany, many of the gunners reported seeing strange glowing lights in the sky, bright enough to be seen by day. They gave off this intense incandescence and zipped through the bomber formations at incredible speeds. "The Foo-Fighters", they called them. The name came from some comic strip that was popular at the time. Most flyers thought they were some strange German secret weapon.'

Intrigued by where this was going, she prompted: 'And were they?'

'There were investigations after the war. Officially, they were optical illusions.'

'And unofficially?'

He hesitated. 'Official Secrets Act?'

'Signed, sealed, delivered.'

'Then I'll tell you about the Foo-Fighters.'

Thirty-one

T-Force: Germany, 1945

They found the two deserters just before dusk. The T-Force convoy was deep into the mountains by this time. The great cathedrals of pines towering around them as the road switchbacked uphill had given way to thinner cover and bare rock. They began following the route of deep, jagged gorges with silvery flumes of water at the bottom. Grey clouds were rolling in, gravid with snow. Even if they didn't dump their load onto the hillsides, it would be a freezing cold night up there.

As they slowed for another gear-grinding bend, Cook, the hawk-eyed gunner, spotted something in the scrappy undergrowth. 'Jerry!' he yelled.

Towers instinctively ducked as his ears were pounded by the stutter of the Vickers, and hot ammunition casings rained around him. Corporal Dobson skewered the Jeep over to the gravel at the cliff-face side of the road.

The firing ceased and there was a silence filled by the hum in his ears. From the spindly bushes lining the gorge side of the road came two white-faced helmetless soldiers, their hair filled with bits of twig and leaves and their hands pointing heavenwards. They must have charmed lives, thought Towers, for all those shells to have missed them.

The convoy halted and the two frightened Germans took a step into the road. Dobson reversed the Jeep so he drew level with them. Towers produced his pistol and aimed it at a point vaguely midway between the pair. Beneath the grime and terror, they were probably not more than sixteen.

'You two,' he said in German. 'Where is the shade factory?'

The pair looked at each other and shook their heads, as if bewildered by the request.

'Come on,' he insisted. 'The *G-Werke*. It's around here somewhere.'

They looked even more terrified now, which suggested they knew exactly what he was talking about.

Towers was about to speak when the Vickers chattered again. One of the boys lifted off the ground and his front opened as if unzipped. Blood, bone and tissue spurted high into the air, coating his friend, who collapsed onto his knees. The other twitched three or four times, huge spasms that produced groans from what was left of his lungs, and then lay still.

'Cook!' shouted Towers, his face flushed with fury. 'What the fuck are you doing?'

'Finger slipped, sir,' said the Liverpudlian. 'Sorry, sir.'

Even Dobson had the decency to snort in derision.

Towers should put him on a charge, stamp his authority, but the last thing he needed was to alienate the men at this point. 'You are bloody—' he began, but became aware of the surviving soldier running towards him.

'Don't shoot! Don't shoot,' he sobbed. Over the spiky smell of fresh blood, Towers caught the ammoniacal whiff of urine from him. 'I'll take you there.'

'Where?' asked Towers, just to be certain.

'I'll take you to the shade factory.'

*   *   *

The boy told them they had missed the turning. Three kilometres back down the mountain was a well-disguised logging track, which ran alongside the face of a cliff. It wasn't the main route up, the soldier explained to Towers; there was also a heavily camouflaged funicular railway through the forest, big enough to transport men and materials to and from the railhead at Bronsdorf, the nearest town.

The boy, crouched behind Towers at Cook's feet, admitted that he and his friend had been guards at the shade factory and had deserted upon hearing the Russians were searching the countryside for installations like theirs. That was why he didn't want to go back. They hanged deserters. Towers promised to protect him, the way he couldn't his chum, and tried out some of the scientific words he had heard: *Kugelblitz* and *Feuerball*. The boy knew nothing of them.

The strange lights in the sky were believed to be experimental radio-controlled missiles and saucer-shaped objects that would play havoc with the B-17 and B-24s' electronics using proximity interference. Had the boy seen any saucer-shaped flying craft?

Another negative. Towers gave him a cigarette that he consumed greedily. Perhaps this would prove to be a dead end. After all, the Foo-Fighters were rumoured to be in Austria, then in the Schwarzwald *Zeppelin Werke* or at the *Forschungsanstalt der Deutschen Reichpost* of Aach bei Radolfzell on Lake Constance. And now the Harz Mountains.

The logging road widened out, although the edge still presented a hazardous drop down into a valley. They should put their headlights on, but Towers wanted to delay that until the last possible moment. There was no point in advertising their presence more than necessary,

The road ended at a plateau, a vast semi-circle scooped out of the hillside. To their left, its entrance shielded by a series of fences and barriers, was the darkened mouth of an enormous cave. On the cliff edge to their right was the concrete blockhouse housing the funicular gear and heavy lifting equipment, draped in layers of camouflage netting, like an old-fashioned veil. Bright steel rails, still polished from constant use, ran from this terminus into the side of the mountain. But there were no troops or workers to be seen. There was no sign of life at all.

Towers signalled for them to halt and the vehicles pulled abreast. He turned to the German prisoner.

'I want you to go in there and show my men around.' The boy glanced up at Cook who leered back. 'Not him, don't worry. Are there charges? Explosive charges – for demolition?'

'Yes, but I don't think they are set.'

'Booby traps?'

'No.'

'You realise you'll be going into every room first, just in case?' The boy nodded. 'No traps.'

Towers put together an advanced party of technicians, an explosives expert and armed escort and sent them towards the cave, while he and Dobson went over to examine the funicular.

Dobson fetched himself a Thompson submachine gun and they walked over to the rim of the plateau. The forest ran down from the blockhouse at forty-five degrees and, here and there, they could glimpse the netting that disguised the funicular's single track. The inside of the control room was deserted. The actual train was missing, too. It must be down at the other terminus. Towers touched the metal mug of coffee that was next to the control levers. 'Cold,' he announced. This was no *Marie Celeste*; the operator had been gone some hours at least.

Two things happened at once. The rails began to sing, a high-pitched whine, and the cable drum jerked into life. 'Someone is coming up,' said Dobson, pulling the bolt on his weapon.

Then the lights of the tunnel behind them came on, and Towers could see that the opening in the mountainside was far larger than he had imagined. It wasn't curved, but looked like a half-hexagon, with two sides sloping up to the crosspiece. The floodlights around the perimeter snapped on too, and the night retreated a little.

'What shall we do?' asked Dobson.

But Towers's attention was taken by one of the Sergeants who was sprinting out of the vast entrance and across the clearing towards them. Towers went out to meet him.

'What is it, Sergeant?'

The man slowed to catch his breath and reslung his rifle. 'I think they're scientists, sir,' he gasped. 'Not soldiers or workers, anyway. Well-fed, well-dressed. A half-dozen. Scared shitless but otherwise fine.'

Towers felt a surge of excitement. This was more like it. 'Bring them out.'

'Sir. But there's something else you should see. Something inside.'

Towers glanced over his shoulders. He wondered how long the funicular took. Should he just blow it? But what if it was the Yanks coming up? He could abandon Allies on the roadside, but he couldn't murder them. 'Sergeant, I'll go in. You stay here. I want machine guns set up to cover that funicular, make it a proper killing zone, so if we don't like what's on the train, we can blast it to kingdom come.'

Towers saw a gleam in the man's eye. 'Absolutely, sir. But . . .'

'Yes?'

He inclined his head towards the factory entrance. 'You'll need a strong stomach, sir.'

He didn't linger long in the labour quarters. He'd heard about them, of course, but nothing prepared him for the smell of decay and disease, the feeling of infection entering his body with every breath. They were on bunks, six deep, stacked six high, and most of them were dead or dying. A few pitiful eyes stared out of astonishingly deep sockets. When they spoke, he heard Russian and Czech and French.

The low-ceilinged room went on for hundreds of yards, and there were side-dormitories running off it. It was hard to estimate how many slave labourers had once been in this hell, nor how many it must have consumed over the years. He spat onto the floor, raising a splash of greasy dust that looked to be half-rock, half-skin. The sickening stench of gangrene found his nostrils and lodged there.

'Fuck!' he wanted to yell at the top of his voice. 'Fuck you for this!'

Instead, as calmly as he could, he turned to one of his soldiers. 'Break out some rations. Feed the living. Not much – less than a fistful. And a half-cup of water. Then get them out into the main factory area. We're going to seal this room.'

'How?'

'Bring the roof down on it. Give the dead the closest to a decent burial we can.'

'Right.'

'Oh, and Smart?'

'Yes.'

He gritted his teeth. 'Keep that German boy out of my sight for the time being.'

The soldier didn't have time to answer. Even from deep within the tunnels they recognised the rattle of British machine guns.

They were still firing when he got into the open. He could see muzzle flashes coming from the rail blockhouse. He should have blown it, after all. He crouched behind a concrete block that had once held a striped barrier pole. 'Kill the perimeter lights!' he yelled back into the tunnel. The T-Force was too exposed. The string of arcs died.

One of his men took a hit and Towers watched as he rolled backwards, a weak cry escaping his lips. A fresh volley of rifle-fire came from the British trucks, and the blockhouse netting danced as if caught in the breeze.

238

The rocket streaked from the right, not the railhead, blazing a trail of sparks between the lorries before it detonated on the cliff. The percussive thud hit his ears and Towers felt himself stagger.

From beyond his own lorries, three sets of new headlights flicked on, and then off, pulsing over and over again to get their attention.

'Cease fire!' he shouted, but the British troops had already come to the same conclusion. The machine guns fell silent as everyone wondered who had crept along the logging road behind them while a decoy team came up the funicular. *Wehrmacht*? *Waffen SS*? Whoever it was with the rockets, they were outflanked.

Towers broke cover and stood. 'Put the lights on again.'

'Sir?'

'Put the lights on again.' He had to take a chance that whoever it was wasn't fanatical enough to die at the fag end of the conflict. But he could be wrong.

Nothing moved for a few minutes, and his men continued to stare down their gunsights. Eventually, there came the slamming of doors and two officers walked from the newly arrived lorries, greatcoats flapping, pistols at their sides. They might have performed a classic *Wehrmacht* pincer movement by squeezing the British between blockhouse and logging road, but they weren't German. It was the Red Army.

The officers were a Captain, Pavel Ovechkin, and a Political Commissar, Nikolai Pagodin, with the rank of Major, both of whom spoke reasonable English. After they had arranged a truce and ascertained that, although both sides had wounded, there were no fatalities, they discussed how to untangle this mess.

The Russians were part of a Serov Mission, the equivalent of T-Force. Most of their 200-strong unit was in Bronsdorf, at the bottom of the funicular. This was a raiding party to test the enemy's strength. They hadn't expected to find the British.

'So?' asked Ovechkin. 'What do we do now?'

'Well,' replied Towers in Russian, 'we were here first.'

'Ah, but we have more men. And rockets,' Pagodin reminded him. 'However, we don't want a fight with you English. You sent us tanks when you had need of them yourselves.'

'True,' agreed Ovechkin.

'Not very good tanks,' grinned Pagodin. 'But it is the thought that counts.'

Towers laughed. That was also true. The homegrown T-34 won the tank war, not the Grants and Shermans the Allies had sent.

The temperature was dropping and ice was sparkling on the ground. The Liverpudlians and the Soviet troops were beginning a tentative fraternisation, helping treat each other's wounded. The Russian cure-all, vodka, was produced from one side, Woodbines from the other.

'You know what was built here?' asked Ovechkin.

Towers shrugged. Before he had entered the slave dorms he had looked at the main assembly plant. There were no 'flying saucers'. 'From what I saw in the main hall, engines.'

The Political Commissar frowned as if this were a trick. 'Engines?'

'Jet engines.'

His brow unfurrowed. Propeller-less propulsion technology was much sought-after in Russia. Pagodin beamed: 'Are there examples?'

'I would think so. And there are scientists.'

'Which we will both want.'

Towers nodded over at the intermingled troops. 'You think we should pull them apart and get them to start fighting again? They might just think it is simpler to kill us and carry on drinking.'

Ovechkin guffawed, as if that were a perfectly sensible idea. 'I have a suggestion,' he said after some consideration. 'Why don't we split the spoils? Half the engines, half the scientists each. We all go home heroes.'

Stalin's man began to protest, but Towers said: 'It's better than killing each other in the last days of the war. Don't you agree?'

'Our instructions—' Pagodin began.

'Oh, bollocks, you stiff-arsed prick,' said the soldier. 'How about we just shoot you and do it anyway.'

There was a long pause before Pagodin burst out laughing. 'You would, too, you bastard, wouldn't you?'

'Sure, why not? I'd tell my auntie you died a hero of the Great Patriotic War, killing Fascists till the end.'

Pagodin slapped Towers on the shoulder. 'If they knew we were cousins, we'd be separated. A Commissar must never like his charges. Not that I like him too much, but we're blood. How about we leave a guard contingent up here, fifty-fifty Russian and Anglos, and we go down to Bronsdorf. There are barracks your men can use. Warm barracks. And the good vodka is down there with the Colonel.'

There was a roar from the men, and some of the Russians began to clap their hands with joy. They all seemed to be getting along famously. 'Why not?' asked Towers, in the most naïve statement of his life.

Salt of the earth, thought Towers, after his fifth – or perhaps tenth, he'd lost count – toast with the two officers. Bit rough and ready, perhaps, but we couldn't have done it without them. The Russians were every bit as vital to victory as the Americans.

They were in a vast refectory in the centre of the village, which had once been used by the German Olympic teams, when they came on mountain treks for altitude training and stamina building. Later on, the elite 14th Alpine Regiment had used the same facilities. There were thirty tables and benches in the hall, each occupied by a mix of the Russian and British raiding parties.

The locals, who had been coerced into serving the food and drink, were cowed and jittery, clearly terrified of the Soviets. They were encouraged with the odd boot up the backside, but nothing more. After seeing the dormitories at the factory, Towers could not work up any great indignation about the odd slap or kick. The surviving labourers had been brought to town and accommodated in an old schoolhouse until the Red Cross could be notified. Towers made the German boy they had taken prisoner look after them, under British supervision. His first job was to scrounge a change of clothes from the households in the village and burn the existing, lice-ridden ones. Towers explained that he was lucky not to have been shot by one side or the other, and he set about the work without protest.

'Alan,' said Pagodin, tipping another vodka down his throat, 'are you in the mood for some entertainment?'

'Ent . . . enter-whatment?' he slurred. 'Why not. Is it a sing-song?'

Ovechkin laughed so hard Towers thought he would break a blood vessel. 'A sing-song. Yes. Come.'

The trio struggled to their feet and Towers was led outside. The main square was deserted, and the long-promised snow was swirling about them. Their feet crunched on the fresh fall, muffling the sound of the Russians' hobnails. Pagodin passed Towers the vodka bottle he had stashed beneath his coat.

'Where are we going?' Alan asked.

'To the gymnasium,' said Ovechkin.

'The gym?'

'For exercise,' confirmed Pagodin. Both Russians giggled.

The gymnasium was a black-painted wooden hall on the edge of town. Lights were recklessly blazing from the window that had steamed up with condensation. As they opened the door, a fist of fuggy warmth hit Towers, causing him to almost stagger back. The smell, the tang of semen and sweat, was overwhelming.

The air was filled with the slap of naked flesh colliding and low grunts were intermingled with more pitiful sounds. These latter were coming from the women and girls who had been brought to form the 'entertainment' the Russians had promised. They had been placed around the gymnasium, some tied to wall bars, others stretched over vaulting horses, others simply laid out on the floor, too terrified, or broken, to move. Few of them had any clothes left on. Many showed signs of bruising, livid weals and bitemarks.

Each woman had attracted a group of soldiers in various forms of undress. The members of some of these clusters were all sated, flushed and breathing hard, allowing their victim a moment of respite while the men recovered from their brutal exertions. Others were still actively indulging in what had gone far beyond rape, those waiting in line sometimes yelling encouragement to their comrades or demanding he hurry up and get off the bitch.

One young girl lay ignored in a corner in the foetal position, a halo of blood around her head, not moving. An obviously pregnant woman sat next to her, naked, knees under her chin, rocking back and forth on her bruised buttocks. The woman reached out and stroked her immobile companion's hair. Towers realised they were most likely mother and daughter.

An officer was staggering around the hall, flies undone, his erection poking out between the buttons. He pushed his way to the front of the queue for one of the girls spreadeagled over a vaulting horse and noisily entered her. Clearly dissatisfied, he withdrew, shook his head and, with clenched teeth, forced his way into her anus and began pumping. The girl groaned, but as her head lolled towards Towers, he could tell she was past understanding what was being done to her. It was a blessing, he thought.

'Oh, shit,' Towers said softly to himself.

He must have uttered it louder than he thought, because several of the soldiers nearby turned and looked at him. One raised a bottle in invitation. The other pointed to a prostrate woman, face down on the scuffed floor, and indicated she was free for the moment.

The room begin to spin, so fast Towers had trouble separating the bodies from each other, and as they blurred together, he felt the vodka in his stomach rise and burn his insides. A hand gripped his bicep, urging him forward, directing him to participate. He shrugged it off and turned on his heel, staggering as he did so. His heel had slithered on a patch of heavily-clotted blood. He heard mocking laughter and a jeer from the soldiers.

The wave of sobriety that swept through his brain carried him out of the gymnasium and he retraced his steps through the dancing flakes. He paused once to lean against the wall of a house and vomit into the snow, the stream of acid and alcohol eating into his throat. Towers remained there, bent double, for a few seconds, waiting for the fire to subside. He stood and straightened his clothes and ran a sleeve across his mouth. Then he composed himself and entered the refectory, behaving as matter-of-factly as he could manage. He waited for a second before he announced himself. 'T-Force, fall in.'

Nobody turned a hair. They couldn't hear him. There was a ribald singing competition in full voice. The matter-of-fact approach wasn't going to work. He yanked out his pistol and, after some effort, managed to point it at the ceiling. 'T-Force!' The boom of the discharge killed the song in the soldiers' throats. 'T-Force. Time to bed down. Thank our hosts and leave. Now.' He tried to make the words as strong, and as final, as possible, but he knew he was still shaky. 'At once, if you will.'

Unfocused, bleary eyes turned towards him. He could see anger and dismay on the faces of his men and the Russians. A bottle came arcing over from the rear, and smashed against the wall behind him. Somebody cheered.

'Get fucked.'

Who said that? Towers almost asked it out loud, but thought better of it. He felt like a schoolmaster with a class slipping out of his control. He considered another shot, but Corporal Dobson, his driver, perhaps sensing his desperation, rose to his feet. 'Oi' he roared. 'Now you listen here.'

The drunks took their eyes from Towers and glared at Dobson

instead. One of the sappers opposite him stood and pointed an accusing finger. 'You brown-nosed bastard—' he began. Dobson reached out, snapped the accusing digit back on itself and punched the soldier hard in the face. The man swayed back, the bench caught his legs and he crumpled to the floor.

The Corporal softened his tone as he addressed them once more. 'Come on, lads. Drink up. You already look like shit. I don't want you cunts feeling like shit tomorrow. We've got a bloody job to do.'

The silence that followed was eventually broken by a loud belch from one of the Russians. A British soldier topped it with a thunderous bass rumble and there was scattered applause. 'And on that charming fucking note,' said Dobson, pointing to the man he had felled, 'let's get out of here. And somebody pick that wanker up.'

The T-Force Private sitting next to the Corporal threw back his vodka and upended the glass with a crash. As Dobson did likewise and walked away from his table, the others followed, one by one. The Russians carried on grumbling, not appreciating their excuse for a party being snatched so early, before they could drink the British under the table.

As Dobson walked past Towers, the latter murmured to him from the corner of his mouth, 'Get them in the trucks, Dobbo. We're going back to the factory. We'll kip there as best we can.'

Dobson looked puzzled, wondering what had brought on the change of heart.

'I'll tell you why later,' Towers said tiredly. 'These are not our people, Corporal. The party's definitely over.'

Thirty-two

Berlin, 1948

Towers's voice had grown so quiet that Laura had to strain to hear his words. 'The Russians . . .'

He began to scratch his temple in a shaky, obsessive way. Frightened he might break the skin, Laura reached up and took his hand away.

'They had collected women on their way through Germany. Kept them locked in trucks. Every stop, they set up a rape centre. This one was a gym, with wall bars, vaulting horses, a trampoline. They made use of it all. You can imagine. They scoured the countryside for new victims to add to their travelling harem. Any age would do.' Towers took a deep breath. 'We pulled out at first light, taking our jet engines and scientists with us. But Bronsdorf is why I am still here. I felt no great sympathy for the Germans after what they had done, then or now, but there is a limit. This was beyond any limit you can imagine.'

'Good grief. How simply hideous.' It seemed a pathetic reaction to such horror, but she could think of no appropriate words. There probably weren't any.

'Quite. You know, there are those who say the rapes here were tolerated by the Red Army High Command because the Russians

246

couldn't believe that the Germans who behaved like barbarians in their country were so privileged. When they got here, they expected Germany to be more primitive than Russia. Populated by animals. Then they found flushing toilets, central heating, and middle-class homes. They went berserk because it had been a so-called civilised society that had committed the atrocities against them.'

'Do you believe that?'

'It might be part of it. But the Harz Mountains chaps didn't need any social envy to egg them on. They behaved like beasts.' He nodded towards the barracks. 'That's why the 112th Shock doesn't actually shock me.' He gave a feeble laugh. 'That's why I don't want them coming any further than this.'

They sat in silence for a while, the need for conversation negated by the noise from above. Her mouth had gone dry, and she fought to stop terrible images playing across her mind.

'It's a bit of a grim topic, isn't it?' Alan said eventually.

'But it's the truth.'

'Unfortunately, it is. Shall we change the subject? Discuss something cheery like atomic fallout?'

'All right. What's Jimmy Webb like?' Laura asked.

'Jimmy? I'm marginally better on atomic fallout. He's ... I admire him greatly, but I don't really know him. He's hard to get close to. He's not much older than me, but I tend to think of him as a kindly but rather distant papa. You know the type?'

She nodded. 'Sees the children in the library, washed and scrubbed, just before bedtime.'

'Precisely. But I think that's just an act. It's not the same man you see on the running track or on an operation. It's as if he has to create a persona for himself as James Hadley Webb, master spy. I shouldn't be saying this, should I? Personally, I think he analyses all this too much. Spying, I mean. It's not helped by—' He stopped.

'By what?'

'Nothing.' She felt the shutters coming down. Confession time was over. 'He had a strange war, too. But you'd better ask him.'

'Will I meet him then? You'll report back on me? I hope it will be favourable.'

He took a final swig of schnapps and replaced the cap. The smile that came was the old one, complete with twinkling eyes, and the voice was stronger again. 'Very favourable.'

Thirty-three

As in much of Berlin, the dwellings of Kreuzberg had had their façades blasted off by Allied bombs and Russian shells. Here, though, unlike the rest of the West, there hadn't been even the feeblest attempt at reconstruction above the ground floor. Some of the blocks were missing an entire curtain wall. Whole rooms still sat exposed to the elements, fireplaces and wallpaper, plumbing and electrics naked to the world. It was somehow obscene, a public display of the private and personal, like an elderly matron whose skirt had blown up to reveal her bloomers.

Yet people still lived up there, their presence betrayed by the pinpricks of light from the kerosene lamps they fashioned from old gas masks, visible to Webb as he drove through the streets towards Oberbaumbrücke. The bridge over the Spree marked the boundary between the Kreuzberg and Mitte districts, as well as acting as the demarcation line between West and East.

Midnight, the exchange was to take place. As melodramatic as ever, Webb thought. Once it had been established that he had a KI Major to trade for Ernst Henkell, the Russians had haggled only over where the swap should be performed. He had suggested the Brandenburg Gate, they had gone for the Glencoe Bridge at Potsdam; eventually they'd settled on Kreuzberg, in the American sector. But at midnight.

'We're here,' said Towers to the driver. 'Any further and we'll probably lose a tyre.' The headlamps picked out a street that, like so many in this district, petered out into a scree of bricks and mortar.

The two cars pulled up near the canal and Webb got out. Two of the SAS men, Sergeant Gallagher and Private Moss, in plainclothes now, were in the following vehicle, with the snatched Russian Major between them. Webb tried to hold his breath as he signalled them to get out and follow. Raw sewage from ruptured mains still leaked into the city's waterways, a stench that assaulted them now from the canal.

Once Webb had checked the batteries in his torch, the group of five walked quickly through the dark streets, picking their way over the rubble and rubbish that littered the pavements. The road sparkled in the feeble light, as if bejewelled, but it was tiny fragments of glass from a thousand bomb-shattered windows.

The once-beautiful redbrick Gothic bridge over the Spree had been sideswiped by an HE bomb and was unsafe for road traffic and for the U-Bahn, which used to run across an elevated section of it. Now only pedestrians crossed it, walking quickly beneath the twin towers in the central arch, which had also been declared unsafe.

There had been plane trees on the approach at one time, thought Webb. He'd walked here on a couple of dates with an Embassy secretary back in 1936. There had been a coffee-stall, too, which sold excellent gingerbread and *Braune Taler*.

As the buildings fell away, and they could see the dark expanse of the River Spree, Webb saw that the stall and the trees had long gone. Only their stumps remained. Some DPs had set up camp amongst them, but the makeshift tents were still and quiet.

'You armed?' asked Webb.

Towers pointed a thumb at the soldiers. 'Well, I've got two fully loaded Special Air Service men. Are you?'

Webb nodded.

'Truth is, sir, you're a lot safer if I'm not carrying. I'll show you my rifle scores sometime. Any bull is perfectly safe while I'm around.'

'Just don't get in my way if I draw my weapon,' his boss snapped. Clearly, it wasn't a time for levity. Where was the friendly but distant papa figure now, wondered Towers.

'You think there'll be shooting?' he asked, but Webb didn't answer.

They reached the southern side of the bridge and stopped. Their bank and the main span were in silky darkness, but the northern end, the Russian zone, blazed away. *We have electricity to burn*, they were saying. *All the coal and gas we need. How are you chaps doing?* Webb checked his watch. Midnight plus one. There was no movement on the far side of the bridge.

After ten minutes, he turned to their prisoner. 'They're late.'

The Russian shrugged. 'Maybe they don't want me any more.'

A flashlight flicked on and off three times and Webb smiled. 'Oh, I think they do, Major.' He returned the signal. 'Wait here.'

'You want me to come?' asked Towers.

'No. But if I get taken, ask our chaps to shoot him.'

The Russian's head spun around to try and get some indication from the others if Webb was joking.

Webb stepped onto the bridge, keeping as far over to the left as he could. The arches of the U-Bahn track to the right held deep, dark shadows where anyone could be lurking. It was a warm night, but he had a gabardine on all the same. He was carrying a 1911 Colt automatic in what he fancied was a rather Bogart-ish shoulder-holster. It had been Dolan's gift; it seemed churlish not to try it out.

When he was a third of the way across he saw movement on the other side. There was a cluster of perhaps a dozen people in place. He was outnumbered. A figure detached itself from the group and walked briskly towards him. The streetlamps caught the metal on his chest and cap, but it took Webb a few moments before he was sure who it was: Colonel Grusenko from the Staats Opera, of the nose-in-the-glove stunt. Of course, border security coordinated any exchanges. The Russian slowed as he approached. Webb removed his hat, to help identification.

'My dear James Hadley Webb,' the Russian said in his thick accent. He seemed pleasantly surprised, as if he had met an old friend while taking an evening constitutional. 'We seem to have swapped luggage by mistake.'

They met at the apex of the bridge and shook hands. 'Colonel. Thank you for the gift at the Opera.'

'Pah. It was nothing. Those people never know when to stop. It was tit for tit.' Webb let the mistake go. 'It's no way to behave. And thank you for yours.' He sniffed his own armpit. 'The soap is still going strong.'

'It's good we could do business, Colonel.'

'Not for long. I am retiring.'

Red Army Colonels tended not to retire. They were either promoted or shot. 'Really?'

'From Berlin, at least. I have been recalled.' He winked. 'A little weakness for a certain Fräulein.'

'I'm sorry to hear that.' At one time a German mistress was a spoil of war; now it was grounds for dismissal. Such fraternisation was a security risk, Moscow had decided.

'Don't worry, Jimmy Webb, I will be glad to leave this place. Now, shall we do this?'

Webb pointed over Grusenko's shoulder with his torch. 'I need to see his face first.'

The Russian looked disappointed. 'James, James. You think we have marked him?'

'No, Colonel. I just want to make sure it's Ernst. I don't want there to have been another little confusion.'

'Of course.' Grusenko made a gesture behind his back and three people stepped onto the bridge. A flashlight was shone in Ernst's face and he screwed his eyes up in pain. But it was the *Detektiv*, all right.

Webb waved at Towers and the two SAS men advanced onto the bridge. In the tiny gap between his breathing and Grusenko's, Webb heard a movement – the scrape of a boot on stone perhaps. He kept his eyes straight ahead, as if he hadn't noticed anything remiss.

'Colonel, I am going to walk back now. Slowly. When I reach your man, I will send him forward.' Grusenko made to speak, but Webb raised a hand. 'I know this is unsporting, but there is a Special Forces sniper on the apartment block behind me. I would imagine you are in his crosshairs right now.'

'Jimmy—'

'If your man under the arches,' now he let his eyes flick, 'does anything, even shows his face, then . . .' He snapped his fingers to mimic the shot that would take the Colonel's head off.

'A sniper?'

'Yes.'

'Really?' Grusenko's eyes grew wide, challenging him in the lie. 'You would do that?'

Webb held his gaze. 'Care to find out?'

'When I am due to see my beautiful wife so soon?' He laughed at the very thought. 'Take care, Jimmy Webb.'

'You too, Colonel Grusenko.'

Webb backed away, placing his feet carefully, his eyes never leaving the Russian, wishing he had thought of a sniper for real. After twenty metres, he turned and strode briskly. When he reached his group, he clicked his fingers once more and the Russian Major pulled himself free and began to walk north.

The Kripo *Detektiv* also started forward, slightly unsteady on his feet. It was unlikely he had had much sleep for the last few days. At least, Webb hoped that was all that was wrong with him.

The two hostages passed on the central span, exchanging the

slightest of nods. On the home leg, Henkell picked up speed and Webb moved forward to greet him.

'Ernst. Thank God. Are you all right?'

The German threw his arms open and hugged the Englishman, who steadied himself as Ernst let his weight go. The *Detektiv* took a deep breath and pushed himself upright. 'Yes. Thank you. Thank you for the exchange. Jimmy, I have to tell you this—'

The shot rang out from the arches, and Webb saw the stab of the muzzle flash briefly illuminate the shooter under the arches, and then he was gone. The report echoed along the water. A startled heron burst from the reeds, its ghostly shape flapping into the sky.

'Shit,' cursed Webb.

On the bridge, the Russian Major swayed once, twice, and then collapsed into a formless heap. At that moment, the lights on the northern bank died and there was the sound of hobnails on asphalt and a body being dragged unceremoniously away.

Eager hands grabbed Webb and the *Detektiv*, and the two SAS men pulled and pushed them off the bridge. 'Come on, move it!' Gallagher barked. With the soldiers providing cover, the group moved quickly to the cars. They were almost there, when Ernst tugged Webb to a standstill. 'Just in case anything happens, I have to tell you this.'

'What?'

'When they questioned me, before Grusenko took me, they seemed mostly interested in one thing.'

'What?'

'Librarian. That's what they kept saying: what did I know about Librarian?'

Webb squeezed his friend's arm to let him know it was OK, and pushed him on towards safety, but he felt ice running in his veins.

'There's more, Jimmy.'

'I know.' There always was. 'It can wait until you get some sleep, Ernst.'

But he knew he didn't have that much patience. It was going to be a long night for both of them.

Thirty-four

The next morning, a bleary Jimmy Webb found the letter in his brown suit, the one he had travelled in from London. He had opened it on the plane, but forgotten about it. He had, in fact, all but forgotten about Olivia these past few days. He made himself a cup of tea, opened the windows on the balcony and read it, a despondency creeping over him as he did so.

My Dear Jimmy,

I hope you are well. It was lovely to see you in Henley. Of course, I did everything all wrong, the way I always do, badgering you to do this and that. I am sorry. I hope you take the time to read this letter. And try to understand the spirit in which it is written.

I love you, Jimmy. Even though I am about to say some difficult things, please remember that. I tried my best to convince myself that what happened between us in the war was nobody's fault. And that Philip, especially, would not begrudge us. Every time, though, I get close to you, I can feel him, standing at my shoulder. I know it sounds crazy, but I think you do, too. It is what stops you from wanting to be with me all the time. I remind you too much of what happened.

The thing is, Jimmy, I have met someone else. Someone who

256

doesn't conjure up the spirit of Philip. I know you'd like him. A widower. He has two delightful boys, whom I've met, and as long as I am up to date with my Wisden *I am sure we will get along just fine. His wife was killed in one of the first V-1 attacks. He was on Monty's staff for most of the war. Nothing glamorous, no heroics, no cloak and dagger ballyhoo either.*

But he is kind and he is cheerful and I think he might be where my future lies.

I do hope you forgive me, Jimmy. I also hope you find the peace and happiness that I clearly can't give you.

All my fondest wishes, as always,

Olivia

Webb reread it one more time, then screwed it up and placed it in the grate. It was probably for the best, he told himself, reaching for a bottle of schnapps. Probably for the best. He kept repeating it between sips until he almost believed it.

'Why did they kill the Major?' asked a puzzled Towers. 'Why do it right under our noses?'

They were in Canteen Four (Civilian), which was built under the stands at the Olympic Stadium, struggling through a Spam and tomato stew. It was a grim windowless room, the walls glossy with lurid green paint, the bulbs bare, the chemical smell of reconstituted food thick in the air. It matched Webb's mood perfectly.

'I think to make a point,' he answered tiredly.

Towers drank from his white enamel mug of tea. He was surprised by Webb's appearance. His superior hadn't shaved and his shirt collar was grubby. Even the tie had been carelessly knotted. 'The point being?' asked Towers.

'They will have guessed we tried to turn him. Even though we didn't succeed – which they had no way of knowing – they wouldn't have let him continue in Kl after being contaminated by us. Best just to make a show of strength, illustrate how little a human life means to them.'

Towers snorted. 'I don't think we need to be told that.'

'No. Quite.' Still, he thought, the sniper's bullet had saved the Major from a slow death, breaking rocks in a punishment camp. By Soviet standards, it was almost humanitarian. Webb pushed his food away, not even half-eaten, and took solace in a Senior Service.

'Did you get anything else from Ernst?' asked Towers.

'Yes – that the coffee is even worse over there.' He puffed on the cigarette. 'So . . . Laura McGill. What did you make of her?'

'I like her. She's a strange mixture of fragile and fierce. That's attractive. I know that wasn't why you sent me. In the old days we would have called her a filly.'

'Alan,' he said wearily. 'Stick to the point for once.'

'She told me the whole story. Says you knew her sister well.'

Webb felt a pain in his chest that he wasn't entirely sure was indigestion. 'I did. Diana – pretty thing. Brave, too.'

'Laura thinks she is still alive.'

Webb grunted. 'If only that were true.'

Towers let the next sentence drop carefully. 'And she thinks you are hiding something – about why Diana's file is blocked.'

Webb took a longer drag on the cigarette. He needed some fresh air. 'She's right. I am.'

'Are you going to share it?'

He was already extracting the next Senior Service from the packet, poised to light it from the stub of the current one. 'Philip and Diana were betrayed by one of their group. Turned over to the Gestapo.'

'Who was it?'

Webb took out his hip-flask and poured a generous measure of whisky into his mug. He took a gulp, and Towers could smell the malt, fresh on his breath, as Webb leaned forward, shocking him with what he whispered next. 'The man they knew as Georges.'

'The Frenchmen? The *chef du terrain*?'

'Yes.'

'Blimey. Is that why there was a Blue on the file?'

'Yes and no. We got Georges at the end of the war. By that time, he'd been running with the Germans so long, he could pass for one. We turned him again.'

'Even though he betrayed your friend—'

Webb didn't want to hear any admonishments from a boy who didn't yet understand what it was like to make these sorts of decisions. He hoped he never did. 'Georges was an asset. A good one. It overrode any personal feelings.' Something, Webb realised, at which he had become far too accomplished. 'Thing is, Alan, Georges the Resistant is Librarian.'

Hindenburg Park, in the southern part of Wilmersdorf, was where James Hadley Webb liked to go to think. As with the Zoo, large swathes of the lawns had been given over to growing vegetables, and he enjoyed watching people weed and dig and compare the size of their onions or cabbages. There was laughter here and a feeling of purpose, the city at its best. There was also camaraderie of danger – digging into the soil anywhere in Berlin was risky. Only the previous week one of the toilers had discovered an unexploded *katyusha* rocket, the howling banshees known as Stalin's Organ, which had rained down on the city in 1945.

They were mostly women who dug, of course; the occasional older man and some young boys were in evidence, but a whole generation and gender was absent. There was one solitary lad in his twenties, but he didn't work the vegetables, he simply looked on as his mother tended her tiny patch, his eyes dull and empty. She occasionally tried to chivy him into helping, but he always refused, with a frightened shake of the head. Webb could only imagine what scenes all the digging and hoeing conjured up for the lad. He usually stayed for an hour until his *Mutti*, tired of an uncooperative audience, shooed him home.

Sometimes Webb got strange looks from the workers, especially any newcomers who hadn't seen him before. He understood why. In the cloying heat of summer many of the women stripped off to their camisole tops or vests and often tied up their skirts. His interest could be construed as prurient, but he wasn't here for vicarious sexual thrills. He just wanted to be part of the furniture, lost in thought and their easy, familiar ritual.

Webb sat on his usual bench near the children's playground at the eastern end of the long, thin stretch of greenery, the scorched letter he had retrieved from the fireplace tucked into his pocket once more. He could feel the heat of it, though, as if it were glowing, radioactive, a poison seeping into his blood. If only he knew what the antidote was, but he had exhausted every possibility. He was losing her to someone safe and steady. Strange, he had never thought of Olivia taking the soft option, of settling for suburbia, all *Wisden* and wisteria.

The problem was, he couldn't offer that. Nothing like it. Nor did he want to try. She had to take him on face value, a man who would work in espionage for as long as he felt he was doing some good. It was just that the definition of 'good' was becoming more woolly by the day. Olivia was right – in one sense, he did miss the certainties, the extraordinary clarity of the recent war. He envied that McGill woman her clear-cut sense of purpose: to find out what became of her sister. One declared aim and an empirical way of judging success or failure. He no longer had that luxury.

Webb could feel the swollen, black river of depression snaking towards him. It had only engulfed him three or four times in his life, but when it did the results were terrifying. A paralysis had come over him, preventing him from making even the most trivial of decisions. He couldn't afford to have it happen again, not now. He crushed the vision of the dark, swirling water, hurling it to the back of his mind.

He held her letter to his nose to try and catch a last hint of her perfume. There was nothing there, not even a vague trace, just the dry aroma of old ashes from the fireplace. Without bothering to read it again, he tore the missive into tiny pieces. James Hadley Webb, the spy, dumped the confetti into the cast-iron waste-bin next to the swings and left the diggers to their work. He needed two things. First, he would visit Lee Crane in the holding cell, and explain what a Pavlovsky was. Then Jimmy Webb, the human being, would have a drink. A big one.

Thirty-five

'Keep the McGill woman busy,' had been Webb's instructions to Towers. Well, he didn't have to be asked twice. So Alan Towers thought long and hard about where to take Laura for their night out. The Blaues Zimmer was too louche, too full of familiar faces and gossip. There were some places in the East such as the Polp that were fun, in a seedy kind of way. But there were always those thin, undernourished women hanging around. It had been a while since he'd succumbed – Webb discouraged that kind of fraternisation, East or West – but there was a potential for embarrassment all the same. The Café Nord, a converted department store, was little more than a giant marketplace, where you were constantly offered a *Zentner* of Eastern potatoes in exchange for packs of cigarettes. It wouldn't be the best start for a date, walking around with sacks of smuggled spuds.

In the end, he settled on the Hotel Endel as a good bet. It was in northern Schöneberg, in the American sector, and although it had its fair share of *Amiliebchen*, girls cruising for GIs, it was big enough to absorb them and the management maintained a cap on the numbers of predatory women.

He dressed casually, in what was known as the Ami-style, with an open-necked shirt, a lovat sports jacket and flannel trousers. When he picked her up from the Charlot, Laura had on a skirt and blouse with a wide belt that accentuated her waist. They would do.

The ballroom of the Endel had been carved in half by a screen of artificial miniature palms, making the dance-floor smaller, but allowing for a larger area for tables and, most importantly of all, a much longer bar, which the Yanks seemed to appreciate. Many of them preferred sitting there, perched on stools, than being out on the main floor.

The celebrated vaulted ceiling, with its golden cherubs and bucolic *trompe l'oeil* hunting scenes, remained intact, although the once-famed chandelier, a gift from the Tsar, had been an early victim of the RAF. The less grandiose replacement looked rather forlorn up there, its cheap cut-glass pendants failing to sparkle.

When they arrived, a willowy German singer was attempting an American accent, mangling the vowels of 'Fifteen Hugs After Midnight'.

'Golly,' said Laura, taking it all in. 'This is quite a place.'

'It's not much, but it's home,' said Towers.

They found a table at the far end, near the row of plastic palms, and he ordered champagne.

'Extravagant,' she said.

'Not really,' he said, thinking of the favourable exchange rate, even at black-market prices. 'I mean to say, yes, nothing but the best. Are you hungry?'

'Not yet.'

'Good, because the food here isn't really up to snuff. The chef learned everything he knows on the Eastern Front. Horse, dog and rat he can do wonders with. Give him a steak and he's flummoxed.'

'That's not true!' she exclaimed. Then: 'Is it?'

He raised his eyebrows, as if surprised she should challenge him. 'Everything is true in Berlin.'

'You like this city, don't you?'

He shook out a cigarette and offered her one. She refused but said she was happy for him to smoke. 'Like is the wrong word, but there is nowhere else quite the same. Oh, it's maddening even when you aren't besieged like we are now. But there is a sense of doing an important job and drawing a line in the sand. This far and no further.'

'And the champagne is cheap.'

He let out an explosive laugh. 'Goodness, didn't I sound pompous? Yes, and the champagne is cheap. But also, you have to admire the Berliners.'

'Really?'

'Really. They've got what London had – a kind of Blitz spirit. And a sense of humour, too. Don't you believe it about them all being dull and humourless.' He winked. 'That's just the Prussians.'

When the drink arrived, he raised a glass. 'To Diana.'

'To tonight,' Laura said.

The champagne was sweeter than she expected. She wondered if it was real or a Sekt relabelled, then felt uncharitable. It was chilled, bubbly and had alcohol in it.

'Did you have a chance to speak to Mr Webb?' she asked.

He nodded. 'I did. He's a little . . . what's the word?'

'Busy?'

'Distracted.'

'The airlift?'

He couldn't tell her the news about Librarian, so he just nodded. She probably wouldn't understand why Georges had been allowed to live, after such treachery. He wasn't sure he did, either.

The singer took a break and the band struck up some shaky Glenn Miller. Towers was aware that gloom threatened to overwhelm their table. 'Dance?' he asked.

'You dance?' She sounded surprised.

'Oh, yes. Anything as long as it's a foxtrot.'

'All right.'

In fact, Towers moved her around the floor well, holding her lightly, but directing her with a pleasing positiveness. He wasn't much taller than her, which she liked. She never felt comfortable staring at a man's chest. And the alternative wasn't much better. 'You get much practice at this?' she asked.

'You mean – do I have a girlfriend?'

'Oh, there's no fooling you spies.'

'Sssh,' he hissed with mock-severity. 'But now you mention it, that is a problem – being in the Firm. Girls tend not to like being kept in the dark.'

'You need a girlfriend who knows the job.' He bit his lip on his reply. She coloured slightly when he realised what she had said. 'I wasn't offering.' She laughed. 'It's the champagne making me silly.'

'Then let's get some more.'

They broke off and went back to the table, hand-in-hand without even noticing the transition. This time she accepted the cigarette.

'What about you? There must be boyfriends. Scores of them.'

She shook her head. 'You know that song "Don't Get Around Much Any More"?'

'Duke Ellington,' he said. 'They usually play it later.'

She coughed as the smoke caught her throat. 'Well, it's rather been my theme tune for the last few years.'

'What about during the war?'

'There was this one chap I thought was sweet on me. American. Turned out he'd been ordered to spy on me to find out what we British were up to in Kunming.'

'Yanks, eh?' he said in mock disgust. 'Still, not a bad assignment.'

'What?'

He topped up her glass. 'Spying on you.'

'I—' She never finished the sentence, silenced by the look of shock on Towers's face. She followed his gaze to the man weaving his way across the dance-floor. He had on a three-piece suit, but the waistcoat was misbuttoned and the tie pulled loose. He reached their table and leaned his full weight on it, spilling champagne from the glasses. It frothed and hissed on the table like hot acid.

'Jimmy. I didn't know you were out tonight.'

'Looked everywhere for you,' he slurred, then swivelled towards her. 'Laura McGill?'

'Yes.'

He mouthed the next words with the exaggerated precision of the very drunk. 'James Hadley Webb.'

He held out a hand and, for a moment, she thought he was going to overbalance, so she grabbed it quickly.

'Just as pretty as your sister. And twice the bloody nuisance.' He tipped an imaginary hat, as if that were a compliment. 'I'm sorry about the way you were treated in the hospital in Kent.' He was, too. He hadn't realised she'd been put down for what they called, with horrible aptness, 'D Grade treatment'. 'Very sorry. You come to my office tomorrow. Alan knows where it is. Well, he should do – he's next door. We'll talk about Diana.'

'Yes, of course.'

'Tomorrow. Nine. May I?' He took a slug of the remnants of Towers's champagne. 'Or better yet, ten. G'night.'

They watched him move off, negotiating the tables unsteadily, both wondering what on earth *that* had all been about.

After dinner at Carlo's, a bogus Italian trattoria not far from the park, Towers walked Laura back to the Charlot through streets silvered by moonlight, skirting her around the feral kids and the half-glimpsed figures engaged in all things carnal and criminal. At one point he made her stop and listen. They could just make out the wail of bagpipes, incongruous and vaguely comical in this place. It made them both giggle.

Jimmy Webb had dominated the evening, though. She could tell Towers was concerned by his boss's erratic behaviour; Laura herself was anticipating the meeting, another step along the road to discovering the truth about Diana.

'Does Webb do that often?' she asked as they crossed over the railway tracks into Wedding. There were two British sentries on the bridge, which was regarded as a 'pinch point' for any Russian invaders, and Towers wished them a good evening, getting a grunt in reply.

'Get quite so plastered? No, not really.' Alan paused for a moment then continued. 'I suppose I shouldn't really tell you this,' he said, as they cleared the bridge and the Bren-gun emplacement on its northern side and moved into the shortcut that would take them through to the Charlot. 'There is one thing about Jimmy. He doesn't know I know. I mean, he told me, but he was in his cups, much like tonight, so I am not sure he remembers. He certainly hasn't mentioned it again. It concerns Diana.'

From the twisted metal doorway of a destroyed factory, a swaying figure lurched forward onto the pavement. She gripped Towers's arm more tightly and he instinctively stepped forward to shield her, but the man staggered harmlessly by in a waft of the mind-rot the derelicts brewed from whatever vegetable matter they could get hold of. Perhaps he should have called a car after all, Alan thought, but he had wanted to prolong the evening.

In the neglected isolation of the industrial district, the night had grown darker as clouds danced across the moon. Towers took his Ever Ready pocket torch from his jacket and switched it on. A family of rats scampered away from the yellowy beam, but Laura appeared not to notice.

'About Diana,' she said, picking up the conversation. 'You don't mean that Diana and Jimmy Webb were . . . ?'

'Gosh, no,' he said quickly. 'I meant it was to do with Diana's mission. Jimmy put it together, didn't he?'

'Yes. It's what I wanted to talk to him about.'

'Well, at one point Jimmy wanted to go himself, but they wouldn't let him. Too valuable, not experienced enough, whatever.'

Towers slowed as they reached a better-lit section of the city.

There were just two more streets to go. 'So he sent Philip Maxwell?' Laura prompted.

'Yes. Because . . .' He felt uncomfortable now, wishing he had never started on the story. 'Because he was having an affair with Olivia, Philip Maxwell's wife. They wanted some time together.'

He jerked to a halt as she stopped dead, her jaw open. 'That's terrible.'

'It seems so now, yes. Look, the war was full of love affairs. They wanted to see whether what they had was, well, worthwhile.'

'Worthwhile? Nicely put, Alan.'

Towers didn't answer for a while. It was probably best not to add that Philip had been Webb's best friend from school. It made his behaviour seem all the more despicable. 'You think he doesn't feel beastly about it? Like your sister, Philip was meant to be back within days. Instead he ended up—'

'At Flossenburg. That's why Webb went looking for him at the end of the war, didn't he? Out of guilt. I suppose he and this Olivia are happily married now.'

'Oh, far from it,' he muttered, realising at last what the cause of Webb's misery must be. He could take the deaths of agents in his stride, but he hadn't been himself since his return from England. 'The exact opposite, in fact, I suspect.'

'Well, there is some justice, then.'

For once, Towers was lost for a quip. 'My father knows Webb from well from before the war, and he knew Philip. I discussed it with him once. He says Jimmy is an honourable chap. I think so, too.' There was no reply. He pointed at the hotel. 'Here we are.'

'Thank you.' Laura hesitated on the ruined steps of the darkened hotel. 'I hope someone is up.'

'Don't worry, we'll bang on the door until someone comes.'

'I had a nice evening,' she said.

'Good. I'm pleased. Perhaps we could do it again. The good bits, I mean, without Jimmy butting in. In the meanwhile, I'll pick you up tomorrow morning. Nine-thirty all right?'

'There's no need.'

'I insist. I'll be here.'

She smiled, walked up the steps, yanked the bell-pull and, after a second attempt at rousing the porter, a feeble light flickered on within. She waved to Alan as bolts slid back and the door opened, wondering as she stepped into the foyer, how she could now face Webb, knowing what she did.

Thirty-six

James Hadley Webb stood in the shabby bathroom down the hall from his office, looking at himself in the blackened mirror, which seemed to shed more silvering each day. 'Just a minute,' he shouted as someone tried the door and grumbled. He ran a comb through his hair and risked a splash from the bottle of Bristow's Astringent to try and stop the tiny blobs of blood that were oozing from his chin. He sucked air in through his teeth as his face exploded as if hit by nettles.

Apart from two purple crescents under his eyes, and the shaving cuts, he had survived the previous night quite well. He'd sobered up after seeing the girl and Towers, and had ended the evening at the Blaues Zimmer, talking with Dolan and being stood whiskies by a grateful Ernst, who had been given a fortnight's leave to get over his ordeal. Every time the *Detektiv* was distracted, he'd managed to dump most of the drink.

The door handle rattled once more and there was a thump. 'Can you hurry along, please?' There was a note of desperation to the voice.

Webb flushed the lavatory to indicate he was, indeed, hurrying along. As he rebuttoned his braces and slipped on his jacket he ran through the whole scheme he had dreamed up with Dolan one more time, convincing himself that it was worth the effort.

He hoped the outcome would be to his satisfaction; he suspected it wouldn't be. They had kept Ernst out of it, of course; it was a 'need-to-know' operation and Henkell didn't need to know. He'd find out later.

With a heartfelt sigh, Webb popped a lime drop into his mouth, hoping to mask the stale sourness of the alcohol, brushed the lapel of his blue pinstriped jacket, gathered up his washbag and unlocked the door. Time for James Hadley Webb to face the music.

Before he began, Webb poured himself a tumbler of Fachinger mineral water. He offered one to Laura McGill, but she shook her head. He tore open a sachet of BiSoDol and tipped the powder into the water, swirling the glass absent-mindedly. 'Thank you for coming, Miss McGill.'

'Thank you for seeing me, Mr Webb.'

'I hope Towers showed you the sights, such as they are.'

'He did, thank you. A perfect gentleman.' There was acid in her voice, she realised, and was careful to tone it down. She mustn't be aggressive and judgemental. 'It was a very pleasant evening. How was yours?'

He laughed at this and downed the glass of water and indigestion relief. He suppressed the bubble of gas that rose from his stomach. 'Pardon me. I just need a little remedial treatment and I'll be right as rain. So, about your sister.' He settled back in his chair and put the tips of his fingers together. 'I met her, of course.'

'I know. Tell me about that, if you wouldn't mind.'

Webb pinched the bridge of his nose. 'I can't remember much, to be honest. One tended not to get too involved. I do recall she was quick, intelligent, sharp.'

'But you remember Philip Maxwell?' she blurted out.

He looked up at the sharpness. When he replied, he sounded stung. 'I knew Philip before those days – from before the war. She couldn't have had a better partner, if that is what you were wondering.'

271

She waited until she was calm to say: 'No, of course not. That wasn't what I meant. Just that, you know, with Diana people seem to remember things like her looks. She was pretty. Vivacious. That kind of thing.'

'Did I say that? Bloody hell, we didn't judge a woman brave enough to go over by her looks. They were a special group of people.' He picked up a pencil and began to fiddle with it.

'I'm sorry. I don't seem to be making my points very well.' She brushed her hair behind her ears. 'Mr Webb . . .'

'Call me Jimmy,' he said. 'Everybody else does.'

'Jimmy, then. I am so used to being fobbed off, lied to, patronised, told I am wasting my time, that I should go off and live my life . . .'

'Oh, me too. Me too.' He allowed himself a broad grin, and for the first time she realised he wasn't simply a grumpy spy who liked to go one over the eight. There was a flash of an attractive person buried under the hangover. 'I am not going to lie to you.' He leaned forward, his eyes clear, seemingly invigorated. Perhaps the BiSoDol was working, she thought. 'Your sister was betrayed.'

She gulped at the four words. Her heart spasmed in her chest and she pressed on her sternum to alleviate the pressure. 'Betrayed?'

'Yes. They knew about the prison bribe, about the sisters.'

'Who told them? Was it the go-between at the prison?'

'No.' Webb paused, as if unwilling to take this step. 'It was Georges.'

'Georges? But he was one of ours.'

'*And* one of theirs. A double.'

'Betrayed? Is that why there was a Blue? Because there would be outrage if the public knew there was a double agent operating in SOE?'

Webb scratched an earlobe. 'Not exactly. The block was because we didn't want anyone trying to track down Georges, to discover what happened to him after the war. He is still alive, you see. Still working for us, in fact.'

It came to her quickly. 'In the East.'

'Yes. His codename is Librarian. He is valuable. Very valuable.'

'So valuable you could forgive him for betraying your friend and my sister? Turning them over to those butchers?'

'Yes, I am afraid so. That valuable. In fact, we recruited worse than Georges. Oh yes, we prosecuted and hanged every Nazi war criminal and traitor and double agent we could get our hands on, unless they were of some use to us. Then it was a different story.' He cleared his throat. 'You have to separate the practical from the personal.'

She let this sink in. '*You* might, Mr Webb. Does he know what happened to Diana?'

Webb poured himself some more water; Laura shook her head when he mimed another offer of some for her. 'Very possibly. He was at Avenue Foch enough times, was friends with Hans Keppler and his superior Boemelburg, the heads of the *Sicherheitsdienst*. The thing is, if Diana knew the traitor was Georges, then she would have been kept in solitary, just in case she found a way of getting a message back to London or to the Resistance that a *chef du terrain* had been turned. I would imagine that Georges would have kept close tabs on what happened to her.'

Laura was appalled. 'And you have never asked him about my sister?'

'It's part of the pact with this particular devil. We pretend that the other doesn't know the worst of his background. That's why he agreed to stay in deep cover.'

Laura stood up, feeling dizzy. She needed fresh air. 'Why are you telling me this now? After the lies in Paris?'

'Because Librarian is in danger. We need to get him out. The hounds are closing in on him. It will only be a matter of time before he is blown.'

She sensed something else. 'But?'

Now he fixed her in the eye once more, but his hands played with a pencil stub, rolling it over his knuckles. 'Georges is worried about coming back to the West, specifically to France, because of the *Juries d'Honneur* – old Resistants who run kangaroo courts and execute traitors. It's highly illegal, but tolerated by some in the French government. I am worried that he might try and take his chances over there and go to ground in the East. If he does, and they catch him . . . well, we don't need a show trial at this precise moment.'

'What can you do?'

'Go and fetch him. Persuade him to come – offer him protection. I know you'll find this hard to believe, but he has redeemed himself.'

Not in Laura's eyes, not by a long shot. 'And if he won't?'

'Then I'll give you fifteen minutes alone with him to discover what happened to Diana. You are likely to get further than me as regards your sister. You'll be speaking off the record, you see.'

It hit her like a runaway train, driving the breath from her body once more. 'Go East?' she gasped. 'What – you mean into the Russian zone?'

'Yes. Mountains and Mohammed and all that.'

The hospital room flashed back in clammy clarity, the stinking bucket, the lousy bedding, the rhythm of the cockroaches tap-tapping on the floor and the endlessly burning filament of the light bulb. 'Isn't that dangerous?'

'It's not without hazard, certainly. If you don't want to go, I'll understand.'

She didn't know what to say. It sounded like madness, but on the other hand, he was laying out an opportunity to question a man who might – only might – know what became of Diana.

'You need to think it over,' Webb said. It wasn't a question.

'Yes.'

'There is a mess down the hall. Take this.' He handed her a dining chit. 'There's some rather nice Aylmer's soup on the menu today, I believe. On your way out, send Towers in, will you?'

*   *   *

Go East? Just on the off-chance that a despicable little shit might have seen or heard something of Diana? It was crazy all right. East was where the Russians had reactivated the KZs as 'special camps', where they had slave labour down the mines, firing squads, prisons of cold, concrete boxes. Being apprehended over there would make the mental hospital seem like a day on Blackpool Pier.

She shuddered and sipped some more of the stewed tea the canteen girls had served from a large copper urn. It was too early for lunch, not even close to midday, but there were small knots of people tucking into soup and bread and Spam fritters.

She thought about the 112th Shock Battalion, the rapes and the venereal disease. The story that Alan had told her about the gymnasium, it was so horrid, it had to be true. Nobody could invent that. No wonder he wanted to stop the Reds coming across. Anyone would, after witnessing that. Yet she was going to cross over into that sickening world of her own free will?

Diana would have gone for you. She went across to France when the Germans were there.

And look what happened . . .

So you won't do the same thing to find her? There, we have finally come to the moment when you discover if you and Diana are the same. When you have to put up or shut up, as the Americans say. And you have been found wanting, Laura. Diana will know you aren't coming, that you have let her down.

A chair scraped opposite her as someone sat down. There was the rattle of a spoon on tin as they stirred their drink.

I am not a coward. I flew into China.

It's not the same.

The person opposite lit a cigarette and grey wraiths of smoke curled over her arms.

Maybe not, but I did my part, she answered her inner voice. This is deranged. It doesn't make sense. Surely you have to weigh up benefit against risk. The risk is definite; the rewards less than guaranteed.

She'd do it for you.

Yes, yes she would. I'll do it for her, then. I'll do it for Diana.

Laura knew that what had happened at the mental hospital had introduced a seam of fear into her, a horror of being in that situation again, at someone else's mercy. And that realisation also made her accept that she had to fight against it, or *they* had won. She had to dig deep and find the resolve to go East. Just like Diana would.

'Laura.'

It took a second for her to place the voice. She looked up, and felt a wave of shock hit her.

'You OK?'

He reached over and touched her wrist and she realised he was real, not a product of her overheating mind. 'Lee? Lee Crane?' She felt her hand fly to her mouth and forced it away. The last time she had seen this man had been in China, thousands of miles and another life away. 'What on earth are you doing here?'

He gave a lopsided grin. 'In a roundabout way I still don't fully understand, I'm here working for Webb,' he said. The Englishman had had him 'arrested' by MPs and had laid out his scheme. After a drag on the Camel cigarette, he added: 'I know what he is proposing, Laura. He told me. We're going in by air. If you want to go over there, I'll be the one who'll be taking you.'

Her eyes widened at this. 'You?'

'Yup. I'm Jimmy's Cab Company, it seems. We fly anywhere, anytime. We just don't tell anyone about it.'

'I don't believe it.'

'I can show you my logbook,' he replied.

'No, not that. I can't quite grasp it's you, here, now.'

'It is. I am your man. Take it or leave it.'

As she sat there, trying to make sense of what he was saying, she knew one thing. Their relationship, such as it was, may have ended badly back in China, but there was never any suggestion that Lee Crane wasn't excellent at his job. And that job had often been getting her from Calcutta to Kunming in one piece. The man could fly better than she could walk.

Laura McGill accepted that, if Lee Crane was at the controls of this crazy enterprise, then she would be going over.

Thirty-seven

Over the next few days Lee Crane put together an 'intruder' crew, with the help of Webb. Crane told him what kind of men he required, Webb pulled strings and studied personnel records until he found suitable candidates.

First to join the team was Leonid 'Len' Stanislaw, a Pole, who would act as co-pilot. Webb had found Len working as a clerk. After serving with RAF Transport Command, he'd returned to Poland after the war and fled when he'd discovered exactly how exalted an ex-Allied flyer would be under the new regime: work camps beckoned. He came to Berlin on one of the refugee trains, lucky not to have frozen to death en route, as hundreds did. Fortunately, he'd kept all his old service papers and, although he couldn't re-enlist, sympathetic officers had found him a civilian desk job.

Next up was Donald Turnbull, a softly-spoken Geordie. He was another ex-RAF man who had been employed in the UK on a civilian engineering contract and brought across to Berlin. Webb had located him in the Royal Engineers' workshop at Spandau, fitting plugs and changing valves.

He introduced them to each other at the hangar in Gatow where *Three of a Kind* was awaiting her big adventure. Then he introduced them to the plane, going over her carefully, hoping they'd be as appreciative of her as he was. He felt like a suitor bringing his fiancée home for inspection. When he had finished the tour he asked: 'So what do you think?'

'Is fine,' said Len in his heavily accented English.

'So, Lennie, you clocked how many C-47 co-pilot hours?'

'On Dakotas? Is what we called them. Dakotas.'

'I know.'

'Troop drops D-Day, gliders over Arnhem, target towing, over two hundred hours.'

'You like them?' Crane asked casually.

'The Dakota?' He touched *Three of a Kind*'s fuselage with his fingertips, brushing the metal gently, as if it were skin, not aluminium. 'Best plane ever built.'

It was the right answer, the only one that would have satisfied Crane. Didn't matter whether it was the finest or not – and he could think of some B-17, Mosquito, Spitfire, P-51 and P-47 pilots who'd put up a convincing counter-argument – it was blind loyalty he liked and wanted. You had to trust and admire the plane you flew, even if all the evidence told you it was a dog. And the Gooney Bird was anything but.

'Captain Crane. Can I have a word?' It was Donald Turnbull, raising his finger timidly, as if he were asking to go to the john during class, thought Crane.

'Sure.'

'Just the two of us?' He looked guiltily at Len, who picked up immediately.

'I go check in cockpit that I remember where everything is. OK?'

Crane nodded and then walked Turnbull under the Pratt & Whitney of the starboard wing, checking for leaks as he went. Outside, one of the flying gas tankers of Flight Refuelling Limited was being unloaded. He could smell the fumes, and it made him nervous. If one of those ever went up at Gatow, there'd be an almighty crush at the Pearly Gates.

'What's on your mind?' he asked.

'I have been looking at these frequencies you gave me—'

'That Mr Webb gave you.'

'Yes. The ones he wants scanned on the flight.'

'Uh-huh?'

Turnbull began to recite from his notes. 'I have 2695 to 2715 MegaHertz, 2900 to 2990 MegaHertz, 2715 to 2750 MegaHertz, 2990 to 3025 MegaHertz—'

'Beano! Well, bingo. It was beano in my time. You know the guy that wrote all those bingo cards with the numbers on them? Apparently, he did six thousand of them and then went insane.' Crane couldn't help himself; he loved seeing the English puff up at what they considered an American's insufferable flippancy in the face of really serious matters. 'Sorry. Read it in *Ripley's Believe It Or Not*. OK, what about them?'

'But then also 95 to 210 Megahertz. The Freya range.'

'The point being, Don?'

'Donald.' The Geordie swallowed. Crane liked him, even if he was over-earnest. Someone had referred to him as a 'grammar-school boy', but he had no idea what that meant. Probably just a lame Brit putdown for someone who got his hands dirty once in a while.

'Mr Webb has also requested Boozer and Tuba.'

'Sounds like quite a party. They a double-act?'

Turnbull was quite tetchy now and his accent grew broader. 'Captain Crane. They are jamming devices. For Luftwaffe radar.'

'Right. Don, we kind of hoped you'd know that. It's why we chose you.'

'Donald. There is also something called Lino.'

'Yes, there is.' A Wing Commander who'd baffled him with science and codenames had brought Crane up to speed on all this. A history of radar in thirty minutes was cramming it, he felt. But he knew Lino was a development of WW2 radar decoy systems.

Turnbull was on the home run now, sounding certain of his

ground. 'The Russians are still using some of the better German radar, but they have brought their own in as well. Which is, I suspect, the higher frequencies Mr Webb gave me. It seems to me you have a full set of receivers and jammers here to cover all eventualities.'

'Don, Donald, did you sign that piece of paper for Mr Webb? The one that said: *Very, Very Official Secrets Act*?'

'Yes,' the other man snapped, sensing another diversion. 'But I need to know: are we flying into Russian airspace?'

'We told you, all will be revealed—'

'Just before take-off. That's all very well, Captain, but I need time to prepare the gear. I flew radar interference on Mosquitoes towards the end of the war. I suspect that is how Mr Webb found me and why he chose me. Back then, it took me two days to calibrate everything so it didn't just generate white noise in my ears. It'll take longer now.'

Crane said quietly: 'You might not have longer.'

Turnbull clenched his teeth and asked once more: 'Are we flying into Russian airspace?'

Crane took off his greasy forage cap and ran a hand through his hair. You don't know the half of it, pal, he thought. From the corner of his eye he saw that Webb's sidekick, Towers, had arrived. So he said softly: 'Yes, we are, Don. But if you let anyone know I've told you, I'll have to walk you into a spinning prop blade and claim it was an accident. Understood?'

The Geordie let out his breath and flashed a smile. 'Right. Just as long as I know, I'll get her as ready as she can be.'

'Good man.'

As he turned away, Crane thought, There's another Limey who needs his head testing.

Berlin had grown clammy, a foretaste of the long airless days of August to come. And the inevitable stink that came with them. Most days, all over the city, people could be seen on the rubble at dusk, burying small parcels of their family's waste because the lavatories were blocked. In winter, these froze into harmless, odourless lumps. Then came the thaw. Summer was, in some ways, worse than the bone-freezing winters.

James Hadley Webb was sweating as he climbed the stone stairs to Karin's apartment. Below him, still acting as the building's ad-hoc gargoyles, was the usual selection of snot-smeared kids, some as young as six. As he entered the block he was offered cigar-ettes, booze, Russian amphetamines, a gorgeous sister and stolen papers. He ignored them all.

At the top of the final flight, he waited while he cooled down. It was no good arriving red-faced and sweating. He leaned over and looked down the stairwell. The kids were playing cards, their voices distorted as they swirled lazily up to him, but the language was unmistakably ripe. What they needed was guidance, parents, fostering. He could imagine the response from the MilGov if he suggested it: 'Mother is a whore, father is a POW in Russia as far as we know. Would you like to take them on?'

No, he had enough problems of his own. He was moving towards an endgame, one he hadn't planned but improvised. It was like that AFN jazz he had come to love – a simple idea, elaborated on until the original melody was buried in complex switchbacks of sound. No matter how wild it became, though, the tune, the heart of the piece, always re-emerged intact, somewhere down the line, taking the players to a safe, familiar coda. That's what he hoped would happen here.

Webb knocked on the apartment door and the haggard Frau opened it, her face even more sunken than he remembered, anger showing across it. 'No,' she said in English. 'No more. My daughter—'

'I know.'

From behind her, he heard the voice of a young boy. He was playing, making machine-gun noises, imitating the older kids who re-enacted the Fall of Berlin on the bombsites. It was amazing

282

how many of the Germans wanted to be Marshall Zhukov in their games.

'I know about Karin. Here.' From the inside pocket of the grey worsted that passed as his lightweight suit, Webb took an envelope. He handed it to the women who, suspicious, held it between thumb and forefinger. It dropped to the linoleum floor and some of the shiny new Deutschmark notes slid out.

'Oh.'

'For the boy,' he said, and repeated: *'Für den Junge.'*

'Ja.' The Frau cautiously bent down, looking around as she did so, frightened this windfall might be transitory. *'Wollen Sie dafur nicht einen Kaffee?'*

Webb didn't want coffee. He should have just shoved the money under the door. He had just wanted to make sure it got into the right hands. 'No. *Nein danke.* I have to go.'

As he left, he heard the woman utter a disbelieving thank you. Over his shoulder, he said, *'Ihre Tochter war ein gutes Mädchen. Ein tapferes Mädchen. Erzählen Sie ihrem Sohn das.'*

Your daughter was a good girl. A brave girl. Tell her son that. He hoped she would.

'Wie war Ihr Name, Herr?'

What was your name, sir? But Jimmy Webb hurried on down the stairs as if he hadn't heard.

After a night flight to Wunstorf in the West, ostensibly to test the instruments but in reality to rate Len, who passed the test comfortably, and to fetch a return load of Pom – a mix of powdered milk and potato – Crane managed four hours' sleep. He then persuaded Laura to take the S-Bahn with him out to Grunewald and the Teufelsee. There, the lake and the surrounding forest offered relief from the city heat. Under the pines, the air was slow to lose the damp coolness of night.

It was a weekday, so the route to the lake wasn't too crowded. They walked down past the beer gardens, populated at that hour by just a few lugubrious customers, and skirted the massive spoil-heap known locally as Devil's Mountain, which consisted of all the unwanted hardcore from the city. Overhead, a giant Sunderland banked into its climb, heading back West for a fresh load of salt or coal. They watched it shrink in the clear blue sky.

'It's a beautiful day,' she said to herself.

He stopped and bought a watery coffee and a cake from a *Schnellimbiss* cart and they shared them as they continued. 'For now,' he said. 'Weather's coming. A storm from the east.'

'Does that mean we can't go over?' Now she had made her mind up, the thought of having the chance of talking to this Georges snatched away, of not being able to take that step closer to Diana, was unbearable.

Laura was wearing a simple white dress dotted with tiny yellow flowers. Her hair was up, her face scrubbed and without powder or make-up. She carried a straw bag containing a Thermos and some bread and cheese, a bathing costume, a blanket and two towels. Crane thought she looked even more beautiful than she had in China. He remembered another picnic, watching fishing junks, when he should have told her the truth: that the OSS had asked him to spy on her. Had he levelled with her then, it would have worked out better. It had been naïve and stupid. So why was he making the same idiotic mistake again?

'Hello, Lee? Tower to Lee Crane. Tower to Lee Crane.'

'Sorry. Miles away.'

They had reached the car park, which was empty, and headed down the dirt track under a canopy of trees. As the soil became sandier, the deciduous woods gave way to dramatic stands of tall, flame-barked pines. After fifteen minutes they reached the southern edge of the lake. Dragonflies were patrolling the water in their usual jerky stop-start fashion, and there was birdsong – something that had been driven away from the town centre by the constant roar of aero-engines. From one of the trees, a heron eyed the water, choosing his moment carefully.

'Will the weather affect the mission?' she persisted.

'No. Bad weather is good for us. Rain, thunder, hail – it all screws up radar. After we take off, we'll report an engine malfunction, just in case anyone's listening on the Russian side. The weather should hide our tracks.'

'Where were you just then, Lee? You weren't with me for a second.'

'I *was* with you – just not at this precise time. I was thinking of our picnic at Kunming.'

She gave him a thin smile, but said nothing. Walking away from the growling of the water-pumping station, they passed a family group, the under-nourished children frolicking naked in the water, splashing each other and squealing, the mother doling out their meagre picnic onto five plates. 'Did you ever find her?' she asked.

He knew whom she meant. During the war in Burma he had fallen in love – or become infatuated with, which he figured amounted to the same thing when you were a kid – with Kitten Mahindra, an Anglo-Indian widow. She was lost in the turmoil of the Japanese invasion and vanished without a trace. He had spent the rest of the conflict and several years afterwards searching for her, until he had given up hope. That was the day she had reappeared on the radar. 'Kitten? Yes. I tracked her down.'

'And?'

'Alive, married. Happy, I hope.'

'You told her you'd been searching for her?'

'Yeah. I think she was pleased someone cared. Then she told me to get on with my life.'

'And have you?'

'I came to find you, didn't I?'

'Oh.' She coloured slightly and said: 'Here? Will this do?'

Without waiting for an answer, she laid the blanket down on a patch of grass that ran down close to the water's edge, where it became shingle and sand, while Crane felt obliged to skim stones on the lake's surface, cursing himself. He hadn't meant to be that blunt.

He watched the heron flap from its perch and start its run along the length of the lake. It would be good to be able to do that, he thought: bale out when the going got tough.

When Laura had smoothed down the blanket, she said: 'Is that really why you came to Berlin?'

'Part of the reason. Look, your pal Towers, he's seemed pretty pissed at me since I came on board. He's a good-lookin' kid, isn't he? If there is something cookin' there tell me, because—'

The laugh was hollow. 'You've got a nerve, Lee Crane. If there was something "cooking" as you put it, what business would it be of yours?'

'None. Obviously.' He made to light a cigarette but her look suggested that was a no-go area too. Fresh air was what she wanted. He slid it back into the carton. 'But is there?'

'Is there what?'

'Something cookin'. Because I want to know whether to watch my back. You know how jealous some men get. After all, we have shared experiences he can't imagine.'

She shook her head in despair and then began to shake. He stepped over, thinking she was sobbing, but she was laughing. 'What's wrong?'

'I don't know where to begin. Stop it, I'm fine.' She wiped her eyes with a napkin. 'Coffee, Captain?'

'I guess.'

The coffee, instant, was powdery and tasted of metal, but he congratulated her on it. For an Englishwoman, it wasn't a bad effort. 'Sugar?' he asked.

'No. Sorry, I didn't think to bring any.'

'It's OK.'

The sun had bullied away the wisps of early-morning cloud and was beating down on them. Crane folded himself onto the blanket, loosening his collar. 'Didn't start too well, did I?'

'Could have been worse,' she grinned.

'How?'

'You could have tried to persuade me not to go East. Said that I was wasting my time.'

He nodded solemnly. 'I was coming to that part.'

'I'm going, Lee. You know that. Or you don't really know me at all. Shared experiences or not,' she teased.

'Indulge me. Let me just rehearse this part.' He took a hunk of bread and cheese from her. 'Thanks. OK, Webb is going because it's his fish he wants to reel in. Right?' She nodded. 'For reasons best known to himself, he wants to do this face to face, and flying is the best way in because every damn road out of Berlin is corked tight. Your pretty-boy pal Alan Towers is nominated because he speaks Russian. So if we get rumbled, we got a native speaker on the radio. That I approve of.'

'Go on.'

'*I'm* going because I can fly the plane and if I'm caught, I'm not RAF or USAAF. Neither is my plane. So, no big political incident there. Len wins his spurs because he can fly a C-47 if I can't. And he's a Pole, so again, no big prize for them. Don is our – what do you call them? – boffin. But an out-of-date one, you know what I'm saying? He's fine for us, but his experience is three, four years old. So he's not worth interrogating. And then there's you. Where exactly do you come in?'

She finished her crude sandwich, stalling for time by over-chewing each mouthful. 'The "fish" doesn't want to be reeled in. He might want to stay in the East.'

'Why?'

'He's got form. History. He might be risking his life by coming back as much as by staying. I'm not sure I should tell you any more.'

Crane lay back, closed his eyes and put his hands behind his head. 'Pretend I am not here and you are talking to yourself.'

He listened to the lazy buzz of insects, the distant yells of kids in their universal language of joy and outrage, and the thrum of plane engines. Eventually, she began to speak, low, as if the drooping branches of the willow beside them held microphones. She gave him the abbreviated history of Diana's mission and the treachery of the Frenchman.

'Jeez,' he said when she had finished. 'I can see that there might be a few people who'd want to meet this Georges in an alley with a Rawlings bat. In fact, I could sell tickets. But if he won't come, what can you do?'

'If they can't extract him, Webb has promised to give me time with him to talk about my sister. See if he knows anything about her in Avenue Foch and beyond.'

Crane propped himself up on one elbow, but she knew what was coming and cut him short. 'I realise Georges might know nothing. So I move on to the next source. And the next if need be and the next.'

'Laura?' He swatted a persistent fly away. Out on the lake a small motorboat chugged by, the occupants holding their fishing rods vertically, like oars waiting to dip into the water. 'How long can you keep this up – the search?'

She returned his gaze, steady and determined. 'If need be? Till my dying day.'

Thirty-eight

As predicted by the Met boys, the weather broke the next day. The sky turned a hard, metallic grey that sat like armour over the city, albeit an armour that leaked icy rain. Crane stood in the hangar with his plane, watching the downpour create a curtain of milky spray across Gatow four feet high. Aircraft were still landing, even though visibility was less than a mile, all on instruments. It was worse at Tempelhof; the US base had suffered a mid-air collision that morning. The news flashed across Berlin, increasing the gloom among flyers.

The storm should ease by that night, Crane knew. It would still be messy enough to confuse radar operators – and pilots – but the wind and rain were going to abate. They needed to, if he were to pull this off.

'Crane!'

When he turned, Freddie Laker looked fit to burst. 'What the hell is going on? What about our arrangement?'

Crane shrugged. 'Sorry. My hands are tied.'

'Tied? Tied?' he blustered. 'Last I heard, they were handcuffed.'

'Mistaken identity.' The US MPs had been rather theatrical when they had detained him at Webb's request. 'All cleared up.'

'And what about my plane?' Laker pointed to *Three of a Kind*.

'*My* plane,' Crane corrected.

'You leased it to me. I got two rotten flights out of you—'

'They were good flights, Mr Laker.'

The man's face went puce. 'You know what I mean! We had an agreement, a contract.'

'He's got a contract with me now.'

Jimmy Webb entered some way behind his voice, pumping his Fox umbrella to clear the rain. He laid it against the side of the hangar and took off his Trilby, shaking water from the brim.

'And you are?' snapped Laker.

Webb coolly looked Laker up and down. It gave Crane goosebumps. 'This man's new employer.'

'Now, look here, this is impossible. The British government—'

'– is very grateful to you.' Webb seemed to rise to his full height, his chest puffing out, as if taking on the mantle of HMG. Crane had never seen him quite so haughty before. 'We are very grateful to you. We will even compensate you. And, with a bit of luck, Captain Crane here will be back flying with you before the week's out.'

Laker looked suspicious. 'Compensation?'

'For days lost. I'd put the bill into the Board of Trade – the Quartermaster's Office. I'd then wait and see, Mr Laker.'

Crane couldn't quite identify the nature of the threat, but it was there all right, a little barb hidden inside soothing words. Laker could sense it, too. He didn't like to back down from a confrontation, but it was obvious he was dealing with someone who could easily make his life harder rather than easier. The man's manner suggested deals in dark corners and bureaucratic barriers subtly lowered into place with no redress.

'Can I take a name?' Laker asked.

'James Hadley Webb.'

'Thank you, Mr Webb. We'll speak again, Crane.' He took his leave, his brow furrowed, wondering what he had stumbled into.

Webb allowed himself to deflate a little and dismissed Laker from his mind. Laker and his civilian chums were doing a good job, but they were also making money from the airlift. The least they could do was lend an unknowing hand to the other war.

'You all set?' asked Webb.

The American nodded. 'Sure. Ten o'clock briefing, as agreed.'

'One more thing. You have a gun?'

'Yup. Am I likely to need it?'

Webb thought for a moment. 'Yes.'

After he had spent an hour running technical checks and making sure Len and Turnbull knew their roles, Crane took centre-stage for a briefing. The little group of men and one woman who were about to risk political dynamite by violating Russian airspace gathered around the tail of *Three of a Kind*, with the hangar doors pulled tight, so they were hidden from the curious.

'You all know the purpose of this incursion,' said Crane. 'It is to pull out a very valuable agent. It's not without some risk, but Mr Webb and I think we have minimised that. So now I can tell you the target for tonight,' he went on. It felt unreal, as if he were Jimmy Stewart about to tell the Eighth Air Force they were going back to bomb Schweinfurt.

He stabbed at the map of Germany he had taped to the rear wall of the hangar. 'Mochnow,' he announced. 'It's an old Luftwaffe night-fighter base. Here.' They all looked blank. Unsurprisingly, none had heard of it. It was just a tiny pinprick in the East. 'There is nothing for a good distance around. No Russian barracks, right?' He looked at Webb, who nodded.

'Landing lights?' asked the ever-practical Len.

'Mr Webb has people on the ground who will light flares. Usual routine, low pass to tell them we are there, circle and approach. Now, we are going to fly the first leg normally, as if we are en route to Wunstorf. A regular airlift flight as far as anyone is concerned. But we'll declare a problem somewhere in the Central Corridor.' This was the universal reporting point for all aircraft in the stream. 'We'll ask for permission to descend out of stream, then we'll drop off the radar. That's when Donald steps up to the plate. Right, Don?'

The Geordie cleared his throat. 'To the wicket, yes. It's fairly undulating terrain, but with no large hills, which is good for us in one sense, but it does mean we have nothing to hide in. However, most of the radar is facing the other way.' He indicated the main border between East and West Germany. 'They will be looking for B-29s heading towards them. Even so, we'll have to stay low.'

'If they do lock on,' asked Towers casually, 'what is likely to be their response?'

'There are radar-guided flak guns around some of the larger cities,' stated Turnbull, 'but all things being equal, we won't be flying anywhere near them.'

'True,' said Crane, 'but let's not fool ourselves. There is a squadron of all-weather interceptor jets which have been deployed here.' Another jab at the map, on a point near Leipzig. 'That's what we'll be facing. Top speed, oh, six hundred, seven hundred knots. Armament is four cannon and four machine guns. We can manage a hundred and eighty knots and I carry a Colt .45 under my seat.' He paused to let that sink in. 'Now, anyone changed his or her mind? No? Well, I suggest you start packing your sandwiches and coffee because we leave in,' he made a show of checking his watch, 'fifty minutes.'

Crane let out his breath and walked away, hoping nobody else could hear the great whooshing of the butterflies' wings in his stomach.

Crane had checked manifold pressure, mixture, fuel, propellers and that he had the right number of crew on board. *Three of a Kind* was ready to go. 'Pre-flight check completed,' he said.

'Pre-flight check completed,' echoed Len, his happiness evident. It was all a big game to him.

'You want to call the tower?' offered Crane.

'You bet.' He pressed the mike button. 'Hello, Gatow control, this is Dakota Papa Alpha.' Crane had got used to the British habit of only using the last two of the five registration letters, and calling his C-47 a Dak. 'Repeat, Dakota Papa Alpha, requesting clearance for take-off en route to Wunstorf. Roger.'

'Roger that, Papa Alpha. You are fifth in line. Repeat, fifth. Should have you airborne within fifteen minutes. Await our instructions. Roger.'

Crane unbuckled himself and walked down the fuselage to the main cabin. Donald Turnbull was hunched over his makeshift desk, studying the radio beacon charts. Crane squeezed him on the shoulder and got a finger and thumb 'OK' circle in return. Beyond Turnbull, there were two groups of passengers. Webb, Towers and Laura were at the front in conventional seats, which had been bolted to the floor that morning. Webb had a large briefcase between his feet. Crane didn't know what was in there, but he could guess. *If all else failed, offer money and lots of it.*

All this effort and expense, he thought, for one agent. He hoped it was worth it.

Laura looked pale, the whiteness of her skin making the thin layer of freshly applied lipstick look startlingly scarlet. She caught Crane's eye and smiled and he tried to make the one he gave back as positive as possible.

Further back, on the unyielding metal benches that lined the fuselage, were SAS Sergeant Gallagher and Privates Moss and Wetherall, all in anonymous coveralls with no regimental markings. Their weapons were a mix of German, Russian and Czech. They were there in case things got sticky on the ground. Jimmy Webb reckoned each one was worth a dozen Russian conscripts. *They'll have to be if I screw this up,* Crane thought.

'OK, folks, listen up,' he said aloud. 'We'll be starting engines presently, ready to taxi. As you can hear and see, the weather is poor. And the Russians won't let us fly over ten thousand feet, so we can't go above it. The flight may be bumpy, but it's nothing to worry about.' He glanced at Laura, who appeared unflustered by the idea of a few seesaws. She'd flown The Hump, so she knew all about bumpy. This would not even come close.

'What you might worry about is the sudden dive about ten or fifteen minutes in. That's me and Len fooling around a little. The flight's wheels up to wheels down of around thirty to thirty-five minutes. I can't promise peanuts or tea en route, but I'll get you there in one piece.'

'And back,' shouted one of the soldiers. There was a ripple of nervous laughter.

'Yeah,' said Crane. 'And back.'

As agreed, they waited until they were in the Central Corridor before they began their little piece of theatre. He reported the fictitious mag drop of the starboard engine, without any panic in his voice. Gatow asked if he wanted to descend to below 3,500 feet, the emergency height which would take him out of the stream. He told them he would.

Ahead was just blackness. The wipers scraping feebly at the windshield were struggling with the sudden splatters of rain. *Three of a Kind* was juddering a little, but not too much, more like a nervous shiver of anticipation, as if she knew what was in store. On the central air corridor there was no tricky terrain or wind shear, unlike the southern, exclusively American approach. They could breathe easy for a while.

'Lady and gentlemen,' Crane announced over the intercom. 'We are about to send out a Mayday. Do not be alarmed. As I said, we know what we are doing.' He endeavoured to make the last part ring true.

Len began his script: 'This is Dakota Papa Alpha, out of Gatow, en route for RAF Wunstorf. We have a starboard engine failure. Repeat starboard engine failure. Also a rev drop on the port. We are experiencing electrical prob—'

Crane pushed the nose down without warning, giving Len a

sickeningly realistic lurch to his stomach and hiccup in his voice. 'Mayday, this is Dakota Papa Alpha—'

'That's enough,' said Crane, turning off the radio. 'We'll turn up tomorrow and say we overreacted, that we diverted. That the radio failed.'

Webb poked his head through the cockpit door, gripping the edge of it. 'Well done, chaps, but you left the intercom open.'

'Sorry,' Crane said. He made to switch it off.

'No. Leave it. On second thoughts, sitting back there not knowing what the hell is happening is worse.'

'You sure?' Crane asked, surprised.

'Certain.'

'It's your ballgame,' he said. 'We're just dropping below one thousand five hundred.' He turned to Len. 'You have the aircraft,' he said.

Webb watched Crane write on a chart with a chinagraph pencil and slash a thick blue line that was remarkably straight for free-hand. He guessed he'd done this before. Crane punched on a stopwatch and laid it down between the seats. 'First leg, four and a half minutes.'

'Four and a half.'

'What are you doing?' asked Webb.

'Zigzagging, just in case they put up a search plane. It's unlikely, but they tell me you never know with the Russians.'

Crane wrote the time and heading down on a pad on the instrument panel. After two minutes had swept by, he announced: 'Lady and gentlemen, welcome to Soviet airspace. Don?'

'Yes?'

'Your show, pal.'

As they outraced the weatherfront, the rain eased a little. It was still dark above, with no stars or moon, but there were hints of light from below. Not many, but enough to remind Crane how low he was, skimming over flat farmland, mostly potato and cabbage fields, and scaring the bejaysus out of an occasional hamlet.

Webb had returned to his seat and there was no sound from the back of the plane, as the C-47 rocked from side to side. The air was rough down there, enough to make the passengers feel queasy and quell conversation.

'Heading change in thirty seconds,' said Len. 'You have the aircraft.'

'I have the aircraft. Don?' Crane asked.

'Got a blip from behind, like. It went, though.'

'Making the turn.'

'Next leg is ten minutes and forty-six seconds.'

Crane looked at Len and grinned. 'Forty-six?'

'You said you wanted accurate.'

'I did, I did. Good work.' They were both playing their parts. He shouldn't start criticising the crew, even in a joking way. Tonight wasn't for joshing. Or for shortening names just for the hell of it. Donald, not Don, he reminded himself.

The C-47 shuddered on, pulling a steady 140 knots under its belt, and they all shrank back into their thoughts. But not for long. Turnbull came back on in his ears.

'Captain, I got radar.'

'Where?'

'Starboard.'

'Strong?'

Turnbull hesitated. 'Weak. Ah, from the port, too. Stronger. They are both getting us. Shall I use counter-measures?'

'No. Not yet.' Crane shook his head to emphasise the point. Using jammers was an admission of guilt, confirmation that you weren't where you should be. It was best saved until absolutely necessary, when they were ready to cut and run. He checked the altitude and let her drift down. Somewhere on the ground they were a little scarab of glowing green crawling across a circular screen, pulsing brighter with each sweep of the radar dish. He imagined a controller scrambling a Yak or a Mig to take a look. He shook his head, trying to cool his imagination down. *It isn't going to happen. OK?* he told himself.

Turnbull spoke again. 'Radar still there. Counter-measures?'

He imagined a few sweaty palms out the back. He hoped Webb knew what he was doing, letting them listen in. 'Only on my mark.'

Len chipped in: 'Turn in one minute forty seconds.'

'Port getting weaker. Pulsing now. If we just dropped . . .'

'I'm down as far as I dare,' Crane snapped. 'Aren't there any bloody hills in Germany to hide us?'

Len: 'Thirty seconds.'

'Fading on the starboard as well.'

'Ten seconds to turn.' Len scribbled the new heading on the pad.

'Turning.'

'Port gone!' Turnbull yelled triumphantly. Then, after a nervous minute, 'Starboard gone. Some from behind. Weak, though.' Thirty seconds crawled by. Even if they were still a dot on the radar at this height, it would have faded now, down to a ghost on an operator's screen. The controller would be wondering if he was reading it correctly, or if it was a stormcloud playing tricks on him. 'Gone.'

Crane let out a breath. He glanced back through the open cockpit door. He gave Laura a thumbs-up; she flashed it back.

'Last leg,' said Len. 'Ten minutes exactly. Then approach.'

'Nothing,' came Turnbull. 'All quiet.' He played with the dials, scanning the radio frequencies. 'Got some chatter. Ground controllers or radar stations, I can't tell. Speaking Russian. You want Mr Towers to take a listen?'

'Are they shouting?' asked Crane.

'No. They sound calm.'

'Tell me if they start shouting.'

Thirty-nine

It was a better landing than they deserved. The abandoned strip had last seen regular use when it sent its squadron of radar-bristling Junkers 88s with upward firing canon against the USAAF and RAF bombers. *Schräge Musik*, 'slanted music', they called the guns. More desperate Nazi ingenuity. In the three years since the last sortie, the runway surface had cracked and collapsed into potholes and fissures, many full of robust weeds. The only landing-lights they had were burning oil drums. It was a recipe for disaster, but *Three of a Kind* bounced twice, gave herself a little shake like a wet dog and hugged the earth. The frame twisted and bucked over the potholes, but Crane cut the power quickly and swung the C-47 towards the line of ruined hangars visible in the dying glow of the flares.

'Where do you want me?' he asked Webb, who was crouched at his right shoulder.

'Wherever you feel happy. Well done, Crane.'

The pilot turned in his seat. 'I have a feeling that was the easy part.'

'You could be right.'

The Gooney Bird jerked to a halt and the engines began to whine down. 'Welcome to the Workers' Paradise of East Germany,' said Crane to himself as he looked out into the darkness, wondering who was looking back at them from their invisible hiding-places. He felt naked, sat out there in his big shiny bird, a long way from home. Wherever that was.

From the rear, Gallagher barked an order. The three SAS men were exiting first to sniff out any trouble. If there was firing, Webb had said, then they would take off, with or without the soldiers.

Webb left the cockpit and returned to Laura, who was looking very pale.

'The moment of truth,' she said, as cheerily as she could manage.

'Perhaps,' he warned, 'but you can't tell with these people. I didn't promise anything.'

'I know. But I'm getting closer to her. I can feel it.'

'Good,' he said sceptically.

Alan Towers joined them. 'Gallagher says it's all clear out there, as far as he can tell. Should we go out?'

Webb nodded. Len and Turnbull stayed inside but everybody else piled out into the damp air. Droplets of stinging rain were being blown by an east wind, which made it feel colder than it was. Crane began to look over *Three of a Kind* in the fading flare-light, making sure there were no major issues to address before what he guessed would be a fast take-off.

'Where is he?' Laura asked Webb.

The last of the landing fires spluttered and died. An inky black-ness enveloped them, the only noise the tick-tick of the cooling engines and the moan of the wind. The air carried the acrid smell of fumes from the oildrums. Webb switched on his flashlight, the beam masked by muslin. The SAS soldiers did the same. He flashed his light three times towards one of the hangars. A brighter, undif-fused light flicked back.

'Wait here,' Webb instructed.

'No,' she said, trying to sound firm rather than petulant.

'*Wait here*,' he almost snarled at her. 'This is my operation. You are here under sufferance.'

She felt tears burn hot in her eyes at the aggression in the remark and took a step backwards. Furious at her sudden weakness, she was about to follow him when a hand grabbed her elbow. It was Towers.

'Don't worry. He's just on edge,' the younger man said. 'He needs to make sure the field is clear. He's protecting you.'

'I don't need protecting.'

Towers let out a low laugh. 'We are miles behind enemy lines, God only knows where – well, God and your friend Crane – and I think we *all* need protection.'

The way he said the word 'friend' was somehow unsavoury. She let it go. Men. Maybe they'd start clashing antlers soon. The cheek of it.

'Kill those lights!' It was Crane, barking orders at the SAS. They did so without being told twice. A few seconds passed and then they all heard it, the soft drone of a small aero-engine. Crane knew it wasn't a transport, more likely to be a high-wing mono-plane spotter. Whoever it was and whatever it was, Crane didn't want it coming in to bust up the party, or sending other gate-crashers along. He scanned the low clouds, but there was no sign of navigation lights. The buzzing swelled and then faded as the plane passed to the south of them. One of the SAS belt torches came on.

'Not yet, guys,' he warned. It was extinguished. He counted to a hundred and said: 'OK. We're clear.'

Webb's leather soles smacked urgently across the pitted asphalt as he returned. 'Laura.'

'Yes?'

'Georges is just inside the nearest hangar.'

She felt a moment of fear. How do you confront the man who cold-bloodedly threw your sister to the wolves? How do you stop yourself scratching his eyes out before he has a chance to tell you what you need to know: is she dead or alive? And, no matter what the answer: *where is she now?* Laura licked her lips and asked: 'Is he coming back with us?'

'He says not.' Webb looked even more careworn than the night he'd been drunk, if that was possible. 'It's your chance now. Talk to him. See what he knows about Diana.'

'I will. Thank you.' As Laura strode forward, Towers fell in beside her.

'I'll come with you,' he murmured.

'Why?'

'Just in case . . .'

'In case of what?'

A dozen lights hidden in the eves of the rotting hangars snapped on simultaneously. The night became a supernova, exploding with such pure brilliance it caused their eyes to become aching slits.

'Jesus!' someone shouted.

Crane put a hand to his forehead, trying to create enough shade for his pinpricked pupils to focus.

The blurred outlines of the SAS figures showed they were already moving into a defensive position. There was the flat crack of rifle-fire and Laura screamed as Gallagher stumbled and went down, rolling on the Tarmac and then lying still.

'Stay where you are!' The command came from beyond the glare of lights. Private Moss raised his sub-machine gun and there was the pop of unseen carbines. Moss crumpled into a heap, gasping at the pain, then flopped to one side and was also immobile. Wetherall dropped his gun with a loud clatter and shoved his hands as far up in the air as they would go.

Now Laura could see the silhouettes moving at the edge of the runway, dozens of them, the steel domes on their heads clearly visible. Russian soldiers. It was a trap. A bloody trap. Georges had struck again, selling them out. He'd got both the sisters now.

'Drop your weapons,' came the command.

Crane held his arms straight to show he had none. 'Laura, come to me,' he said.

She took a step back.

'Stay where you are!' the voice yelled again.

'OK, so stay where you are,' Crane repeated in a low voice. 'Just be ready to run if I say so.'

Webb took out his pistol and let it drop. 'Alan, if you are armed, best do as he says.'

Reluctantly, Towers produced a Walther PP, checked the safety, and let it bounce onto the ground. 'What the hell is this?'

Crane laughed, an empty, grating noise. 'Well, it looks like an ambush to me, pal.'

As their eyes adapted to the lights, they could see the soldiers had dragged a man from the hangar. Georges – Librarian, Crane assumed. The Objective of this incursion. Rough jabs with rifles forced the man to kneel and a pistol was placed against his head. Crane looked away and at Laura. She was transfixed. The man she had come all this way to see was about to have his brains spread on the Tarmac. So he hadn't been the traitor, then.

'Hey,' Crane said to Laura, trying to catch her attention.

She gave a mirthless smile. 'I'm OK.'

'Remember China?' he asked softly. They had once been attacked by Chinese bandits and had narrowly escaped with their lives. Unlike the bandits. 'We got out of that one.'

But Laura had returned to looking at Librarian, her body tensed, waiting for the bullet that would kill him.

The expected execution shot, however, never came. Instead, with a hiss and a puff of smoke, new flares ignited, marking the far end of the field, and Crane heard the drone of the little aircraft once more, circling this time. 'Webb—'

The Englishman cut him short. 'I know.' He, too, was examining the night sky.

'Bloody hell,' hissed Towers.

Two Russian soldiers moved among them, one pointing a carbine at each in turn, and the other gathering up the weapons. A second set of troops kicked at the two prostrate SAS men, causing a protest from Wetherall. The surly Reds settled for rifling the pockets of the dead.

The aircraft came low over their heads, the propwash cold and gritty. It was a drab olive observation plane, the kind with room for a pilot and a couple of spotters. It touched down gently and rolled to a halt at the far hangar, 400 yards away. As the engine cut and the disc of the propeller slowed, the stretched canvas door opened. A figure emerged and spent a moment refitting a comically tall cap. The medals on the man's tunic glinted in the arclights.

'James Hadley Webb,' he boomed. 'What brings you to my neck of the woods?' It was Colonel Nikolai Zakharovich Grusenko.

Forty

The Russian Colonel marched across from his plane, a grin plastered over his face. At least someone here is enjoying himself, thought Crane. He half-expected the guy to start dancing.

'Dear me, Jimmy. Where shall we start? Bringing your terrorist group into sovereign Russian territory.' He indicated the SAS men. 'Violation of airspace. Espionage.'

'We declared a Mayday,' said Crane. 'This was an emergency landing. As allowed under civil aviation—'

The Colonel cut him short. 'And if I asked the men still inside the plane to start it up, it would cough and splutter, would it? Or would we find a very healthy American plane?' He spat out the nationality.

'Greek,' offered Crane, but was ignored.

'And I see you are here to pick up a piece of scum.' He indicated Georges. 'Must be a very valuable piece of scum for you to come all this way. So many of you, too. He must be quite a catch.'

'Not really,' said Webb unconvincingly. 'You can have him, but you can't keep all of us, Colonel. It would be a diplomatic incident.'

Grusenko laughed. 'A diplomatic incident is exactly what we want right now. Besides, I only have to keep a few of you.' He glanced at Crane and curled his lip. 'We have enough good pilots of our own, but you and your young friend . . .' He pointed at Towers, who winced at the thought of what was to come if they took them to Karlshorst. 'I might not even have to leave Berlin if I return with you two in my back pocket. What is the phrase: feathers in my cap?'

There's enough room on that hat for a whole war bonnet, thought Crane, but said nothing. There was a pause when the whole scene became frozen, a stand-off while each side pondered the next move.

It was Towers who broke the silence. 'Jimmy, can I have a word with the Colonel? As our resident Russian speaker?'

Webb frowned. 'Go ahead. If you think it will do any good.' He didn't sound convinced.

Towers said something in rapid Russian that caused Grusenko's eyebrows to rise. '*Da*,' he replied, the one word Crane understood.

'What do you have in mind?' Webb quickly asked Towers.

'A long shot,' he replied softly. 'We don't have much room for manoeuvre here. Trust me.'

Towers walked over to the Colonel and the pair of them moved towards where Georges was kneeling, his head forced down to expose his neck, where the pistol rested. The weasel-faced officer who held it looked impatient to pull the trigger.

Crane began to shiver and noticed Laura was doing the same. 'What's he up to?' she asked.

'I think I know. Horse-trading.'

'Trading what?'

'Let's hope it's not us, eh?'

They watched Towers and Grusenko in huddled conversation. Minutes ticked by. There was much gesticulating by Towers as he pleaded his case. They heard a snort of amusement come from the Russian. Then he began to nod. Finally, after slapping Towers on the shoulder, Grusenko led them back to Webb.

'Your man is a good man, Jimmy. Worth his weight in gold.'

'How much?' Webb asked wearily.

'A quarter of a million Marks,' said Towers. It was the price of their freedom. Either a little or a lot, depending which side of the gun barrel you were on. Right now, it seemed like a bargain. Grusenko could go back to Moscow a very wealthy man and some or all of them got to avoid the KI interrogators. Towers had done well.

'Deutschmarks, I suppose,' said Webb.

'Of course,' said Grusenko. 'Where would I spend Ostmarks?' The currency that Russia had introduced in the East to counter the Western Marks was already considered worthless as hard cash.

'You have that much?' asked Towers.

'In the case,' Webb admitted. 'In the plane.'

'Plus I had to give him some guarantees,' added Towers.

'Let's start with the money,' Webb said. 'The rest is just face-saving, so he doesn't seem like the cheap crook he is.'

Grusenko pretended not to hear.

'I'll go and get it,' said Towers.

'And Georges?' Webb asked, trying not to betray his impatience.

'Georges stays,' said Towers, his words heavy with regret. 'That was one of the conditions.'

'No.' It was Laura, the words blurting out. 'I need to speak to him. Please.'

'It's too late for that,' said Webb. 'Isn't it, Colonel?'

'It is just as you say, James Hadley,' intoned Grusenko. 'Too late.'

'Is it?' There was disappointment in Webb's voice.

The Colonel's oversized head nodded solemnly. 'Yes, it is. All as you suspected. Towers is your man.'

Towers was almost at the cargo door when he realised what those words meant. As soon as he saw the dead Sergeant Gallagher get to his feet, Towers put it all together in a flash of clarity. He broke into a run.

Towers ducked under the front of the plane and headed for the woods fringing the airfield. There was a series of metallic snicks as weapons were cocked to bring him down, but Webb yelled, 'No, he's mine!'

Towers had the sense to put the DC-3 between him and the rest of the group, running in the long shadow of the plane towards the woods. But he wouldn't have it easy, thought Webb, as he put his head down and kicked off as if he was after Jesse Owens himself. Arms pumping, he, too, sprinted beyond the plane. He blinked hard, trying to distinguish the shapes ahead of him, praying for some night vision after the floodlights. He identified the black smudge zigzagging towards the safety of the trees as Towers.

Now he could see the man clearly, Webb's legs thudded down in a drumroll rhythm, closing the distance, reeling him in. His muscles were burning and the blood vessels in his head thumping a wild tattoo, but he didn't let the pace drop. The shape grew larger, solid, and he fancied he could hear his quarry's breathing, forced and more ragged than his own. He allowed himself a little smile.

Then, he was almost on Towers, could almost reach out and touch him. If only, he thought, he had played rugby instead of rowing, he might know how to do a flying tackle, but he couldn't risk launching himself and grabbing thin air. He had to grasp the collar, and he was more than an arm's length away. Webb managed to move up a gear, pleased that his lungs were still inside his body, that he could go the distance.

And then Towers stopped, spun, and was aiming a fist at him. *Stupid boy. Fifteen yards from safety and he makes a stand.* He had probably expected Webb to stop, but he didn't; he barrelled into Towers at full speed, sending them both skidding over the coarse asphalt and into frozen mud.

Webb was aware of two punches landing on his bad ear, but he took his time levering himself up and driving a fist into the younger man's face. He felt the nose burst and there came a soft grunt of pain. A second blow wasn't required. The SAS men were there, panting hard, machine pistols covering the traitor. Webb stood up and uttered one word.

'Bastard.'

And then he turned away.

'Oh my God,' Laura was saying as the spy limped back into the light on the other side of the C-47. 'Oh, my good God. What the hell—'

She looked between Webb, Crane and Grusenko, trying to understand what she had just witnessed. Gallagher and Wetherall appeared with a pale and bloodied Towers between them. Webb brushed down his trousers and checked his sore knee. He must have caught it in the tumble he took, but adrenaline had anaesthetised the blow. He turned and told Gallagher: 'Put him inside the plane. And watch him.'

Towers was too shocked even to speak as he was bundled out of sight. No doubt his protestation of innocence would come later.

'Just one thing, sir,' said Gallagher from the doorway.

'Yes?'

'If it had been for real, not pretend, like, they would never have taken us so easily.' There was hurt pride in his voice. The SAS didn't like even faking defeat.

Webb nodded his reassurances. 'I'm sure of that, Sergeant.'

'Will someone please tell me what in Christ's name is going on?' Laura snapped irritably.

Behind her, Georges stood and began to massage his neck. Within moments, he and the Russian officer were lighting a cigarette each. The Red's low tones betrayed traces of an American accent. Webb caught a glimpse of someone else in the shadows. In the flare of a match he could see it was Bob Dolan, come to collect his fee for setting up this whole charade: first crack at the Colonel. If there were going to be any feathers put in a cap, it would be in Dolan's. That was OK. Webb had his mole.

'Tell her,' said Crane suddenly, with an edgy undertow that

brooked no argument. 'Tell her now. No more crap, Webb. That was the deal.'

'What deal?' Laura was growing angry now.

'We haven't exactly been straight with you,' admitted Webb.

'Really?' she asked. 'How, exactly?'

'Well . . .' He cleared his throat before making the announcement. 'Let's see. We aren't in East Germany. The border is ten miles that way. We are still in the West.'

'What? But . . . all that zigzagging?'

'The air corridor is twenty miles wide,' explained Crane. 'It'll take a little zigzagging if you know you have the space.'

'What about the radar? I heard it. We were being tracked by the Soviets. And Donald—'

'And when the next Academy Awards are due, I'll nominate Don. We were being tracked, but we always are. Most of the time, Don was searching for other planes we might bump into, or for Russkies who might get curious about us. But you see, we didn't pull out of the corridor until we were over the West, then we looped back here.'

'But why?' Then she remembered why she had hitched a ride in the first place. 'Look,' she said. 'Can I talk to Georges now?'

Webb examined his scuffed shoes. 'I know what you are wondering. Why did we run this little pantomime? For Towers's benefit, that's why. He had to buy this all one hundred per cent. Had to believe he was in the East. Which meant you had to believe it, too. And as for Georges . . . he isn't Georges, I'm afraid. He's an American impersonator.'

'You've dragged me all this way for nothing?' Crane wasn't at all surprised by the exasperation in her voice, although, in fact, she was taking it better than he had anticipated. 'And what's his story?' She pointed at Grusenko, who was still beaming with pleasure.

'The Colonel decided to come over to us. He's defected. Being called back to Moscow early is, I believe, never a good sign.'

'Never,' Grusenko confirmed.

Ernst Henkell had come back over the bridge with a message from the Colonel, asking for sanctuary. The delivery of the nose and the shooting of the KI Major on the bridge had been Grusenko's perverse form of courtship. It was useful timing, because it enabled Webb to work him into the role-play. 'He agreed to assist in our little performance.'

Crane decided enough was enough. 'OK, Webb, the rest can wait. I'm taking her.' He placed a hand on Laura's elbow and spun her round.

'As for you,' she hissed, 'you really take the biscuit.'

'Oh, shush now.' He pushed her as quickly as he could towards the little spotter plane.

'What now? Where are you taking me?'

At last, he was able to tell her the truth. 'To see Diana, I hope.'

Forty-one

Crane spoke quickly as they walked – so quickly, in fact, that Laura feared she would miss something. She tried to process each and every word, to make sense of what she had just observed.

'I never knew the Colonel was coming by plane,' Crane said. 'Honest. That took me by surprise. But I knew what they were up to. It's called the Pavlovsky Gambit or Game.' She was about to speak, but he cut her dead. 'No, listen to me. I've had a crash course in Advanced Spying these past forty-eight hours and I'm hanging on by my fingernails. It's a Russian scam originally. I'm guessing it was devised by someone called Pavlovsky. When the MGB discover someone is about to defect, they set up a meet with an American handler who arranges a pick-up. The defector is bundled into the boot of a car and driven to the West, to a CIA safe house in the forest where he is debriefed by agents who feed him bourbon and burgers. Except they aren't in the West. The car is driven round in circles. And the American crewcuts are really Russians who've been through some school they have near Moscow. So the defector spills his guts to his new best friends and then they know what he was about to tell us and then, I dunno, they shoot him.'

'So . . .'

A gust of rain caught them full in the face and they both winced.

311

There was a wind whipping up, moaning through the super-structure of the abandoned hangars.

'So we did the same,' Crane shrugged. 'Except with a plane going around in circles. Towers, thinking we were all about to be dragged off, told the Colonel he had to let him go, that he was on the Russkies' side. That he was valuable where he was, and to have fallen into Russian hands, even temporarily, would compromise his career curve. Not knowing Grusenko had already jumped ship, of course.'

'So they'll shoot Alan now?'

'Oh, I don't know about that. I think Webb will try and use him.'

Laura shook her head, still not understanding it all. 'But Alan hates the Russians.'

'Yeah, with good reason.'

'I don't understand.' She sounded close to tears now as incomprehension threatened to overwhelm her.

'You will. Later.'

They were at the spotter now, and she steeled herself for another flight. 'Where are we going?'

'Nowhere. I just want you to know, I only agreed to do this – to keep you in the dark – because of what they were offering as bait. I thought you'd think it was worth it. I hope I was right.'

The little plane rocked on its wheels as Diana stepped out onto the asphalt. She was dressed in a shabby raincoat, her face was pinched and drawn, and even Crane could tell she had a bad haircut, but when she smiled it rivalled the arc lamps overhead. This, Laura knew, was the genuine Librarian. Her longlost sister.

'I'll be over here, counting my lucky stars,' said Crane, examining the sky as he left. He could see the ceiling was lowering rapidly. The weather they had outrun had come looking for them.

The hug between the two sisters lasted a long time. Laura could feel how bony Diana was through the coat. Her hair smelled of lignite and dust, and her skin was rough against her face. She didn't care; she squeezed harder, holding on until it became clear to both of them that they were just putting off the first words.

'Diana—'

'Laura. I'm sorry. So sorry.'

'Where have you been?'

'It's such a long story.'

Laura's laugh betrayed an edge of bitterness. 'They told me you were dead. Everyone told me you were dead.'

'It was a close-run thing.' She ran a hand through her stiff hair. 'Ugh.' She nodded at the C-47. 'Tell me there is a hot shower on that plane I can use.'

'No. But there will be when we get back.'

There was a pause that grew to an awkward silence. It was lengthy enough for Laura to guess what was coming.

'I can't fly home with you,' Diana said eventually.

Laura's eyes filled with tears at the words. 'Why not? Why can't you? I've been looking for you for so long—'

'I can't. So don't argue. There it is.'

Laura's palms hurt where her nails dug into them. 'You mean you *won't* come?'

'Hey, girls.' It was Crane, handing over a hipflask, the universal panacea in Berlin, it seemed. 'Sorry to interrupt. Here, it's American whiskey – but good American whiskey.'

They both took a gulp from the steel container, raising a toast to each other, and the tension passed, for the time being.

'I traced you as far as the canal in Paris,' said Laura.

'Really? Well done.'

As patronising as ever, Laura thought, but suppressed the urge to say so out loud. She had to give them a chance to mesh once more. 'I saw Raymond Bec, briefly.'

'Did you? How is he?'

'Fine. He said to send his love if I ever saw you. I could tell he thought I was crazy to think you might have survived.'

'I'm sure he did.' Diana took another gulp of the spirit. 'Anyone else would have given up. Not my little sister.'

Laura sucked in more deep breaths to stay calm. 'You are going to have to tell me where you've been. At least try and make me understand.'

'I don't know if I can.'

'*Try!*' She found herself hissing the word.

Taken aback, Diana nodded. 'OK. So you traced me to La Villette? After the abattoir, I made my way back to Le Mans. It took the best part of a week. I wanted to see Georges, tell him what had happened, so he could punish the warders who betrayed us with the sisters, I suppose. I turned up at the café we used, and . . .' she flinched, the fury still raw enough to make her snarl '. . . Georges and the French Major, Major T, were there with the Gestapo. Or the Abwehr – I don't know for sure. But they were German, that much was obvious. And there they all were, laughing and drinking with a couple of tarts. I knew then that Georges had betrayed us in Saint Denis. That he hadn't done a deal for the sisters at all. The proprietor of the café tried to warn me to get out, but it was too late. Georges had spotted me. I got away from there, but the Gestapo lifted me at the train station. They had a perfect description.'

'From Georges?'

Diana nodded and took another mouthful of the whiskey. 'So, I knew one of SOE's *chefs du terrain* was really in league with the Germans. That was dangerous knowledge. It was too risky to put me in with other SOE prisoners who might get a message out, so I was put into Night and Fog. You know about that?' Laura nodded. 'I was taken to Paris, to Avenue Foch and kept *en secrèt*. There was a special floor for us at number 84. I saw a few Germans, like Keppler and Boemelburg, and double-agents, like Georges.'

Laura glanced back at the faux-Georges, who was still smoking with his pretend captors. 'So the genuine Georges . . .'

'. . . is dead, as far as we know. But this Georges – Librarian, supposedly – was a decoy for Towers. A bait to get him over and blow his cover.'

'Surely the Colonel would have known if Towers was a traitor.'

'No. Grusenko's border security, but he's not KI. That's their Intelligence. He couldn't access any list of agents. And even if he could, you can't necessarily believe it when a Red tells you so-and-so is a traitor. They lie, you know, spies.'

'I've noticed.'

'So there had to be a way of getting Towers to blow his own cover.'

Laura realised they had drifted off-track. 'And then what happened to you? After Foch?'

'Germany. Mecklenburg – a sub-camp of Ravensbrück. I was lucky not to be shot or hanged.' She quivered at the memory. It was impossible to describe, sometimes even to remember in any kind of detail, the horror and terror that punctuated each day. This gradual slide out of focus was a blessing. But sometimes the whole of her experience in the camps got mixed up with those hours in the La Villette slaughterhouse. It was the same process, but with humans rather than animals. 'Someone, an orderly, helped me switch identities with a Frenchwoman who died of TB,' she said in a low voice.

'A German helped you?'

'A good German. A Luftwaffe man, injured on the Eastern Front, who found himself in that hell, just like me. Only on the other side of the wire. He saved my life, several times, and risked his own. I know you might find that hard to credit, in that place. When the Russians liberated the camp, I returned the favour, pretending he was an SOE agent. Jürgen, his name is. You'll like him.'

'You're still together?'

Diana nodded. Now Laura could see there was something odd about her face. One pupil had failed to contract in the glare of the arclights. She had heard that a hard blow could do that, damage the nerves. Or a severe beating. 'It's one of the reasons I have to go back.'

'The other?'

'Once the fuss has died down, I have to make sure the Colonel's girlfriend gets out to join him. It's part of the deal.'

'Oh, fuck the Colonel. What happened after the war? Why didn't you come home then?'

'I suppose I went native. To be with Jürgen. To make sure nothing happened to him. I eventually made contact with the British who put me onto Webb, who was searching for Philip. Poor Philip. When I told him my story, Jimmy asked me to stay in deep cover – codename Librarian – just for a while. I wasn't alone. They planted agents all over countries likely to come under Soviet control. Operation Counterbalance, they called it. It wasn't that much of a hardship, not really.'

'"Just for a while"?' Laura repeated. 'That was three years ago, Diana. Three years, in which I watched our mother—'

'Please.' She took Laura's hands. 'Don't make me hate myself any more for that. I am so sorry.'

'But what are you doing over there?'

'Jürgen is with the Ministry of Supply. I work for the railways. Lowly jobs on the face of it. The Russians don't trust the Germans, you see. But when an army moves, it needs food, it needs transport. When they shift thirty thousand men to labour in the mines at Erzgebirge and close off the entire region, they still need to move the products out and food in. If the Russians drop the order for bread rolls and coffee, you can be sure they aren't crossing the border to invade tonight. Little things, but they tell us lots. It's not all Minox cameras and cyanide pills, you know.'

Laura didn't know how to answer. It seemed like such a waste. A life being thrown away for train movements, for one tiny piece of the jigsaw that surely could be sourced elsewhere.

Diana sensed the confusion. 'It doesn't sound much. But it is.'

'You'll never come back.'

'I will. Once this crisis is over. Jimmy has promised; *I'm* promising.'

The pilot of the spotter leaned out and said: 'We have to go now, miss. Weather's closing in real fast.' The words came with a deep Southern drawl.

'Diana, please.' Her sister didn't reply, but stepped in and kissed her on the mouth.

'Oh, God, lipstick, how I miss it. I have to go. I must be dropped back into place now before anyone realises I have gone. I love him, Laura. Remember that.'

Laura found herself sobbing, wanting to beg and plead but knowing it would be no good. She never could dent Diana's resolve. And this time she couldn't offer to go in her place. 'Please, please, please be careful.'

The engine of the spotter plane stuttered twice and then caught, the slipstream snatching at their final words. 'And come back.'

'I will.' Diana lowered her voice until it was soft like velvet. 'And thank you.'

'For what?'

'For believing in me.' She climbed into the little aircraft. Laura held out her hand for a last touch of her sister's skin, but the door slammed shut.

The plane snatched forward as the brakes were released and the revs increased. The monoplane trundled towards the far end of the field, turned into the wind and was soon climbing into the blackness of the night. As it gained height, the delicate spotter swayed and crabbed in the cross-winds and then its silhouette passed into the clouds, out of sight.

Laura stood immobile until the drone of the engine faded and was lost to the howl of the incoming storm. Only then did she really crumple, putting her head into her hands. She was talking to herself, but Crane could not make out the words. However, the anger and frustration were clear enough. He watched her shoulders shake as she sobbed, waited for the spasms to subside, the mumbled recriminations to run dry. When they did, he put an arm around her and she leaned into him. She blinked away the tears and wiped her nose. As she spoke, she glanced up once more at the thickening darkness. 'What a bloody mess.'

'Your sister is a brave woman.'

She looked up at him, her voice hiccuping as she spoke. 'And brave people sometimes get used, don't they? By manipulating bastards.'

Crane couldn't deny it. He pulled her closer and let her cry some more.

Forty-two

The flight back to Berlin was more conventional than the outward run. With Wunstorf control's help, Crane fed them back into the corridor at Walstrode, flying at 3,500 feet and at 160 knots. Then it was a simple route to Egestorf, Egestorf to Restorf and then Restorf to Frohnau before calling Gatow.

As the storm passed, it left an unnatural glow in the east, a fuzzy, luminous pyramid, tilted to one side. Crane knew what it was: the misleading fake dawn variously known as 'the shining hour', 'zodiacal light', or, to the Germans, *Falschschein*. It was caused, meteorologists thought, by sunlight dancing off cosmic particles out in space, as stray rays found the debris left by the beginning of the universe. Whatever caused it, the phenomenon was unsettling, with the fraudulent promise of a new day that was in reality still many hours away.

There was a strange atmosphere on the aircraft, too. It was almost as if the mission had failed, not succeeded. Yet it had all unfolded according to plan, as far as Crane could see: Towers had identified himself as a Russian-controlled double-agent to the Colonel in order to keep his cover intact.

Yet, Crane got the impression that Webb was disappointed to be proved right about Towers's treachery. When he came forward to the cockpit, Crane asked him in a low voice: 'Are you going to tell Laura how you knew about Towers?'

319

'Not unless she asks. It's upsetting.'

Crane shook his head. 'Not half as upsetting as saying goodbye to a sister you've just found isn't dead, after all.' Laura had, Crane appreciated, been through her own shining hour – the dawn of a new day in her life had been revealed as an illusion, snatched away by Webb and his schemes.

'Perhaps.'

It was when he had been talking to Ralph Tyler that Webb had become suspicious of Towers. It was clear that he had already made approaches to try and join SIS. By destroying Webb's reputation, he would hasten the day when he was moved across, shifting closer to the centre of power. So if it was Towers, he had been turned. But when? The only time Webb was certain he had been in contact with Russians for an extended period had been at the Harz Mountains. That was what Webb had done with Tin-Eye's CSDIC files at the London Cage: he had gone over every post-war inter-view in the region.

There he found an overlooked war-crimes interview with a woman in Bronsdorf, who had been raped by the Russians. She had suffered horribly in the gymnasium they had converted into a rape centre. She had told her interviewer of an Englishman, an officer, who had been present and who, after a skinful of vodka, had joined in.

One Russian, a Commissar, had egged him on, jokingly insulting his manhood and the feeble English sex-drive and Western decadence. Reticent at first, the unknown officer had eventually thrown himself into the fray with enthusiasm, she claimed. Not only that, but while the Englishman was distracted with another woman – she had been cast aside until later – she had seen the Commissar filming him. The evidence was all on celluloid. The war-crimes interviewer at the time had scribbled a comment that this was clearly 'fanciful'. No Englishman was capable of such monstrosities.

Towers always insisted that he'd pulled out T-Force as soon as he discovered the rape centre, appalled at the behaviour. So Webb had tracked down Dobson, the T-Force driver, who confirmed that they didn't leave Bronsdorf until the next day, after sleeping it off. They'd had quite a party with the Reds, but Dobson and the others knew nothing about the gym; the Russians had deliberately snared only Towers in their net.

Putting the rest together wasn't difficult; the NKVD and its successors had perfect blackmail material on Towers. They had used it well.

How, though, was he going to deliver this awful news to Towers's father? It would break Charles Towers's heart. He imagined the shame would be hard to bear for the son, too.

Webb had a lot of questions for Alan Towers. Who was his handler? Why had they killed Otto in the first place? The German had said he had discovered 'something scary'. It must be to do with the uranium mines. Which meant it concerned the Russians' progress towards the A-Bomb. Of course, killing Otto in the West had that other advantage – it made SOB, and Webb, look foolish and ineffectual, hastening the day when it shut down and Towers was transferred to MI6. There, he would have risen smoothly through the ranks, perhaps even one day ousting Philby, who was no longer the Golden Boy. Imagine that. A Russian plant running the Soviet desk. Who would ever even suspect it?

And poor Karin? Someone had tortured her to try to find out the route to Librarian. Karin had resisted, it seemed, not even giving away the tiny amount she knew. But how had they got on to her? He thought he'd shaken his shadow that night. Perhaps they'd used CS – chain surveillance – which involved agents with powerful field-glasses in radio contact with half-a-dozen men who swapped with each other, so the Objective was unaware he or she had been tagged. If done well it was virtually undetectable, especially when carried out by the Russians.

Towers would not give up the truth easily; they rarely did. It would have to be teased out carefully, while the traitor put the best possible interpretation on his actions. You had to allow them that, at least initially. But Webb would get as close to the genuine facts as he could, even if it took him and John Findlay months. Patience, that was the key.

Crane called Gatow with his height, direction and speed and his ETA at the Frohnau Beacon. He was given the airfield state of runway, windspeed and direction in return. The wind was strong but not unmanageable.

'What will happen to Towers? Will you guys hang him?' Crane asked.

'Not if we can turn him. Use him back against them. We'll see. Even so, we no longer hang spies.'

Crane began his descent to 2,500 feet. 'You sound like you regret that.'

Webb managed a smile. 'It was a little more clear-cut in the war.'

'Jimmy.' It was Laura, squeezing into the already crowded cockpit.

'Yes?'

'Diana told me about the two men who betrayed her – Georges and this Major T. What happened to them?'

Webb said quietly: 'You won't like the answer.'

'I rarely do these days,' she replied.

'Major T is now a General. He is also a senior figure in de Gaulle's Rally of the French People Party.'

'But he was a traitor.'

'Of sorts.'

Crane turned around. 'There are degrees of traitor in your world, are there?'

'Indeed. His mission was to weed out Communist Resistance groups before D-Day. Le Mans and Paris were very heavily Communist. De Gaulle wanted to make sure that his men were seen as the backbone of the Resistance, not FTP, so that when it came to post-war government, he and his chums would be the saviours of France. Whether you approve or not, the Major did his job well. De Gaulle rewarded him.'

'And did the British approve of that?' Her voice was ice.

'Oh, we didn't know about the targeted betrayals of Communists to the Germans, otherwise we wouldn't have sent Diana over. When they arrived, Georges and the Major needed to make sure she didn't discover the real reason the sisters were arrested.'

'So Georges set up the phony prison break, hoping Diana and Philip would be caught,' said Laura, her words laced with bitterness. 'And it would be nothing to do with him because he would be in Le Mans. No dirt would stick.'

'That's right.' Webb rubbed his forehead, which was suddenly hot. 'And for what it's worth, no, I didn't approve of Georges's actions. The FTP was the first to rise up against the Germans. Their deliberate betrayal was monstrous.'

The word triggered a memory in her. 'Alan told me a story about you once,' said Laura softly. 'I wasn't sure I believed it. About you sending Philip to France with Diana, so you could . . .'

Crane pricked up his ears, but she didn't complete the sentence. Len called Gatow for clearance and turned onto 180 degrees magnetic, homing for the Grunewald Beacon.

Webb gripped the back of Crane's seat. 'Yes. That's true. It was hardly my proudest moment.' How could he explain to her that each and every time he had gone over the mission to France, as dispassionately as he could, it always came back to the same conclusion? Take Olivia out of the equation and he still would have sent Philip. The man was a pro, he had experience, and he knew what he was doing. Philip Maxwell was the best man for the job, the finest protection Diana could have. So Webb had sent him. Somehow, it didn't help, didn't make it any better. 'Philip was ideal.'

'Maybe. But it shows me exactly how you think. You used Philip then and now you used Diana, Crane and me to nail Towers. So you had a watertight case.'

'If I'd just voiced my concerns about him, there would have been an enquiry. In my experience, the best operatives just wriggle out of those. I couldn't take that chance.'

Laura, though, didn't seem to hear. 'And you'll never let her come out, will you? There'll be no end to this crisis, because there will always be another. And another. It's what you thrive on, isn't it? It's what makes you think you have some bloody importance in this world. "Just one more year, Diana, then you can come home, just one more mission".'

Webb didn't disagree. Already he could feel the black river of depression spreading through him.

'What about the other Frenchman? The real Georges? The one who gave her to the Gestapo at the railway station? Did he survive?'

Webb shook his head. 'Georges was really Henri Court. He was killed in a plane crash in Laos in late 1946.'

Crane was about to speak when a roar filled the cockpit and a cyclone burst among them, swirling maps and papers into the air. Webb and Laura lurched forward and the plane began to crab wildly.

'You have the aircraft!' Crane yelled to Len above the din, as he unstrapped himself and pushed his way aft. Len coolly strapped on his oxygen mask and gave the plane enough right rudder to correct the crab.

The wind was whirring through the main body of the plane, howling as it went, flinging droplets of water in faces and stinging eyes. Yells of panic mixed with a thumping noise from the outside, a dull ringing on the metal fuselage.

The first thing that explained the scene to Crane was the emergency door release, right where the three riveters had scratched their names. The big red lever that should be up and locked with a captive cotter pin was in the down position. The cargo doors had been blown off by the explosive bolts. Someone had gone out into that raging night.

Gallagher, the SAS Sergeant, was lying prone, both his hands out of the plane, his face contorted in agony. Holding onto him was Moss, who had wrapped his own legs around one of the steel bench legs for extra purchase. Wetherall, was, in turn, gripping Moss.

From the outside came that repetitive thunk-thunk sound.

Now Crane knew what that was. It was Towers's head, banging against the fuselage as the slipstream buffeted him. They'd hand-cuffed him, but not behind his body. So he had managed to pull the lever – the instructions were next to it in big red letters, large enough for Mr Magoo to read – and he had tried to jump. Gallagher must have reached him just in time. The SAS man now had hold of an ankle with both of his meaty hands, but the strain on his arms was tremendous. Towers should have been plucked into the heavens as he clearly intended. Only Gallagher's extraordinary double-handed grip was preventing him from getting his wish.

'Get a line on him,' the SAS man yelled through gritted teeth. 'We can pull him in.'

The sickening crash of flesh and bone against metal continued.

Crane knew Towers would be senseless by now, at the very least. He wouldn't feel a thing. He said, 'Let him go.'

'No!' Webb yelled from behind. He tried to push by. 'We need him alive.'

'Stay back,' instructed Crane, jabbing his finger towards Webb. 'I don't want anybody else going out there. Stay where you are.' Crane looked at the expectant faces staring at him, open-mouthed. Then he remembered it was his crate they were in and he was Captain. 'I'll do it.'

From the rack on the wall, he extracted one of the webbing safety belts, made sure it was clipped onto the fuselage and dropped to his hands and knees. He crawled over to Gallagher, the wind from the open hatch roaring in his ears, and latched the spring-loaded carabineer clip on to the metal loop on the soldier's belt. At least he wasn't going anywhere now.

Crane repeated the procedure for the safety line to his own belt, then he tied a length of nylon rope to one of the anchor points and fashioned a slipknot at the free end. Again, he went down on hands and knees.

'I'm going to crawl over the top of you, Sergeant, and loop this over Towers's foot. Think you can take the weight?'

Gallagher managed to turn his head. 'My girlfriend weighs more than you.'

Crane pulled himself on top of the Sergeant and followed the line of his arm towards Towers. In the strobe of the navigation light, flashing like a neon sign, he could see that the hands gripping the ankle were colourless and waxy. 'I can reach him. The loop should pull tight just below your fingers.'

Crane tensioned his muscles against the force of the wind as he edged the rope out. Hair whipped across his face, blinding him and he shook his head. His eyes were watering, but there was a distinct lessening of the blast. Len was letting the airspeed drop, giving him all the help he could. 'You OK?'

Gallagher grimaced. 'I can't feel my fingers, but I can hold on. Just watch where you put your knees, will you?'

'Sure. Almost there.'

Crane was aware of someone in the doorway to the side of him. Irritated, he turned his head, his eyes burning from the wind. 'Be careful—'

It was Laura. She was wisely flattened against the fuselage, so she was in the little pocket of calm on the forward side of the door. From there, she had a good view of the tangled trio and of Towers flapping in the wind. Good enough anyway to raise Crane's Colt .45 auto, squeeze the grip safety and loose off three rounds.

'No!' Crane yelled ineffectually.

Whether she hit Towers or not they would never know, because the shock of the booms and the flashes made Gallagher release his grip. As he rolled away to safety, Crane slithered forward on his stomach, the rush of air sucking at him. He imagined Towers tumbling away over the German countryside, and felt himself following. With half his body out into thin air, Crane squeezed his eyes shut as the wind tore at his face. It was like being punched with a brick. His safety line snapped taut as Gallagher yanked it and Crane was pulled inside, just in time to see Webb snatch the gun from Laura, dropping it as he burned his hand.

'What the hell are you doing?' Webb roared.

'You'd try and use him – and he could find a way to tell them who Diana was, couldn't he? Some code you didn't know about? You might have tried to be too clever and lost me Diana. I couldn't take that chance.'

Crane bent down, picking up the weapon by the handle and dropping the magazine. There was one in the spout and he ejected it. Guns and planes, he thought, were never a good combination. She'd known from China that he always kept a .45 in the cockpit and he'd reminded everyone at the briefing that it was there. Dumb.

Webb didn't say a word. He slumped down into his seat, and wondered what he would tell Charles Towers now. It was more than likely the thought of the disgrace and humiliation for both father and son that had caused Alan Towers to jump. Perhaps he had come to the conclusion that, with him gone, there was no need to disillusion the old man about his only child. He could be right, thought Webb. The report could easily be sealed for fifty or more years, with the public thinking only that there had been a tragic accident. Towers wouldn't be the first or last to die during this blockade. And the lie to his father would simply be another in the long, endless list that was part of his job.

After he had unsnapped his safety line, Crane led Laura to her own seat and lowered her in. Her eyes were wet, and he brushed the hair away from her face. He thought that was it, that she was finished for the day, but she said to Webb: 'You bring her back, you understand? You bring Diana back alive. Do something decent for once in your miserable life.'

Crane expected some kind of riposte, but the Englishman stayed silent, as if digesting the words carefully. Eventually, Jimmy Webb simply nodded.

Crane made his way back to the cockpit and all but fell into the pilot's seat, the place where he at least knew which way was up. He said to Len, 'Tell Gatow we are missing a part. Cargo door accidental discharge. It may have smacked the tail as it went, caught a control surface.' As might Towers, he thought. 'Priority approach.'

Over the Grunewald Beacon they turned to 260 degrees magnetic and dropped to 1,500 feet. The night had cleared, and there were a few tiny stars pulsing above them.

Ahead were the twin rows of the high-intensity lights leading to Gatow. His arms felt like sacks of wet cement as he lined up the plane, a weariness washing over him as he tried not to think of the twisted body of a once-handsome young man lying crushed in a potato-field and a beautiful woman, still choking back her disappointment.

'Gear down?' asked Len.

Crane nodded. 'Gear down.'

'I tell you, Captain,' said his co-pilot, reaching for the under-carriage lever, 'I'll be glad when this is all over.'

Crane gave him a tired smile. It wasn't finished yet, not by a Mississippi mile.

Epilogue

Three weeks later

Lee Crane had never kidnapped anybody before. Nor had he been party to cold-blooded murder. His body was tensed, waiting for the sound of the gunshot. It had been that way for close to fifty minutes now, and his neck was getting stiff. He looked at the sky once more. It was darkening from the brilliant cornflower blue it had been all day and the sun was almost at the top of the tree canopy. It would be dusk soon and this gravel airstrip, used mainly by crop-dusters, had no lights for a take-off.

They were 100 miles south-west of Paris, in the countryside, at the end of a fine summer's day, the still, warm air full of crickets' stridulations. Six hours previously, he and Raymond Bec had helped Laura bundle a man called Henri Bevier into the boot of a car and had than driven here from Paris, where *Three of a Kind* was waiting with Len.

He could see his co-pilot now, making frantic signals from the cockpit. 'Lee,' he mouthed. Crane raised a hand. They all wanted to get out of there pronto. But there was a woman in the ramshackle shed that passed for an Ops building holding Crane's Colt .45 on a man he had tied to a chair, and Crane thought they ought to just hang around long enough to see if she was going to pull that trigger. If she did, then *Three of a Kind* would be making a long loop out to sea and dumping a second body into thin air.

They were there because of a hotel in Vientiane, the capital of Laos, called the Riviera. It was built when the French thought they'd have the place forever; it had a mansard roof modelled on Versailles, fancy tiles, metal-framed windows with sky-blue shutters, a swimming pool and a garden that needed a whole army of workers to keep it under control. Which was why it now looked like something from a Tarzan movie. The hotel had two restaurants and a couple of bars. Everyone who drank there called the one at the rear, overlooking the garden, the Boeing Bar. There had been an attempt to rename it the de Gaulle Salon after the war, but it never stuck.

The Boeing Bar was where you held the wakes for jungle pilots who didn't come back. There was a roll-call on the wall. It was a fabric panel from an old Boeing Model 40 fuselage that had been stretched and varnished. Painted on it were the crew names for each incident, the year – with a gap for 1940–1945, when there were too many to count – and the locale. Or, this being back-country flying, the best guess at the locale.

Crane knew most of the names on there, at least those since 1945. Because when you heard of a guy going down, you had three questions. Where was it? What was he flying? Was it pilot error or an act of God? These led to the fourth, the Big One. *Could it have happened to me?* Because sometimes you knew the guy's luck had just run out, and there but for the grace of God went you. Other times, you heard he had ignored the weather forecast or an oil-pressure drop, or had insisted on that extra passenger or agreed to carry a couple more crates than the aircraft's specs suggested was sensible.

Crane knew, then, that no Henri Court had died in a plane crash in Laos in 1946. No Henri anything. There had been a Frenchman killed, but he'd been in Indo-China since the 1930s. He'd cabled the hotel to double-check, and the manager had replied that he was right. So Webb had been lying. 'Georges' *hadn't* been killed in a Laotian air crash.

It had taken them a fortnight to get to the truth, with the help of Raymond Bec. He had figured out that, if Major T had been rewarded by General de Gaulle for weeding out Communists, there was a good chance that his partner in crime would also have been. It was Raymond who, once he had imagined him without a beard, had identified one of de Gaulle's senior aides as Georges aka Henri Bevier.

So why did Webb lie? Well, Bevier was most likely engaged on his old double-dealing tricks, as a plant who would tell the British what de Gaulle was up to. And to protect him from exposure as a former Gestapo informant, his younger brother, Jean-Marc Bevier of the DST, had helped concoct the cock-and-bull story with Charbonneau, the camp guard, so Laura would stop digging. The subterfuges of SOE didn't end with VE Day, that was for sure.

Although Crane had been expecting it for close to an hour, the crack from the hut still made him jump. He turned around, and watched her walk across the crushed rock towards him, pistol at her side. The sharp noise came again, and he was relieved to see it had been the door banging open, then shut once more. When Laura reached him, he took the gun from her. The handle was warm, but the barrel was cold to the touch.

'I couldn't do it.' The shame and defeat shone through. 'It was too long ago, it would be too cold-blooded.'

Crane nodded. It was going to be difficult for her to understand that this was no bad thing. That she had already had enough material for a lifetime of nightmares with Towers. But she'd shot him to protect Diana, not for revenge, and that was a subtle, but crucial difference.

Crane looked back at the hut over her shoulder, wondering what he would do if Henri came out, if he could execute him for her. Probably not. This one wasn't his fight.

'She did make it, Laura, remember that. Despite Henri's betrayal.'

'I know.' Her words became steel. 'But he doesn't know that, does he?' There was no way on earth she could risk admitting that her sister was still alive to such a worm. 'As far as he is concerned, she died in the camp he made sure she was sent to. And Philip Maxwell didn't survive. Who knows how many others owe their deaths to him? So I told him that one day, somewhere and somehow, we'd settle the score.'

Crane wasn't sure about that 'we', but he let it go. 'I think that's rather a tall order. Once his brother in the DST finds out what we did, we won't be very welcome back in France.'

'I don't care – because Georges will never know, will he? No matter where he is, he will never know if the stranger at the bar has come to get him. He will never feel at peace again. At least, I hope not.'

As she said it, all the energy seemed to drain out of her. The coiled spring inside her finally unwound and she fell against Crane. He put his arms around her and held her close. All that had happened between them in the war, all the stupid games, had ceased to matter over these last few weeks. There had been just Laura and Lee, looking for Henri, searching for an end to all this. Just how secure that bond was remained to be seen, but he had to hope, because it was anchored pretty damn well at his end.

Crane gave the spinning sign to Len that told him to start the engines. Moments later, he heard the noise that still made him tingle – the sound of a well-maintained Pratt & Whitney catching first time.

'He's still tied up,' she said, glancing at the hut.

'We'll call the cops when we land, tell them where he is. Or get Raymond to come down and free him. The guy can't tell the truth without giving the whole game away about his own history, can he? Meanwhile, we've got nearly full tanks. Where do you want to go?'

'Berlin,' she said wearily. 'But you don't have to fly me back there. I can take the car and get a commercial flight to Hanover and then go across to Gatow.'

'You sure you can face it?'

She knew what he meant. It was going to be agony, with Diana possibly just a few miles away, yet to all intents and purposes, as far away as the planet Mercury. 'Yes. I have to make sure Jimmy Webb keeps his promise about getting Diana out.'

Something told Crane that Webb would do so. He'd have to, or Laura would come around borrowing that Colt again. Webb had gone back to London for a few days at the same time as they had left Berlin, saying he had a few personal matters to sort out. Laura told Crane what it probably was. Olivia Maxwell. Crane only hoped the man hadn't left it too late to salvage some happiness from that situation. Despite what Laura had said in the heat of the moment, and the mess of deceptions, Crane thought Webb was probably a pretty decent guy underneath it all. As much as a spy can afford to be decent, that is.

'What about you?' she asked him.

'I thought I'd, oh, head back to Berlin too. There's still a blockade on. See if I can pick up some transport work, try and meet a nice girl.'

'*Are* there any nice girls in Berlin?'

He almost didn't say it. But then his mouth moved without being told. 'I know one,' Crane said quietly.

Laura gave a tired smile. 'Oh, her.'

'Let me take you back?'

'What about the car?'

'Leave it. Didn't cost much.'

She thought for a moment and said: 'OK, Lee. But no promises, eh?'

He finally unwrapped his arms and ushered her towards the waiting plane. The sun had hit the canopy, its lower edge blurring into the treetops. He wished he could drive Laura to a local village, find a restaurant and crack open a bottle of *vin rouge*, listen to the clack of *boules* in the square, watch the bats race around the church tower at dusk, and find a little hotel for the night. But that kind of thing could wait until another day.

Inside *Three of a Kind*, Crane made sure Laura was secure in her seat and walked up to the cockpit, where Len had the C-47 all ready to go. They taxied round on the rough cinder, past the still-quiet hut, and he gave the plane emergency throttle levels, because he wanted to be away from there that bad. They lifted off into the falling sun and, in the end, Crane was glad that the only blood red they were going to be seeing that day was streaked across the sky in front of them.

He took *Three of a Kind* round in a long, shallow turn, putting the glare of the sunset firmly behind them, pointing the nose towards Berlin.

'Len,' he asked.

'Yes?'

'You married?'

'Yes. Last year.'

'How did you propose to your wife? How did you pick the moment?'

Len looked across at him, puzzled. 'Why?'

Crane touched the pocket of the leather jacket to make sure the ring he had bought along rue de la Paix in Paris was still there. He felt the hard circle of gold under his fingers and smiled to himself. 'Just wondering, Len. Just wondering.'

Glossary

ABWEHR   German military intelligence organisation (1921–44), run by Admiral Canaris. Not part of the SS or Gestapo, and Canaris was eventually implicated in the plot to assassinate Hitler in 1944.

AFN   American Forces Network. Radio for US troops in Europe.

CBI   The China-Burma-India theatre of World War II.

CSDIC   The Combined Services Detailed Interrogation Centre was concerned with the questioning of all enemy personnel, including spies.

DST   Direction de la Surveillance du Territoire, the French version of MI5.

ELAS   Acronym of the Greek National Liberation Army, controlled for the most part by communist leaders.

FANY   First Aid Nursing Yeomanry. A volunteer group of women formed in WWI, initially to provide ambulance drivers at the front. In WWII it supplied signallers, coders and couriers to Special Operations Executive.

335

Foo-Fighters	Mysterious lights in the sky observed by Allied pilots over Germany and thought to be secret weapons of some description. Later dismissed as optical illusions by official reports, rumours that they were early flying saucer experiments by the Nazis persist.
FTP	Franc-Tireurs et Partisans, the communist-led French resistance organisation.
G2	A staff officer in a US Army battalion responsible for all military intelligence matters.
GCCS	Government Code and Cipher School (now GCHQ).
G-Werke	Nazi code word for the complex of factories hidden – often by burrowing into mountainsides – to protect them from Allied bombing raids. The best known example is Dora, at Nordhausen, where the V-2 rockets were produced and many thousands of slave labourers died.
JIC	Joint Intelligence Committee, the body charged with giving direction to and co-ordinating the UK's various spying organisations, at home and abroad.
K-5	The Fifth Department of the Criminal Police – a political police force (not unlike the later Stasi) operating in the eastern zone of Germany.
KI	The Committee of Information, a central clearing house for all counterintelligence from the many Russian and East German agencies.
MGB	Ministry of State Security, 1946–53, one of many Russian secret police organisations, concerned in East Germany with denazification.
MPD	Missing, Presumed Dead. Appended to the Personal Files of missing SOE agents at the end of WWII.

MVD	Ministry of Internal Affairs, one of several fore-runners of the KGB.
OSS	Office of Strategic Services, the US clandestine organisation that eventually became the CIA.
PF	Personal File. The SOE's record of an agent's recruiting, training and missions.
SD	Sicherheitsdienst, the SS intelligence service responsible for hunting down spies and sabo-teurs. Its Paris HQ was on the elegant Avenue Foch.
SHAEF	Supreme Headquarters Allied Expeditionary Force, in charge of all tactics and policy regarding the European theatre.
SIS	Secret Intelligence Service, also known MI6.
SMERSH	Soviet Counterintelligence in WWII, an acronym of the Russian for Death to Spies.
TAT	A Technical Assessment Team, composed of specialists, including engineers, who would analyse German factories, weaponry and instal-lations. Part of T-Force.
T-Force	Technical Force. An armed, mobile unit designed to race ahead of advancing troops in order to secure German scientists, science and tech-nology. Both the Americans and Russians had equivalent teams.

Author's Note

After a controversial war, the Special Operations Executive was disbanded in January 1946. Some of its personnel transferred to MI6, and for a short time, a unit known as Special Operations Branch operated in Europe. Eventually, SOB was replaced with a Directorate of War Planning (DWP), run by the former Head of Middle East General Staff Intelligence, Brigadier John Nicholson. Its task was to establish 'stay-behind' networks in the East, including Berlin. Librarian is based on one of those.

Possibly SOE's biggest wartime disaster in France was the treachery of double-agent Henri Dericourt ('Gilbert'), an Air Movements Officer who inspired the character of Georges/Henri. Debate still rages about his exact role and the extent of his betrayals. Certainly, he was partly responsible for the collapse of SOE's Prosper network in 1943.

Dericourt was tried and acquitted by the French after the war, with the help of testimony by Nicholas Bodington, an old friend, who was also Deputy Head of SOE's F Section. He testified that the British had known about Gilbert's contacts with the Abwehr/SD all along and had encouraged them. Many in the Intelligence community were appalled by this. But then before the war, Dericourt and Bodington were also friends with Karl Boemelburg, the Head of Paris SD, one of the prime agencies responsible for hunting down SOE agents. It was, and remains, a tangled web.

Dericourt is said to have died in an air-crash in Laos in 1962; his body, though, was never found. There has been much speculation that it was a CIA/DST set-up.

At the end of the war there was confusion about what had happened to some of the SOE operatives taken by the Germans to camps such as Ravensbrück and Dachau. One woman, Vera Atkins, who had been Intelligence Officer in F Section, tracked down the missing names. Even she, though, made mistakes in identification that were not cleared up until well after 1945.

For a definitive account I thoroughly recommend *Vera Atkins: A Life in Secrets* by Sarah Helm. Rita Kramer's *Flames in the Field* is very good on Sonia Olschanesky, one of the last agents to be identified, who is also the subject of Kramer's novel *When Morning Comes*. An earlier work, *The German Penetration of SOE* by Jean Overton Fuller tells the whole Dericourt story by the woman who initially exposed the double-agent to the public.

Rose Miller is a fictional character who first appeared in the earlier novel in this series, *Early One Morning*. Lee Crane is the protagonist in *The Last Sunrise*, which also features Laura and Diana McGill.

The blockade that made the Berlin Airlift necessary was triggered by the currency reform, although the Russians were actively seeking an excuse to force the Allies out. The siege began on 24 June 1948; it ended on 12 May 1949, although flights continued until September, just in case the Russians were playing more games. During that time, General William Tunner oversaw the delivery of 2,325,509 tons of goods by air on 277,569 flights. Unlike the Americans, the British did use civilian outfits. There were twenty-three of them in all (one of them run by airline pioneer Sir Freddie Laker). The civilian companies, which included flying tankers, suffered twenty-one fatalities. In all seventy-eight were killed as a direct consequence of the operation: thirty-one Americans, thirty-nine Britons and eight Germans. There is a monument to the men who flew the air bridge near Tempelhof Airport in Berlin, curving into the sky towards its mirror image at Rhein-Main air base.

Background on the airlift can be found in *City Under Siege* by Michael D. Haycock; *Battle Ground Berlin* by David E. Murphy, Sergei A. Kondrashev and George Bailey; *The Berlin Airlift* by John and Ann Tusa; and *To Save A City* by Roger G. Miller.

I also used *Growing Up In Hitler's Shadow* by Kimberley A. Redding; *Battleground Berlin Diaries 1945–48* by Ruth Andreas-Friedrich; and *The Bonfire of Berlin* by Helga Schneider.

Among general books on Intelligence, I would recommend *The Hidden Hand* by Richard J. Aldrich, an excellent overview of the Cold War. Although it isn't set at the time of the blockade, David Stafford's *Spies Beneath Berlin* is excellent on the kind of characters who were operating in Berlin and Vienna after the war.

Bad Nenndorf did function as described (and Tin-Eye Stephens was court-marshalled for excessive brutality – and acquitted), but it was closed down in 1947, not 1948 as I have here.

I am indebted to Ken Moore who got in touch with me regarding T-Force and its extraordinary role in racing ahead of troops to find German technology and scientists. My placing them in the search for 'Foo-Fighters' (which did exist, or at least the reports of the strange phenomena did) is pure invention. However, the 5th Kings No 2 T-Force did have some remarkable successes, including capturing the most advanced German submarines of the day, capable of 25 knots underwater.

The Pavlovsky Gambit was a genuine ploy for convincing would-be deserters that they had crossed over to the West, when in fact they were still in the East. The Russians used it successfully for several years in the late 1940s. There was a *Truman Show*-style school outside Moscow where agents were Americanised and used in such deceptions.

SMERSH did exist outside Ian Fleming's imagination, and it

was named after a contraction of the phrase 'death to spies'. The organisation was at its most active during WWII and hunted ex-Nazis in Germany after the conflict. It was eventually absorbed into other Russian military intelligence units.

As usual, agent David Miller and editor Martin Fletcher played their pivotal roles in the gestation of *Dying Day*, as did many others at Headline. Thank you all once more. Also, I am grateful to Sabine Edwards and Susan d'Arcy.

I was also lucky enough to have Squadron Leader Frank Stillwell (navigator) and Wing Commander James F. Manning (pilot) of the British Berlin Airlift Association read the book and advise on various technical aspects of the air bridge. Any inaccuracies or exaggerations left in the book are, of course, my responsibility alone. I would like to thank other members of the BBAA who shared their ex-perience with me.

Thanks once more to Lorna MacAlister, who is Laura McGill's alter ego. Finally, the largest debt of gratitude goes to Lorna's good friend John Debenham-Taylor and his wife Gilly; the latter put up with my pestering her husband with her usual good humour and prepared marvellous lunches while I did so. It was while we were talking about John's role in SOE in the Far East (material that I used in *The Last Sunrise*) that he let slip about the time he was in Berlin, waiting for an agent called Otto, who had been investigating activity in the uranium mines, to come across from the Russian Zone. Almost in the West, and right in front of John, the German was snatched just before he reached safety and was never heard from again.

John kindly gave me his impressions of Berlin in 1948 and the business of espionage at that time, and read an early version of the manuscript. He tells me that a character like Webb, operating separately from direct SIS control, was perfectly feasible. After all, the Intelligence Division of the British Control Commission, Germany, numbered hundreds of officers and thousands of agents. We shall never know how many, because ID files were destroyed at some point and the American equivalents are posted as 'missing'. Nevertheless, John is in no way responsible for the liberties I have taken with the truth. Without him, though, there would be no *Dying Day*.

Robert Ryan
London

Now you can buy any of these other bestselling
Headline books from your bookshop
or *direct from the publisher*.

FREE P&P AND UK DELIVERY
(Overseas and Ireland £3.50 per book)

Run The Risk	Scott Frost	£6.99
Stripped	Brian Freeman	£6.99
Flint's Code	Paul Eddy	£6.99
Dead and Buried	Quintin Jardine	£6.99
Smoked	Patrick Quinlan	£6.99
Copper Kiss	Tom Neale	£6.99
The Death Ship of Dartmouth	Michael Jecks	£6.99
The Art of Dying	Vena Cork	£6.99
After the Mourning	Barbara Nadel	£6.99
Guardians of the Key	Clio Gray	£6.99

TO ORDER SIMPLY CALL THIS NUMBER

01235 400 414

or visit our website: www.headline.co.uk

Prices and availability subject to change without notice.